Dear Reader,

Mischief & Mayhem introduces two unusual and captivating heroines whose attempt to solve mysteries puts them at great personal risk.

We hope you enjoy these stories about our two Regency "detectives." Their exploits are gripping and often amusing as they attempt to outwit the men in their lives.

In May we will be putting the spotlight on men in a two-book collection called *The Reluctant Bridegrooms*. We hope you will enjoy it as much as we did.

Happy reading,

The Editor

MISCHIEF & MAYHEM

Janet Edmonds
& Petra Nash

Harlequin Books

TORONTO • NEW YORK • LONDON
AMSTERDAM • PARIS • SYDNEY • HAMBURG
STOCKHOLM • ATHENS • TOKYO • MILAN
MADRID • WARSAW • BUDAPEST • AUCKLAND

ISBN 0-373-31217-2

First North American Publication 1995.

MISCHIEF & MAYHEM

A NABOB'S DAUGHTER
Copyright © 1993 by Janet Edmonds

HEIR APPARENT
Copyright © 1992 by Petra Nash

CONTENTS

About the Author

Janet Edmonds was born in Portsmouth but lived for years in the Cotswolds, where she taught school before deciding that writing fiction was more fun. A breeder, exhibitor and judge of dogs, she now lives in an isolated house in the Fens. She also has a son and a cat and avoids any form of domestic activity if she can.

A NABOB'S DAUGHTER

Janet Edmonds

HISTORICAL NOTE

SMUGGLING HAS ALWAYS been rife round our shores and East Anglia has never been an exception though I'm told that today drugs and illegal immigrants have replaced brandy, tea, lace and silk. Anything that carried heavy duty was smuggled and the smuggling of any commodity stopped as soon as the duty was discontinued—tea is perhaps the most notable case in point. Smuggling was a two-way traffic. For several centuries, in order to protect our weaving industry, it was illegal to export raw wool, so fleeces were smuggled out continuously until the Industrial Revolution lessened our dependence on one industry.

Almost everyone in rural areas, especially those near the coast, was involved to a greater or lesser extent. The customs service—interestingly, a much older institution than the police—was inadequately manned, heavily outnumbered, and widely hated even by law-abiding citizens. Its organisation was complex and hierarchical and those who worked for it did so at great personal risk.

The Fens have been systematically drained and extended since the seventeenth century, after previous sporadic attempts, and, ever since the Romans, earthworks have been used to keep back the sea. The coastline of the Wash is no longer what it was during the Napoleonic Wars and Eaden's map of the area, surveyed in 1792, is the one I've used. Wisbech in those days was at the narrowest end of the wide estuary of the River Nene. Since the middle of the nineteenth century, the Nene has been deepened, straightened, narrowed and extended so that Wisbech is now over ten miles from the present estuary, though it remains a working port. Instead of a long and hazardous ford by Cross Keys House, there is now a Victorian swivel bridge across a much narrower stretch of water and Cross Keys House is now a hotel.

Impressment into both navy and army were lawful from the thirteenth century—1206 in the case of the navy—and at least one of the events in this book is based on a true incident: a press-gang really was attacked by village women to the South of King's Lynn, in order to gain time for the men of the village to go into hiding, though this happened some years later than my book.

Janet Edmonds

CHAPTER ONE

"I SHOULD BE very much obliged, madam, if you could keep this young blackguard on a tighter rein in future." Lord Bardolph's voice froze the small parlour as dramatically as his tall figure dominated it.

India Leigh lifted her chin defiantly and drew herself up, irritated by the fact that even at her tallest she was at the disadvantage of having to look up into eyes which were as cold and unwelcoming as the waters of the Wash. "Your language is extreme, my lord," she said. "My brother is only fourteen, after all, and he seems to have been aided and abetted in this little escapade by your own brother who is, I believe, the elder of the two."

The Viscount had no choice but to concede the point. "Bartram is sixteen, but I take leave to tell you he gave me no cause for concern until you and your brother came here."

"Which does he lack—spirit or initiative?" India snapped. "He must be remarkably easily led if he goes along with the hare-brained schemes of a fourteen-year-old."

The fact that the same thought had often occurred to Lord Bardolph did not make it any easier to accept the comment when it came from an outsider whose origins, in so far as she was known to have any, appeared to have been trade. He was unmoved by her considerable beauty and by her undeniably fine eyes, and if his opinion had been asked he would have said that she dressed in a way most inappropriate to such a remote spot. True, the green velour of her dress would certainly keep at bay the Fen winds, but the skilled cut by which its simple lines were achieved, the quality of its braid and lace trimmings, all pointed to a London dressmaker—and an expensive one at that. None of this had anything to do with the matter in hand, but all conspired to fuel his annoyance.

"Bartram has not been allowed to run wild," he said repressively. "I have endeavoured to inculcate in him a sense of duty, of what is fitting. Ultimately I hope to see him embark on a career in the church and such episodes as this are hardly helpful."

"Goodness me!" India exclaimed. "How very pompous you are! I wonder if it has crossed your mind to ask Bartram if he wants to go into the church? From what I've seen of him—admittedly not very much—I'd have said he was quite unsuited but, naturally, I bow to your superior understanding of him."

The Viscount's mouth grew tight-lipped with fury. "You're too generous, madam," he said icily. "You'll forgive me, I'm sure, for not wishing to see my brother model himself upon yours."

India bestowed her sweetest smile on him—no mean achievement when she was boiling with anger. "I'd be similarly concerned if I thought Richard was modelling himself on a twelve-year-old," she told him.

Lord Bardolph's anger was directed as much against himself for having laid himself open to such a remark as with India for having uttered it. It wasn't often that someone succeeded in putting him at a disadvantage and he couldn't recall a woman ever having done so before. It wasn't an experience he was enjoying. He delivered a pretension-squashing *coup de grâce*.

"I find you impertinent, madam," he said.

To his amazement, instead of flinching or shifting her gaze—which was the very least he had anticipated—India threw back her head and laughed. It was a full-throated laugh of genuine amusement which, had the circumstances been different, he might have found intriguingly attractive. As it was, it was so totally unexpected that it left him mystified. What woman with any pretensions to gentility could possibly find it amusing to be called impertinent?

India wiped her eye. "Do forgive me, my lord," she said. "It really is too bad of me to laugh at you, especially when I suspect it isn't something you're used to. Pomposity really is counter-productive, you know. I'm surprised you haven't learned that." Her tone became more confidential. "I know one should never listen to gossip, but they say in the village that your bride elect left you quite literally at the altar. Now that isn't a humiliation I'd wish on anyone, but I feel bound to say that if you were half as pompous and downright rude to her as you have been to me, and so totally unable to see the lighter side of a situation, then, frankly, I'm not in the least surprised."

No sooner were the words uttered than India knew she had gone too far by any standards. Had it been within her power to recall them, she would have done so. As it was, her colour rose in almost precise counterpoint to the paling of Lord Bardolph's. She opened her mouth to apologise but his retaliation was too swift.

He inclined his head in an ironic bow. "You are no doubt aware of the speculation locally as to why a personable young woman such as yourself, the daughter, it's believed, of a nabob, should have returned unwed at the ripe age of twenty-three or four from the country after which she was named . . . a country where, one gathers, Englishwomen—especially single ones—are rather thin on the ground. Local speculators have obviously not been privy to the benefits of your shrewish tongue. I no longer find it remarkable that you returned an old maid, despite your fortune. Good morning, madam."

India opened her mouth to protest that he was unfair and closed it again on the realisation that she was hardly in a position to complain. Before she could collect her thoughts sufficiently to enable her at least to try to smooth things down, he had gone, letting himself unceremoniously out of the house before the maid could be summoned.

India drew a deep breath and turned to the object of Lord Bardolph's visit. "And what have you got to say for yourself, Richard?" she asked.

He was very nearly as tall as she was and it wouldn't be long before she would be at as big a disadvantage in dealing with him as she had been with Bardolph, she thought.

Her brother merely grinned. "My, that was a set-to, and no mistake," he remarked. "Do you know, you're trembling."

She did, and was trying hard to control it. "Don't change the subject. What's your version of this morning's events?"

"In general, I suppose Bardolph hasn't got it so very wrong, bearing in mind the source of his information," Richard began.

"*Lord* Bardolph," India corrected him. "I don't think he'd welcome any familiarity from you, just now."

Richard's grin broadened. "I got the impression there wasn't going to be much opportunity for it from any member of this family," he said.

Since there were only two members of it, this comment was more pointed than India liked to admit. "Never mind that," she said. "What have you and the Honourable Bartram been up to?"

Richard's normally cheerful face clouded over. "Will you listen to me? Really listen, I mean?"

"You know I will."

"But you won't automatically believe Lord Bardolph just because he's an adult?"

"Not automatically or for that reason but it's only fair to say that, whatever difference of opinion we might have had, he didn't strike me as untruthful," India warned him.

"I don't suppose he is," Richard agreed, "but the thing is, he took Mr. Huggate's word for everything."

"Then you'd better tell me your version of events," his sister suggested. She pointed to a chair. "Sit down and start at the beginning. I'll try not to interrupt."

"Bart doesn't want to be a churchman, you know. He's got his heart set on being a sailor. Bardolph's got a yacht and sailing on it is the thing Bart most likes doing, only his brother's too busy most of the time to take him out. Bardolph says he wouldn't really like being a sailor at all because life in the navy isn't remotely like sailing on a private yacht."

India felt that Lord Bardolph might have a valid argument there but she wasn't very clear what connection this had with the morning's brouhaha. "This morning's events, Richard, if you don't mind. Get to the point."

"I am. The thing is, wanting to be a sailor so badly means that Bart's made himself very knowledgeable about ships and the sea and all that and, barring going for a sail, there's nothing he enjoys quite so much as going out on to the salt-marshes and just watching." He paused. "As a matter of fact, Bardolph—*Lord* Bardolph, I mean—ought to thank me for trying to change Bart's ideas: I told him he wouldn't enjoy the sea so much if he had to come all the way from India on it. I told him it was a bit different from sailing up and down the coast on a diet of quail's eggs and champagne."

"Quail's eggs and champagne?" India echoed, bemused. "Am I supposed to believe those are the staple foods on board Lord Bardolph's boat?"

"I don't suppose they're the *staples*, exactly," Richard admitted. "I mean, you'd need to eat an awful lot of quail's eggs to fill you up, wouldn't you? It's just that they seem to be part of the attraction for Bart."

"I doubt if much of either is served in the navy," India remarked. "I don't wish to be unkind, Richard, but Bartram does seem to be lacking in common sense."

"Oh, he's quite stupid about a lot of things," Richard agreed cheerfully, "but he really does know a lot about ships and related things. He knows all the birds we see and a lot about their behaviour and all that. That's why I enjoy his company so much. After all, if I'm going to be a farmer, I need to know about these things, and if I decided to farm in this area, which Bart says is quite unlike any other—and I'm inclined to believe him—then the more I can learn from someone who really knows, the better."

Since Richard's ambition was as big a bone of contention between them as Bartram's evidently was in his family, India, who had no stomach for another argument just yet, tried to turn the conversation away from the detour it appeared to have taken. "This is all very fascinating, but I'm no nearer understanding what happened today."

Richard shook his head. "You're no nearer *knowing*," he told her, "but you're much nearer *understanding*."

India sighed. Sometimes she wished Richard were not quite so bright. She also wished he had waited another six or seven years before developing their late father's precision of argument. It might be very mind-forming and educational but in a fourteen-year-old boy it smacked of unwelcome precocity. "It's *knowledge* I'm after," she pointed out. "You can *explain* after."

"I shan't need to," Richard chuckled. "That's why we go to the marshes, and we go there often. From time to time there's a ship hove to some way off-shore, usually at low water just before the tide turns. Bart says it's a very dangerous thing to do because of the mud and sand shoals and that the master must be very skilled indeed. They weigh anchor as the tide rises and head off towards King's Lynn. We know that because we thought they were probably waiting for high-water so that they could get up the Nene to Wisbech, but they didn't. Bart thinks they must go on to King's Lynn, or maybe back to Holland."

"Why Holland?" India asked.

"He says he can tell by the rigging, she's a Dutchman—a ketch, he says. He explained it all to me, but I'm not really interested in all that business about gaffs and jibs and what-have-yous, so I only half listened and I certainly can't explain it to you. Does it matter?" He looked at her anxiously.

"Not in the least," India assured him. "In fact, it's probably quite a blessing because I wouldn't understand, either, and then you'd get annoyed. Go on."

"As a matter of fact, I've only seen her once—the time we raced along the estuary to see where she went—but Bart's seen her several times, always previously at night."

India frowned. "Does that mean he has a bedroom overlooking the Wash?"

Richard grinned cheekily. "No. He knows when the tide and the moon are going to be right and just slips out of the house. He says people come ashore. Smugglers, he says."

India thought of the flat expanse of the salt-marsh backed by the embankment that stopped the sea encroaching on to the equally flat drained siltfields behind. "I see. And where do they hide whatever it is they smuggle? In caves?"

"Don't be silly, India. How could they? Bart says, given the ketch's origins, the most likely contraband is Hollands. Gin, you know."

"Yes, I do know what Hollands is," she said. "What does Bartram think they do with it?"

"They haven't really got much choice, have they? They must have an accomplice ashore who has somewhere where they can hide the goods until they can be moved."

Light began to dawn. "Do I infer that this is where this Mr. Huggate enters the story?" India asked with misgivings.

"That's right. Got it in one. Bart says the place of possible concealment nearest to the spot where they land is Huggate's big barn. The one he built about ten years ago when he started to keep sheep. He said it was to store the fleeces and I dare say it was except that it seems a bit stupid to store a valuable crop so far from the house and the dogs. Anyway, Bart says the ketch was there last night. Now we'd previously agreed that next time it was there we'd go out first thing and root around that barn and see what we could find out. Before old Huggate's had time to shift it, you understand."

"Mr. Huggate," India corrected automatically. "Didn't it occur to you that this might be just a smidgeon dangerous?"

"Why? He wouldn't dare do anything in broad daylight, would he?" Richard said with the blithe confidence of extreme youth. "We weren't going to be *obviously* searching for anything. We made it look as if we were just playing games around there."

"What sort of games?"

"Hide-and-go-seek, that sort of thing; it justified one of us poking and prying into all sorts of nooks and crannies."

"Including, presumably. Mr. Huggate's barn."

"Exactly. Well," he amended, "it would have done, only the barn was well and truly padlocked and there wasn't a chink anywhere."

"Which is precisely what you'd expect if it was being used to store fleeces," India pointed out.

"Or contraband."

"You don't think this idea of contraband gin is a consequence of two boys having over-active imaginations and not enough to occupy their time?" India suggested.

"Then think of an alternative explanation," Richard demanded, ignoring the insult.

"Maybe the Dutchman is buying the fleeces."

"Then why not transport them to Wisbech—or Lynn—and ship them out from there? It would be a lot safer. Or it would be if it were legal."

"Perhaps they go direct to Holland or somewhere else."

"Perhaps they do but it's as much against the law to export English wool as it is to import Hollands gin without paying duty. Either way it's smuggling." A thought struck him. "Maybe we haven't considered the half of it. Maybe he's smuggling Hollands in and paying for it by smuggling wool out. Now there's a thought to ponder!"

India judged this to be an idea that was better not pursued. "I take it Mr. Huggate caught you?"

"We told him we were just playing games but I don't think he believed us. He said we were a bit old to be playing hide-and-go-seek."

"I'd have to agree with him on that," India commented.

"He marched us off to Bardolph—*Lord* Bardolph—and told him he'd caught us in his outhouses—which wasn't strictly true since you can hardly call a barn two hundred yards from all the other buildings an outhouse, can you? He told his lordship we'd been using Bart's spyglass to set straw on fire, which is absolutely untrue. Even if we'd wanted to, the sun isn't strong enough and we're not so stupid that we don't know *that*. Anyway, Lord Bardolph believed him and said he'd make good any damage if Mr. Huggate would let him know what it amounted to, and Mr. Huggate said fortunately he'd found us in time and it hadn't come to that but he'd be obliged if his lordship would make sure it never happened again and his land was now out of bounds to both of us and would his lordship please speak to you about me and make sure I was punished as well. Which he did," Richard concluded.

"It seems to me I've maligned Bartram by saying he lacked spirit and initiative," India said ruefully.

Richard shifted uneasily. "Not entirely. I mean, he's the one that guessed what was going on but it was my idea to see what we could find out."

"I see. Well, at least you've owned up to that. Tell me something which puzzles me: if Bartram really believed smuggling was going on, why on earth didn't he say something to his brother? Lord Bardolph is the biggest landowner in the area and a magistrate. He would be able to authorise 'rooting around,' as you put it, by the proper authorities and all this unpleasantness would have been avoided."

"The thing is, Lord Bardolph isn't what you'd call a sympathetic brother. He's a half-brother, really: Bart's mother was the late Lord Bardolph's second wife and she died when he was born. There's sixteen years between them so they haven't much in common. Lord Bardolph is very good at administering set-downs, Bart says—and after listening to him just now, I can quite believe it. Bart says any suggestion of his gets a set-down and leaves him feeling about five years old and five inches high. He says his brother would just have laughed at him."

India privately thought Bartram was probably right but judged it unwise to say so. "All the same, that's whom he should have mentioned it to. Even if Bardolph didn't march straight over there, he might well have had the place watched, just to see whether there was any substance to Bartram's story."

"He might, I suppose," Richard said grudgingly. "On the other hand, think how gratifying it would have been to be able to go to him with some *real* proof. That would have made Lord Bardolph think twice before being quite so dismissive of his brother's ideas in future."

India supposed it would and had to concede that the boys' scheme, seen from the perspective of fourteen and sixteen, had a logic of its own. She sighed. "I'm not saying I disbelieve you when you tell me Mr. Huggate was lying, but I do think you've both been letting your imaginations run away with you and I think the Viscount has a case. I don't want you to have anything to do with Bartram for the time being and you can stay indoors for the next week. I'll see to it that you have some studying to do."

He looked at her in horror. "You mean I can't go out at all?"

India relented. "You'll accompany me to church, of course, and I think I could allow you to come shopping with me. That ought to give you a bit of fresh air and exercise."

"Thank you *very* much," Richard snorted. "I think I'd rather write essays."

"That can be arranged. Now go up to your room and leave me in peace for a while. You've interfered with my day quite enough already."

Richard took the hint with alacrity but paused by the door. "How long is 'for the time being'?" he asked.

It took a moment or two before India realised what he meant. "Till you can see Bartram again? I don't know. Till I say so, I suppose."

"An indefinite sentence, in other words."

"Something of the sort—and it serves you right."

When Richard had left the room, India sank on to the sofa with a sigh of relief. Bardolph and her brother had between them given her more than enough to think about and now she needed time to work out the ramifications and decide how best to deal with it.

Since their parents had died within days of each other in an outbreak of cholera in Bangalore, India had found herself her brother's legal guardian with all the responsibilities that that entailed, chief among which was that of deciding their immediate future. Bardolph's gibe struck a raw nerve, not because she had any particular urge to acquire a husband just for the sake of it, as so many women seemed to do, but because a husband would have been a very useful asset in the present circumstances, due to the fact that the responsibility for those decisions would have been his. India was by nature far from indecisive and, had there been only her future to consider, things would have been much easier. Richard's future was another matter altogether.

She wondered whether, with hindsight, she had been foolish to reject all the suitors who had offered for her hand in India. Every summer her mother had taken her on the interminably long journey north to the mountains, to cities like Peshawar and Rawalpindi where it was reasonable to assume she might well find a husband among the government officers or the garrison. Her parents had had every reason to feel optimistic about her chances: India was not only extremely beautiful but was blessed with an exceedingly wealthy father—not quite what one might call a gentleman, perhaps, but rich enough for that to be overlooked by younger sons and ambitious civil servants. It had been known that a small fortune would be settled on her upon her marriage and a larger one on the death of her father. No, there had been no shortage of suitors.

Unfortunately all of them had fallen short of India's expectations in one way or another. There were those whose way of life suggested that it would take them very little time to get through her fortune and, since her parents' assessment of their qualities coincided with that of their daughter, they could only congratulate themselves on having raised a daughter with such discriminating good sense. They were less pleased when she rejected a suitor because he was too worthy or too serious, too domineering or too humourless.

"But that's just what one *needs* in a husband," Mrs. Leigh had protested on learning of the rejection of one eminently suitable young man. "Your husband will have absolute control over you and your fortune. Worthiness and solidity are very necessary virtues in a husband."

"But if I have to live with them for the rest of my life, unrelieved by any mitigating humour, I shall go quietly mad."

Mrs. Leigh could see her daughter's point though she had no intention of saying so. "Nonsense," she said. "You refine too much upon humour. You can have too much of a good thing, you know."

"Indeed you can. That's why I'm anxious to avoid too much worthiness or solidity. Papa strikes the right sort of balance so, Mama, if you can find me a young man with Papa's business acumen and his sense of humour, I'll do all I can to live up to your expectations."

But it seemed that no such man existed or, if he did, he didn't live in India.

This wasn't as dispiriting as it might have been. Neither India nor her brother had ever been to England but both their parents had been born there. It stood to reason that there might well be a man—possibly even men—in England with characteristics closer to those she sought in a hus-

band. Her mother smiled and shook her head when India
suggested as much.

"Men are men, my dear," she said. "You'll find the full
range in India. I'm afraid the idea that they're different in
England is a case of the grass looking greener in the next
field."

Their parents' death changed all that. It was unthinkable
that a young, unmarried woman should live alone in Bangalore with only the protection of a fourteen-year-old boy
and some native servants. She must marry or return to
England. This was the advice she received from all sides and
India knew it to be sound even though she found it incongruously amusing that her counsellors invariably used the
word "return" despite the fact that she had never set foot
in England in her life.

She gave marriage more serious consideration than ever
before but could detect no improvement in the candidates
for her hand and, in any case, felt that a lifelong commit-
ment was not best entered into at short notice and when she
was grieving deeply for her beloved parents. She and Richard would 'return' to England.

Another factor influenced her decision but it wasn't one
she was prepared to mention to anyone else. Richard was
young but he was also intelligent, ingenious and resourceful far beyond his years. He had a natural ability for getting into mischief and for leading others into it, too. India
knew her parents had been keen to send him to England
where they had felt that a few years at Oxford or Cambridge would not only complete his education in the way
from which he was most likely to benefit, but also give him
enough intellectual occupation to keep him out of the mischief his parents were sure was inspired as much by boredom as by naughtiness. Their satisfaction with this scheme
was tempered with concern that at either place he might well
gravitate towards the least desirable elements of university
society without the mitigating influence of his family to re-
direct his activities into more desirable paths.

Both problems would be solved by going to England: she might find a compatible husband and Richard could go on to university while still remaining within reach of his sister's influence.

They had initially rented a house in the capital, a city which exceeded their highest expectations and reduced India to a wide-eyed schoolgirl up from the country. The shops, the warehouses, the mantua-makers and the milliners, to say nothing of the theatres, were a delight and India had been seriously considering acquiring an appropriate chaperon who could introduce her to respectable society, when she began to realise that Richard had become a cause for concern.

It had seemed quite reasonable for a spirited boy to resent being tied firmly to his sister's apron-strings and India had no initial qualms about letting him explore London on his own, just so long as he was home by the time she asked and told her where he was going. He was unfailingly obedient on the first score but she wasn't so sure about the last. That was to say that, while he might very well have visited the places he said he was visiting on any given day, she suspected that he added one or two less salubrious destinations to his itinerary. His conversation became interlarded with cant expressions at the meaning of some of which India could only guess. He became more careless of his appearance and, although India could refuse to let him leave the house until she was satisfied, she noticed that on his return he was a great deal more dishevelled than half a day's exploration of a great city warranted. When he told her that the allowance she made him was not nearly enough for "a man about town," as he described himself, she became seriously concerned, knowing it to be on the generous side.

The lawyer who handled the family's affairs endorsed this view and tentatively suggested that Miss Leigh might be well advised to consider removing to a quieter town where there would be fewer distractions. He also suggested that she demand to know exactly what, where and with whom Richard spent his days, but this was not a piece of advice India was prepared to follow, knowing it would only be resented and, if Richard guessed she would disapprove, result in his lying to her. Far better quietly to find somewhere else to live and present him with a *fait accompli*.

Deciding where to go had been a problem because she had the whole of England, Scotland and Wales to choose from. The choice was really too great for comfort and she finally limited it to the areas of, but not too close to, both of the great university cities. After a lifetime spent in the Deccan, India thought it would make a pleasant change to live near the sea, a decision which further restricted her choice to the area north and east of Cambridge. She knew nothing of the Fens nor of the nature of the German Sea and barely noticed the quickly disguised surprise of the London agent she engaged to find a suitable house for them.

The house was entirely suitable and the location exactly what she had asked for but she was totally unprepared for the reality. She was quite unprepared for the high earthen embankment that kept the sea from flooding in across the fields created over the last hundred years by draining the marshes and consequently lower than the besieging sea itself, an embankment that effectively cut off any view of the sea unless one stood on top of it. She was quite unprepared for the merciless wind that howled interminably across the flat, open landscape. She was equally unprepared for the deeply suspicious reserve of the inhabitants of an isolated village, a reserve that was almost secrecy and contrasted starkly with the openness, the noise, the colour and the gossip of an Indian village.

The climate had a lot to do with that, of course: the wind, the cold and the rain were effective deterrents to the street life that was so much a feature of India. It was hardly surprising that people scurried home to shut out the weather behind stout doors and closed windows. It was primarily Richard who broke down the barriers of acceptance. He went everywhere, poking his nose into this and that, learning to catch moles and trap eels, wildfowling from a flat-bottomed punt at dawn, and even struggling to master the stilts with which Fenmen traditionally crossed flooded stretches of land. And because the brother was invariably cheerful, no matter how wet and muddy he might be, the villagers gradually began to accept his sister too, especially as they began to realise that her fine London clothes and her undoubted wealth did not lead her to put on airs or "fancy herself" as they had feared.

Even so, the social life of the little village was strictly limited. There was the vicar, the doctor and their families. There was a handful of farmers who kept themselves to themselves, a philosophy adhered to more stringently by Mr. Huggate than by any of the others, and there was Edward Chelworth, Viscount Bardolph of Old Fen Hall.

Unfortunately the conventions of society held good even in this remote spot and it was therefore only possible for India to receive and be received by the married ladies of the parish. The vicar and his wife took pity on her and decided that, for social reasons and despite his youth, Richard could be invited, too. It was clearly impossible, however, for the Viscount to pay a morning call on Miss Leigh or vice versa, a situation which, the vicar confided to his wife, was plainly ridiculous since it kept apart the two parishioners most eligible to be introduced to each other. He took very little comfort from the fact that both parties seemed entirely happy with the situation.

They met in church, of course. Or, to be more precise, they encountered one another entering and leaving. A courteous inclination of the head acknowledged the other's presence, together with a murmured, "Good morning."

On the basis of this level of acquaintance, India formed the impression that Lord Bardolph was cold, arrogant and decidedly high in the instep. For his part, the Viscount took one look at Miss Leigh's extravagantly modish apparel and dismissed her as a shallow, hen-witted butterfly—though admittedly a beautiful one—whose wealth had given her vulgar pretensions to gentility. On the rare occasions when he thought about her at all, it was with amazement that she had chosen to live in the Fens when London was so obviously very much more the sort of milieu in which she saw herself. It was most unlikely that she would stay here very long.

India was unsure whether to be relieved or worried that Richard had made himself so very much at home here. He loved the Fens. Where his sister saw space, he saw skyscapes like none he had seen before. The lingering, spectacular sunsets and the glorious dawns more than compensated for the winds which drove the rain relentlessly before them. The people made him welcome, cautiously at first and then with amused willingness to let him into the secrets of surviving in this strange land. It was a land that spoke to his condition and he marvelled now at the degree of resentment he had felt when he first learned they were leaving London and coming here. He had always known that his parents intended him to complete his education at one or other of the great universities and he was neither surprised nor dismayed that India intended their wishes to be carried out. It was something to which he looked forward and the only regret he had on that score was that the present political situation ruled out any chance of undertaking The Grand Tour. What he had learned already from the Fens was what he intended to do with the rest of his life once his education was complete. He would be a farmer. Preferably a sheep farmer.

He had thought India would be pleased that he had settled on his future and was taken aback by her reaction, which was at first laughingly dismissive and then, when she realised this was no passing fancy, dismayed. Business was what they had been brought up in and one of the professions was what their parents had assumed Richard's education would lead to. Farming was what peasants did, though India had to admit that that wasn't a word that fitted their farming neighbours, least of all Viscount Bardolph. What neither of them knew was that both their parents had come from farming stock, so that a love of the land was as firmly bred into Richard's bones—if not into his sister's—as the sea was in those from maritime families. It remained a source of friction between them, so Richard let the matter drop. If that led his sister to believe he had given up the idea, it was too bad because, India notwithstanding, he had every intention of pursuing that livelihood and if India withheld the wherewithal once he had finished his formal education, then so be it; there would only be a few years before he had control over his own fortune and then he could farm to his heart's content. And he had every intention of doing so.

LORD BARDOLPH returned to Old Fen Hall in a humour that was far from sweet. He had been bettered in a disagreement and had not enjoyed the experience. It was particularly galling to know that he had largely himself to blame and to recognise that, although he had fired a telling parting shot, the nature of it meant that he had lowered himself to India Leigh's level, and there was little gratification from that. Had she been a woman one could admire, he might have applauded her quick thinking, but there was very little to admire in Miss Leigh. There was her beauty, of course, and he had already remarked upon her eyes, which were large and dark, well-spaced and set very slightly at an angle, giving her an expression reminiscent of a deer. She had a neat figure, too, and there was always her fortune. Lord Bardolph had no interest in the latter and had long ago learned to be wary of beautiful women whose main purpose in life seemed to be the desire to trap a title. To be fair, that didn't seem to be India Leigh's ambition—or, if it were, she was going a very strange way about achieving it—but there was no denying she had struck a nerve.

Laura Newton had been beautiful and she had used all her wiles to entrap the young Viscount into a proposal of marriage. He had been quite besotted with her fragile, pink-and-

white beauty with its fluttering eyelashes and breathless little voice that made her seem infinitely vulnerable and very
much his junior instead of two years his senior. He hadn't
realised until after the proposal was uttered that underneath that delicately palpitating exterior lay a will of forged
steel with a relentless determination to have its own way. He
hadn't realised until it was too late that the smiles and the
tinkling laughter were social attributes, not indications of
any real humour and that, except where her own best interests were involved, her mind was completely unformed.

He had been able to overlook most of the warning signs
until the day when she'd made it perfectly clear that she had
absolutely no intention whatsoever of spending any part of
their married life in the country, much less in his beloved
Fens. She hadn't visited them but knew them to be remote
and, it was said, desolate, empty and, worst of all, unfashionable. From then on his infatuation had faded and died
but the realisation had come too late. He had proposed, he
had been accepted—with considerable alacrity—and the
betrothal had been announced. It was impossible for a gentleman to withdraw. The old adage about making your bed
and lying on it was unpleasantly apposite.

The Viscount had stuck to his proposal. He had also
stood unexpectedly firm over the choice of church for the
ceremony. They would marry in the village church which
served Old Fen Hall, the groomsman moving out of his own
home and into the hall so that the bride elect could be suitably accommodated until after the wedding.

Lord Bardolph had left London three weeks before the
wedding to make sure everything at the Hall was as it should
be; he had still harboured hopes that perhaps Laura might
change her mind if she could be presented with perfection.
He had been surprised but not disconcerted to receive a note
from her to say that she was going to be delayed and
wouldn't, in fact, arrive until the day before the wedding,
and when the groomsman had arrived in the evening saying
she still hadn't come Bardolph had experienced the first

faint flutterings of hope. The most likely explanation, of
course, was the mists or the state of the roads, and it was
quite possible the ceremony might have to be postponed.
Nevertheless, in the absence of any message to the contrary, the Viscount and the vicar had agreed they must carry
on as if all were in order.

The messenger had arrived when everyone was at the
church and Bardolph often wondered whether his timing
had been at Laura's instigation. The message was brief and
to the point: Miss Newton was crying off. She no longer had
any wish to become Viscountess Bardolph.

The congregation had gasped with speculative dismay and
genuine sympathy for the jilted bridegroom. Bardolph's
feelings were mixed. It was not a pleasant experience to be
an object of pity and probably—later—of ridicule. On the
other hand he had had a lucky escape and resolved that he
would take very good care never again to let infatuation
warp his judgement.

The note had contained no explanation for the bride's
action and Bardolph, knowing by now just how important
his title had been to his intended, had asked the friend who
had unnecessarily relinquished his home to go to London
and find out. The Viscount drew immense satisfaction from
the outcome. Miss Newton had made good use of his three
weeks' absence from the capital to flutter her eyelashes at
the Marquis of Quorndon, who had maliciously enjoyed
playing her at her own game until she genuinely believed
that it was only a matter of days before he, too, would propose—if only Bardolph were out of the way. Since a mar-
quisate and later, when Quordon's father died, a duchy, far
outranked anything she could hope for from Bardolph, she
had decided the gamble was worth the toss. Some years later
a well-bred but minor clergyman had rescued her from the
shelf and he was now being pushed very effectively towards
a bishopric with, Bardolph suspected, his wife's blue eyes
fixed firmly on one or other of the archepiscopacies.

Bardolph grinned as he thought of it. It had been a lucky escape, all right, and well worth the nudges and whispers of the next few months, even years. No one knew his true feelings for the very simple fact that, if he had tried to explain them, people would only have thought he was putting a brave face on it. It was therefore no wonder that India Leigh had heard the popular version, and he certainly wasn't about to disillusion her. Her wealth had come from trade and her wardrobe was ostentatious in that it was costlier than either her status or her surroundings warranted, and it was therefore vulgar. That disposed of Miss Leigh, and if the thought occurred to him, however fleetingly, that such a conclusion endorsed her assessment of him as pompous, he was angry enough to be able to dismiss it out of hand.

He wished he could dismiss her brother equally easily. He recognised in Richard Leigh much that he would have liked to see in Bartram. Until today, he hadn't deplored Richard's origins half as much as those of his sister. While he would have preferred Bartram to choose a friend of his own age, it was difficult to see how he could do so when village boys of sixteen had a living to earn and there was none of his own class. Richard Leigh was intelligent, with an enquiring mind and a maturity of judgement that belied his years. He was a born leader in a way that Bartram would never be. One of Bardolph's reasons for so strongly opposing his brother's ambitions to join the navy was not the rigours of the life, useful an excuse as that was, but his sad acknowledgement of the fact that, while he could buy Bartram in, it would be much more difficult to buy his promotion once the boy had demonstrated his unsuitability for any rank higher than lieutenant. Richard, on the other hand, would do exceptionally well in the services. It was ironic that his interests lay entirely in the land.

He had no hesitation in assuming that the events of the morning had been at young Leigh's instigation, especially since Bartram had once artlessly let slip India's reason for coming here, and he could hardly blame Huggate for being annoyed. Nathaniel Huggate was not a man to whom one warmed. He was a prosperous farmer who made very little noise about his success and had the reclusive nature not uncommon in Fenmen, but none of that made him a liar and, in the absence of any rebuttal by the boys or any attempt to justify their actions, he had no option but to accept Huggate's word.

Richard Leigh had been dealt with, though Bardolph had little faith in the ability of a butterfly like India Leigh to exert any lasting influence on a boy of Richard's strong-mindedness. Bartram, however, was under his control and that was a very different matter.

He had told Bartram to go to the nursery and stay there until he got back. It looked as if he had done so. Bardolph handed his cloak, his hat and his gloves to the manservant who came forward for them and was about to ask him to tell Bartram to attend his brother in the library when it occurred to him that it wasn't always a good idea to make too much use of the heavy hand. Instead, he went upstairs and opened the nursery door.

Bartram was sitting on the window-seat, looking down into the yew-framed garden below, but he turned a discontented face towards the door when he heard it open.

"Oh, it's you," he said. "You've been long enough."

Bardolph held his temper in check and sat down in the old rocking-chair. Nurse used to tell him bedtime stories in this chair and its associations were of comfort and relaxation. He needed both just now. He forced himself to be pleasantly reasonable. "I could hardly march young Leigh home and drop him on the doorstep without some sort of explanation, could I? Miss Leigh had to know what's been going on."

"I'll bet *she* stood up for her brother," Bartram said bitterly.

"I had the impression she was extremely angry about the whole business," Bardolph said with perfect truth.

"Did she believe you as easily as you believed old Huggate?"

"She didn't accuse me of lying; she didn't even suggest I might be mistaken. I think I can assume she believed me."

"And Richard? What did he have to say?"

"Nothing. He had the grace to look suitably crestfallen. I don't think he's a boy who sulks."

"Unlike me, you mean."

"Your words, not mine."

"Didn't she ask him for an explanation?"

"Not while I was there—any more than I'd have asked you for one if the positions had been reversed. I don't doubt they were demanded as soon as I'd left the house, however."

Bartram snorted. "I'd be very surprised if they were. Richard says he can do want he wants, that his sister doesn't interfere."

Bardolph might have implied as much to India's face but, even if he believed it—and he wasn't at all sure he did—it wasn't a point he was prepared to concede to his brother. "That wasn't the impression I got, but what Miss Leigh does or doesn't do is none of my concern. You are. I've listened to Huggate. Now I'll listen to you. What's your version?"

"My 'version,' if I chose to give one, would be the truth but you're not going to believe me, so I might as well save my breath."

Bardolph sighed. "Come on, Bart—you know me better than that."

Bartram hesitated. If ever there was a time to tell Edward of his suspicions and the way they led up to this morning's escapade, it was now. Two considerations stopped him. He didn't doubt that sooner or later Edward would compare notes with India Leigh and if Richard had told a different story he'd be in even deeper trouble for lying than he already was for what, with any luck, would be interpreted as thoughtless mischief. The second cause of his hesitation was his deep-seated fear of ridicule. Everyone knew smuggling went on along the East Anglian coast and everyone knew that everyone else—well, everyone except Bardolph—took advantage of it to a greater or lesser degree even if they didn't actively participate. The cellars at Old Fen Hall were probably the only ones in the county where there wasn't a drop of liquor which had escaped paying duty. But to accuse a man like Nathaniel Huggate of wholesale smuggling would incur anger, which Bartram could cope with, and ridicule, which he couldn't. He and Richard might have convinced themselves it was true; convincing Edward was a different matter. At the very least, his story must tally with Richard's. The best thing would be to say nothing until they'd had a chance to talk about it.

"Do I? You never take anything I say seriously. You treat me like a child. Why should this be any different?"

"When you talk like a petulant, spoiled brat, it's hardly surprising if you're treated like one. Why don't you grow up? Or at the very least be your age? For God's sake, Bart, Richard Leigh is more of an adult than you are, for all he's two years younger."

If Bardolph intended that remark to act as a spur, he misjudged it. Bartram sniffed and tossed his head in what was suspiciously like a flounce. "Oh, yes, you'd much rather *he* was your brother, wouldn't you? His sister's sending him to Cambridge but I've noticed that although you went there, and so did Papa and Grandpapa, you've never mentioned sending me. I suppose you think it would be a waste of money."

Bardolph frowned, unable to see any connection with the complaint at hand and his brother's future. "Then I'm sorry, Bart. I had no idea you harboured ambitions of a deeper education. If Cambridge is what you want, rest assured you shall have it. I thought your sole goal was the navy. You know my views on that. Believe me, I'd infinitely prefer to see you at university."

Since Bartram hadn't the slightest interest in extending his education any further than was absolutely necessary and had only mentioned it at all out of pique, this immediate acceptance by his brother of a hitherto unknown ambition was decidedly unnerving. If he wasn't careful, he'd end up doing even more Latin and Greek than his tutors had already foisted on him.

"Yes, well, I might surprise you yet," he said, retreating into childish dark innuendo.

"You already have," Bardolph told him. "However, perhaps we may discuss that another time. I'd like to return to the matter in hand. Since neither you nor young Leigh has been prepared to give me an alternative explanation for this morning's little fracas, I have no option but to accept Huggate's evaluation. You're gated for the next week—and I do mean gated: confined to the house. I'd like to say you can ride in the park, but quite frankly I don't trust you not to stray. Furthermore, you'll have nothing to do with Richard Leigh for the time being," he concluded, unconsciously echoing India.

"And how long is that going to be?" Bartram asked. "He's the only person round here that I've got anything in common with."

"Until I say so. It will depend largely on your behaviour and your attitude."

"In other words, you're forbidding it altogether."

"That isn't what I meant and it isn't what I intend. Richard Leigh is probably the most suitable friend you're likely to find round here." Bardolph paused. "This is one of the problems of living here and it's one that would be solved by Cambridge. If that's really what you want, Bart, you've only to let me know."

But Bartram wasn't going to let himself be trapped into something which held no appeal at all. He ignored the plea. "If I'm confined to barracks, I might as well go somewhere more congenial than this," he said, conveniently forgetting that the old nursery remained one of his favourite haunts. "I'm going to my own room," and, when there was no objection from his brother, he departed, taking very good care to slam the door behind him.

Lord Bardolph leaned back in the rocking-chair and absent-mindedly set it in motion with one small push of his booted foot. He did not enjoy taking the place of a father to his sulky, resentful brother. He knew he came down far too heavily on the boy; he lacked that lighter touch that their father had had, a touch which encouraged an affectionate respect. As Bartram got older, he had tried to become less didactic with him, but it was difficult to sustain when Bartram himself seemed unable to recognise any change. Perhaps the answer was to encourage him to join the navy in the hope either that fraternal encouragement would make him change his mind out of sheer perverseness, or that a year or two in his chosen profession would bring a request to be bought out. The trouble with that scheme was that, in a time of prolonged war, there was an uncomfortable probability that Bartram wouldn't live long enough to make the request, and Bardolph didn't think he could face the feeling of guilt that would ensue.

He had no real objection to the friendship with Richard Leigh and if it resulted in some of the younger boy's initiative rubbing off on the older one it would be a very good thing. It was a pity Richard was in the care of so pert a female. Had there been a father to consult, Bardolph would have suggested they put their heads together and agree on a term to the boys' separation. It would at least preclude their playing one guardian off against the other, as Bartram had tried to do. Bardolph had little to say in favour of Miss Leigh but she hadn't struck him as being a woman who would let her brother do as he pleased. He would be quite interested to know exactly what sort of punishment she had decided to mete out, because he had no doubt at all that as the door had closed behind him Richard had reaped the benefit of that highly accomplished tongue.

It was a problem to which he gave a great deal of thought.

CHAPTER TWO

INDIA READ the note again.

> Lord Bardolph hopes that Miss Leigh will consent to receive him on Tuesday morning, or at an alternative day and time that better suits her convenience, to discuss aspects of their brothers' friendship.

It was short and to the point and if he intended them to reach some sort of agreement on how best to deal with the boys it was a very good idea. If it meant she was going to be subjected to another tirade about her brother, it wasn't. India had no desire whatsoever to meet Lord Bardolph again, much less exchange words with him. Still, the wording was carefully chosen, the request entirely reasonable, and it would be both churlish and unreasonable to refuse him. It was an interview which would be easier if Richard weren't around, so India told her brother, with perfect truth, that his behaviour in the last few days had been impeccable and she was therefore prepared to relent a little and allow him to go fishing, provided he kept his word not to see Bartram Chelworth.

Richard couldn't believe his luck and India knew that, when he was fortified with a flagon of ale, a loaf of bread and a hunk of cheese, she wouldn't see him between an early breakfast and dinner.

Lord Bardolph was obviously making every effort to be civil, and India had no intention of being outdone when it came to civility. He declined an offer of refreshment, how-

ever. "You're very kind, Miss Leigh, but since my visit will
inevitably have set tongues wagging perhaps it would be in
both our interests to make it as brief as possible."

"Would you feel happier if I asked the maid to attend
us?" India asked demurely.

He looked at her suspiciously, unsure whether he was
right to detect sarcasm. He decided not. "I don't think we
need go to quite those lengths. I'll put my cards on the table, Miss Leigh. I don't know what you may have learned
from your brother, but mine has given me no explanation at
all for this business with Huggate and, although I know you
hold Bartram in low esteem, I assure you he isn't usually as
irresponsible as Huggate's story seems to suggest."

Thus courteously reminded of her own discourtesy, India coloured and drew a deep breath. "Lord Bardolph, I'm
very conscious that on your last visit here my concern got
the better of me and I made statements that went beyond the
bounds of politeness. Will you accept my apology?"

Apology notwithstanding, it was gratifying to see him so
completely taken aback. He smiled, and India observed that
his normally saturnine features were changed utterly by the
genuine warmth in his normally cold grey eyes.

"I think we both said things in the heat of the moment
that we may later have regretted," he said. "I know I did.
Shall we try to put that unfortunate exchange behind us?"

"Nothing would give me greater pleasure," India agreed
warmly. "Richard told me quite a lot. I think he was telling
me the truth—apart from anything else, he is usually truthful—but they do seem to have been . . . well, misguided."

"Would you be betraying a confidence to tell me what he
said?"

India considered. There were some aspects of Richard's
revelations which she would prefer not to divulge, if only
because Bartram's somewhat partial interpretation of his
brother's attitude was probably unjust and its retelling was
not calculated to enhance the possibly fragile accord they
had just established.

"The general gist of it seems to have been that they've got it into their heads that Mr. Huggate—who, I must say, has always struck me as an eminently respectable man—is not just involved in smuggling but is in some way a mastermind behind it."

"On what do they base this assumption?"

India shook her head. "Largely because he has a very large barn some way from the main buildings, and on the observation of ships occasionally at anchor in the Wash."

"What nonsense! Everyone locally knows exactly what that barn is for. He stores fleeces until he has enough to send to the clothiers."

"That, in the boys' opinion, is all bluff," India told him. "In fact, while Richard was telling me all this, it occurred to him that Mr. Huggate was involved in a two-way trade: contraband in and fleeces out. I'm afraid he does have a very vivid imagination," she added apologetically.

"It's a characteristic of youth, I believe." He smiled at a suddenly recollected memory. "I remember when I was about twelve being firmly convinced that Jem Patrick, who was sexton at the time, dug corpses up again when the mourners had gone home, and served them to his family."

India stared at him, fascinated. "What on earth gave you that idea?"

"Evidence every bit as convincing as any the boys have got hold of, I assure you. For one thing, he looked like a hobgoblin and his wife like a witch and she did all her cooking the old way, in a huge iron pot hanging over the fire—you could see it through the open door of the cottage when you rode by. What else would you need such a big pot for? The fact that they had eight children and Jem was known to be one of the most successful poachers in the Fens didn't seem to me to have any relevance at all."

"Did you tell anyone about it?"

"I kept it to myself until one summer when there hadn't been any deaths for several weeks and it occurred to me that the family must be getting pretty hungry and maybe, in the

circumstances, Jem might supplement the pot with the odd
naughty boy, so I decided I was only doing my duty by
warning the younger children in the village to stay at home
and be extra good. Their parents soon found out why the
poor mites were terrified to set foot out of doors and, just
like Huggate, they descended on the Hall to complain to my
father."

"What did he do?"

"He was appalled, of course. That was the only time in
my life he ever gave me a thrashing—and that was the easy
part of the punishment. I had to go to Jem Patrick and his
wife and apologise. That taught me a lesson I've never forgotten. What made it all the harder was that the Patricks
were so forgiving about it. In a way, I'd have felt better if
he'd given me a thrashing, too. I can laugh about it now—
mainly because those two poor souls are dead themselves so
I no longer feel embarrassed every time I see them—but it
wasn't funny at the time."

India chuckled. "I can imagine—and I must say it's a
great comfort to know that you weren't *always* a pillar of
rectitude. That makes you *much* more human."

He stiffened. "Is that how you see me? As an inhuman
pillar?"

"Oh, dear, why don't I learn to think before I speak?"
India lamented. "Just when we seem to be getting on so
much better, too. Mind you," she added, consideringly, "I
suppose a pillar must by definition be inhuman. Still, it
wasn't civil and I'm determined to be civil. I'm sorry."

Disconcerted that, while India should apologise for her
rudeness, she felt no need to modify her judgement of him,
Bardolph suggested they return to the matter in hand. "If
Bartram really believed that story, why on earth didn't he
come to me with it? He must have known I'm the person
best situated both to look into the allegation and to do
something about it if it proved true."

"You didn't go to your father with a far more bizarre
story," India pointed out gently.

"True, and I suppose the reason was that I knew he wouldn't believe it." He paused and looked at her. "Is that why Bartram didn't come to me?"

"You'll have to ask him that, my lord. I've not spoken to him and it would hardly be right for me to repeat anything I might have heard at second hand."

"Which means Richard has told you the reasons and I'm not far off the mark," he said shrewdly. "Dare I ask if you're punishing your brother?"

"Yes, of course. As much for giving Mr. Huggate cause for concern as anything else."

"Good. I think we ought to see whether we can co-ordinate the punishments we've meted out so that they're being treated more or less equally. I've gated Bartram for a week and told him he can't see Richard for the time being. When I was pressed to define that limitation, I told him it meant till I said he could. He wasn't very pleased. What's so funny?"

India had thrown back her head and was laughing that full-throated laugh that had so annoyed him before. He found it rather less annoying on this occasion, for some reason.

"We seem to have had identical conversations," she told him. "Mind you, I did concede that Richard could accompany me to church and to do the shopping." She chuckled. "He didn't think that was much of a mitigation to what he described as an indefinite sentence."

Bardolph smiled ruefully. "At least we're in perfect accord on one thing," he said. "Will you tell him the purpose of my visit?"

"He won't need to know anything about it. I told him that, since he'd been on such exceptionally good behaviour, I was going to relent for just one day and let him go fishing. He won't be back until dinnertime."

"Didn't he think that rather odd?"

"I shouldn't think so. He'll just attribute it to my being
in a singularly good mood today. I thought it quite likely
might not wish to discuss your visit with him."

"Especially since he was present during my last one."

"Precisely."

"For how long do you suggest we sustain the ban on thei
meeting?" Bardolph asked.

"It must be long enough to be a punishment but not so
long that they take to meeting clandestinely. I don't think we
should do anything to encourage deceit, do you?"

"What would you say to a week confined to the house
followed by a fortnight honour bound not to meet?"

"That sounds reasonable," India said thoughtfully. "Do
we tell them we've set a limit?"

Bardolph considered the matter. "I think not. A fortnight isn't really very long. If they don't know, it will seem
much more severe than it's going to be."

"Mmm. Are you sure that's wise?"

"It's only two weeks, for goodness' sake."

"I suppose so," India said doubtfully. "They can't get up
to much in that time, can they? Not on their own."

NEITHER INDIA nor Bardolph saw the surreptitious passing
of a note between their brothers on the way out of church
that Sunday. By that time, both boys had been told that
their confinement to the house would end on Tuesday but
that the ban on their meeting would continue 'indefinitely.
Richard had accepted this decision with resignation, but
Bartram had grumbled for the rest of the day about its being unfair and he betted no such harsh fate had been allot-
ted to Richard. Since Bardolph had no intention of telling
his brother of his visit, he bore the grumbles with a better
grace than Bartram had expected, thus depriving the
younger of the self-righteous sense of grievance in which an
outburst of anger would have allowed him to indulge.

It really was too bad. There was no justice in the world
Edward was out to thwart him at every turn and if Bartram

weren't very careful he'd find himself packed off to Cambridge without a by-your-leave. It was no good talking to Edward, who was past being able to see reason. He would just have to take matters into his own hands. *That* would make Edward sorry.

Richard wasn't happy about the ban and objected to it as much on principle as because it bothered him unduly. He had plenty of other things to do even if they weren't as much fun on his own. Common sense told him that "indefinitely" probably meant three or four weeks—less if he played his cards right. Common sense also told him that the better the grace with which he accepted it, the sooner it was likely to come to an end. He wasn't at all pleased to receive a note asking—no, demanding—that he and Bartram should meet on the outmarshes behind the sea-bank on the first day of their freedom.

His initial reaction was to reject the idea but when he reread the message there was something about the wording which made him feel uncomfortable, especially since he wouldn't be able to let Bartram know he wasn't coming. It was brief yet managed to be both hysterical and despairing and hinted at some awful fate Bardolph had lined up for his brother. Richard couldn't see what that might be other than his well-established refusal to let Bartram go to sea, though perhaps the Viscount had come up with an alternative career for his brother. It was typical of Bartram to read too much into something his brother had said, just as—admittedly aided and abetted by Richard—he had read too much into Mr. Huggate's activities. As Richard was now shamefacedly prepared to admit, they had let their imaginations run away with them.

The obvious thing to do—and certainly the most sensible—would be to take the note to India and ask for special dispensation, just this once, to let him meet his friend. He rejected it only because he wouldn't be a bit surprised if India, presumably still seething under Bardolph's insults, didn't go straight over to the Hall and demand that this time it should be the Viscount who kept a tighter rein on his brother. In that eventuality, Richard had no doubt that once India had left Bartram would get one of the sarcastic tongue-lashings he so dreaded. No, he couldn't tell India any more than he could leave his friend on the outmarshes feeling he had been deserted. It went against the grain to be deceitful and if India found out...well, he'd just have to cross that bridge when he came to it.

At least he wasn't obliged to lie. When India saw him going out her only words were a reminder to be back for dinner. No "Where are you going?" or "You won't see Bartram, will you?" He was perfectly willing to agree to be back for dinner. He had no intention of being anything else.

Bartram was already there and, judging by his manner, had been for some time. "I began to think you weren't going to be able to give your sister the slip," he said.

"Didn't have to," Richard replied. "I'm not gated any more. Just a week of that. I can go where I like, provided I don't see you."

"Same here," Bartram said, surprised. "Do you think they've put their heads together?"

"Shouldn't think so," Richard said positively. "You weren't there when Bardolph took me home. Believe me, they didn't part good friends. I should think they'd both find it difficult to be barely polite to one another if they met in the street. What's this all about? I don't mind telling you I was in two minds whether to come. I don't like deceiving India, not when I've given her my word. I grumble about her but she's not a bad sort. Even let me go fishing once when I was gated because I'd been taking it well. This had better be worthwhile because if she finds out she's going to be *really* angry."

"Bardolph's sending me to Cambridge," Bartram said dramatically.

Richard considered the matter. "It's not exactly the Grand Tour—it's not exactly London, if it comes to that but I should think there's plenty to do there. How long for?''

"You don't understand. It's to study."

"What's wrong with that? He's not the sort to starve you of funds and from what I've heard there's plenty going on if you've the ready. Not that I've mentioned that to India, you understand," he added hastily, "and I'd be obliged if you wouldn't, either."

"Don't you understand? It's his scheme to stop me going into the navy."

"Maybe he just feels you should have a good education first," Richard suggested.

"What use is Latin and Greek on the high seas?" Bartram asked. "None, that's what. No, he's going to push me into the church."

"Has he said so?" Richard asked, surprised. He wasn't at all sure what qualities were needed in a churchman but he somehow didn't think Bartram had them, and he didn't altogether share Bartram's opinion of his brother.

"No, of course not. He's not that stupid. He must know I wouldn't go along with it."

"Then what makes you think that's his intention?"

"I can't think of any other reason for sending me to Cambridge," Bartram said. "Besides, I've got a sort of hunch about it."

"Look, I don't want to upset you, Bart, but haven't you noticed that these hunches of yours aren't exactly reliable?"

"You didn't see him. He sat in that rocking-chair cool as a cucumber and he wasn't the least bit concerned about what *I* wanted. Still, I've had plenty of time to think about it now, and I've decided what we're going to do."

"'We'?" Richard echoed. "What has all this got to do with me? Where do I come into it?"

"You're my friend, aren't you? I'm the first to admit that I've got the imagination but you've got the common sense—

quite a lot of it, considering your age—so we make a good combination, so naturally we do things together."

"What things?" Richard asked suspiciously. He liked this conversation less and less the further it progressed.

"Has your sister told you how long this ban on seeing each other is going to last?"

"No. She said it would be till she saw fit."

"Exactly! Edward said much the same. He said it would be when he judged I'd had long enough to learn some sense. You know what it means, don't you?"

"That if we play our cards right and don't get up to any mischief in the meantime they'll lift it," Richard reasoned.

"Don't you believe it. This ban will last until after Edward's packed me off to Cambridge. I expect he's already writing to his old college to ask them to take me."

"Would that really be so bad? I mean, the trouble with this place is that there's absolutely no one to do things with—there's you and there's me. Apart from us everyone is either working or too old to be interested in fun. At least at Cambridge you'll make lots of friends in the same situation as yourself. I'm the one that'll be worst off, stuck here with nothing to do."

"Which is why I've come up with this scheme," Bartram told him, thinking that if ever there was a hot iron to be struck this was it. "We run away. In the night," he added.

Richard looked at him pityingly. "I didn't imagine you meant in broad daylight," he said scathingly. "And what then? I've always thought running away sounded very uncomfortable: no proper food," he explained with some feeling.

"We take food with us—there's bound to be plenty in your larder and mine—and we take lots of money. Well, as much as we can scrape together. I thought we could run away to sea. That way the navy'd feed us *and* pay us."

"Oh, no, we don't—at least, I don't. I've had enough of the sea to last me a lifetime, thank you very much, and can't imagine a rating in the navy—which is what we'd be—

lives anything like as well as passengers who've paid for their cabins. And that isn't all that well, I can tell you. No, Bart. I am definitely *not* running away to sea.''

''I suppose it doesn't have to be the sea—not for you, at any rate. What about the army? That would be exciting. You could be a drummer-boy, right at the forefront of what's going on.''

Richard gave the proposal due consideration. There was no denying its attractions were greater than those of the navy. There were one or two snags involved, though. ''The ones at the forefront get killed,'' he said. ''Or else they lose bits, which is probably worse. I don't think the army's going to be much of an improvement on the navy, to tell you the truth.''

''And I thought you were adventurous!'' Bartram said cuttingly. ''You just want a nice, easy life tied to your sister's apron-strings. At least I'm prepared to get up and *do* something about my situation.''

''That's not fair,'' Richard retorted, stung. ''It's just that I don't want to join the army or the navy. I want to be a farmer and once I come into my own money that's what I'm going to do. In the meantime, I just have to pick up what I can about it, but I can't see that running away to sea is going to be any help at all.''

''Don't understand the attraction of farming, myself,'' Bartram commented. ''I've lived in the country all my life and all I can see you get from it is tired and dirty and endless conversations about the price of grain or the prevalence of foot-rot. Still, if that's what you want, why not come with me and when we're far enough away you can get some work on the land—which you must admit will be first-class experience for you—and I'll enlist. What do you think?''

As an idea, it was a distinct improvement on its predecessors and a far more attractive prospect than sitting out the next seven years until he was controller of his own life. Seven years, even broken up by the diversions of Cambridge for some of them, was a very long time and Bartram was right: it was time which could be usefully spent gaining practical experience.

"They'd come after us as soon as they read our notes," he said.

"Who said anything about leaving notes? We just disappear."

"If we do that, they'll worry," Richard objected.

"Edward won't. He'll be annoyed, because I'll have got the better of him, but deep down he'll just be relieved."

"India will. She'll worry herself sick."

"She'll soon get over it. She's not one of these silly, vapourish females and if she hasn't got to worry any more about keeping you out of trouble—which you told me you thought was why she'd come here in the first place—she'll be able to go back to London and find herself a rich husband or a title, or even both. At least she won't have to die an old maid, which is what'll happen if she has to stay here, because there are *no* eligible men at all."

"Except your brother," Richard said doubtfully.

"Edward? Don't be funny; he *hates* women. Besides, he's very high in the instep. I don't want to be rude about your sister, Richard, but let's face it, although she's an heiress and not the least frumpish, she just isn't the class that men like Edward marry."

"And after the set-to they had the other week, I don't think she'd have him if he asked. Besides, she's not after a title. Never has been." All the same, Richard knew that India had given up much that she enjoyed to get him away from the influence of bad company, which she had eventually admitted had been her purpose in coming to the Fens in the first place. He also knew that her chances of getting married diminished rapidly with every passing year. She was twenty-three already, an age which many regarded as beyond further hope. Perhaps by running away with Bartram he would indirectly be doing her a service. He still didn't like the idea of not telling her. Bartram might think what he chose, but Richard knew India would be both worried and upset. "I don't mind coming," he conceded at last, "but we've got to let them know what we're doing."

Bartram sighed with exasperation. He could think of no better guarantee of being ignominiously dragged home than letting Edward know his plans. Edward would simply alert every harbour-master and every enlistment officer on the east coast—probably even further afield than that—and ask them to have him delivered back to Old Fen Hall if he turned up and, since the reward would be generous, they would. If, on the other hand, there were no notes, it would be some time before he realised Bartram had run away and wasn't just off fishing. Then Edward would have to out-think him and decide not only where he was going but also which route he had taken. By the time he had worked it out and made a few false casts, Bartram would be on the high seas, out of his reach. It didn't occur to Bartram that his brother might be more than capable of out-thinking him.

"I'll tell you what we'll do," he said. "We'll compromise. We'll wait till we're well away from here and then you can write your sister a note assuring her that you're all right, and I'll post it when I've signed on. That way she won't know where *you* are, and I'll be at sea before she can let anything slip that might get back to Edward."

"You would post it? You wouldn't forget?"

"Trust me. I'm your friend. In any case, why should I forget?"

Three nights later Bartram waited until the only sounds were the creaks and sighs of a sleeping house and crept downstairs and out through the kitchen and the dairy. There was no sound from the dogs who knew him well and the thick straw of their bedding deadened the restlessness of horses unaccustomed to be disturbed at this hour. It took precious time to muffle the hoofs of two horses before fetching their tack and saddling them up but they were essential minutes: it was one of Edward's obsessions that the stable yard was kept free of mud and straw, which meant that the sound of iron on granite cobbles would carry with absolute clarity to the coachman in his house adjacent to the yard, even if it didn't wake Edward himself.

He led the horses across the yard and round the bend of the drive to a spot where he could mount without fear of being spotted and then rode off at a fast trot to the place outside the village where he had agreed to meet Richard.

"You took your time," Richard grumbled. "I've been here hours."

"I bet you haven't. I bet it just feels like hours," Bartram said shrewdly. "I had to wait till everyone was asleep and it took longer than I expected to muffle their hoofs. It was quite tricky trying to do it in the dark." He was removing the cloths from the hoofs as he spoke. "Did you get the food?" he asked as he straightened up.

Richard held up two sacks. "Plenty. Cook will be furious when she finds out. There's bread and cheese, of course, the remains of today's mutton pie, a veal pie we're supposed to be having tomorrow—or today—and the remains of a roast chicken."

"That ought to see us through a day or two. What about money?"

"The rest of my allowance and all of India's housekeeping money—about three guineas in all. I didn't like taking that. It felt like stealing."

"Rubbish. You'd have eaten the food bought with it, wouldn't you? Well, then, you've just taken money to feed yourself when the victuals we've got run out. She'll be able to economise once you're gone, so she'll gain in the long run."

It was a specious argument at best and did little to ease Richard's conscience. "What about you?" he asked. "Did you get any?"

Bartram smirked. "A bit more than you," he said. "Edward had the rents in last week and they were still in his desk. The lock was quite easy to break. I didn't take it *all*, of course," he said magnanimously. "I haven't counted it, either, but there must be about fifty guineas in my pocket."

Richard whistled through his teeth. "Bardolph'll kill you if he gets hold of you," he said.

"He's not going to get hold of me, is he? In any case, I doubt if he'll notice it's missing. What's fifty guineas to him? I've known him put more than that on a horse at the races and not bat an eyelid when it lost."

Richard, accustomed to the society of wealthy merchants in Bangalore, any one of whom could have accounted for every last penny in their coffers, doubted whether Bardolph was any different but judged it wiser not to say so. He mounted his horse instead. "Where are we going?" he asked.

"We'll make for Cross Keys House and the Wash Way," Bartram said. "I want to get to King's Lynn as quickly as I can and I'm sure you'll be able to find work the other side of the Nene. Or you can go further afield if you prefer. I've got to enlist before Edward catches up with me."

"I don't much fancy crossing the river at night," Richard objected. The Nene was fordable only at low water by the mile-and-a-quarter-long strip known as the Wash Way. On either side were treacherous stretches of mud and sand and when the tide swept in upriver it did so with deceptive speed and dangerous currents.

"Don't worry. I was born here. I know it well," Bartram said with a confidence his friend couldn't entirely share.

"I don't think it's wise, anyway," Richard said. "By the time we get there, there may be one or two people about. They'll be able to tell Bardolph they saw us."

That put a different complexion on it altogether and Bartram decided that hoodwinking his brother had better take priority over enlistment for the time being. "We'll go along the Nene embankment to Wisbech and cross the river by the bridge there. We won't be so noticeable among the crowds. Then we'll go across to Downham Market to cross the Ouse and after that we can head north to King's Lynn.

Or I can, if you've found yourself some work by then,'' he amended.

"That sounds better," Richard said. He rather thought he might part company soon after Downham Market and head across to Norwich where he must surely find some sort of work to tide him over until the next hiring fair. It would be very much easier to remain undiscovered in such a big city, too. One way and another, apart from the continuing feeling of unease about the way he had treated India, things looked as if they were turning out rather well.

CHAPTER THREE

LORD BARDOLPH'S valet tapped on his employer's door and, when there was no reply, turned the handle and went in, coughing discreetly. It took quite a prolonged bout of coughing to wake the Viscount, who was a heavy sleeper, but eventually he stirred.

The room with its heavy curtains was still dark. Lord Bardolph frowned. Sleep was still dulling his mind but something wasn't quite right. He was usually awoken by Folksworth's pulling back the curtains to let the morning light stream in.

"Draw the curtains, man," he said. "I can barely see you."

There was an infinitesimal hesitation before the valet did as he was told and the thin, pre-dawn grey struggled manfully over the windowsill, lightening the room without illuminating it. Bardolph groaned. "Good God, Folksworth, what time is it?"

The valet coughed again, apologetically this time. "A little after a quarter-past five, my lord."

"Quarter-past *what*? No—don't repeat it." Lord Bardolph sat up and looked steadily at his valet. "You know me too well to risk waking me up unnecessarily. Something's happened. Out with it."

"I think perhaps you'd better speak to Gidding, my lord. He's waiting outside."

"Gidding? The groom?"

Folksworth gave a small, deferential bow. "We only employ one of that name, I believe, my lord."

"Yes, of course we do. I'm still only half awake. Send him in."

Bob Gidding was acutely embarrassed at being ushered into Lord Bardolph's bedroom and would infinitely have preferred the valet to convey the news but Mr. Folksworth had seemed to think it would be all right... He pulled his forelock. "Good morning, my lord," he began.

"Good morning, Gidding, though I've a strong suspicion this visit means it isn't. What's the matter?"

"It's the horses, my lord. Well, two of them. Fanfare and Clarion, my lord."

"What's wrong with them?"

"I don't rightly know as anything is," Gidding replied, punctiliously truthful. "The thing is, there's no way of knowing, seeing as how they're not there."

"Not in their boxes, you mean?"

"That's right, my lord."

"Have you checked the paddocks? They haven't been turned out?"

"First thing I thought of, my lord, just in case they'd been needed in the night—though why they'd be put back in a paddock to catch their deaths instead of in their boxes is beyond me. No sign of them. Their tack's gone, too."

Lord Bardolph's eyes narrowed. "When you say 'their tack', do you mean quite specifically their tack or just the tack for two horses?"

"No, my lord. I mean their tack."

"Right. Get back to the stables and have a look round to see if you can find anything to indicate which way they've gone," Bardolph instructed, throwing back the bedclothes and swinging his legs on to the floor. "Folksworth, my riding clothes."

He was washed, shaved and dressed in record time even if, Folksworth thought regretfully, it showed. His visit to the stables only confirmed what the groom had already told him and a close examination of the scythed grass bordering the drive revealed nothing. Whoever had taken them had used the right tack and the dogs hadn't barked. The implication was clear: it hadn't been strangers.

"Have all the grooms turned up this morning?"

"Yes, my lord, I checked. Mr. Folksworth and the housekeeper are checking the indoor staff. It did cross my mind, my lord—if you'll forgive the impertinence—that, seeing as how Fanfare is Mr. Bartram's mount, maybe he's taken them."

"The same thought had occurred to me but you know as well as I do my brother isn't noted for getting up early."

"Except when he's fishing."

"True, but he doesn't take a horse with him, much less two. I'll go and check. If he's not there at least we'll know who to look for."

Despite the fact that he could think of nothing with sufficient lure to get his brother out of bed in the middle of the night, Bardolph wasn't entirely surprised to find Bartram's room empty and his bed unslept in. The counterpane had been removed and the blankets turned back by the maid the previous evening and an indentation suggested that it had been lain on but not in.

Bardolph called his valet. "Folksworth, would you be so kind as to find out for me what my brother has taken in the way of clothes and ask Cook to check the larder? I shall be in the library if I'm needed."

Lord Bardolph's desk was in the library. It was a large and very beautiful escritoire with drawers and pigeon-holes above the cherry-wood writing surface. Two doors closed over these so that a clean line with intricate marquetry was what met the eye when the desk wasn't in use. As he crossed to the chair at which he conducted much of the estate's business, Bardolph noticed that the lock had been forced and the doors stood slightly ajar. He frowned and then remembered the rents that he had locked away until he next rode in to Wisbech to deposit it in Jonathan Peckover's bank.

He opened the drawer in which three bags of coins had been placed and was initially surprised to find them all there, but when he took them out one of them weighed very much lighter than he thought it should. He opened it. It was the bag containing guineas and a quick count proved it to be forty-eight guineas short.

Bardolph frowned. A common thief would have taken all the money, not a relatively small part. A common thief would not have taken one horse, let alone two, because of the danger of the dogs waking up the household or, even if they could be quietened, the sound of hoofs waking the coachman. What was more, it was highly unlikely to be sheer coincidence that the money, the horses and his brother were all missing from their beds at the same time. The missing money suggested that this was no schoolboy prank, no midnight steeplechase and he had a sinking feeling that the only possible explanation was that Bartram had run away.

There remained the puzzle of two horses, unless Bartram had taken enough clothes with him to need a baggage horse. It seemed unlikely and then he recalled that Clarion's riding tack had gone and a saddle was not much use for transporting baggage. It followed therefore that there were two horses because there were two riders.

Richard Leigh?

The Leighs maintained no stable. When Richard wanted to ride, he hired a hack from a small local livery stable and they certainly wouldn't hire a hack to a fourteen-year-old in the middle of the night. Bartram would have faced no such problem.

Richard Leigh.

If that young scoundrel had persuaded Bartram to put up the horses and the cash, what was he providing? It would be interesting to find out. It would be even more interesting to discover what their game was and where they were headed but, since there was still an outside chance that Richard Leigh had nothing to do with all this, the first imperative must be to find out whether he was still soundly asleep in his bed or whether he, too, was missing. It was a pity the recently improved relations with Miss Leigh would have to be jeopardised but that couldn't be helped. He would ride over there straight away.

But first he had to try to discover which way Bartram and two horses—and probably a second rider—had gone. While someone saddled his horse, he told Gidding to organise everyone who could ride into teams which would quarter the Fens in the hope of finding someone who had seen them. Every farm was to be visited, every drove explored and the people at every settlement questioned. Since Bartram's ambition was to go to sea, and since his achievement of it would place him beyond his brother's reach for some years to come, the searcher's first priority must be the Wash Way. It was the shortest route to King's Lynn and, although the present state of the tide made it uncrossable and delay therefore inevitable, there was a very good chance the boys would have been spotted. Both Bartram and the horses would have been recognised in that area, an additional advantage which wouldn't necessarily hold true if they had gone elsewhere.

INDIA'S MAID was as diffident about waking up her mistress as ever Lord Bardolph's valet had been a short while previously, though her method was more direct. She shook her.

India stirred and sat up. "Eliza? Whatever's the matter? What time is it?"

"Seven o'clock, Miss Leigh, and I'm sorry, I really am, but there's a gentleman in the parlour to see you."

"At seven in the morning? Don't be ridiculous. And if there is, tell him to go away and come back at a more civilised hour."

"From the look on his face, he'd refuse point-blank," Eliza told her. "In fact, I wouldn't be a bit surprised if he came straight up and hauled you out of bed himself. It's Lord Bardolph," she added as if this explained everything.

India frowned. "Lord Bardolph? What on earth can he want at this unearthly hour?"

"I'm sure I couldn't say, Miss Leigh. He didn't look about to tell the likes of me. 'Just fetch her,' he says when I asks what it was about. Shall I tell him to come back later?"

India resisted the temptation to say yes. She couldn't delude herself that Bardolph was in the habit of paying morning-calls at this hour so whatever had brought him here must be important. "Tell his lordship I'll be with him as soon as I'm half presentable."

While Eliza conveyed this message to its destination, India hastily put on a peignoir of sapphire-blue edged with swansdown and held together under the bosom with a jewelled clasp. She freshened her face in cold water and hastily re-braided her dark hair in one plait which hung over her shoulder. It would do, in so far as such intimate attire could be held to 'do' when entertaining an uninvited man. Only the obvious urgency indicated by the hour could possibly excuse her not dressing properly and taking her time over it. If he didn't approve, that was just too bad—he should at least have sent a warning message.

Despite the fact that he was in no mood to approve of anything connected with the Leighs until and unless Richard proved to be sound asleep in his bed, Lord Bardolph was distinctly appreciative of the picture India presented when she came into the room. A woman who could look so good so early and at such short notice was nothing if not resourceful, though, in India's case, he had to admit she started with the very best in raw materials.

He bowed. "I apologise for the hour, Miss Leigh."

"And so you should. I fully intended to have you sent packing but my maid seemed to think it was important."

"Your maid was right. I certainly don't customarily make morning-calls at this hour, and not on single ladies. At least, not on those with pretensions to gentility."

"In precisely the same way that I don't customarily receive men in my dressing-gown. Gentlemen, of course, don't make it necessary."

Bardolph felt his lips twitch. "*Touché*, Miss Leigh. And now may we consider the pleasantries completed? The purpose of my visit really is rather urgent. Tell me, do you happen to know where your brother is at this moment?"

"I've always heard that some members of the aristocracy are noted for their eccentricity," India told him, "but I didn't guess it might extend to checking up at unseemly hours on where lesser mortals might be. It isn't any of your business, my lord, but since it isn't of the slightest importance, either, I take leave to tell you that Richard is still sound asleep."

"In his bed?"

India appeared to consider the question. "In India he sometimes slept on the veranda but it's very warm in India, you understand, and the wind doesn't blow you off your feet. Besides, we don't have a veranda here. Don't be silly—of course in his bed."

Lord Bardolph held his temper in check with an effort. "I wonder if you'd do me the very great favour of checking?"

India looked at him in silence for a few moments and then went over to the door. "Eliza!" she called when she'd opened it. "Would you go and wake Richard up and tell him to come down here immediately, please?" She turned back to her visitor. "Will that satisfy you, sir?"

"Admirably. Believe me, Miss Leigh, I hope he materialises."

It was Eliza who materialised. "I'm sorry, madam, but he's not there."

"Not there? He must be. Snuggled under the bedclothes, perhaps."

The maid shook her head. "The bed hasn't been slept in and Cook says can she have a word?"

"Tell her not now. It will have to wait until I've worked this out. If he's not in bed, where is he?"

"With respect, madam, I think you should see Cook," Eliza suggested.

"You think she can throw some light on this? Very well, ask her to come along."

Cook had come with the Leighs from London, largely because she knew a good position when she saw it. She was very Welsh, very red in the face and very angry. "There's a load of snide, underhand and deceitful wretches these Fen-men are," she began. "I can cope with the wind, I can even cope with their heathenish language most of the time but I can't and I won't cope with thievery and that's the truth, madam."

"What thievery?" India asked.

Cook held out one massive hand and counted off her losses on her fingers. "There's yesterday's mutton pie gone, what's left of it, and today's veal pie as well. There's no sign of the cold chicken and the bread-crock's empty. And that's not the end of it for there's no sign of that lovely cheese we'd only just cut into. There's gone they all are, madam. Quite gone and what I'm going to feed us all on today is more than I know."

"I'm sure you'll succeed in conjuring something up," India told her, "and as soon as I'm presentable we'll see about replacing what we can."

"What are you going to do about the thief? That's what I want to know," Cook declared.

"I'm sure Lord Bardolph will be able to tell us," India told her. "His lordship's a magistrate. Who better?"

"Rest assured he'll be hanged, drawn and quartered," the Viscount interjected.

Cook nodded. "I suppose that'll have to do but it doesn't go far enough, if you ask me." She turned back as she reached the door. "That wasn't quite all, come to think of it. There's two empty flour sacks gone missing. I keeps them, you see. They comes in useful for all sorts of things, but two of them's not there now."

"I dare say the thief used them to transport the victuals," Lord Bardolph suggested affably.

"I dare say your lorship's right," the cook agreed and left the room to conjure up a breakfast of pancakes, ham, scrambled eggs and kidneys, which was the most she felt able to concoct after so great a shock.

"I shouldn't think you could go much further than hanging, quartering and drawing," India remarked as the door closed behind Mrs. Newport's broad beam.

"Believe me, I'm considering it," Lord Bardolph said grimly. "Two of my horses and forty-eight guineas have also been taken."

"There can't be a connection," India protested. "The items missing are so disparate. Unless..." Her voice tailed away and she looked at him in alarm as the implications of this news coupled with the very fact of his being here dawned on her.

"Quite," he said sardonically. "Miss Leigh, would you be kind enough to check whether you have any money missing?"

"But I keep very little in the house—just enough for our day-to-day needs. Nothing like forty-eight guineas."

"Nevertheless, I'd appreciate it if you'd check."

"I shall have to leave you for a moment."

"I dare say I shall survive."

When she returned, she was both chastened and angry. "I owe you an apology, my lord," she said. "All my housekeeping money is gone. I can't tell you exactly how much it was because it was all in small change but it doesn't compare with your loss. I'd estimate it to have been very slightly in excess of three pounds. It begins to look as if the boys have gone together, your brother providing the mounts and the money, mine providing sustenance and such money as he could find. Richard will have had some of his allowance left but that won't amount to more than a few shillings. Why on earth have they run away?"

"That's a question they can answer when we've caught them. For the moment I'm more concerned to know where they're heading."

"You don't think perhaps that the 'why' might give some clue to the 'where'?" India asked.

"It might, I suppose. Do you know of any reason your brother might have had?"

"No, none," India said, shaking her head. "One is tempted to think the recent bother with Mr. Huggate may lie behind it but I don't think Richard was at all resentful of his punishment. He took it remarkably well considering he had no idea how long it was going to last."

"That's more than I can say for Bartram." He hesitated. "I don't wish to be unkind, Miss Leigh, but do you think Richard's clever enough to pretend to accept his punishment while actually planning to do something about it himself?"

India considered it. "I think he's clever enough," she admitted. "I don't think he's sufficiently devious, though. Apart from anything else, I don't think he'd want to cause me the anxiety he knows I'd suffer."

"Yet he seems to have done precisely that," Lord Bardolph said gently.

"He does, doesn't he?" There was a wistful note in India's voice which made her seem suddenly very vulnerable and the Viscount was conscious of a desire to protect her from any further anxiety—a desire which, since he held her responsible for her brother's behaviour, was quite irrational in the present circumstances. Then she visibly brightened as a thought struck her. "You don't think they've taken it upon themselves to prove that their suspicions of Mr. Huggate are correct? That they intend to keep watch until they're in a position to produce irrefutable evidence of his involvement?"

"That's logical enough and I certainly wouldn't put it past them—goodness knows, they're silly enough." Then he shook his head. "It's an attractive idea but it won't fadge:

there's an outside possibility they might be able to conceal themselves for what might amount to several weeks, but they'd never be able to hide two horses. Besides, they wouldn't need horses—they'd only be a few miles from home."

"Their goal might be London," India offered reluctantly. "Richard was very put out when he learned we were leaving. Would that appeal to Bartram?"

"It might well, though he's never expressed any interest. If he were on his own, I'd say he's run away to sea. His great ambition is to join the navy—a career for which I consider him totally unsuited."

"Have you told him so?"

"Frequently," he replied, surprised.

India nodded. "Yes, you would. So that's very likely what Bartram would do if he were on his own, but he's not, and no one will ever persuade Richard to run away to sea. I've no reason to believe he ever harboured any dreams in that direction but, if he had, the voyage from India will have killed them. He hated it. He said he intended never again to set foot on a ship no matter what. His ambition is to be a farmer."

"I've never heard of anyone running away to work on a farm," Bardolph commented.

In spite of her anxiety, India chuckled. "Neither have I," she admitted, "but they must have had some destination in mind."

"It begins to look as if the steps I took before coming here are our only hope," the Viscount told her. "I've taken every available man off his work and they're quartering the whole locality in the hope of picking up the boys' trail. Someone must have seen them, and if two boys on horseback don't attract attention *per se* the quality of their horseflesh will."

"They must be aware of that," India said doubtfully. "They may very well sell them and buy more mundane mounts."

"If they do," Bardolph said grimly, "I'll make them wish they'd never been born."

"And Cook will help you," India said, trying to lighten his anger.

He laughed in spite of himself. "She'd probably do an even better job than I. In the meantime, I'll let you know as soon as I've any news."

India reached out without thinking and laid her hand on his arm. "You will let me know immediately, won't you?" she pleaded, looking up into his grey eyes. "I mean, you won't leave telling me until you've sorted everything out?"

Bardolph laid his hand on hers. "Immediately, I promise. As soon as I have any news at all, I'll ride over and let you know." He smiled reassuringly. "Don't worry, Miss Leigh. Both boys are more than capable of looking after themselves for a few days. It's only a matter of finding out their direction, following them and bringing them back. If it's any comfort to you, I promise any punishment meted out to Richard will be at your hands, not mine."

India smiled ruefully. "Thank you, my lord, though I feel bound to confess that Richard might take rather more notice of you. You're quite formidable when you're angry, you know."

"Am I? I'd never have guessed you found me so."

India dropped her gaze and her long dark lashes fluttered over her eyes. "I'm a very good actress, you see," she said.

"Ah, is that what it is? I'm afraid I attributed it to your having the hide of one of your Indian elephants. I'm delighted to learn I was wrong."

It was jokingly, almost flirtatiously said and India was unsure how to respond so she hid her confusion by changing the subject.

"We're wasting precious time, my lord. I'll look forward to hearing news."

He bowed. "And I shall look forward to delivering it, Miss Leigh."

Lord Bardolph returned to the Hall in a far better humour than might have been expected. Nothing had transpired to change his opinion that, whatever the boys were up to, Richard Leigh lay behind it, but he no longer judged that young man's sister to be in any way blameworthy. On the contrary, her reactions had been everything he could have hoped for, if not what he had dared to expect. He was beginning to wonder whether he might not have misjudged the lady altogether.

BARTRAM AND RICHARD reached Wisbech in very good time and, more importantly from their point of view, without having been observed, so far as they could tell. Plenty of people saw them in Wisbech but none seemed to take undue notice of them. It was market day and buyers and sellers, regular tradesmen and itinerant peddlers, were congregating on the marketplace, while the quay was crowded with fishing-boats and cargo-ships. Bartram looked at them wistfully as they rode over the bridge upstream of the main basin.

"We could always sign on one of these," he told his companion.

"I'm not signing on anything," Richard told him. "Besides, this isn't the place. It's far too close to home. Someone would be bound to recognise you and it wouldn't take Bardolph long to get here—I dare say he could make it before the next high tide. In any case, I thought you wanted the navy? No chance of that here."

Both arguments were irrefutable but Bartram was deep in thought all the way to Downham Market. Here they agreed they were far enough away and had a big enough start to risk stopping for a rest and some luncheon. Each boy was so sunk in his own thoughts that he scarcely noticed the other was, too. Bartram was the first to break the silence.

"I've been thinking," he said, "and I've come up with a scheme that will suit both of us better than our original plan. It was seeing all those ships in Wisbech that gave me the idea. I know you don't want to go to sea, but why don't we sign on together to work our passage over to the Continent, then I can join a *foreign* navy and you can farm there? There are some very good farms in the Low Countries, I've heard, to say nothing of Belgium and France."

"You don't think it might be a bit dangerous farming in a country that's at war with my own?" Richard suggested.

"Well, not France, perhaps or Belgium, but there's always Denmark and any number of German countries— Hanover, Saxony, places like that."

"Don't you ever read any newspapers?" Richard looked at his companion in amazement. "Almost everywhere is under French rule. Denmark isn't and neither is Prussia, and I don't fancy either of them. I'm not going to Norway or Sweden, either. As for you joining a foreign navy, you must be quite demented. *What* foreign navy? Most of them will clap you in irons as soon as they see you."

"Yes, well, it was just an idea," Bartram said sulkily.

"And just about the worst one you've ever had," Richard told him with the bluntness of a true friend. "I've been thinking, too. It seems to me that this is a good place for us to separate and go our own ways. You can head back northwards to Lynn and enlist, while I go west and south into Bedfordshire and Hertfordshire where I'm not going to have any difficulty finding a good farm. What do you say?"

Bartram said nothing for some time. Richard's suggestion came as a very nasty shock. At the back of his mind he had never really believed that the younger boy would want to separate when it came down to it. He had been quietly confident that he would be able to persuade Richard that the sea was really quite good fun. He might himself have to relinquish his naval ambitions in order to persuade Richard to sign on for a spell on a coastal trader—something that didn't make the sort of voyage that had given Richard so pronounced a dislike of sea-travel. Why, such ships were rarely out of sight of land and it stood to reason that, while the sea could undoubtedly be, well, a little choppy round the coast, it couldn't compare with what one might expect to meet in the middle of the Atlantic. So pleased was Bartram with this plan that he had convinced himself that he had only to put it to Richard for his friend to accept it but his rejection of Bartram's modified version was so adamant that Bartram hesitated to put its predecessor in case that, too, was rejected with the minimum of thought. And now here was Richard wanting to split up already, fired by a thoroughly selfish wish to pursue his own ambition no matter how inconvenient it was to his companion.

"I think it's much too soon," he said at last. "Let's both carry on to King's Lynn. It'll be much easier there to cover our tracks, and if you do decide to stick to this bizarre idea of farming you can head towards Norwich. Better agricultural land round there."

"Is there? Maybe I should strike out for there from here. Get there all the quicker."

This was not at all what Bartram had in mind. "Well, you won't," he said spitefully, "because you'll have to walk. I couldn't let you go on unsupervised with one of my brother's horses. He'd kill me."

"Only if he caught you, and I thought the whole point of this was to get away from him," Richard said, startled by this sudden change in his friend.

"Figure of speech," Bartram said lamely. "The thing is, these aren't the sort of bloodstock you're used to riding. Much better stick with me for a bit longer till you've really got the hang of them. Actually, once we get to Lynn and I've signed on, I shan't need either of them, so you might as well have them both then. You can always keep one and sell the other. That would compensate for the small amount of money you brought with you."

Richard hesitated. The prospect of walking any great distance, especially in riding boots, was not an appealing one. On the other hand, there was much to be said for continuing to Lynn if at the end of it he came away with both animals. He wasn't at all sure that Bartram could be entirely trusted to keep his word since he was already taking for granted certain alterations to the original agreed plan. However, if Richard did stay with him to Lynn, Bartram could hardly then turn round and refuse to let him keep Clarion, even if by that time he'd decided not to include Fanfare. It didn't, after all, make very much difference where they split up but it made a considerable one if obstinacy lost Richard a mount.

"All right," he said. "I'll come with you to Lynn."

WHEN LORD BARDOLPH called at Abbot's Lodge towards evening that day, India jumped up to greet him, oblivious to decorum.

"You've some news?" she asked. "You've heard something? Do tell me, my lord. Don't keep me in suspense. You've no idea how worried I've been."

Lord Bardolph took her outstretched hands and guided her towards the sofa. "I've come here for no other purpose than to tell you what I've discovered. Now be a good girl— sit down, take three deep breaths and when you're a little calmer I'll tell you."

India found it surprisingly reassuring to be spoken to as if she were once more a child, and did as she was told. "Now, my lord," she said, "I think I'm calm enough. What have you discovered?"

"Fortunately for us, country people, no matter how reticent they may be, are both extremely observant and quite remarkably inquisitive. I'll wager anything you like that Richard will believe them to have been totally unobserved and Bartram—who's lived here long enough to know better—is probably of the same opinion. In fact they were seen approaching the Wash Way but changed their minds and rode along the embankment to Wisbech."

"The person who saw them was quite sure it was them?" India asked anxiously.

"I gather the light was too poor to identify the riders, but he was quite sure about the horses. A fisherman landing his catch at the Nene Quay in Wisbech recognised Bartram, who was riding over the bridge into the town. No one seems to have taken any particular notice of two horsemen in the town itself, but since it was market day that's hardly surprising. They were next spotted at Outwell. At least, the horses were and note was taken because the riders seemed rather young to have been entrusted with such prime horseflesh." He frowned. "I hope they give those animals a good, long rest. To get as far as they have, I'd hazard a guess based on the distance they've travelled in the first day that there haven't been too many rests so far and I doubt if they've dismounted and led the horses much today, either. It looks as if Downham Market is their immediate destination so I've sent someone there to find out which route they've taken. I'm still putting my money on King's Lynn, in which case I shall be there before them tomorrow, but I shan't know for sure until someone gets a message back to me, and I don't expect that until the early hours. It's a full moon and I've arranged changes of horses so that there's no unnecessary delay. At all events, I shall leave the hall as near as possible at first light. My guess is they'll sleep very soundly tonight and wake up feeling sufficiently safe from pursuit to be in no particular hurry."

"I do hope they choose a clean inn for the night," India commented.

"Whatever happened to your romantic soul, your sense of adventure?" Bardolph asked. "Where would be the fun in running away and sleeping in an *inn*? No, they'll be wrapped in a blanket under the stars. Much more the thing, I assure you. Besides, an innkeeper would remember them."

"Then I hope it doesn't rain," India insisted.

"I, on the other hand, hope it does. Serve them right."

India laughed reluctantly but it seemed to Bardolph she was preoccupied.

"Is something still bothering you?" he asked gently.

"I was just thinking—do you have such a thing as a side-saddle in the stables?"

"Several. Why?"

"I think I ought to come with you."

If she had intended to startle the Viscount, she couldn't have succeeded more gratifyingly. "Come with me? I've never heard such nonsense in my life. Totally unfitting," he declared.

"I can ride, you know," India said indignantly. "Quite well, as a matter of fact. The only reason I don't do so here is that the livery stable doesn't have a horse that will carry a lady's saddle. I've ridden quite long distances in India so you needn't be afraid I shan't keep up."

"That isn't the point," Bardolph said. "I'm going on my own so there'll be no chaperon and, in any case, I'm likely to be away over at least one night. Your reputation would be ruined."

"Now who's talking nonsense?" India retorted. "I'm an old maid—hadn't you heard? Quite on the shelf, I believe. Old maids don't have reputations to lose."

"If there's any truth in that outrageous statement at all— which I beg leave to doubt—you're not nearly an old enough old maid for it to apply to you."

India, momentarily diverted, looked at him speculatively. "I *think* you've almost been betrayed into a compliment," she said. "You really must be careful, my lord. When you're alone in a room with a woman, such remarks could be used to compromise you. I understand you're generally considered a *very* good catch," she added ingenuously.

"A good catch I may be, but no one who knows me would take me for a big enough flat to lay myself open to being compromised by a nabob's daughter. Which, madam, is precisely why you will not accompany me, no matter how outstanding a horsewoman you may be. In fact, now I come to think about it, although we still have some side-saddles in the tack-room, we no longer have any horses trained to carry them."

"That would appear to clinch the argument, wouldn't it?" India said with deceptive meekness.

Bardolph looked at her and frowned. It was certainly an irrefutable argument, though he doubted whether she believed it, but his admittedly brief acquaintance with her had not accustomed him to such tame acquiescence on her part. "One would have thought so," he agreed.

"Then nothing remains but for me to thank you for keeping me informed and to wish you good luck for tomorrow," she said.

He bowed. "I hope that next time I call it will be as the bearer of good news."

"To say nothing of a brother," India pointed out.

"That too, of course. Goodnight, Miss Leigh. I hope your mind is sufficiently at ease for you to be able to sleep well."

"I'm quite sure I can depend on you, my lord. Goodnight."

Lord Bardolph paused briefly before swinging himself into his saddle. He had an uncomfortable feeling that, although everything indicated that he had won the argument, there was nevertheless something behind it. India Leigh had capitulated far too easily. It was hard to see what else she could have done in the circumstances and she certainly didn't lack enough intelligence to recognise that fact. All the same, he couldn't help feeling slightly uneasy.

When the door had closed behind him, India sat in silence for several minutes before going over to the looking-glass that hung over the fire-place. It was a large, ornately framed glass and if one stood far enough back one could almost see oneself from top to toe. She was only very slightly taller than Richard; an inch, no more.

She went over to the little writing-desk, dipped pen into ink and wrote. Then she called Eliza.

"Get the gardener's boy to take this round to the livery stable," she said.

CHAPTER FOUR

A NIGHT UNDER the stars might be romantic and adventurous and what one did when one ran away but it was also exceedingly uncomfortable and, in Richard's opinion, just plain stupid when one was barely a mile from Downham Market and had a total of over fifty guineas. He thought the risk of a landlord's remembering them was a small chance to take when set against the advantages of a hot meal, a comfortable bed and a proper breakfast. Bartram disagreed.

It was Bartram's concern for the horses that had kept them from pushing on any further yesterday. He said they had pushed them as far and as fast as they had dared in order to put as much distance as possible between them and their relatives—by which Richard suspected he meant Lord Bardolph, since India could pose no threat in that respect. They would lay up somewhere snug for the rest of the afternoon and the night, and go on their way in the morning, but this time they'd put the horses' well-being first.

While no one could possibly criticise a desire to look after the horses, Richard found it distinctly odd that Bartram's primary motive still seemed to be to avoid aggravating his brother's ire. Bardolph would undoubtedly be furious if his horses were ruined but, since Bartram would be on the high seas and Richard the other side of Norwich, it was hard to see how the Viscount was going to find either of them even if his horses did somehow get back into his possession.

Richard sat up and rubbed the stiffer parts of his anatomy before clambering over the bank in the lee of which they had spent the night, and slaking his thirst in the drain on the other side. These wide, canal-like water-courses had been built over the last century and a half to drain the water from the marshy fens and turn the resulting siltfields into some of the richest farmland in England. They stretched in a huge, man-made, geometric web across the landscape, some of them no more than a narrow dyke, others twelve, sixteen, twenty feet wide. They made cross-country travel more difficult but no traveller in these parts need ever die of thirst. Nor need his horses. When Richard returned, Bartram was still asleep, so he removed the horses' hobbles and led them down to drink.

He came back to find Bartram on his feet, panicking. His friend heaved a sigh of relief as Richard and the horses crested the bank and came back down the landward side.

"You scared me to death," he said. "I thought you'd made off and taken the horses with you."

"Thank you very much," Richard retorted with heavy sarcasm. "Is that how you trust your friends?"

Bartram was immediately embarrassed. "Well, no, I didn't mean that, exactly. It's just...well, I'd just woken up and all that. I wasn't thinking straight."

"I'm beginning to wonder if you ever do," Richard told him. "The horses are watered and so am I, and I could eat an ox but I'll make do with Cook's veal pie. She makes a very good veal pie, does Cook."

The boys were on their way again within the hour, heading north and keeping the Great Ouse on their left. Neither of them knew the road but both of them knew that this way they couldn't possibly miss King's Lynn.

Progress was slow because Bartram insisted that they ride for an hour—at a walk—and then dismount and lead the horses for a further hour. The excitement of the previous day had evaporated into an anticlimactic calm. It would have been a pleasant, peaceful journey if there hadn't also been something a little dispiriting about it. The feeling of adventure had gone and Richard began to feel more strongly than ever that he should have stood firm against Bartram's persuasions. He put himself in India's shoes and tried to imagine what she must be going through. She had been sufficiently concerned for his welfare to leave London, which she had loved, just to get him away from undesirable influences. She must now be tormenting herself with the thought that perhaps she hadn't acted in his best interest after all. Once they reached King's Lynn, he would write to her and, disloyal though it might be to think it, he was disinclined to trust the dispatch of the note to Bartram. He would find a more reliable way.

Bartram, too, was beginning to wonder whether his flamboyant gesture of defiance and independence had been altogether a good thing. Very likely Edward hadn't even realised he was missing yet, though a groom would have told him about the horses. In that case, the Viscount had probably decided he'd gone visiting and had had to stay overnight. Bartram was inclined to think that his decision not to leave a letter had been a mistake. He should have composed one very carefully calculated to hit exactly the right note and leave Edward flattened, humiliated and guilty at his insensitive treatment of his young brother—no, halfbrother, Bartram corrected himself. At least Edward would have known. As it was, he probably wouldn't even begin to be concerned until tomorrow, and then as likely as not he would simply shrug his shoulders and bid his brother good riddance. It didn't strike him as at all inconsistent that a young man who was so convinced his brother would care neither about a missing relative nor two extremely valuable horses should be so worried about what would happen when the elder brother caught up with him.

The boys' progress was not only slow, it was silent.

Bartram broke the silence. "What's that?" he asked.

They were leading their horses at the time. Richard stood still and listened. He could hear a rhythmic sound that was little more than a vibration but he could see nothing. "I don't know. I'm not even sure I heard anything. Unless it was horses' hoofs."

"I don't think so. It's more like a drum."

"Who'd be banging a drum out here?"

Bartram shook his head. "I don't know."

They listened more attentively but the sound died away and they soon forgot about it.

Their desire not to be spotted led them to circumlocute any small settlements they came to but they knew it was a wasted effort where more populous villages were concerned and these they rode through; a man on horseback occasioned less comment than one walking because the latter was clearly on a long journey, a question-provoking eventuality in itself.

They had left one such village a mile or so behind them and had dismounted once more when a sudden turn in the road brought them face to face with a small contingent of seamen: a lieutenant, ten men and a powder-monkey.

The seamen stopped, blocked the road and raised their muskets.

"Well, well, well," said the officer. "What have we here?"

"Nothing that need concern you," Bartram said loftily in what he hoped was a fair imitation of Edward's most depressive manner.

The officer was unmoved. "I can't agree with that. Seems to me you're just what we're looking for: two able-bodied young men. What better to turn into able seamen? Wouldn't you like to serve King and country in this time of crisis?"

"Not particularly," Richard said. "I intend to farm."

"Do you now? And what about your friend here? What's your ambition?"

"He's on his way to King's Lynn to enlist," Richard said, totally unaware of the significance of a contingent of sailors this far inland.

"Now there's a happy coincidence," the officer said, grinning broadly. "And what sort of farming are you going to be doing in King's Lynn?"

"None, of course. I'm taking the horses on to Norwich."

"Ay, yes, the horses." The lieutenant walked carefully round them. "Now I'm not an army man," he said, "but I'd say these were prime bloodstock and not at all the sort of beasts that I'd expect to come the way of two scallywags like you. Where did you steal them—?"

"We didn't," Bartram interrupted. Unlike his companion, he had a shrewd idea that this was a press-gang, though he'd never encountered one before. The navy suddenly became extremely unattractive. "They belong to my brother, Viscount Bardolph of Old Fen Hall in Lincolnshire."

"My, oh, my, a scion of the aristocracy, no less, and trying hard to acquire the manner born. What about you, young man?" he went on, turning to Richard. "No doubt your father's a belted earl?"

"No, sir. My father's dead. I live with my sister. We returned from India only a few months ago."

"Did you now? What a fortunate coincidence. After a voyage like that, a life at sea will hold no terrors for you, will it?"

"As a matter of fact, it gave me a profound dislike of the whole thing," Richard said bluntly.

"The navy'll soon put that right. Now then, we'll do a deal with you—you come with us without any fuss and we'll make sure you're not picked up as horse-thieves."

"But we're not horse-thieves!" Bartram protested. "I told you, they belong to my brother. He lent them to us."

"I thought I'd made it clear that I don't believe you, and if you could see yourselves you'd understand why. No, we'll take you along to serve your country and we'll take the horses along, too, until I've decided what to do with them."

"If you do anything other than return them to my brother, it's you who'll be the horse-thieves," Bartram said angrily. "And horse-thieves hang."

"Something you'd do well to remember. I'd have thought the navy would be preferable. Maybe I'll contact this Viscount Bardolph and offer him his horses back—for a reward. No doubt he'll be glad to know the thieves have been dealt with."

Neither Richard nor Bartram commented on this suggestion but the same hope occurred to both of them: that any message about the horses should reach Bardolph before they were at sea. Both of them had the good sense not to voice this; if it hadn't already occurred to the lieutenant, far be it from them to suggest it.

It seemed as if the lieutenant had found some snag in his own scheme, however, and before they reached the next village he stopped, had the horses' tack removed and hidden in a dyke, and the horses turned loose to fend for themselves.

"Why have you done that?" Bartram asked, dismayed.

"Don't worry. They'll find plenty to eat and there's no shortage of water. Besides, it won't be long before someone takes them under his wing."

"I thought you were going to try for a reward," Bartram persisted.

"Had second thoughts. Wouldn't want anyone to think I came by them illegitimately, would I? Now step out a bit more lively. We don't want to be all day."

It was the carrier from Downham Market who saw the horses. He drew rein and sat on his cart, and studied them while he sucked on his clay pipe.

"Ther in't many round 'ere like that, bor," he said, though whether he was addressing himself or his horse was unclear. "They's the right sort—and the right colour, too," he went on. "But wheresa tackle? Thass what I wanssa know."

He climbed down from his board seat, fished behind it for the iron weight that served as tether when there was nothing else and dropped it on the ground on the end of the tethering rein. Then he looked around him. After that he climbed to the top of the broad bank that kept the river from flooding the lower siltfields on either side and looked along it in each direction. Nothing. He turned round and studied the landscape on the other side. A dyke looked distinctly hopeful and it wasn't long before he found what he was looking for. He hauled the saddles and bridles out of the rushes and turned them over. Under the flap of each saddle, on each girth and stirrup leather and on every separate piece of leather in the bridles, was stamped a "B."

"Thass what I was lookin' for, bor," he said and lugged both saddles over to his cart and settled them in among the sacks and bales and covered them with the tarpaulin. Then he caught the two horses and tied them to the cart-tail. He climbed back on his seat and considered his options.

"Now wass for the best?" he asked the world at large. "Back to Downham and mebbe catch that groom and mebbe not and be a day late delivering and no mebbe about it? Or on to Lynn and ask around or mebbe find a magistrate."

Lynn won, despite his natural reluctance to have anything to do with magistrates. The reward for the horses mentioned by the groom in Downham was substantial but it was a gamble at best; people, especially screw-jawed nobs, had a nasty habit of forgetting their promises, particularly when they were made to people in no position to press for them to be made good. Payment for the delivery of goods was certain but a day's delay might lose future business. He climbed down and replaced the tethering-block behind the seat. When he set off again he was some three hours behind the press-gang and travelling much more slowly.

INDIA STUDIED HERSELF in the glass. Not bad. Not bad at all. It was a pity the boots were too big but at least she wasn't going to be doing much walking. Richard's cut-away coat fitted her quite well, despite being a bit tight round the chest. The breeches were a good fit and the problem of her long hair she had solved by braiding it from the top of her head and coiling it round and pinning it so that it was hidden under his high-crowned beaver. From a distance she didn't look at all like a female. She was unsure how readily anyone meeting her at close quarters would be deceived.

A tap at the bedroom door was followed by its cautious opening before India could say, "Come in," and Eliza, who clearly expected to find her mistress still in bed, began to tiptoe in, saw India fully, if most indecorously dressed and almost forgot her errand.

"Whatever are you thinking of, madam?" she asked. "Whatever will you do if someone sees you? Whatever will they think?"

"Are you here to tell me they've brought a horse round?" India asked, ignoring the maid's horrified questions.

"Yes, madam. Leastways, they've brought Master Richard's cob round, seeing as how they had a note from you last night. I nearly sent them packing, what with him not here and all, but I thought if you'd sent the order round—and I remember getting the gardener's boy to take a note for you—maybe you knew what you were doing and I'd better check first." She looked her mistress up and down. "And at the risk of being turned off for being pert, madam, I take leave to say you *don't* know what you're doing."

"I beg to differ," India told her. "Now go into the kitchen and fill a bag—one of Cook's hoard of flour sacks will do—with food I can carry: bread and cheese, some ham, some of the replacement pie she made yesterday. Plenty of it because I don't know how long I'll be gone."

"She'll kill me, madam."

"Tell her it was my orders and you didn't dare disobey. Tell her she can kill me when I get back."

"Are you going after Master Richard?"

"Something like that," India admitted.

"You shouldn't go alone, madam, not dressed like that."

"I'm dressed like this because that cob Richard rides doesn't take a lady's saddle and neither do any of their other mounts. As for my being alone, I can only reassure you that I haven't the slightest intention of being on my own for very long. Does that put your mind at rest?"

"No, it doesn't," the maid said bluntly. "Not when I think of all the possible implications of the remark. What do I tell the household?"

"You'd better tell them something approximating to the truth. Say that I've had some positive news about Richard and have gone to fetch him back."

"And your clothes?"

"Why mention them? No one but you will know what is or isn't missing from my wardrobe—or from Richard's. Don't answer anything other than the question asked. There's no need to volunteer information."

"And Cook? She's not going to be satisfied with that."

India thought quickly. "The men who brought me the news were hungry and had to be fed. That ought to do. If she queries the sack just shrug and assume either that she counted them wrong in the first place or that Richard must have taken more than she thought. After all, it's not your job to keep track of flour sacks if she chooses to hoard them."

It was Eliza's sensible suggestion to tell the ostler to tie the cob to the fence and go home, on the pretext that Master Leigh wasn't yet ready. "He may be nothing but a country boy, madam, but he's not a natural and you'll fool no one else at close quarters."

India thanked her and looked at the clock. She had plenty of time. Bardolph could only cross the Nene at low water and, while she needed to be fairly close behind him to avoid the turning tide—to say nothing of following his hoof-prints for safety's sake—she had no desire actually to catch him up until she was across the river and the rising tide made her immediate return impossible. She guessed that in his eagerness to reach King's Lynn ahead of the boys he would cross at the earliest possible moment. Timing would be crucial for both of them.

Hers was made more difficult by her mount. Richard had often complained about the cob which he apostrophised as a Jerusalem race-horse, a cant expression she accurately deduced to mean a donkey. He was built for stamina, not speed, and would therefore have been ideal for India's present purpose had he not also had a straight shoulder and quite the hardest mouth she had ever had to deal with. The jolting discomfort caused by his forehand construction wasn't helped by her own lack of familiarity with riding astride and getting accustomed to both horse and style took longer than she had planned.

When she reached the river, the far bank was swathed in the mist that the sun had not yet got high enough or hot enough to dissipate. Of Lord Bardolph himself there was no sign but the tide was still firmly out and there were comforting hoofprints in the mud.

India took a deep breath, shortened her reins and put the cob at the barely discernible causeway. She prayed that he was both sure-footed and endowed with a well-developed sense of self-preservation. She had never crossed the river before except by the bridge at Wisbech but she knew how notorious this route was, not only because of the suddenness with which the tide came in and the currents it brought with it, but because it was said the mud in places was enough to suck a man under. Hadn't King John himself and all his baggage-train drowned in these very waters, according to legend? India shivered. These were not the sort of thoughts to encourage except when one was safely on the bank.

The crossing seemed interminable, an illusion created not only by its inherent dangers but by the invisibility of the opposite bank, and India was reassured to discover that the cob was indeed sure-footed and not the least put off his stride when the mud beneath his hoofs became wetter and the prints they were following filled with water that blurred their edges as the passage continued. The tide was turning.

India looked downstream with some alarm and could just detect those infinitesimal changes that heralded the sea's inexorable advance. She dared not urge the cob to greater speed for fear of his inadvertently putting a foot wrong, and her relief when the mists lifted and she saw the far bank was almost upon them was unbounded. Twenty paces, twenty-five at most, should see them safely ashore but even so the water was fetlock-deep as the cob scrambled up the muddy bank to the safety of dry land.

Now the danger was over and the tide well on its way, India need have no hesitation in catching up with Lord Bardolph. The inaptly named Prince saw no immediate necessity for breaking into a trot and resisted both heels and whip for as long as he could before succumbing and his gait was so uncomfortable that India wasted no time forcing him into a more congenial canter.

The mists were rising rapidly now and ahead of her India glimpsed a horseman heading south-eastwards at a steady, collected canter. Given the superior quality of Lord Bardolph's bloodstock, it was unlikely in the normal course of events that a livery hack would ever gain on him but, fortunately for India's intentions, collection was an equestrian concept unknown to the cob, who thundered stoically along, slowly eating up the distance between them. Such was his single-mindedness, to say nothing of his hard mouth, that he lumbered past the Viscount's half-bred hunter regardless of his rider's efforts to rein him back. By the time she had succeeded in slowing him down, they were so well ahead of Lord Bardolph that she had to stop him altogether and wait for the other to catch up.

Since Lord Bardolph could only have seen her retreating back and was therefore unlikely to have recognised her, India decided that the sooner she made herself known to him the better, and get any unpleasantness out of the way. The alternative would have been to stay behind him all the way to Lynn and have the ensuing scene—for she had no doubt there would be one—acted out in front of an audience of fascinated passers-by.

"Good morning, my lord," she called out as he approached. "We seem both to be making good time."

His head jerked up and only instinctive good horsemanship stopped him jabbing at his horse's mouth. "Miss Leigh? Surely not?" He came closer and stared more penetratingly. "Good God, it *is* you! What in the name of all that's holy are you doing here?"

"You have a short memory, my lord. I did tell you only yesterday that I wanted to come with you."

"And I told you—quite bluntly, as I recall—that you were not coming with me because it would be most indecorous."

India smiled very sweetly. "Our recollections don't entirely tally," she told him. "That argument was demolished by my drawing your attention to the fact that, as an old maid, lack of decorum didn't enter into it. The clincher—as I recall—was the fact that, although your tack-room contains ladies' saddles, your stables don't contain a horse used to carry them. As you see, I've been able to overcome that objection."

Lord Bardolph cast a knowledgeable eye over the cob. "I hope you're enjoying the experience," he said with heavy irony.

"As a matter of fact, this is quite the most uncomfortable animal I've ever ridden," she told him frankly. "Still, it's very sure-footed, it got me here, and I fancy he can go on for mile after mile without wilting, just so long as he isn't asked to do it too fast."

"Serve you right," he said cheerfully. A thought struck him. "Does this mean you crossed the Wash Way?"

"Of course." Since there was no alternative, India was surprised he should need to ask.

Lord Bardolph scowled. "You silly little fool. Don't you realise how dangerous it can be? Or have you made yourself familiar with it in your brief stay in the Fens?"

"No, I've never seen it before and, yes, I've heard of its dangers. I used my common sense, that's all."

"What common sense? You can't have much if you even attempted it. I know it well and gauged my time with care, and when I crossed there was no one else in sight. You must have been some way behind me."

"I was hidden in the mist, I expect, as you were from me. I guessed you'd cross at the earliest possible moment. When I reached the crossing it was plain someone had just gone over. I simply followed the hoofprints."

"The tide must have been coming in by the time you reached the other side," he said shrewdly.

"It was beginning to," India said. "I was a little worried for a few moments until the mists lifted and I realised we weren't too far from the bank."

"'A little worried,'" he echoed. "If you were only a little worried, you must be quite mad. Don't you know how fast the tide can come in over that ford?"

"I have heard but I dare say they exaggerate," India said defiantly. "In any case, I made it—and I don't mind admitting I gave thanks for this stolid beast who knew exactly what he was doing."

"Which is more than anyone can say for his rider," Lord Bardolph retorted. "Dare I ask what you intend to do now?"

"I'm coming with you to look for Richard—and Bartram, of course."

"Dressed like that? You most certainly are not!"

"I thought it was rather a good idea, myself," India said, outwardly unmoved by either his anger or his sarcasm. "I can see that you might be concerned at the gossip if you're seen riding with an unchaperoned lady, but no one's going to think it least bit odd to see you with . . . a nephew, for instance."

"And for how long do you think anyone will be deluded into thinking you a nephew—or any boy at all, if it comes to that? Not once they see you close to, I can tell you."

"Then we must take very good care they don't get that close. I'll pull my hat further down," India suggested, doing so.

"I haven't got a nephew," Bardolph objected.

"You have now," India said affably.

He put his heels to his horse's side and moved off, closely followed by India, quietly congratulating herself on having won her case.

Her congratulations were premature.

"It won't do, Miss Leigh. You'll have to go back."

"The tide will be in by now. It'll be hours before the Wash Way is fordable again. Probably not until evening. I should think it was even more dangerous in the dusk, shouldn't you?"

"There's nothing to stop you heading south and crossing the river at Wisbech."

"Unaccompanied? When I wouldn't get home before dark? Is that more *comme il faut* than dressing like a boy and having your protection? Or were you going to come with me—for safety's sake, you understand—and lose a day in the search for the boys?"

He made no answer and they rode on in silence for some time. When Lord Bardolph spoke, it was in the tone of a man who had been giving the matter a very great deal of thought.

"I think the easiest thing to do in the circumstances—and certainly the most appealing—is to strangle you."

"You'd hang," India told him, unmoved.

"I believe the aristocracy is beheaded," he corrected her. "It would be a small price to pay."

"You wouldn't be so sure of that as the axe descended," India told him confidently. "Do they keep it sharp these days, or do they have to have several tries, like for Mary, Queen of Scots?"

He gave a short laugh. "Do you have an answer for everything, Miss Leigh?"

"Not invariably," she said after giving the matter some thought. "But I do think you ought to get in the habit of calling me something other than Miss Leigh if there's to be even the slightest chance of our deceiving people.''

"What do you suggest?''

"'India' is sufficiently unusual but I suppose it does have a female sound to it. This is rather fun, you know. It's not often one has the chance to choose one's name.''

"Then for goodness' sake make it something ordinary,'' Lord Bardolph warned her.

"You don't like Aloysius?''

"No, I do not. Quite apart from its intrinsic demerits, it's exactly the sort of name to attract attention—and about the only thing we seem to be agreed upon is that that would be undesirable.''

"Very true,'' India agreed. "What about Jem?''

"Too ordinary. Besides, viscounts have grooms called Jem, not nephews.''

"Has anyone ever told you you're extremely difficult to please?'' India said.

"Frequently. What about Harry?''

India tried to find fault with it and failed. It was perfect. It struck exactly the right note of boyishness, at the same time carrying a hint of having been used in the family for generations. "All right,'' she said. "I'll be Harry.''

The Viscount grinned. "Dear me, couldn't you find *any* objection to it at all?''

"I dare say I could if I tried,'' India told him demurely, "but I thought it was about time I let you have the last word.''

They clattered into King's Lynn by the Southgate and Lord Bardolph was immediately accosted by a man who had clearly been waiting for him.

"Gidding!'' the Viscount exclaimed. "I thought you were coming home after spending the night in Downham?''

"And so I was, my lord, but, seeing as how young Master Bartram and his friend was headed out towards Lynn, I thought I'd come on here and see what I could find out.''

"And what have you found out?''

"I think we'd better go somewhere where we can talk, my lord. In private, that is. There's a carrier wants to have a word with you."

"I'll meet you at the Customs House in ten minutes," his employer told him. "That will give me time to hand Phantom over to the ostler."

"Let me take him, my lord," said the groom, conscious that it was, after all, what he was employed for.

"You've got to find this carrier," the Viscount replied. The last thing he wanted was for Gidding, who knew perfectly well there was no nephew, to realise that youth on the cob was not only with his lordship but was also no youth.

As soon as the groom was out of sight, Lord Bardolph beckoned India to follow him and they treaded their way through the narrow streets to an inn which was sufficiently crowded for no one to have enough time to peer closely at young Harry. It seemed respectable enough, if not Bardolph's first choice in normal circumstances. He took the horses into the stables, which seemed well enough run, and engaged a private room, asking that they serve a substanial luncheon.

"My nephew—who will be here in a moment—eats like a horse. I have to go out on business but I'll be back shortly. Just leave him to get on with eating. You know what boys are," he said.

The landlady said she did, indeed, having raised six of them herself, and what about a flagon of ale?

This presented a small problem: any nephew of Harry's presumed age would be happy with ale and insulted by lemonade but Bardolph doubted very much whether India had acquired a taste for beer. "Ale for the boy, certainly," he said. "Can't stand the stuff myself. Perhaps you'd make some lemonade for me?"

Shaking her head over the eccentricities of the gentry, the landlady said she'd be delighted and Lord Bardolph went back outside to warn India to pour herself half a tankard of ale, so that it looked as if she was drinking it, and to make sure her back was to the door whenever anyone came in. "I think they're too busy to be curious," he said, "but just in case."

"When you've seen this carrier and listened to whatever your groom wants to tell you, you won't go hareing off without me, will you?" India said anxiously.

"Worried about being abandoned in wicked Lynn?" he chided.

"Not worried, exactly, but I wouldn't put it past you to leave me here while you pursue the search."

"And if I promise not to?"

"Then I shall enjoy a good meal."

"I'll be back, if only to tell you what I've learned. That's a promise. Whether I take you with me on the next stage is a matter for discussion when we know what the next stage is. Agreed?"

"I don't think I have a choice."

"You're learning fast."

India tried to relax sufficiently to enjoy the plain but plentiful food the landlady sent in. It was difficult because her mind kept straying to Lord Bardolph, where he might be and what he might be doing. Her great fear was that he wouldn't return just to tell her what he had learned, but would choose instead to act upon it, returning only when he could present her with a *fait accompli*. He *had* promised he wouldn't and India was quite sure that promise had been sincerely given. Furthermore, her instinct was to trust the Viscount, despite the fact that they seemed unable to spend more than five minutes in each other's company without falling out.

All the same, when that promise was given, Bardolph had had no idea what might be the nature of the information the carrier had for him and it might well prove to be something she would be happier not knowing. He might therefore break his word in order to spare her. She had no very clear idea what sort of situation this might be, since if it were very bad news indeed she would have to be told sooner or later and sooner must surely be better. So, despite her hunger, she found her appetite had largely deserted her once the door had closed behind her companion. She forced herself to eat because she knew she needed to and because what was on the table was much more appetising than the food that had been jolting across the county tied to her saddle.

When the door opened to re-admit Lord Bardolph, relief flooded her face and she jumped up to greet him.

"You did come back, after all," she said.

He raised one quizzical eyebrow. "I told you I should. Did you expect me to break my promise?"

"Not when you gave it," India said candidly, "but when you'd gone and I had time to think about it I thought it might be something so dreadful that you'd prefer to deal with it on your own and not tell me anything about it until afterwards."

He inclined his head in a sardonic bow. "Thank you for your faith in my integrity."

India flushed. "I'm sorry. I didn't mean it in quite that way. It's just that once I was on my own I had time to think and to imagine." She smiled fleetingly. "I suppose I gave my imagination too much rein."

"Much too much, but I'll put it down to a natural anxiety and not hold it against you."

India's smile was mischievous. "Until I do it again, whereupon I don't doubt you'll remind me."

"Of that you may rest assured," he said, unperturbed. "And now, if it's all the same to you, I'll repair the damage to my own appetite." He glanced at the table. "You said you were hungry but you don't seem to have eaten much."

"I was too worried—and it isn't all the same to me. You can't sit down to luncheon without telling me what happened."

"I can, however, eat and tell you at the same time, which—if you'll forgive the bad manners involved—will mean saving time by explaining everything to you either before or after the meal," he pointed out.

"Then let's begin," India said, pulling up a chair on the opposite side of the table.

Lord Bardolph cut himself a hunk of pigeon pie. "The carrier, who had been in Downham when Gidding was telling all and sundry there was a reward offered for the recovery of the horses and the boys, found the horses on the road to King's Lynn. Since bloodstock isn't very often found grazing at will on the Fens, he did some hard thinking—his expression, not mine—and decided someone had turned them loose to suit their own ends. He guessed they hadn't strayed very far from where they were released and thought he'd have a look for their tack. He found it more or less concealed in the rushes at the side of a dyke. He was quite positive they'd been concealed, not just put down for later collection. He had enough sense to guess they were marked and when he found the "B" imprint on the leather he knew he was in line for a reward so he caught the horses, tied them behind his cart and carried on into Lynn with them. He left them at the tavern that baits his own horse, hoping that the magistrate to whom he intended to turn them over would pay the bill and pass on the reward.

"Fortunately, Gidding had taken it upon himself to go on into Lynn instead of doing as he was told and returning home from Downham. By sheer good luck, he happened to see the carrier's cart come into town. He followed it to the tavern and introduced himself. It wasn't really necessary because the carrier remembered him, but Gidding hadn't known that. So both horses and tack are safely back."

"But what about the boys?" India asked. "Surely they wouldn't have abandoned the horses?"

"That's the problem. Gidding has checked both animals over. Neither has lost a shoe, neither is lame or saddle-sore, so there's absolutely no reason why they should have been abandoned. I questioned the carrier very closely and he's quite positive that there…" he hesitated "…that there were no signs of anything untoward having happened."

"You mean the boys weren't lying in a ditch with their throats cut," India said baldly.

"Well, yes, but I didn't want to put it quite so bluntly."

India, who felt the present exigency was far too important to allow for time-wasting euphemisms, said, "I can't think why not. After all, if I've no pretensions to gentility, my sensibilities aren't likely to be easily offended, are they?"

"Very true. I should have remembered that," he retorted. "Very well, as you will. No, Miss Leigh, they do not seem to have had their throats slit or their heads stove in, or, if they have suffered either fate, it wasn't in the locality in which the carrier found the horses. Frankly, that isn't much help in ascertaining just what *has* happened to them. Perhaps your ungenteel mind can offer some thoughts on the subject."

"No, none at all. Could they have fallen in the river or in a drain?"

"It's unlikely that both of them would have done so and no bodies have been found. Nor does that account for the hidden tack. The horses would have been grazing but they'd still have been saddled and bridled."

"True." India grew thoughtful. "It means we're not very much further forward, doesn't it?"

"I wouldn't say that. We now know for certain what we'd previously only speculated upon—they were heading for Lynn. We now know we're looking for two young men on foot."

India frowned. "Doesn't that make it more difficult?" she asked. "They'll be much less noticeable anyway, and Norfolk must be full of two young men on foot."

"I'm afraid that's so."

"So what do you propose we do now?"

"'We' aren't going to do anything. I'm going to retrace the carrier's route to where he found the horses and a little beyond in the hope of finding some trace of them. You will remain here until I get back."

India shook her head. "I don't think that's a good idea at all," she said.

"Then what do you suggest I do? If you've a better idea, I'm happy to listen to it."

"There's nothing wrong with what *you* plan to do. It's your plan for me that I disagree with," she said.

"Does that mean you think you ought to come with me?"

"Of course it does! I'm not staying here on my own, worrying myself into a frazzle."

"I understand that," he said, his voice unexpectedly gentle. "But don't you see, whatever's befallen them may prove to be exceedingly unpleasant and it may take unpleasant methods to get them back."

"Such as what?" India asked, intrigued.

"If I knew, I wouldn't have to speculate," he said tetchily. "One thing that has occurred to me, however, is that since both Bartram's family and Richard's are known to be wealthy it isn't beyond the bounds of possibility that ruffians are holding them with a view to demanding a ransom."

India considered the matter. "Wouldn't the kidnappers have sent the horses back to you as corroboration of their story?"

"That's why I don't consider that to be the most likely explanation."

"I see. So you only put that idea forward because you hoped it would frighten me off," India suggested shrewdly.

He gave an exaggerated sigh. "I suppose I might have known it wouldn't work."

"I wouldn't ordinarily describe you as an obtuse man," India agreed. "I'm coming, my lord. Action is infinitely preferable to inaction."

Since this was the Viscount's own opinion, he had no argument to set against it and gave in with at least a semblance of good grace. "Will you at least give me an undertaking that, once on the road, you'll be guided by me even if you find it irksome?"

"I'll give you an undertaking that I'll try," India conceded. "I can't give an *absolute* promise when I've no idea what may arise."

"I suppose I shall have to be content with that," he said.

"I suppose you will," India agreed. "There is one suggestion I don't think you'll object to. Since you've got the horses back, would it be possible for me to transfer to one of them? Either of them must be a better ride than that cob."

"I don't doubt it, but very much more difficult to handle, especially in a style of riding with which you're not familiar."

"I'll cope. Prince has done a pretty good job of breaking me in. Besides, would the nephew of a viscount be riding a cob-horse while his uncle was decently mounted?"

Lord Bardolph gave a reluctant laugh. "I suppose not," he said. "At the very least, it may lessen the chances of people looking twice at you. Very well, I'll tell Gidding to saddle Clarion for you."

"What reason will you give him?"

"That, Miss Leigh, is for me to know and you to wonder."

"What a very vulgar reply," India said affably.

"I wanted to be quite sure you understood," he replied with equal affability and added, his voice serious once more, 'Trust me, India. You can, you know."

The use of her first name seemed so natural that India did not at first realise it had taken place. "I'm sure I can, my lord," she said.

He had left the room to instruct the groom before the use of her given name registered in her conscious mind and she blushed, partly because of its impropriety and partly because she was afraid her own use of the formal address when she answered him might be interpreted as an attempt at a set-down.

If Lord Bardolph had seen it as such, there was nothing in his manner when he returned to suggest it.

"Ready, Miss Leigh?" he asked, apparently quite unconscious that he had ever called her anything else. "The horses are waiting and I'm anxious to get as far as we can before nightfall."

DOWNHAM MARKET was well within a day's ride for horses of the calibre of Lord Bardolph's but by the time they left King's Lynn they had only an hour or so of daylight left and both horses had already had a long day's work behind them, thus obliging their riders to take them slowly. India wondered whether it wouldn't have been better to set out early next morning but Lord Bardolph shook his head.

"I can't pretend I'm not anxious about the boys. If there's the slightest chance of finding them this evening, I want to be able to take advantage of it."

The handful of people they encountered were uncommunicative—strangers riding abroad at dusk were best avoided—but one old man volunteered the information that, while he couldn't rightly claim to have *seen* two boys, on or off horses, he had heard tell that a press-gang had been out that day. Unfortunately, he couldn't rightly say where it had been operating, seeing as how he hadn't seen it for himself, and it might only be a rumour, mightn't it?

"Do you think that's what's happened to them?" India asked as they pressed on.

Lord Bardolph frowned. "It could be. I can't imagine a press-gang would risk taking two young men who were mounted, especially when their appearance and the quality of their horses would suggest that they had the sort of parents who would be in a position to exert some very unwelcome pressure on the authorities to release them."

"Can they be released once they're taken?" India asked.

"Legally, no. In practice, it happens. It depends upon who does the asking."

"You mean it depends upon how rich they are."

"Quite, though discretion is also needed. Fortunately the navy is very badly paid and their pay is often months in ar-ears. That's a great incentive to a flexible interpretation of he rules.''

They rode on in silence for a while. ''We don't know when r where or why the boys left their horses,'' India said. 'They might not have been on horseback when they met the ress-gang—and I should think they were so dusty and di-hevelled as to disguise any quality that might otherwise ave been apparent.''

''I was hoping that neither of those facts would occur to ou,'' Bardolph told her.

''Very kind of you, my lord, but I'm really not some del-cate flower that needs to be protected from every adverse vind.''

He grinned. ''So I'm beginning to realise.''

Before the last remnants of light filtered from the sky, hey stopped at a small inn which regretted that it could only ffer one bedroom for the gentlemen but there was a ruckle-bed in it that would do his lordship's nephew quite vell.

Lord Bardolph groaned. ''The boy needs the comfort of good bed,'' he said. ''He's not used to the heavy riding ve're doing, so if it's all the same to you I'll have some clean lankets and a pillow and take myself off to your hay-loft.''

The landlord was horrified. ''My lord, surely that isn't ecessary? The truckle-bed is too short for you, I admit, but our nephew'll not have a problem and it's comfortable nough.''

''I'm sure it's admirable,'' Lord Bardolph told him. Unfortunately my nephew snores. I'll see him settled first. hen I'll be quite happy over the horses.''

He glanced round the little room they were led to and odded approvingly. ''This will suit you very well,'' he told ndia when the landlord had left them to find some more lankets. ''Make sure you lock the door when I've gone and on't open it until you're ready to come down.''

''I'll have you know, my lord, I do *not* snore,'' India told im indignantly.

"I shouldn't think you could possibly know one way or another."

"No one has ever so much as *hinted* that I do," she insisted.

He raised one eyebrow. "Really? Do I infer from that remark that you've been in the habit of sharing your room with a variety of people who might reasonably have been expected to comment?"

"I have no control over what you may choose to infer," India retorted. "However, it certainly isn't what I intended to imply. It isn't the case—and I suspect you're very well aware of that and are only trying to provoke me."

"And succeeding rather well, don't you think?" He laughed and chucked her under the chin. "Can you think of a better excuse to oblige me to sleep elsewhere?" he asked. "Or would you have preferred to share the room with me?"

"No, of course not," India said hastily. "I just wish you could have found an excuse that didn't make me look ridiculous."

"Ah, but then the very ridiculousness of it makes it all the more probable that you're my nephew. Now go to bed like a good girl—and lock the door."

India did as she was told, torn between annoyance at being spoken to as if she were still in the schoolroom and relief that he was prepared to go to such lengths of discomfort to safeguard her reputation.

She was both disconcerted and more than a little shocked to realise that she didn't actually want him to sleep somewhere else. Lord Bardolph was arrogant, overbearing and unnecessarily rude but he had a dry sense of humour that was more than a match for her own verbal indiscretions and, above all, he induced in her a feeling of absolute confidence that he knew exactly what he was doing and would see to it that she came to no harm. It would be a lesson to her not to make snap judgements on people in future. And on this pious thought, she fell into a deep and dreamless sleep.

They set off as early next morning as India's deep sleep and a hearty breakfast allowed, Lord Bardolph consoling himself for the delay with the thought that at least it meant the horses had had a good night's rest, even if he hadn't himself.

Since footpads might well have hidden the tack once they discovered it was marked but were unlikely to have abandoned horses which could easily have been disguised by the application of dye and a tooth-file, both India and the Viscount accepted that the most likely explanation for the boys' disappearance was the press-gang. Had that been the only explanation, Lord Bardolph would have returned immediately to King's Lynn to seek them out and bring his very considerable influence both as a landowner and a magistrate to effect their release. But there were other possibilities, chief among them some sort of accident to one of the boys which might have led the other to seek help at the nearest cottage, which, in this locality, was not necessarily on a road, much less in a village.

Their journey was therefore a far cry from a straight ride to wherever the horses had been found, and questions asked *en route*. Every outlying cottage was visited and then their steps had to be retraced to the road before they sought the next cottage or reached the next little settlement. By the end of the morning they were no more than halfway towards Downham Market and still hadn't reached the spot where the carrier had found the horses.

Then they had their first bit of good luck—good luck in the sense that it was word of two boys who might possibly be Bartram and Richard, that was, for it was also definite word of the press-gang. People at Runcton Holme reported having seen it the previous day "with two of they poor involuntary recruits," as one man put it. By the time they had reached Watlington, the press-gang had acquired another "recruit" and was clearly on its way back to King's Lynn, and the landlord of the tavern confirmed that they had taken the less populated road along the river, not having been greeted with any great affection in Watlington.

"Back to Lynn, I think," Lord Bardolph said. "And at the best speed we can muster."

They took the same road as the press-gang, largely because they might pick up more detail from the occasional cottage, but they didn't stop to knock on doors, only pausing to question people who were in their fields or gardens and easily hailed.

Calamity struck barely two miles from the town walls. Clarion cast a shoe.

India dismounted and looked up at Lord Bardolph. "You'd better go on, my lord. If you'll let me have some money, I'll lead Clarion to the nearest smithy and follow you when he's been shod."

"Oh, no, you don't, my girl," he replied. "There's a hamlet over there. Let's see what it has to offer."

Sandwiched between the Ouse and the Nar, it offered not only a smithy but an inn, which, though small, was both clean and respectable.

"Leave me here, my lord," India urged. "The smith can take care of Clarion and I'll stay at the inn until you return. It's far more important that you trace the boys. I should imagine that the navy gets pressed men to sea as fast as they can to prevent them from running away and, frankly, while that might suit your brother, it won't suit mine. His ambitions lie elsewhere."

"I don't know about its suiting Bartram," Bardolph said grimly. "It would certainly serve him right. You're right, however. I do need to catch up with them as a matter of urgency for precisely the reason you gave but I can't leave you here, unattended and unchaperoned. It's unthinkable."

"Nonsense," India said bracingly. "If I were diffident little Miss Leigh, I'd concede the point, but I'm not. I'm your young nephew Harry. Not, perhaps, old enough or wise enough to be left entirely to my own devices but certainly old enough to be left in charge of a horse with firm instructions not to leave the village until you get back to settle the bill—though I think I'd better have some money for food and a bed in case you're delayed until tomorrow."

"I doubt if you were ever diffident little Miss Leigh," he told her, laughing in spite of his concern. "And I'm not sure you look enough like anyone's young nephew for it to be wise to leave you at all."

"But all the same, you'd be quite relieved if you felt you could do so," India said, voicing his thoughts precisely.

"It would be very ungallant to do so, however."

"Only you and I need ever know about it," India pointed out. "And if I promise never to allude to it—or, at least, only under *very* extreme provocation—and if I further promise to be very circumspect indeed while you're away, what harm can there be?"

"You tempt me, but it's against my better judgement."

"It's my brother as well as yours who's at risk. Please, my lord—you *must* give their cause priority."

He hesitated but succumbed. "Very well, but you stay in your room as much as you can and don't draw attention to yourself. Above all, try not to get involved in the sort of conversation that makes people take notice of you." He chuckled. "Quite apart from anything else, it will strike them as distinctly odd if they never see you without your hat."

"I suppose I could hack my hair off," India suggested helpfully.

"Don't you dare! Will you do as I ask?"

"Yes, my lord."

"Very well, then. I'll engage a room for you and tell them to send you up some food. That ought to occupy you for a while. I've observed you don't subscribe to the view that ladies should peck at their food in order to enhance their gentility."

India chuckled. "That's probably because I haven't any to enhance," she said.

"Will you never cease reminding me of one injudicious—and highly inaccurate—remark intended purely as a set-down?" he asked.

"I shouldn't think so," she said cheerfully. "It gives me that advantage, you see."

India ate with gusto the meal sent up from the kitchen and then put the tray outside the door so that she could take off her boots and her beaver and lie down. She might have slept very well the previous night but a morning in the saddle and a substantial meal left her quite ready for a nap.

She was awoken by a commotion from somewhere outside the inn. It took a few minutes to register the fact that it was not only outside but a little way off, and then curiosity took her to the window to discover what it was all about. She had to open the casement and crane her neck before she saw the tail-end of what appeared to be a bunch of very angry women, one of whom was brandishing a broom and another a pitchfork.

Intrigued, India pulled on her boots, pinned up her braid more securely and crammed her beaver back over it before running downstairs and out into the street.

The shouting increased as she got nearer and when she rounded the corner she realised that virtually all the women of the village must be there, each of them armed, if only with a rolling-pin. These weapons were being brandished at a small group of uniformed men who were trying to come ashore at the little wooden landing-stage. The seamen were armed with muskets but they were obviously unwilling to use these for anything except inadequate shields against the blows being rained down on them by brooms, shovels, rolling-pins and, in one instance, an expertly wielded riding-crop.

India kept well out of the fracas. It was an entertaining scene even if she couldn't quite make out what it was all about; she wasn't always able to understand the speech of the Fens and when it was uttered by women who were excited and angry and all speaking at once she found it virtually impossible. She leaned against a cottage wall unobserved by the women, trying to make head and tail of what they were saying, and when this amusement palled and she turned away she decided to wander down to the other end of the narrow, straggling street to see how Clarion was coming on before retiring once more to her room.

She might have been unobserved by the women but the press-gang had seen her soon enough. The sight of a youth lounging against a wall grinning at them while the women hurled abuse and declarations that there were no men or boys in the village at all was too much and the officer in charge detached two men with hurried instruction to creep round the back of the village, enter it from the other end and take the insolent youngster while the rest of the party kept the women occupied.

Thus it came about that, as India strolled back towards the smithy, she met two smiling sailors coming towards her. Although she had guessed by now that what she had seen had been a press-gang which had come upriver instead of by road, the implications for herself entirely escaped her. She might be dressed in Richard's clothes but she didn't think of herself as a boy in any sense except the purely superficial one. All the deeper implications had passed her by, largely because she knew her present role was intended to be of extremely brief duration.

So she smiled back and touched her finger to her hat-brim in, she thought, appropriate salute.

She was close to the smithy now and the smith, glancing out, realised the danger his lordship's nevvy was in and called out a warning, but it was too late. Both sailors sprang and seized her "in the name of the King," bundling her back the way they had come in order to avoid the wrath of the women through whose ranks they would otherwise have to pass. India had time only to shout to the smith to tell Lord Bardolph what had happened before she was being half dragged, half pushed back to the river and the press-gang's boat. The men raised a triumphant cheer as they saw their comrades' success and the young officer with them grinned broadly.

"No young men or boys in the village, eh?" he shouted at the women. "Now we all know just what a bunch of lying crones you all are." He gestured to his party to retreat to the boat.

One of the women, whom India recognised as the landlord's wife, shouted out, "But that ben't a young man—thass Lord Bardolph's nevvy. You take him and his lordship'll have you in chines like an owd dawg."

The lieutenant had heard far too many excuses for not taking this youngster or that to fall for that one, though he had to admit it was original. "You tell his lordship to have a word with the captain of the *Pelican*," he called out. "That's if he can reach him before she sails."

"And don't think I won't," the landlady shrieked back. India blessed her but secretly doubted whether it would do any good.

She had fortunately crammed her hat hard on her head before leaving the inn and now she sat slumped in the skiff with her shoulders bowed so that her face was as much concealed as she could manage.

She thought fast. One way to get out of this predicament was to tell the officer she wasn't what they thought she was. It would be easy enough to prove it but she doubted whether it was necessarily wise to do so at this stage. She could prove she was a woman easily enough, but what sort of a woman? She could hardly blame the seamen if they took her for a lightskirt. Respectable women didn't wear men's clothes. Why, there were even those who condemned the wearing by women of riding-habits with cuffs and lapels in the military mode. The possible consequences of making such a revelation didn't bear thinking about. She had no doubt they would let her go—sooner or later. And in the meantime? They wouldn't be amused at having been so completely deceived, and the longer the deception continued, the greater would be their displeasure, especially when they had been, as now, so close to her. No, she could be reasonably certain that they wouldn't let her go with a pat on the head and an exhortation to be a good girl in future.

If any revelation was to be made, the time to do it was before the *Pelican* set sail. Doubtless the press-gang would suffer gibes about having been at sea too long, but she didn't doubt the captain would get rid of her as fast as he could—and if the *Pelican* was the ship she was destined for, it wasn't beyond the bounds of possibility that Richard and Bartram were also aboard, in which case, even if she was unable to persuade the captain to let them go, too, she would be able to tell Lord Bardolph where they were.

The lieutenant had a notebook out. "Name?" he snapped.

India hesitated. Truth or falsehood? "Harry Chelworth," she said.

"Harry?" he queried.

"I mean Henry," she amended. It wasn't easy to pitch her voice at a level that wasn't at variance with her appearance and it wasn't going to be easy to sustain it. The fewer words she spoke the better.

"Just Henry?"

She thought quickly. "Henry Edward," she said.

He looked at her suspiciously. "And where are you from, Master Chelworth?"

"Old Fen Hall. It's between Holbeach and the Wash."

"Is that so? Then you were a long way from home."

"Yes, sir."

"I'll tell you, something, Master Chelworth. I don't believe a word you've said. I don't believe that's your name and I don't believe you come from between Holbeach and the Wash."

Oh, God, India thought, he's realised. She hunched herself over even more and modelled her tone on her admittedly limited acquaintance with Bartram. "I can't help that," she muttered sullenly. "Your not believing it doesn't make it untrue."

"I'll tell you why I don't believe you, lad," the lieutenant went on. "It's because I've been landing along these shores and up and down these rivers on and off for a very long time and in all that very long time I've never met a local youngster who spoke the way you do."

"What's wrong with it?" India grumbled, guessing that some sort of reply was expected from her.

"Nothing, that's what's wrong with it. No trace of the local speech, no local words, not even the local intonation. No, you're not local. In fact, if I were to go just by your voice, forgetting the state of your clothes, I'd say you were an educated young man. Would I be right?"

"Sort of," India said gruffly.

"And this Lord Something-or-other one of those harridans was shrieking about. Are you his nephew?"

There was a brief, tell-tale hesitation before India said, "Yes."

"You're lying," the officer said with the certainty of one speaking from experience. "Maybe you tricked her into believing it. You won't trick me."

"Beggin' your pardon, Mr. Swanmore," broke in one of the two men who had captured her, "but 'e shouted something to the smith about a-lettin' a Lord Someone know what'd 'appened."

"Did he now? And what do you think people in a tiny hamlet south of the Ouse know about some nobleman who lives, if this scoundrel's to be believed, some way north of the Nene? Very little, if you ask me. This nobleman—if he exists at all—may be known in King's Lynn among the right sort of people but do you really believe a settlement of illiterate bog-dwellers know him? I take leave to doubt it.

"I'll tell you what I think we've got here, Mr. Warsash. We've got the makings of a first-class gammoner. Now it seems to me the best thing for him is going to be a spell in His Majesty's Navy to turn him into an honest man. What do you think, Mr. Warsash?"

The sailor grinned. "I reckon the navy might do the trick, sir—providin' 'e don't get washed overboard or hit by cannonfire or choked by weevils. Yes, sir, in seven or eight years I reckon he'll be a weritable pillar of the community."

Being totally unfamiliar with flash vocabulary, India had no idea of their precise meaning but she gleaned enough of their drift to be quite sure that it was unfavourable. If Lord Bardolph were here, she could seek enlightenment. She had no doubt at all that he would know what a gammoner was.

If Lord Bardolph were here, she'd have no need of an explanation because she wouldn't be in her present unenviable situation. It was a depressing thought, not made any less so by the fact that he had left her largely at her own insistence and, furthermore, that if she had done as she had been told and stayed in her room none of this would have happened. The women would have routed the press-gang—with hindsight India guessed that all the young men of the village had hidden in cellars and barns while their womenfolk held the press-gang at bay—and India would not have been spotted. It served her right.

That was likely to be Lord Bardolph's first observation when he learned of this and India thought she would meekly, even cheerfully, accept any objurgation he chose to throw at her if only he were there to throw it.

He might well be sardonic, sarcastic and cutting, but he would get her out of this mess first. Right now there was nothing she would welcome more than the sight of his tall, arrogant figure riding along the bank towards them.

The problem with that little pipe-dream was that both banks were now a long way off. The Ouse had widened and deepened as it approached King's Lynn. Their journey downstream had been fast and now the oarsmen needed only the occasional stroke to keep the little boat on course, the river itself doing most of their work for them. Only as the quays themselves hove into view did the sailors swing the skiff closer to the land.

"There she is," the lieutenant said, pointing ahead. "There's the *Pelican*, your home for the foreseeable future."

For the first time since boarding the boat, India raised her head to see their destination. Anchored in mid-stream—probably, she thought bitterly, to discourage pressed men from leaping overboard—the frigate seemed enormous in comparison with this little rowing-boat, though she was sure it was smaller than the East Indiaman that had brought them back to England.

Another small rowing-boat was in the process of returning to the *Pelican* from the quayside and India's glance involuntarily strayed towards the spot from which it had come.

Two men, their hands tied behind them, were being helped into the saddle by a third who then swung himself on to his own heavy-boned bay. India recognised both man and horse.

Oblivious of the risk to everyone in the little boat, she sprang to her feet and shouted as loudly as she could. "Bardolph! I'm over here! Bardolph! Come back, Bardolph!"

The sailors grabbed at her coat-tails and pulled her back from a precarious stance which threatened them all. The bystanders on the quay could hear her shouts but they couldn't make out the words. They had little difficulty in interpreting the actions of the youth in the boat and rightly guessed him to be a victim of the press-gang, and one with a bit more spirit than most.

They ambled closer to the edge. This could prove to be good sport and if the lad succeeded in overturning the skiff...well, there would be more than one pair of hands to help him out of the water and into a hiding-place before pleading total ignorance to having seen or heard anything untoward.

Lord Bardolph hadn't heard anything but he noticed the drift away from his own little theatre of activity to something more immediately entertaining and his gaze followed theirs, falling on the tableau in the boat just as India was forced back into her seat.

"Good God," he breathed. "Not her as well!" He turned to the two ruffians he had prised away from the *Pelican*'s captain on the grounds that they were wanted for horse-stealing and capital crimes took precedence over the requirements of His Majesty's Navy. "Don't either of you two dare move," he told them. "They've got India as well."

"India!" Richard exclaimed. "What's she doing here? She ought to be at home, waiting."

"Don't waste your breath preaching to the converted," Lord Bardolph snapped. "Just pray you have a chance to tell her yourself."

The boat had drawn alongside the *Pelican* now and the crew and their captive were preparing to board it, the latter horribly convinced that her effort had been unnoticed by the very person at whom it had been directed.

Lord Bardolph thought quickly and hastily revised his tactics. He led his "captives" down a narrow street that was little more than an alley, cut their hands free and passed his own reins to Bartram.

"Keep your hands behind you as if you were both still tied," he said. "I'm going to have to try to get India away and I'm not sure the captain is going to fall for the same story twice, particularly not when he realises that it's no youth that's been brought ashore. He'll let her go, of course, but he's going to have his doubts about you two and about my original story. It wouldn't surprise me if he demands to have you back so you need to be ready to leave here fast and in full control of your horses."

Bartram looked scared. "Why don't we go on ahead?" he asked. "You can catch us up with Miss Leigh later."

"Because it will be easier if she rides pillion behind one of you," his brother said, his face darkening with anger at this further demonstration of Bartram's selfishness. "And because I have no intention of letting you get into another scrape from which I shall be expected to extricate you."

Back on the quayside, a coin acquired the services of a waterman to row him back to the frigate.

"Captain Curdridge, please," he said to the rating who received him on board.

The captain stood up as his visitor entered his cabin, both men obliged to bow their heads under the low-slung beams, supporting the deck above. "A rapid return, my lord," Captain Curdridge said politely. "I do hope those two scoundrels haven't given you the slip so soon."

"No, Captain, they're quite safe—and have turned suddenly co-operative, doubtless under the entirely mistaken belief it will save them from the noose."

"Oh?" The captain's interest was more polite than sincere.

"It now appears that there were three of them—and the third has just been brought aboard by another of your parties. They claim this one is the ring-leader."

"Indeed? May I ask if it's your intention to deprive this ship of all its crew?"

"No, of course not. I just want the last of this particular trio."

"Of whose existence you were hitherto entirely ignorant," the captain pointed out, reasonably enough. "What guarantee can you offer that he won't be followed by a fourth or even a fifth horse-thief?"

"I think that's rather improbable."

"Frankly, my lord, I find it improbable that there were two and then three. I allowed myself to be convinced over the two by virtue of the fact that you're a magistrate as well as a peer of the realm. I find a third a little hard to take. Perhaps an element of share and share alike should enter into this. You've had your first two. Now it's my turn to keep the next brace."

"At least let me question this one—in your presence if you'd prefer."

The captain looked at him in silence for a few moments. "Yes, I should prefer," he said, and sent his midshipman to request Mr. Swanmore to deliver to his cabin the pressed youth just taken.

The lieutenant pushed India through the door and then ducked in behind her. "Take that hat off," he snapped. "Show some respect." And, to force obedience, he knocked the beaver on to the floor.

A silence fell on the room. In Lord Bardolph's case, it was due to the need to think quickly. The captain and his lieutenant were quite simply stunned and it was the former who collected his wits first.

"Dear me, a mistake appears to have been made, Mr. Swanmore." He looked piercingly at the younger man. "I take it it *was* a mistake?"

The lieutenant blushed scarlet. "Yes, Captain. I . . . we . . . had no idea."

"I can see I shall have to suggest to their lordships at Admiralty that seamen should have longer ashore even if they can't have shorter periods at sea. You, are not, I believe, a married man, Mr. Swanmore?"

"No, sir."

"Perhaps, your efforts have hitherto been misdirected." The captain turned his attention to Lord Bardolph. "Were you aware that this third horse-thief was female?"

"No, I wasn't. It was a detail her confederates omitted to mention. It makes no difference to whether or not she hangs, of course, but I suggest, Captain, that it considerably simplifies your decision."

"In what way?"

"You can hardly knowingly allow a woman to serve on board ship. I believe the regulations expressly forbid it. You'll have to let her go."

"Yes, I shall, but it only serves to increase my doubts about this whole story of yours. It was farfetched to start with, my lord. I'm more than half inclined to disbelieve the whole and send a landing party out to bring those other two back.''

Lord Bardolph grew very still and it seemed to India that he had somehow, without apparently moving a muscle, become both haughty and more than a little menacing. Then he gave a thin-lipped smile and raised his eyebrows as if conceding a point. ''I can't stop you doing that if you insist,'' he said and transferred his attention to his fingernails, which seemed suddenly to require scrutiny. ''I wonder how quickly word would get round the fleet that an officer, ten ratings and a powder-monkey, all from the same ship, can't tell a young woman...'' he glanced at India as if studying her for the first time ''...a remarkably personable young woman when she's cleaned up, I should think, from a youth? Not even when they've rowed downriver with her in the enforced proximity of a rowing-boat?''

''Below the belt, my lord,'' the captain told him.

''Quite, but in prize-fighting it's a matter of no holds barred.''

The captain turned to his lieutenant. ''That will be all for now, Mr. Swanmore. Perhaps you'd be kind enough to attend me when Lord Bardolph has gone ashore.''

The lieutenant shot the Viscount a surprised glance and opened his mouth to say something, looked at his captain's face and thought better of it, so closed it again. ''Yes, sir,'' he said.

Captain Curdridge sighed as the door closed behind him. ''I don't know what this is all about, my lord, but I've a pretty shrewd and increasingly sure idea you're gammoning me. I know—and so do you—that I ought to get to the bottom of it, but since I'm due to sail on the tide I'm going to let it go.'' He glanced at India. ''I'd have had to let her go, anyway. What were the fools thinking of? But I'll be blunt, my lord, and uncivil enough to tell you to your face that I hope I never see you or either of those young blackguards again, least of all on board any ship of mine. And that goes for this female, too.''

Lord Bardolph gave a brief smile. "I don't think you're alone in that wish." He took the collar of India's coat in his fist. "As for you—out!" he said, propelling her through the door ahead of him.

The lieutenant was waiting outside and they heard the captain's shouted "Mr. Swanmore!" as they climbed the companionway to the deck above.

"Did you call him Lord Bardolph?" the lieutenant asked when he stood in front of his captain.

"Yes. Why? Do you have reason to think he isn't?"

The young man shook his head. "No, nothing like that. It's just that one of the women who tried to stop us landing shouted out that she'd tell Lord Bardolph because the boy was his nephew and the boy—I mean the young woman— also protested that she was. The men say he—she—shouted something to the blacksmith about letting Lord Bardolph know what had happened." He paused. "But she can't have been his nephew, can she? I mean, not his *nephew*."

"And I very much doubt whether she's a horse-thief, either. Mr. Swanmore, this business leaves me more confused than a pint of rum. If it's all the same to you, I suggest we regard it as one of the unsolved mysteries of the universe over which we have no control and with which we will therefore not concern ourselves further."

The lieutenant grinned. "Thank you, sir. An admirable suggestion, if I may say so."

"So glad we concur," Captain Curdridge murmured. "You may go, Mr. Swanmore."

CHAPTER FIVE

"THANK GOD you came," India said as she was bundled across the quay and down the narrow street towards the horses, under the interested eyes of loiterers playing pitch-and-toss on the flagstones.

"Don't talk. March," the Viscount replied and India obeyed. The sooner they were out of here, the sooner she would feel safe.

Richard and Bartram stared at Bardolph's companion, momentarily mystified. They recognised India simultaneously, caught each other's eye and promptly roared with laughter.

"If only you could see yourself!" Richard gasped. "You look a sight!"

"I thought it looked rather...becoming," India retorted.

"I suppose it might have done when you left home," Richard replied. "It certainly doesn't now. And isn't that my coat?" he added.

"Your coat, your breeches, your shirt, your cravat, your boots and your beaver," his sister told him, unrepentant.

"All without so much as a by-your-leave—and they won't be fit to wear when you eventually take them off," Richard said indignantly.

"I couldn't ask you for them when you weren't there, and if you had been there I shouldn't have needed them," India pointed out reasonably.

"I'd be obliged if you two would stop bickering," Lord Bardolph interrupted. "Just remember we're not out of the navy's reach yet. I've a suspicion they'll be watching to see how we leave Lynn—whether as a magistrate with three malefactors in tow or as four friends. We're going to have to ride along the quay in full view of the *Pelican*, so we're going back to the waterfront and along the South Quay before turning off again and back into the town. I want you boys to keep your hands behind you as if you were tied, and I'll keep hold of the leading-reins. That will all help to sustain the illusion. I don't think I'm going to put Miss Leigh up pillion behind either of you. She'll ride in front of me, hands apparently tied in front of her. Are we agreed?"

"Do we have a choice?" Bartram grumbled.

"Yes, you do," his brother told him affably. "You can do as I say or I'll cheerfully hand you back to Captain Curdridge and allow you to fulfil the lifelong ambition of the last four years to make the navy your career. Is that what you'd prefer or am I correct in deducing that it's lost some of its appeal?"

"I never intended to start off as a pressed man," Bartram said peevishly. "I thought you could buy me in as a midshipman at least."

"Ah." Lord Bardolph smiled blandly. "So it was the gold braid that appealed, rather than the sea. I did wonder."

Bartram flushed with anger. "That's not what I meant! There's no future in the service if you start from impressment. No pressed man ever became an admiral." His tone was scathingly sarcastic but it had little effect on his brother.

"Precisely," he said. "And now perhaps we may go?" Lord Bardolph swung himself into his saddle and then leaned down to pull India up before him, a difficult task made easier by utilising his stirrup as a step.

"Ready?" the Viscount asked when everyone seemed to be settled. "Right—and for goodness' sake look dejected even if you can't manage contrite."

The little caravan, three of its members looking appropriately downcast, rode back along the South Quay, past a Dutch ketch, the *Amelia*, whose crew were obviously just completing the battening down of the hatches prior to catching the tide and following the *Pelican* into the estuary and on into the German Sea.

So far as Richard was concerned, it was just a ship, bigger than some, smaller than others, but Bartram was a connoisseur to whom no two ships were ever quite the same. He had seen the *Amelia* before, anchored just off-shore in the waters of the Wash.

He was debating how best to draw Richard's attention to it when the necessity of doing so was removed from him by the appearance at the top of the gangway of a familiar sturdy figure about to descend.

There was no mistaking Mr. Huggate in his gaiters, the old-fashioned cut of his coat and his low-crowned beaver. The rest of the party spotted him at the same time and India heard a muffled curse from Lord Bardolph.

"Just the person I least wanted to run into," he muttered. "Be uncivil, Miss Leigh. Keep your back to him."

India had no objection to doing as she was told. She therefore was in no position to observe that Mr. Huggate seemed no better pleased to bump into Lord Bardolph than Lord Bardolph was to bump into him. However, since recognition was mutual, neither could pretend otherwise. Lord Bardolph touched his hat. "Good day, Huggate."

"And to you, my lord." The farmer's glance rested briefly on India's back and then travelled on to the two boys, noting the leading-reins and the position of their hands and not, Lord Bardolph prayed, seeing that there was no rope holding them in position. "Having a spot of bother, my lord?" he asked.

"Boys will be boys," Lord Bardolph explained. "This time the mischief's rather more serious and I don't think a bit of public humiliation will do either of them any harm."

Mr. Huggate snorted. "If they'd had a good thrashing last time they stepped out of line, they wouldn't have had the urge to get up to mischief again," he said.

Lord Bardolph raised one quizzical eyebrow. "You think so? I lack your faith in the efficacy of a good beating. Mischief is mischief and, while I can't applaud it, I'd be very unhappy about any boy who lacked the spirit to get into it."

"A view not necessarily shared by anyone on the receiving end of it."

"I'm sure you're right. Your servant, Mr. Huggate," and Lord Bardolph urged his horse forwards and turned off the quay down the first narrow street that offered.

As soon as the party had passed through the Southgate, Lord Bardolph relinquished the leading-rein and allowed the boys to control their own mounts. "What happened to Clarion?" he asked India.

"He's still at the blacksmith's as far as I know," she replied.

"Then the first thing we do is make for there and collect him."

They rode in silence for some time and India, now that her relief at her freedom and gratitude to Lord Bardolph as the source of it had somewhat subsided, began to feel a little piqued that his concern for Clarion exceeded his concern for her in so far that he had enquired about the horse but had not asked one single question about what had happened to her. At last she could stand his lack of interest no longer.

"You'll be pleased to learn that I'm perfectly all right," she told him.

"I can see that for myself." He sounded surprised, as if the information was so superfluous as not to merit being mentioned.

"I thought you might have been worried about what had happened."

"No. Why should it worry me? You're not my responsibility and if you choose to gallivant about the countryside most indecorously dressed, then you must take the consequences. If my brother hadn't been involved, I assure you I'd have had no part to play."

"If your brother hadn't been involved, neither would I," India said sharply.

She had a point but Lord Bardolph was in no mood to acknowledge the validity of it. He was only just beginning to realise how concerned he had been to see her in the long boat and how relieved to find that she had come to no harm. He told himself that he would have felt the same about any female in such circumstances but he had a sneaking suspicion that his concern for any other female, though sincere, would have been entirely cerebral. His concern for India was uncomfortably close to being emotional and he didn't like the implications of that at all. Anger was a convenient refuge.

"What in the devil's name were you doing, anyway?" he demanded. "I told you to stay in your room. Obviously, you thought you knew better than I."

"It wasn't like that at all. There was a commotion somewhere outside. I tried to see what was going on from the window but even when I undid the casement I couldn't see anything more than a few skirts and the back of a woman with a pitchfork, so I went down to have a closer look."

Lord Bardolph groaned. "How like a woman! Something arouses your curiosity and all circumspection, all common sense, goes out of the window."

No more was said for some time but it was the Viscount who spoke first because India, unable to think of an immediate riposte and unwilling to acknowledge any justice in his comment, deemed it wiser to say nothing. "What *was* going on?" he asked suddenly.

India smiled to herself in the moonlight through which they were now riding. "Female curiosity, my lord?" she asked.

"Not at all. An entirely laudable request for enlightenment."

She nodded wisely. "A very different matter altogether," she agreed and related the events leading up to her capture.

He heard her out without comment and lapsed into thoughtful silence when she had finished. It was not, however, an unfriendly silence and it seemed to India that the anger she thought she had sensed had somehow slipped away as the daylight had a short while ago. She was glad to be sharing a horse, to have his strength behind her and to feel his arms around her. She knew this was reprehensible, that she should be both shocked and embarrassed at this degree of intimacy; very likely she should ask to be transferred to her brother's horse. But India didn't care. Bardolph would almost certainly despise her for not raising the objections to this mode of travel that any woman with pretension to gentility would raise, but she needed to be realistic. This was as close as she was ever going to get, in any sense of the phrase, to Lord Bardolph, who she knew already regarded her as trade, having money but not refinement, pert-tongued and rashly indecorous and, since she *was* trade and pert-tongued and nothing in her behaviour would have led any man to think she was other than impulsively indecorous and lacking in any ladylike qualities, there was nothing she could do about his opinion of her. She would make the most of what there was and try to think no more about it.

The trouble was, there had been moments when it had seemed as if they were on the verge of reaching a level of understanding that would at least have enabled them to continue as friends, but every time such a moment arrived something happened to put their relationship back several notches. And sometimes, she admitted reluctantly, it was that very same pert tongue of hers that was responsible.

Lord Bardolph had no hesitation in continuing through the early part of the night. There were sufficient of them not to attract the attention of footpads and nothing more sinister was likely to be encountered on these roads. There was a full moon and the road was easy enough to follow. He was anxious to reach the village where Clarion had been left, and not out of any concern for the horse. It would suit his plans very well if they were to arrive at night. He couldn't stop the landlady talking, though he thought a surreptitious guinea or two would ensure that lady's discretion.

Accordingly, when they reached the inn, he instructed the others to wait outside while he found out what accommodation they could offer for themselves and their horses.

The landlady had been dreading his arrival and the explanations he was likely to demand as to the whereabouts of his nephew, and her husband, no less apprehensive than she, stepped forward before Lord Bardolph had so much as opened his mouth.

"Now, my lord, I takes leave to tell you, you in't got no call to blame me or the owd woman for what 'appened 'ere earlier on. Yer 'oss is orright but as fer yer nevvy, well, there weren't much as anyone could do—and they did try."

They were a little disconcerted that Lord Bardolph—who might reasonably have been expected to demand to know what they were talking about—merely drew off his gloves and laid them neatly on the counter.

"Landlord, my nephew is a young fool and deserves everything he got. He was told in no uncertain terms to stay in his room. He chose not to. Very well, then let the navy teach him to do as he's told."

The landlord gasped and his wife stared open-mouthed at Lord Bardolph. Of all possible reactions they had considered, this was not one. What was more, it looked as if no explanations were necessary: his lordship plainly knew what had happened to the boy.

"I've come back for my horse," Lord Bardolph went on, "and I'd appreciate a quiet word with your good lady—a matter of some delicacy, you understand."

"Of course, my lord," the landlord said, though he didn't. "Er—will you be wantin' a room, or shall I send to the farrier to bring the 'oss round?"

"No, I'll settle with him in the morning. I'd like two rooms for tonight, stabling for three horses and a private parlour if you have such a thing."

The landlord shook his head regretfully. Largesse such as this betokened rarely came their way, and in circumstances least likely to produce it. "No private parlour, my lord, but if it's a meal yer wantin' the owd woman can serve it in the bedroom."

Lord Bardolph looked past him to the landlady and bestowed on her his most charming smile. "Perhaps we could first have that quiet word, Mrs. —?"

"Mrs. Ramsey," she confided. "If you don't mind stepping this way, my lord."

My lord stepped, and must then have left the inn by the back door because when the landlady reappeared she was alone, bustling with intrigue and on her face an expression big with importance.

Outside, India did not receive news of Lord Bardolph's plan with anything like Mrs. Ramsey's approval, but that might have been due to the fact that Lord Bardolph made no attempt to use charm. On the contrary, he was arrogant, peremptory and high-handed.

"No, my lord, I will *not*," she insisted. "For one thing it's totally untrue."

"Don't come the self-righteous pillar of veracity with me, my girl," the Viscount retorted. "If riding around the countryside dressed as a boy isn't living a lie, I don't know what is."

"That's quite different. It was forced on me by circumstances. And I am *not* your girl."

"You should be eternally thankful you're not," he told her. "The fact that you are nothing to do with me except by the accident of fate that made you decide to settle in the Fens at least relieves me of the obligation to demonstrate the full extent of my disapproval. As for your dress being forced on you by force of circumstances, well, so is this slight adaptation of the facts."

"Your brother is only sixteen."

"Oddly enough, I'm aware of that fact, Miss Leigh."

"You're perhaps not aware that I'm three-and-twenty."

"I should never have guessed from your immature behaviour that you were so old. I must congratulate you."

"On what?" India asked suspiciously, aware that she was laying herself open to some cutting comment but unable to squash her curiosity.

"On having lived so long without anyone having felt the need to strangle you."

"In any case, the landlady won't believe it—she'll recognise me."

"She won't see you until you've done as I say. I very much doubt she will remember you. Dressed as a youth you look a great deal younger than you do in women's clothes."

"All the more reason why she won't believe it. She'll take one look at me and one look at Bartram and realise it's nonsense—"

"I'm not too happy about this myself," Bartram interrupted. "Who's going to believe that I eloped with a...' dismay drove courtesy out of his head "...with an old maid?"

"Thank you, Bartram," India said with heavy irony. "That was just what I wanted to hear." She turned back to his brother. "All the same, he's right. No one is going to believe a woman of my age would elope with someone who still ranks as a schoolboy."

"Women—especially a certain class of women—will do almost anything to acquire a title," Lord Bardolph pointed out with some relish.

"Bartram hasn't got a title," India retorted. "Not unless you count Honourable, and that doesn't convey any rank on his wife."

"True, but you see, Bartram is at present heir to my title and you've heard that I'm not generally expected to live very long."

For a moment, India thought he was referring to some genuine rumour. She paled. "Why? What's wrong with you?" she asked.

"Something to do with my dissolute lifestyle, I believe."

"Really? I hadn't realised you were so interesting!"

"Thank you, Miss Leigh. Whenever I need my opinion of myself boosted. I shall know where to come."

India chuckled in spite of her annoyance. "I hadn't observed you to suffer very much from that complaint," she said and then added, more seriously, "But you really can't expect me to admit to a *tendre* for Bartram, my lord. It goes beyond the bounds of credibility."

"I agree. Only your greed for a title lends it any credibility at all, and then only in the estimation of those ignorant of these things. Use your common sense, India. If you're dressed as a boy they will recognise you as my "nephew" and will be close enough to realise you're no such thing. Now I've disposed of Harry. He was taken by the press-gang—as they already know—and so far as I'm concerned it serves him right for not doing as he was told and staying in his room. I have to account for needing women's clothing. Having inveigled Bartram into eloping with you, you dressed as a boy to avoid remark and make the pair of you less easy to follow."

"And Richard?"

"He was sent by your family to accompany me. They didn't want to leave you to my notoriously untender mercies."

"I see. And have you also thought of a good explanation as to why, if we're eloping to get married—which has to mean Gretna Green—we happened to be travelling in the opposite direction?"

It was clear that that salient point had escaped Lord Bardolph's notice. "It has to be attributable to something more convincing than poor geography," he said doubtfully.

"The villagers may have some idea where you and Bartram live, my lord," Richard broke in. "They don't know where we do. Bartram—and I suppose you as well—were staying in our locality. India ensnared him in a very short time," he added helpfully.

"You see?" Lord Bardolph said triumphantly. "Between us we have a foolproof story. Now will you go upstairs and put on the dress Mrs. Ramsey will by now have put out for you?"

"She'll see me go in and recognise me," India objected.

"No, she won't. I've stressed the importance of discretion and she'll be in the taproom making sure no one slips out and accidentally catches sight of you. I suggest the sooner you go, the more likely she is to have been successful."

India knew he was right. She had also realised that if she changed into women's clothes now it meant she and Richard could ride straight up to their own front door without the fear of undesirable gossip. So she swung her leg over the horse's neck and allowed Lord Bardolph to catch her by the waist and lift her down. Once on the ground, he did not immediately let go and she found herself looking up into his grey eyes and thought she detected a warmth there, but it was difficult to be sure in that light, it might be nothing more than wishful thinking.

"Believe me, India, this is for the best," he said quietly.

"I know, my lord," she replied with uncharacteristic meekness. "It's just that you're so... provoking."

His finger flicked her cheek. "Only because you rise so delightfully to the bait," he murmured.

India whisked herself out of the remnants of his hold and hoped the moonlight hid her blush. She ran quickly into the inn, refusing to rise to that particular bait, if such it was.

When she reappeared she was wearing a dimity frock that had originally belonged to Mrs. Ramsey's eldest daughter, a mob-cap, and some ill-fitting shoes. She was aware how unfashionable she looked. She did not realise how well the simple dress became her.

Lord Bardolph unfastened his cloak and placed it round her shoulders. "No woman travels without a cloak," he said.

India glanced down at it and smiled. "And capes are such a noted feature of women's cloaks," she commented.

"You hope to set a fashion," he told her.

They entered the inn by the front door and the curious stares they encountered were due as much to the reappearance of a man who had not been seen to leave as to any curiosity about the rest of his party.

On the Viscount's instructions, Mrs. Ramsey had cleared and laid a table for them in the corner of the taproom, Lord Bardolph having been of the opinion that, in the absence of a private parlour, it was preferable for them all to be seen eating in public than to congregate in one or other bedroom away from the common gaze.

They ate well, but it had been an exhausting and trying day for all of them; the night was well advanced and Lord Bardolph wanted to make an early start in the morning in order to reach the Nene at the best stage of the tide. India was the first to beg to be excused and neither of the boys raised even so much as a token objection to Bardolph's suggestion that they, too, should get what sleep they could for what was left of the night.

He was not far behind them, delayed only by Mrs. Ramsey, shaking her head in disbelief.

"Who'd 'a' thought it, my lord?" she said, waylaying him on his way out. "Such a genteel-looking lady, too, and him no more than a lad. Who'd 'a' believed it?"

"Who, indeed, Mrs. Ramsey?" He leaned over confidingly. "Mind you, if she'd been too obvious in her wiles, I think the boy would have seen through her, to say nothing of the rest of the family. Why, I was as much duped as anyone else!"

Mrs. Ramsey was shocked. "And I take leave to tell you, my lord, that you in't no flat, not by a long chalk."

"I flatter myself that's true—which just goes to show how very clever she is."

The landlady nodded. "A good thing you found out in time, if you asks me."

"A very good thing, Mrs. Ramsey. A very good thing indeed."

"You'll take good care she don't run off with your brother again, I'll wager."

"I think I can safely guarantee that whoever that young woman marries, with or without eloping first, it won't be my brother. Goodnight, Mrs. Ramsey."

ALTHOUGH LORD BARDOLPH awoke looking, if not necessarily feeling refreshed, the same couldn't be said for his companions. Clarion was fetched from the smith and a lady's saddle, somewhat the worse for neglect, obtained, which the horse accepted with surprise but without animosity.

Lord Bardolph viewed it apprehensively. "I'll be lucky if it doesn't give him saddle-sores," he commented. "Miss Leigh, will you be very much offended if I keep him on a leading-rein initially? I mean it as no insult to your horsemanship but he's never carried a side-saddle before, let alone anyone on it, and neither of us can have any idea how he'll behave."

The same worry had occurred to India. "I'd be grateful, my lord," she said.

They crossed the Ouse by way of one of the small bridges to the south of King's Lynn and set out across the network of droves that would eventually bring them to the Wash Way. On one stretch, where there was room to ride several abreast, Bartram drew level with his brother and Richard, with whom he had been in close converse, drew alongside his sister.

"What do you think Huggate was doing in Lynn?" Bartram asked.

"How should I know?" Lord Bardolph replied. "I wish he hadn't been. I'd as lief not have it spread about the locality that your behaviour is such that you have to be brought back home in fetters."

"Hardly fetters!" Bartram exclaimed indignantly.

"Rest assured that 'fetters' is how Huggate will tell the story—and it will lose nothing in the telling. You've made an enemy there, Bartram, and for no better reason than your immature behaviour."

"But what was he *doing* there?" Bartram insisted. "Doesn't it strike you as odd that he should be so far from home?"

"No odder than our being so far must have seemed to him. He's an astute businessman. I dare say business is what brought him to Lynn. It's brought me often enough over the years."

"But you're different. You're a major landowner with interests in a number of ventures."

Lord Bardolph laughed. "Don't fall into the trap of thinking that because a man farms just a couple of hundred acres he has no other interests. From what I know of Huggate, I'd be prepared to wager that he has fingers in a great many more pies than I can lay claim to."

"Pies involving Dutch ketches?"

"Why not? Business is business and there are plenty of Dutchmen who'd rather do business with the English than with their French masters."

"Do the French allow them to?" Richard asked.

"I think you'll find that merchantmen are quite skilled at evading men-o'-war when they choose to," Lord Bardolph told him. "And the French are not yet in a position to risk an attack in English waters."

"You make it sound as if the Dutchman's a smuggler," India suggested, and caught a warning glance from her brother.

"That wasn't necessarily what I meant to imply," Lord Bardolph said. "I can't say I'd be altogether surprised if I were told he ran a little contraband from time to time. Most of them do."

"For a magistrate, you sound remarkably unconcerned," India said, ignoring Richard's increasingly anxious expression.

Lord Bardolph laughed. "As a magistrate, I have more than enough to do without initiating searches of every ship that docks on the off-chance that they've contraband aboard. Besides, we have tidesmen to supervise that. Magistrates just deal with the consequences of what they find."

"Don't you have any power to initiate action?" India asked.

"I've the power of any other citizen who suspects contraband is being run. I can alert the proper authorities to my suspicions. I'd have to be very sure of my facts, though. Riding officers are already stretched to breaking point."

India pondered this for a while before pursuing it a little further. "So if anyone thinks contraband is being run, they should tell Customs, not a magistrate?"

Lord Bardolph shrugged. "It would certainly be a quicker route to the same result," he said.

"You sound as if you have a reservation," India commented.

"I suppose it's true to say that if you were able to convince a magistrate of your story and persuade him to alert the authorities his word would be more likely to be believed and it would be difficult for the relevant officer to ignore the warning—"

"But you'd run the risk that the magistrate might be involved himself," Bartram interrupted, rather smugly, India thought.

His brother frowned. "It's not unknown for magistrates to be involved themselves to a greater or lesser degree," he admitted. He gave India a penetrating glance. "Why all these questions, Miss Leigh? Do you suspect someone?"

India caught Richard's imploring expression. She had no right to expose the boys' over-fertile imaginations to Lord Bardolph's scathing tongue. They were in enough trouble as it was. She shook her head. "No. I was just pursuing the idea to its conclusion."

"Dear me. Are you always so dogged?"

"Terrier-like," she assured him.

"Thank you for the warning. I prefer bird-dogs, myself." He glanced down at her and smiled. "They have softer mouths, you know."

As a statement it was unarguable but India had the uncomfortable feeling it meant something else, something that any delicately nurtured female would find offensive. Obviously, she wasn't a sufficiently delicately nurtured female, a fact of which Lord Bardolph was all too well aware and to which he had never been reluctant to draw her attention. She would pretend not to have noticed the innuendo. "How long will it be before we reach the Nene?" she asked.

He laughed and India had the disconcerting impression that he knew exactly what had been going through her mind. "Another hour or so. We should have time to rest the horses while we wait for the tide to fall far enough. Will you be able to bear with me that long?"

"I shall make a truly valiant effort," she told him, and was rewarded with a genuinely amused laugh.

"Then I undertake to make an equally determined effort not to provoke you further—not today, at any rate."

India chuckled. "I'm glad you're honest enough to recognise your limitations," she said demurely, but Lord Bardolph refused to be drawn and only laughed once more.

When the little party drew rein outside the Leighs' house, India heaved an audible sigh of relief. "Thank goodness," she said. "I was beginning to think that 'home' was a figment of my imagination."

Richard dismounted from the hired cob to help his sister to the ground and India immediately made to unfasten her cloak. Lord Bardolph held up a prohibiting hand. "Wear it till you're indoors," he suggested. "The dress you have on underneath is sufficiently unlike your usual style to occasion comment. If you've no objection, I'll call tomorrow and collect it."

"There's no need for that," India assured him. "I'll send someone round with it."

"Does this mean my visit would be unwelcome?" he asked.

India coloured with confusion. "No, not at all. I didn't mean to imply anything of the sort."

"Good, then you may expect me." He looked her steadily in the eye. "If I didn't wish to visit, I could always send one of my own servants, you know."

"Till tomorrow, then, my lord," she said. "And I must thank you for your efforts on behalf of Richard and myself—we are both indebted to you, and most grateful."

Lord Bardolph leaned down towards her, an amused smile on his lips. "May I venture a piece of good advice, Miss Leigh?" he asked.

"Of course!"

"Go in and lie down before this excess of civility gets the better of you. I trust your spirits will be restored by the morning. *Au revoir,* Miss Leigh."

India turned from him with something precariously like a flounce and went up the garden path as quickly as she could without actually running, her indignation fuelled by the chuckle that followed her progress.

"Tea," she announced to the startled Eliza. "Master Richard will be here as soon as he's returned the cob to the livery stable."

Eliza relieved her mistress of Lord Bardolph's cloak and considered the ill-cut, old-fashioned dress beneath with disapproval. She shook his head. "Not an improvement, madam," she said.

"I assure you, it's a great improvement over Richard's breeches," India told her.

"I take leave to hope you didn't exchange the one for the other," the maid went on.

"What else? I was in no position to carry half of Richard's wardrobe around with me."

The maid shook her head again. "You had a bad bargain, madam. Master Richard won't be too pleased, either. You took his best habit."

''Then he will have to regard it as a small price to pay for having run off like that.'' India caught sight of herself in the large glass hanging in the hall. ''On second thoughts, the tea can wait until I've had time to change. You're right, Eliza. This may be more appropriate but it isn't an improvement. Ten minutes will suffice.''

India went early to bed that night and fell asleep straight away, such was her exhaustion. Her sleep was deep and dreamless and, as a consequence, she woke up in the early hours of the morning, wide awake and superficially refreshed. Such had been the events of the preceding days that it would have been scarcely surprising had her thoughts been full of them, and in particular of the very different outcome that could have been expected had anyone—and particularly any member of the press-gang—discovered her true sex. But these considerations were only peripheral to her thoughts. The centre ground was firmly occupied by the tall, arrogant, opinionated and downright uncivil form of Edward Chelworth, Viscount Bardolph.

She exonerated him—with reluctance, but one had to be fair—from her original charge of pomposity: the pompous had, by definition, no sense of humour; Bardolph did have. It was dry, sardonic, frequently self-mocking and usually sarcastic, but it was there. India thought it quite likely that many who were subjected to the whiplash irony of his tongue offered no retaliation but, metaphorically at least, crawled away to die. India was made of sterner stuff. She had a perverse streak that would give no one—and least of all Viscount Bardolph—the satisfaction of knowing they had struck home. She would do her best to give as good as she got and it was in Bardolph's favour that he took a successful set-down with the outward appearance of good grace. In fact it had become almost a positive pleasure to thus spar verbally with a man who never took refuge in a charge of ''feminine logic'' when he was worsted in an exchange.

When India had first made his acquaintance, she had not been at all surprised to learn that his intended bride had come to her senses in the nick of time. Now her sentiments had undergone a complete change and she could only pity a woman with so little perspicacity. Lord Bardolph was provoking, even annoying, but India sensed there was no real malice behind his acerbic wit; apart from that initial confrontation, he had never passed any remark that she wasn't perfectly capable of responding to in kind, and she had asked for that initial set-down by uttering a far more unkind one herself.

Behind the irony, Lord Bardolph had proved himself to be a man upon whom she could depend. He had gone to enormous trouble to rescue the boys. A cynic might have pointed out that, since one of them was his brother, he could hardly have been expected to do otherwise, but India was sure that, had only Richard been involved and had she sought the Viscount's help, he would have gone to just as much trouble. He had tried to discourage her accompanying him but when she had done so his recriminations had been minimal and he had acted throughout in a manner best calculated to preserve her reputation. When he had issued her with instructions, they had been the right ones for the circumstances and only when she had ignored them had she found herself in jeopardy.

India had been brought up to think for herself. She regarded herself as an independent woman and privately acknowledged her good fortune in being in a financial position to be able to indulge that independence. Now, for the first time, she began to see that there might be advantages to having someone else—a man—take many of the decisions, especially if that man should be one whom she had learned to trust. A man like Lord Bardolph, for instance. She tried to think of some other man of her acquaintance who fitted her criteria, and failed. It irked that same spirit of independence to feel that Lord Bardolph was unique: there must be other men capable of filling the gap of whose existence she had hitherto been entirely unaware. There probably were, but since she wasn't acquainted with any of them it was a purely academic exercise even to consider the possibility.

The truth was that Lord Bardolph was the only man she had ever met—apart from her late father, who could hardly be said to count—with whose company she wasn't totally bored within half an hour. Not only did he talk like a sensible man, but managed to do so with humour and without treating her as if she were of lesser intelligence. He never patronised her, and that was a rare accolade.

All of this India was prepared to acknowledge without reservation. It was more difficult to be equally frank with herself about other feelings. Her head played a large part in her assessment of his character. It played no part at all in accounting for the rest of her feelings towards him.

Apart from the ride to pick up Clarion, when he had been obliged to put his arms round her and had done so in an unobjectionably matter-of-fact way, he had touched her only three times: a flick of her cheek, a finger under her chin, and his arms on her waist when he helped her from the saddle. Small gestures, an essential service, but none of them perfunctorily performed—or so it had seemed to her.

Perhaps she had been deluding herself that there had been an unusual warmth in his eyes and a tenderness in the apparently careless brush of a finger. The fact remained that those superficial intimacies, simple as they were, had made her heart beat faster and brought a colour to her cheeks, making her feel as bashful as any schoolgirl in receipt of her first compliment. She wished the boys had not been there and wondered whether, had that been so, Lord Bardolph would have been less circumspect. India chided herself for so unladylike a thought but it persisted and with it came a longing that they should have an opportunity to be together without the presence of anyone else. This longing was in no way eased by the reflection that, were they alone, Lord

Bardolph was far too much of a gentleman to make even such innocuous gestures as he had so far.

And there lay the whole nub of the problem. Lord Bardolph would always be the perfect gentleman. India Leigh, on the other hand, was not only harbouring very unladylike thoughts at this very moment, but had on several occasions recently been guilty of unpardonably vulgar taunts and hardly less vulgar behaviour. The fact that the taunts, at least, were the result of provocation from his lordship was no real justification, and India knew it. Lord Bardolph could have very few illusions about the sort of woman she was, since she had made no particular effort to behave as she ought. It was hardly surprising therefore if, when he himself was provoked, he made it clear exactly what he thought of her. It was a lowering reflection that an opportunity to be alone with him would do absolutely nothing to promote her intense longing to be taken in his arms, to be loved and cherished. If he behaved like the gentleman he was, he wouldn't put her in so compromising a position, and if he did it could only be because he was so convinced of her lack of gentility that he felt free to treat her accordingly.

India, tossing and turning in a vain attempt to sleep, found it ironic that, with so many eligible men in India with whom she hadn't been able to contemplate a life together, she should now have come all this way to fall in love with a man who, while indubitably eligible, was possibly the least likely to seek such a union. Well, she admitted with a surge of unhelpful honesty, not a legitimate union, at any rate, and she didn't think she was sufficiently independent or unconventional to consider the alternative. Not yet.

CHAPTER SIX

THE MORNING was well advanced before India woke up, heavy-eyed and not at all refreshed, as Eliza observed when she put her head round the door to see whether her mistress was awake yet.

"I'll bring your breakfast up to you," she said, pulling back the heavy curtains that cut out the clear Fen light as well as the strong Fen winds. "And if you takes my advice, you'll indulge yourself in the luxury of a day in bed. You looked half dead when you came in and I can't truthfully say you look very much better this morning. I'd have thought you'd have slept like a log."

"So did I. I spent too long in the saddle and even though I was lying down it felt as if I was still riding," India told her. It wasn't a lie. She merely omitted to add that this well-known physical phenomenon was swamped by other, less freely admitted results of her recent escapade. "Breakfast in bed will be most welcome," she went on and was about to add that the rest of the day in the same place would be equally so, when she remembered that Lord Bardolph had said something about calling to collect his cloak. Eliza could perfectly well be entrusted with the task of giving it him, but it was unthinkable that the Viscount should leave without being thanked for his kindnesses of the past days, and who better to thank him than India? "But then I'll get up," she said instead.

"Very well, madam," Eliza replied, not at all surprised at her mistress's decision; no one could ever accuse Miss Leigh of indolence. "I'll put out your fawn cambric."

"I think not," India told her. Her fawn cambric did all very well around the house. It was a useful dress but by no stretch of the imagination a becoming one. "Not fawn. My spirits need lifting. The apple-green lawn will do very well and perhaps you'd put out one of the silk shawls we brought back with us. Isn't there one of a darker green which tones in well with that gown?"

Eliza agreed that there was and took the dress down to be pressed while India ate her breakfast.

Any fear the household might have had that India might be sickening for something vanished when it was seen that she had demolished a very hearty breakfast indeed, and if Eliza thought it at all strange that Miss Leigh should be *quite* so particular that her hair was arranged just so when, so far as the maid knew, she was going nowhere, she knew better than to comment.

When Lord Bardolph sent up his card about an hour later, Eliza smiled to herself. Who'd have thought Miss Leigh could be so very close?

India rose as he came into the room. The borrowed cloak, sponged and pressed, lay carefully folded over the back of a chair. India smiled.

"I'm so glad you were able to come by," she said, extending a hand in greeting.

Lord Bardolph returned the smile appreciatively. Since the inference that he was just passing had not been one that could have been drawn from his words of the day before, he guessed they were for the maid's benefit and doubted very much whether they would have their intended effect of eliminating speculation. He took the proffered hand and raised it politely to his lips. "Your servant, Miss Leigh. I'm glad to see you've recovered from the exertions of the last few days without ill effects."

India watched the door close behind the maid before answering. "Since my mirror tells me I look positively haggard," she said with some asperity, "I beg leave to tell you that that remark leaves me torn between questioning your powers of observation and doubting your veracity, my lord."

"Dear me, and I thought it was nothing more than a social commonplace," he said, more amused than taken aback.

India flushed. "And I had vowed to be nothing but courtesy itself yet here I am already being impolite."

"And on so little provocation, too. I dread to think what reply I could expect if I set out to be provoking."

"At least as good as you gave," India told him. "If it weren't, it wouldn't be for the want of trying! But I really do apologise, my lord. I had intended this meeting to be entirely affable. I was going to return your cloak and thank you for your good offices on Richard's behalf, to say nothing of the care you took of me."

"Perhaps you'd prefer me to go away and come back tomorrow at a previously arranged time—I undertake to be punctual—so that you can have your polite phrases of indebtedness all neatly polished and tripping off the tongue. I, on my part, will polish up a selection of appropriate responses which I shall endeavour to make as bland and inoffensive as I can, though, since you will be working from a text and I shall have to improvise, I must apologise in advance if they don't quite fit."

"Don't be absurd, my lord. You might just as well suggest we sit down now and construct the dialogue prior to enacting it tomorrow!"

"Miss Leigh, your brilliance overwhelms me! A scheme of such originality bears witness to a quite remarkable imagination. Just think—you could double your fortune by assembling a collection of unexceptionable conversations to fit all situations. Men and women alike would buy the volumes—I feel sure they would run into the plural—and learn their parts in the privacy of their own homes. They would emerge equipped to cross all the minefields of social interchange without fear of a *faux pas* and would hail you as their saviour."

India put her head on one side and looked at him speculatively. "I don't think I'm the one with the remarkable imagination," she said. "Mind you, I'm not saying you're wrong. I should think there are a great many shy, unconfident people who would jump at the chance to learn their way through the shoals of social converse." She chuckled. "I think you've just given me a capital way to occupy the long winter evenings. Should I use a *nom de plume*, do you think?"

"Undoubtedly—and, since we're both determined not to annoy each other, I'll refrain from drawing your attention to the fact that you are not necessarily the person best qualified to construct inoffensive conversations."

"And in order to maintain my part of that resolve, I won't make the cutting reply that I might otherwise have done."

"Which really means you couldn't think of one, because I don't believe you could have resisted the temptation."

India laughed with genuine amusement. "In the interest of accord I'll neither acknowledge nor deny your accuracy, my lord." She took the cloak from the back of the chair. "This is what you came for, sir. My thanks for the loan of it."

Lord Bardolph took it gravely. "I could perfectly well have sent my man for it," he told her. "There was something I wanted to put to you if you can spare me a few minutes."

India indicated a chair. "Then I see no need to continue standing. Shall I ring for some refreshment?"

He shook his head. "Please don't bother. I've already stayed longer than I'd intended. If we're not careful this visit will give rise to unwelcome speculation, which I imagine you'd like no more than I. Miss Leigh, whatever opinion I may have on your action in following me in the search for our brothers, I observed that you're a very competent horsewoman. You said something about your not riding because the livery stable had nothing suitable and, since you obviously enjoy riding, I wondered if you'd allow me to furnish you with a mount."

"I thought nothing in your stables would carry a lady's saddle?" she said.

"That's true. Clarion has given that the lie. Either he's been trained to it before he came into my possession or he's a natural. I've told Gidding to do some work on him, using a properly fitting saddle instead of that thing we had to make do with. He will then be at your disposal every day. You have only to send a message over to the Hall, and I'll have him sent round. You'll be able to ride with Richard."

"Thereby keeping both him and Bartram out of further trouble, you mean," India suggested.

"Believe it or not, that was not only not my intention but I can truthfully say it hadn't even occurred to me. In fact, I was going to make quite a different suggestion."

"Yes?"

"I wondered whether you'd allow me to escort you, at least to start with, until we're quite sure of Clarion. You'll get quite a different view of the Fens from horseback and it would give me pleasure to show you."

She glanced up at him from beneath her lashes. "Despite the unwelcome speculation it might incur?"

"If that worries you, I'll have Gidding ride a discreet distance behind."

"That would probably be best," India agreed, privately cursing the conventions that made it necessary.

"Good. Gidding reckons, given Clarion's aptitude, he can have him ready in a week. If you're agreeable, we'll ride out seven days from now."

India's eyes sparkled, and not entirely at the prospect of an enjoyable ride. "I shall look forward to it, my lord," she said.

IF LORD BARDOLPH chose to put an extremely valuable hunter at Miss Leigh's disposal on the altruistic grounds of taking pity on her for being able to find nothing else suitable, it was not within Gidding's terms of employment to tell his master that the other one had bells on it, tempted though he was. It was a very long time indeed since his lordship had mounted a lady—in the equestrian sense, that was, as the groom pointed out to the valet—and if his lordship asked Gidding's opinion he could do a lot worse than Miss Leigh, for all she wasn't strictly speaking gentry.

"You mark my words, Mr. Folksworth," he said over a tankard of ale in the pantry, "that's a young woman as can bring him to heel, if ever I saw one."

The valet was less convinced. "She's not Our Sort, Mr. Gidding, and you're not telling me his lordship won't be the first to recognise that fact. Now I'll agree he normally plays away from home, and that makes this one different, but it's not as if she's a local, after all."

Gidding stuck to his guns and considered his opinion vindicated by his lordship's insisting on his accompanying them. Lord Bardolph had issued no particular instructions to his groom beyond that basic one and it was left to Gidding to decide how to interpret his precise degree of accompaniment. Through villages he was simply a length behind. Away from them, he kept well beyond earshot and, since the Viscount made no comment upon either, he reckoned he'd judged it about right.

India revelled in the pleasure of riding a good horse again. Clarion was a far cry from the delicately boned Kathiawaris with their extraordinary ear-carriage. He had power rather than speed and was undeniably better suited to the often water-logged going than those agile descendents of the Mogul emperors' Arab horses would have been.

Lord Bardolph was on his best behaviour. That was to say, at no time did he utter any remark that could conceivably be interpreted as provoking. It seemed to India that this was the result of a conscious effort on his part and it behoved her to respond in kind. Quite apart from any other considerations, it would do no harm to demonstrate that she was capable of behaving in a conventional way. It didn't

ccur to her that Lord Bardolph's motive might be to pre-
lude the sort of dispute which would make it difficult for
er to continue to use one of his horses in a pastime she so
emonstrably enjoyed.

The consequence was that the atmosphere between them
ecame the relaxed one of old friends and eventually she
ecided that she could broach a subject that still rankled
lightly without jeopardising their current good relations.

"How well do you know Mr. Huggate?" she asked one
ay as they rode side by side along one of the substantial
road-topped banks that separated drains from siltfields.

"'Know' is not the word anyone can honestly use about
Iuggate," he said. "I've been acquainted with him all my
fe and watched him prosper but I can't claim to know
im."

"You surprise me. In such a close-knit community, I'd
ave thought it impossible *not* to."

"Huggate lives in some isolation and doesn't welcome
isitors. He's something of a recluse and I suspect is not at
ase among people. It's not uncommon in isolated farm-
teads, you know. The villages are, as you have observed,
lose-knit to an extraordinary degree. I doubt if in any other
art of the kingdom you would find a group of village
vomen acting so concertedly, not just to fail to co-operate
vith the press-gang but actively to thwart them—and remember, there's nothing illegal about impressment; it's been
England's way of filling the army and navy since the thir-
eenth century. But that sense of community doesn't neces-
arily extend beyond the villages."

They rode on in silence for a while—in silence because the
viscount was clearly deep in his own thoughts and it was he
vho spoke first. "I've not been entirely fair to the Fen-
nen," he said. "In one sense, Huggate isn't a part of the
ommunity; he prefers to be left alone and people are per-
ectly happy to respect that wish, but if there were a dispute
etween him and an outsider they'd take his part to a man,

even if he were in the wrong. Why this sudden interest in him?''

"It isn't sudden. I'm not even sure it really qualifies as an interest. Richard is still smarting under what he calls Huggate's injustice.''

"Was he unjust?''

"I don't know. I wasn't there, but Richard has always been truthful. He says they weren't around the outhouse but a large barn which is too far from the farm to qualify as such.''

"In Richard's estimation.''

"True. Anyway, he also says they weren't trying to set straw on fire and Huggate's degree of anger was out of all proportion to the offence.''

"Does he deny they were on Huggate's land?''

"No.''

"Or that they were in close proximity to one farm building or another, under whatever name?''

"No.''

"Did they have a spy-glass?''

"I gather so.''

"Then personally I think Huggate had every right to be angry, whether or not they were trying to set fire to his straw—which I feel bound to say I always considered very unlikely. Look at it this way—how would you feel if you caught a couple of boys—or young men, since both of them are old enough to know better—skulking in your garden with a spy-glass?''

India thought about it. "Angry," she said. "Angry and frightened, I suppose, but then, it's a very small garden.''

"I don't imagine Huggate was afraid, or at least not for his personal safety, but I think he had every right to be angry. The boys had no right being on his land at all unless he had given his permission. Had it been simply a matter of riding circumspectly through, I doubt if he'd have made any objection, but if they want to play around outhouses—or barns, for that matter—they can play around mine.''

"Put like that, you certainly demolish Richard's case," India admitted. Lord Bardolph's argument was so entirely reasonable that she couldn't bring herself even to mention Richard's more bizarre speculations about the farmer's activities, as she had been in half a mind to do.

"Your partiality to your brother's cause is understandable and very much to your credit, Miss Leigh," the Viscount said. "Don't let it blind you to a less partial view."

"I'll try not to," she agreed with a meekness that earned her a sharp glance. She looked up at him sideways from beneath partly lowered lashes. "My lord, may I say something... perhaps a shade indelicate?"

"What man could possibly say no to a request such as that?" he exclaimed. "You intrigue me, Miss Leigh."

India laughed. "Well, at least that's a friendlier response than telling me you were wondering how long my good behaviour would last," she said bluntly.

"The thought never crossed my mind. This... indelicacy...?"

India blushed. "It's just that... well, a couple of times when we were trying to catch up with the boys, you called me India. It sounds so much more friendly than 'Miss Leigh,' don't you think? I wondered if you'd have any objection to... to using it more often."

Lord Bardolph looked straight ahead between his horse's ears. What India could see of his expression was stern and only he knew how great was the effort with which he prevented his lips twitching.

"I hadn't realised my tongue had slipped," he lied. "Please accept my apologies. I hope it didn't cause you any distress."

India wished the earth would open up beneath Clarion's hoofs. Why, oh, why couldn't she learn to keep her mouth shut? She had taken advantage of the easy relationship that had seemed to exist and with what result? All she had done was to reinforce his belief in her basic vulgarity. "No, my lord. No distress. On the contrary, I rather liked it." I may as well be hanged for a sheep as a lamb, she thought defiantly, though there was no defiance in her tone.

"You do realise that it would be...most improper?" he went on.

"I was assuming it would only apply when we were alone together—not in company," she said miserably.

"I'm not at all sure that that doesn't make it even worse," he commented thoughtfully. He glanced down at her contrite face and guessed with an accuracy that would have surprised India what was going through her mind. He had been teasing her long enough. "On the other hand, friends—especially true friends—are few and far between, so how can I spurn an offer of friendship? I'll call you India, but there's one condition attached to it."

"What's that?"

"You return the compliment and call me Edward."

India studied his face. He seemed to be perfectly serious, but with Bardolph one could never tell. It wasn't beyond the bounds of possibility that he was just leading her on into further indiscretions to underline the opinion he already had of her. Besides, she hadn't thought that far ahead.

"I don't think I could, my lord."

"Dear me, am I so formidable?"

"No, not at all. It's just that...it isn't something I'd even considered."

"Then consider it now."

India did, in silence and for several furlongs. "It doesn't seem natural, somehow," she said at last.

"Yet 'India' does?"

"Yes."

"Don't you think you're being just a shade illogical?"

"Maybe, but it still wouldn't feel right."

"Then I'm afraid we're destined to remain on formal terms until your feelings undergo a change."

"If your tongue doesn't slip first. It has done in the past," India pointed out.

He chuckled. "Rest assured I shall be watching it like a hawk, night and day, from now on."

India opened her eyes very wide in obviously feigned surprise. "Will that be necessary, my lord? Night and day, I mean? I know I suggested it should only apply when we were alone together but I wasn't envisaging that eventuality occurring at night. I'm afraid you've been reading too much into my words."

"A slip of the tongue," he conceded. "Still, slips of the tongue can be surprisingly revealing, you know. Perhaps that one disclosed my true wishes."

The colour flooded into India's cheeks. So that was what he thought of her! She had had enough hints in the past. Now she had been told in so many words. She pursed her mouth.

"I think, my lord, we should confine our converse to the expectations of this year's harvest."

"Very wise, Miss Leigh. Do you know anything about harvests?"

"Not a thing. I'm relying on you to tell me what opinion to hold."

"I'll try not to disappoint you."

The ride continued in silence apart from the occasional courteous suggestion from the Viscount that they go this way or take the left fork, suggestions to which India was too miserable to object even had she wished to. She had only herself to blame. She had laid herself open to misinterpretation and Lord Bardolph was the last person to turn down an opportunity to take advantage of it. She had thrown away, in a few unguarded moments, any hope she might have had of him revising his opinion of her.

Had India but known it, Lord Bardolph was equally unhappy. He had handled badly a situation which India had already indirectly warned him was delicate. He flattered himself that he was normally adept at avoiding misunderstandings. He certainly hadn't proved so on this occasion. What was it about India Leigh that prompted some inner demon to put the worst possible construction on anything she said—and let her be aware of it?

He had offered her the use of Clarion for several reasons, about some of which his motives were unclear even to himself. True, he had guessed that it would give India a great deal of pleasure, and so it had proved. Nor had he himself been unrewarded: he had had the pleasure of her company and, if he had sometimes missed the stimulus of crossing verbal swords with a worthy opponent who neither burst into tears, as most women did, nor became surly, as did many men, that had been compensated for by the easy relationship that had grown up between them. That had been destroyed in a few ill-advised exchanges. He should have known better. She thought he was pompous and arrogant. He had been at considerable pains over the last few weeks to prove her wrong. Nothing would give him greater pleasure than to hear her call him by his given name. He should have agreed to use hers without comment and without conditions. Had he done so, there was every chance she would sooner or later have slipped into the unconscious use of his own name, in much the same way as he had dropped his guard and used hers. Now, no matter what amends he made, they were back on a rigidly formal footing which would make it impossible for any informality in address to slip in by the back door. Henceforth the use by either of them of the other's given name would have a significance that might have been avoided.

There was one thing that could—and must—be avoided. It would be unforgivable if his tactlessness led India to feel that she must discontinue these rides, which so obviously gave her pleasure. Her continued use of Clarion must be salvaged even if all else was lost.

Accordingly, when they drew up outside the Leigh's house, he helped her from the saddle and, instead of remounting his own horse, said, "Would you be kind enough to invite me in, Miss Leigh?"

It was the last request India expected and her surprise was evident. "Of course. This way, if you please."

Both horses were handed over to the groom. "Take them home, Gidding," Lord Bardolph told him. "I'll walk."

India led the Viscount into the front parlour and invited him to sit. "Shall I send Eliza for some tea, or would you prefer some other refreshment?"

"None, thank you." He waited until the door had closed behind the maid. "Miss Leigh, I've been cursing my confounded tongue for the past half-hour. I've embarrassed you and offended you and I intended neither. Will you forgive me?"

She smiled briefly. "There's nothing to forgive, my lord. I was out of order."

"No," he replied, shaking his head. "I should have accepted your request as it was meant and not made a tease out of it."

"Is that what you were doing?"

"Yes, and have subsequently regretted it very much."

"It's very kind of you to put it like that."

"Kindness doesn't enter into it. That's how it is."

"Thank you, my lord. I don't think apologies come easily to you. This one has all the more value on the account."

"You think this is just an apology, offered out of the kindness of my heart to make you feel better?"

"Isn't it?"

"No—yes— Good God, was there ever a more provoking woman?"

"That sounds a bit more like you," India observed without rancour. "Shall we leave it there?"

"No, because that isn't what I came to say. Miss Leigh, I'm aware that I've made it more difficult for us to regain the easy friendship I thought we had. I don't want to see your pleasure in riding sacrificed on the altar of either your pride or mine. If you wish to take your revenge by offending me in return, you will decline to ride Clarion again."

"Wouldn't that be cutting off my nose to spite my face?" India enquired.

"Yes, it would, but I'm not at all sure you wouldn't do that if you thought it worth it."

"If my spite was great enough, you mean."

"No, I did *not* mean that," Lord Bardolph said firmly. "Plain speaking, Miss Leigh, I believe you enjoy riding Clarion. I should like you to continue to have that pleasure. Ideally I should like to be able to continue to accompany you, but if you would prefer to have only the company of Gidding or Richard I shall entirely understand and the horse is still at your disposal. I hope you will accept this as meaning precisely what it says."

India smiled—a little wistfully because she couldn't quite see how they might ever return to the pleasant friendship that had existed before, a friendship which was the most she felt she could hope for and which her own thoughtless tongue had damaged, if not completely destroyed. "I'd like it above all things," she admitted.

"Good. That's settled. Clarion is at your disposal." He hesitated briefly. "And so are his owner's services as a guide, should you wish to avail yourself of them."

There was nothing wistful about India's smile this time. It was warm and generous. "Who better to teach me a true appreciation of the locality in which I've chosen to live?" she said.

So the rides continued whenever the weather permitted, which, in the Indian summer so typical of the Fens, was most days. India was loath to miss an opportunity, not only of riding but of doing so in the company of the man with whom she most longed to be. She hadn't yet experienced the driving rain and biting winds that everyone told her—with an unnecessary amount of glee, she thought—characterised Fenland winters, but if the tales she heard were only half true riding would be out of the question and, with it, Lord Bardolph's company.

She drank in avidly all the information the Viscount imparted. She recognised the hovering flight of the marsh harrier and the melancholy pleading of the curlew's call. She learned to spot the heron waiting for his lunch, as stationary as any lead replica beside a garden pool. She learned to judge when the outmarshes could support a horse and when the tide was far enough in to render the apparently sound grey-green grasses unsafe. By the same token, she knew when not to be surprised that vessels stayed in the deeper channels at the limit of her vision and when to expect to see them close enough to be able to count the men on deck.

As a consequence, she knew enough to be surprised to see a ship at anchor, sails furled, dangerously close to land, though not enough to recognise it.

"Is she aground?" she asked, pointing seawards.

"I doubt it," Lord Bardolph replied. "She's on an even keel, as if the master knows exactly what he's doing. The channel there is narrow and dangerous but for those who know it it's deep enough."

"But why stop there at all?" India persisted. "Why not go on round to Wisbech or to Lynn?"

"Why, indeed. I imagine she'll get under way with the tide and be gone."

"It still seems very odd. My lord, may I borrow your spy-glass?"

He took it from its saddle holster and handed it to her, and if there was a slight reluctance to do so India didn't notice it. When she handed it back to him, she looked puzzled. "Do you think they could be wildfowling?" she asked.

"Most unlikely at this time of day," he said, surprised. "Why?"

"Some seamen have rowed towards the shore—there must be a channel out there leading across the mudflats—and I can't think what else they'd be doing." She watched him put the spy-glass back in its case. "Aren't you going to look?" she asked.

"I don't need to. I'd already noticed it and, yes, there is a channel just about there, running quite a long way towards the shore." He hesitated, as if unsure whether to say more. "You didn't recognise the ship?"

"Should I have done?"

"You've certainly seen it before."

India looked out to sea. "The *Pelican*?" she suggested.

"I would have said it was bigger than that."

"You'd have been right. No, not the *Pelican*, the Amelia."

India couldn't immediately place the name. "The *Amelia*?" she echoed.

"The Dutch ketch berthed at Lynn. Perhaps you were too relieved to have escaped the navy's clutches to notice anything else."

"Of course! That was the ship we saw Mr. Huggate disembarking from. At least, you all saw him. I had to keep my back to him, if you remember."

Lord Bardolph chuckled. "I'd forgotten. I remember wishing him at the devil and cursing the need to acknowledge him. Maybe it was a fortuitous encounter, after all." He lapsed into silence and they rode on without speaking, the Viscount obviously deep in thought. When he spoke again, it was with an uncharacteristic tentativeness. "I don't suppose it's occurred to you that Huggate's land begins just beyond where that channel ends?"

"I don't see how it could have done since I have at best a very hazy idea of the limits of his land and none at all that there was a channel there."

"Do you feel inclined to pay a social call on Mr. Huggate, since we are, in a manner of speaking, passing by?"

"Now why didn't I think of that myself?" India wondered. "What a marvellous opportunity to demonstrate that at least one member of the family is neither a fire-raiser nor a felon to be brought back in chains. I should perhaps draw your attention to the fact that our respective brothers are firmly convinced Mr. Huggate is in league with smugglers.''

"Our respective brothers have too vivid a corporate imagination for their own good," Lord Bardolph said repressively.

"I know, but you must own it adds a *frisson* of excitement to what will probably turn out to be an exceedingly tedious visit."

The Viscount reined his horse in. "Miss Leigh, you will watch your tongue, won't you? For God's sake don't breathe a word of our brothers' stupid suspicions."

"Of course not," India replied, surprised. "I want to mend fences, not smash them altogether."

"Good. Please bear that in mind."

They rode down the sea-bank and could see the Huggate farm buildings huddled among their sheltering trees not very far off.

"Mr. Huggate will be able to see us coming," India pointed out to her companion.

"I should hope so, too. You don't imagine I hide behind banks or skulk in dykes when I pay a social call, do you?"

"How silly of me! There's bound to be a simple explanation, after all."

"And in all probability an exceedingly dull one. Just remember that, Miss Leigh."

"Of course, my lord," India said demurely, and pretended not to notice the sharp, suspicious look cast in her direction.

A large barn lay apart from the rest of the farm buildings and India deduced that this must be the one that had so interested her brother. There were men around it, not in itself an unusual occurrence on a farm. India did think it somewhat odd that they should disappear when they caught sight of the approaching riders. Lord Bardolph, more familiar than India with the innate curiosity of the English countryman, considered it most peculiar, though perhaps no more so than the sight of farm workers going about their agricultural business in waders. He said nothing and betrayed no undue interest in the barn as they rode past it and on to the house.

India had never met Mr. Huggate before but she knew his reputation for being reclusive and taciturn. She was therefore entirely unprepared for the effusiveness of their welcome.

"My lord Viscount, this is indeed an honour. And this is Miss Leigh from India? A privilege to welcome you, Miss Leigh, and, if an old man may be permitted to say so, that continent's loss is our gain. I dare say there were broken hearts left behind when you sailed!"

"You're too kind," India murmured, both overwhelmed and taken aback by this reception.

"You'll take refreshment with me, of course," the farmer went on and raised his voice to call over his shoulder, "Ned, take his lordship's horses and bait them while I bait their master," and he slapped his thigh at appreciation of his heavy joke.

A farmhand appeared from somewhere behind the house and took the reins of both mounts after respectfully touching his forelock to the Viscount. "'Mornin', me lord," he said.

"Good morning, Goldham. How's your wife?"

"Not too bad just now, me lord, though the winter do play hell with her joints, if you'll pardon me sayin' so." And he led the horses off to the stables so that his employer could lead their riders indoors and out of sight of things they shouldn't see.

"I dare say Miss Leigh would like some tea, and what about you, my lord? I can offer you a glass of Madeira or perhaps you'd prefer good English ale?"

"Ale would fit the bill very well indeed," Lord Bardolph told him. "I think Miss Leigh would probably prefer Madeira to tea. We've been riding for some time and I think the warmth wouldn't come amiss, Miss Leigh?"

"Madeira would be perfect," India agreed, unsure whether to be surprised or gratified that he had so accurately read her mind.

Their host poured the wine from a fine crystal decanter and handed the glass to India with a little bow, saying, "I take leave to tell you, Miss Leigh, that you'll not taste a better Madeira this side of the Canaries, and that's a fact."

"Paid duty, has it?" the Viscount asked jocularly.

Mr. Huggate tapped the side of his nose. "You can inspect my cellars to your heart's content, my lord, and I guarantee you won't find a single bottle or a single cask that hasn't paid full duty."

"I'm sure that's so—and I wish I could be equally sure about every other cellar in the district," Lord Bardolph replied.

"Aye, I don't envy you the job of magistrate," Mr. Huggate said with such heartfelt sympathy in his voice that India found herself disbelieving every word.

She wasn't warming to their host. Even had she not known of his reputation for taciturnity, she would have found his present effusive garrulity uncomfortable. She liked him less and less, and was more and more inclined to believe that Richard and Bartram might unwittingly have hit the nail very accurately on the head. She could only be relieved that he was more intent on engaging Lord Bardolph in conversation than her, which at least left her free to glance around in the intervals between smiling politely at his ponderous witticisms.

The parlour in which they sat was old-fashioned and might have been comfortable had it not had the indefinable air of a room rarely used, and then for funerals or, evidently, visits from the local aristocracy. The furniture was solid, the walls dark and the flags uncarpeted. If the boys' theories about Huggate's activities were correct, there was no evidence in this room that he had a substantial alternative income to farming. If he did, it sat in the bank or, more probably, went back into the farm. She had already observed that the farm buildings were in excellent repair and had thought little of it; anyone worth his salt made sure that the tools of his trade were in good condition before attending to his own creature comforts, which was not to suggest that Mr. Huggate went short of much. There was simply no outward show of the wealth the boys attributed to him. That might be a point in his favour but it might also mean he was far too clever to provoke gossip.

The room had just one window and the view from it was restricted by an old yew hedge that cut the worst excesses of the winter winds. India could, however, just make out the shape of the infamous barn—and something else, as well. It would never do to be staring too determinedly out of the window so she had to make do with seemingly casual passing glances. On one of the first of these, she spotted three men running from the barn and, since they were then cut off from her sight by the bulk of the barn itself, she concluded they were heading seawards. That glimpse had been a fortunate one because on every subsequent occasion the limited view was devoid of human life.

All right, her common sense told her. What would you expect on a farm if not workers making use of a barn? There are fields between the barn and the sea. Why shouldn't they be going there? But even India's limited acquaintance with English farming was enough to tell her that there had been no stock and no crops other than grass on those fields. Lord Bardolph might be able to explain what the men might have been doing. She would ask him when they were alone again. She brought her attention back with a jolt to the visit in hand, suddenly aware that their host had turned his attention to her.

"So you're the sister of that young rapscallion I caught with his lordship's brother near my barn a few weeks ago," he said with a joviality far removed from the report she had had of his attitude at the time.

"I'm afraid so," she said, forcing herself to smile. "I must apologise if he gave you cause for concern."

"Think nothing of it. Boys'll be boys and there's not a lot the rest of us can do about it." He turned to the Viscount. "I'll be bound you got up to a thing or two in your young days, my lord."

"Undoubtedly. They did not, however, include setting fire to a barn," Lord Bardolph replied frostily.

"Well, no, and I didn't mean to imply... Still, no harm was done, when all's said and done, so what say you we forget all about it?"

Lord Bardolph inclined his head politely. "Between the three of us I think that would be an admirable policy. However, I suggest that neither Miss Leigh nor I should convey that agreement to our respective brothers. I don't think anyone's interests are best served by letting them think they've been absolved from criticism, least of all theirs."

"I can see you're a wise man, my lord," Mr. Huggate gushed, "and I dare say that's reflected on the Bench."

"I certainly don't endeavour to be foolish," Lord Bardolph replied tartly and stood up. "And now, if you'll excuse us, I think we should be on our way. Miss Leigh will be feeling the strain of a long morning in the saddle if she isn't home soon."

"And here's me thoughtlessly rabbiting on," the farmer said. He stuck his head round the door. "Edith!" he called down the flagged hall. "Tell Ned to bring his lordship's horses round as fast as may be."

When they made their farewells, Mr. Huggate pressed India's hand in a manner that she decided she had better regard as fatherly and peered at her intently. "Are you sure we haven't met—apart from the odd glimpse in church?" he asked.

"Quite sure," India said positively. "I'd have remembered."

Mr. Huggate smirked. "Flattered, I'm sure," he said. "All the same, I can't help feeling there's something familiar about you."

"There's absolutely *nothing* familiar about me— unless, of course, you've been to Bangalore," she said firmly.

He sighed. "That pleasure's been denied me. Still, it's very odd."

"I don't think I've ever been called odd before," she said reflectively, as if she were trying to recall such an occasion, and she was rewarded by his embarrassment at being misunderstood. This had the advantage of enabling them to get away without any further delay, Mr. Huggate being clearly desirous of avoiding any further misunderstandings.

"That was unkind of you," Lord Bardolph said when they were out of earshot.

"Yes, wasn't it?" India agreed affably. "It got us away, though, didn't it? Why, the man's the most appalling toadeater I've ever met!" She glanced up at her companion. "Is that the effect being a viscount usually has on the lower orders?"

"It didn't have that effect on you," he pointed out.

"I am *not* a lower order," India said indignantly and then corrected herself. "Well, I am, of course, but I've never toadied to you like that."

"Very true," Lord Bardolph murmured. "You need to learn the trick, you know. The Prince Regent would be deeply offended if you treated him like an equal."

"Since I'm hardly likely to meet him, I don't think I'll worry too much about that," India replied.

"Still, bear it in mind. You never know what the future might bring."

India considered this statement but she could detect no hidden significance so she dismissed it. "And another thing, my lord. I am *not* feeling the strain of a morning's riding."

"Would you have preferred our visit to be extended?"

"No, of course not! It was well-nigh intolerable as it was!"

"It was, wasn't it?" he agreed cordially. "One might almost suspect that he was trying to keep us there as long as possible."

"Especially since he's not supposed to welcome visitors and to be particularly close-mouthed," India said.

"Precisely. It makes one think."

"Did you notice those men?"

"What men?"

"Yes, I thought he was occupying your attention too efficiently to allow you to glance out of the window. You could see that barn, you know."

"Not from where I was sitting. I'm not totally unobservant. All I could see was yew hedge."

"I could see the end of the hedge and the barn beyond. Early on in our visit I saw some men. They seemed to come out of it and then ran round the back and disappeared. That would be seawards."

"Or fieldwards," he pointed out.

"I thought of that but there was no stock in those fields and no crops that would require attention."

"My compliments, Miss Leigh. You learn quickly."

"Do you think there might be something in the boys' ideas about Mr. Huggate's activities?"

"Smuggling, you mean? It's not impossible but it seems most unlikely—and especially in broad daylight."

"Do you have an alternative explanation?"

Lord Bardolph needed to consider that for some time before answering. "Not at the moment, but that doesn't mean there isn't one."

That was unarguable but although India, too, gave it a great deal of thought she couldn't think of another explanation, either. She changed tack. "Did you believe what he said about there being nothing in his cellar that hadn't paid duty?"

"Implicitly."

"Isn't that rather naïve?"

"Miss Leigh, I'm a number of things, but naïve isn't one of them. Good God, girl, use your head! If the boys' suppositions are correct—and yours, too, for you seem increasingly inclined to endorse them—just about the last place there would be any contraband liquor would be in Mr. Huggate's cellar.''

''Perhaps that's exactly what you're *meant* to think,'' India suggested. ''Now, if it were me, I'd put the contraband in the cellar and have strange seamen skulking around my barn just to convince people like you that it was there, when in fact the barn would be full of straw or fleeces or something equally innocuous. You should have asked to see his cellar.''

''You can't pay a courtesy call and insist on seeing a man's cellar. Not even if you're a viscount,'' Lord Bardolph pointed out in some exasperation.

''But a magistrate can,'' India objected.

''A magistrate can issue a warrant for a riding officer to investigate but before he does so he has to be convinced there are good grounds. I'm by no means convinced that there's anything wrong at all.''

''You were sufficiently interested to go there in the first place,'' India reminded him.

''A mistake,'' he said shortly.

''You disappoint me, my lord.''

''I'm sure I do,'' he said harshly. ''I take comfort from the fact that disappointment is something from which one generally recovers.''

Nothing more passed between them until they had been riding along the sea-bank for some time. India pointed out to sea. ''Is that the *Amelia*?'' she asked.

''It certainly looks like it,'' he agreed and utilised his spyglass. ''Yes, that's the Dutch ketch. Did you recognise it or was it an intelligent guess?''

''The latter—I'm not Bartram. To me a ship is just a ship. Doesn't that rather confirm the boys' suspicions? We saw the seamen heading inland and as soon as we appeared on the scene at Huggate's farm they disappear and are now putting back out to sea.''

''Nonsense. I told you they'd leave on the tide and that's precisely what they have done. Of all the reasons they may have anchored just there in broad daylight, smuggling is the least likely but, whatever their reason, it would have been the height of stupidity to stay there any longer than they had to."

India sighed with exasperation. "You're an intelligent man, my lord. Why do you persist in thinking in straight lines? It's the same as the cellar—what better to throw the revenue men off the scent than to work in broad daylight?"

"You don't think the revenue men have spy-glasses of their own? You don't think they would take an interest at least as keen as yours in what an isolated ship was doing, anchored in a deep channel at low tide for no apparent purpose? Perhaps you should try thinking in straight lines for a change, Miss Leigh. Your life would certainly become a lot less complicated."

He had made a valid point and India was annoyed with herself for not having seen it. She had no desire to cross swords with Lord Bardolph and yet, try as she would, she always seemed to end up doing just that. At the same time she had the unaccountable feeling that there was something behind his argument other than a wish to put her straight. Gentle irony was one of his more effective weapons and all that would have been necessary, yet he had preferred heavy sarcasm. It was, as her father might have said, like taking an elephant gun to kill a fly, and that wasn't Lord Bardolph's usual way.

When they drew rein outside her house, the Viscount helped her from the saddle, as he always did, but, instead of releasing her waist as soon as her feet were on the ground, he held her a little longer and his voice was gentler than it had been at their last exchange.

"I mean no offence, Miss Leigh, when I say that I think you've fallen under the spell of our brothers' imagination. I can't deny that smuggling goes on around these coasts but it really is a very subtle, surreptitious affair. If it were as open as you seem to think, the revenue men wouldn't have half the difficulty catching the perpetrators as they do. I would advise you to put it from your mind. At the very least, you'll sleep easier in your bed.''

India opened her dark eyes wide in genuine surprise. "I assure you that thoughts of smugglers on the outmarshes don't keep me awake, my lord.''

"Perhaps not, but don't you think every horse-hoof you hear is the gentlemen riding by?''

"To tell you the truth, I sleep too soundly to be woken up by a mere horse. Besides, wouldn't they muffle the hoofs?''

He laughed reluctantly. "You're right, of course. You wouldn't hear twenty sets of iron shoes clattering over the cobbles. You confuse me, Miss Leigh. I can't quite decide whether you're an immensely practical, sensible woman, or a romantic with a vivid imagination. It's an intriguing dilemma.''

India glanced up at him through her lashes. "Thank you, my lord. Every woman likes to be considered intriguing—and now, if you don't mind, I think you ought to let go of me. We wouldn't wish to attract gossip, would we? And that's my sensible side coming out,'' she added helpfully.

He smiled wryly. "I hoped you hadn't noticed," he said, letting go.

"Even if I hadn't, you may be sure those behind the twitching curtains had.''

Lord Bardolph sighed. "I wish I could decide which I prefer.''

"My lord?''

"Common sense tells me I should prefer your practical face but the reprobate in me has a pronounced hankering to see more of the romantic.''

India whisked the skirt of her habit out of the dust and chuckled. "I leave you to grapple with your dilemma, my lord,'' she said and made her way up the garden path without a backward glance.

CHAPTER SEVEN

INDIA HAD a great deal to think about when she was back in her room. Eliza took her habit to brush the dirt out of it and press it for its next use and this left India to sit before her glass, brushing her hair but so sunk in thought that the action was automatic. She might be facing her reflection but she saw nothing.

Lord Bardolph's parting words had lifted her spirits out of the depression his previous rebuke had caused. They might almost have been considered flirtatious and for the first time in her dealings with the Viscount she felt she had neither made a fool of herself nor set up his back. She smiled to herself. A flirtation with Lord Bardolph might be very enjoyable, the more so since she had already decided that a more serious relationship was out of the question. It began to look as if he might be rather adroit at it, which surprised her. She had never entirely abandoned her early impression of humourless pomposity. That was to say, she had firmly acknowledged that he was far from humourless, but he was inclined to stand upon his dignity—which, in India's estimation, was very close to being pompous—and flirting, by definition, involved unbending to a degree that India would not have expected of him.

His attitude to the smugglers bothered her. She knew as well as the next man that smuggling was rife all round the coast of England—and Wales, too, in all probability. Something had not been right at Huggate's farm; there had been no plausible explanation of seamen—presumably Dutch seamen—heading for the barn. Yet Lord Bardolph had seemed singularly unconcerned even though, as a magistrate, he must surely be one of those most deeply concerned to wipe out illegal practices. A large part of the population felt the law was quite simply wrong and a sizeable proportion turned it to their financial advantage but that didn't absolve magistrates from their duty to enforce it. The Viscount didn't strike India as the sort of man to turn a blind eye or not to care, and he had certainly been interested enough in Huggate's visitors to ride over for a closer look, yet he dismissed her ideas with some scorn as being the figments of Richard's imagination—which, she had to admit, to some extent they were. They had learned nothing and had merely been subjected to the farmer's effusions. India had thought these very odd but Lord Bardolph seemed to find nothing unusual about them. She could only conclude that he was so accustomed to being treated like that that it struck him as being in no way remarkable. And if that were so, it would certainly destroy India's contention that such uncharacteristic behaviour had any sinister connotations.

Nevertheless, it continued to niggle at the back of her mind and when Richard left his books to join her for a belated luncheon she said, "Richard, what sort of a man was Mr. Huggate?"

Her brother grinned. "A very angry one."

"Understandably, by all accounts, but that isn't what I meant. Forget the anger if you can and tell me what sort of a man he was behind it."

"All I saw was anger," Richard pointed out reasonably. "Bart says he keeps himself to himself and doesn't talk much even when he's among other people—at market, say. He doesn't normally have two words to string together. That's what Bart says but he didn't have any problem finding them when he caught us, nor when he let loose about us to Bardolph."

"How did he treat Lord Bardolph?"

"How would you expect? He didn't have any grudge against *him*, only against us, and he had his temper under enough control for that to be apparent."

"But he didn't toad-eat him?"

Richard considered. "I wouldn't call it toad-eating, exactly. He was very angry, you see, and I suppose he had to be careful not to contradict himself since he wasn't telling the truth in the first place, so he was fairly forthright but that was mixed with a sort of obsequiousness that made me feel a bit sick, to tell the truth."

"What sort of obsequiousness?"

"Oh, you know—your lordship this and your lordship that, never risking letting Bardolph think he'd forgotten his rank and the deference due. Quite nauseating, really, because, to give Bardolph his due, I've never thought he wanted to be addressed like that. Mind you, Bart says that's how a lot of people address him."

"So he expects it?"

Richard shrugged. "I don't know what he expects. I only know what Bart says he gets. Bart himself says Bardolph doesn't like it above half, but if you ask me Bart's a bit piqued about it. I think he'd rather like it if being an Honourable gave him the right to some sort of similar address."

India recalled Bartram's discontented face and thought her brother had probably summed it up rather well. "I know Bartram's a friend of yours and he's told you quite a lot about farming and the Fens, but the more I hear about him and see of him, the less I like him. I do wish there were someone else with whom you could be friendly."

"He's a bit childish," Richard admitted, "and very stubborn when he's set on something and, of course, he doesn't much like Bardolph, but that's envy as much as anything else. It's not just the title. Bardolph's got the money and the self-confidence—which isn't surprising, given how much older than Bartram he is— but he's all right really. All the same, I shan't be sorry to go to Cambridge and make a wider acquaintance."

It was a remarkably adult view for a fourteen-year-old, and India wondered whether life in a colony where Englishmen assumed authority was theirs by right had contributed to her brother's undoubted precocity. It didn't leave her much further forward in her attempt to understand Lord Bardolph.

SHE WAS AWOKEN from her usual dreamless sleep by a sound which she at first took to be an unexpected downpour of rain. As her sleepy brain cleared, she realised that it was too intermittent to be rain and the sound wasn't quite right. Leaves rustling against the window? No, there was none close enough to reach, not even in a gale.

The sound came again, heavier this time, and India sat up. Someone was throwing gravel at the window. Who on earth could want to wake her up but not be prepared to knock on the front door like a reasonable human being?

She climbed out of bed and carefully parted the heavy curtains that hung at the room's other window. Glancing down at the angle forced on her by the desire to disturb the curtains as little as possible, she could make out the foreshortened form of the Honourable Bartram Chelworth, his face expectantly upturned.

India let the curtain fall, confident that he hadn't seen her, and frowned. It didn't take much thought to realise that Bartram had mistaken her room for Richard's, which was across the landing and on the other side of the porch. The big question was why? What did he want—and was it his intention to get the two of them involved in some other mischief? Worse, was it a pre-arranged signal which had misfired only because Bartram had picked the wrong room?

Since the only way to find out was to tackle Bartram himself, India threw on a wrap and her slippers and went swiftly downstairs to unbolt and unlock the door. Locks, bolts and hinges being in first-class order, this was quickly accomplished and the door was opened just before Bartram had time to realise what was happening and make his escape. He clearly hadn't expected anyone to open the front door, much less India.

"I think you'd better come in," she said. "I want to know why I've just been woken up in so clandestine a manner. Or were you hoping to elope with me and my fortune?"

His expression was one of pure horror. "Elope with you? Good God, no!" His eyes strayed to the other windows on the floor above. "I thought I'd found Richard's room."

"Come in," India commanded. "I shall try to overcome my disappointment—indeed, my dismay—that you haven't come to rescue me from the shelf, but I give you fair warning—I intend to know what this is all about."

A shamefaced Bartram followed her into the front parlour. "I didn't mean that I didn't *want* to elope with you, Miss Leigh. I mean, it's not a thing that's ever crossed my mind." It seemed to strike him that, true as this might be, it was hardly the most felicitous way of making amends for an instinctive reply which had been somewhat uncomplimentary. The trouble with Richard's sister was that, as with Edward, Bartram was never entirely sure when she was joking.

"Stop floundering, Bartram," India told him. "I believe it's customary for elopements to be planned by both parties in advance—though I suppose you might have been intending to abduct me. No—" and she held up a hand to check his horrified protest "—I'm only teasing. Was Richard expecting you?"

"If he had been, I'd have taken jolly good care to make sure which window it was," Bartram said sulkily.

"That would certainly have made sense," India agreed, relieved that at least she hadn't stumbled on some juvenile conspiracy. "What's this all about?"

"I'd rather talk to Richard, if it's all the same to you."

"It isn't." She noticed that he was wearing a greatcoat and boots. "Is one of Bardolph's horses standing out there in the cold?" she demanded.

"No. He locks the stables these days."

"Very wise. Maybe he should lock bedroom doors as well. You look as if you're dressed for a journey rather than for a night's poaching."

"I'm not a poacher!" Bartram protested indignantly.

"I'm glad to hear it. I dare say Bardolph will be quite relieved, too." She saw that he had started to tremble despite the coat. "I think perhaps a glass of wine would do you no harm," she said more kindly. "Come into the kitchen with me. There'll be some warmth left in the range and I'll see what I can find." She pushed him ahead of her down the hall and lit the oil-lamp that served the kitchen. Instead of wine, she poured him a brandy. "On second thought, I fancy this will do you more good. Sit down and drink it. You look to me like someone who has stoked themselves up for something and suddenly finds the fire's gone out."

Bartram grinned in spite of himself. "Not a bad way of putting it."

"Something to eat? Cook makes a rather splendid cherry cake." India was not unfamiliar with the weaknesses of young men who weren't quite as grown up as they liked to think.

"That sounds good."

India watched him devour a large portion of tomorrow's cake, knowing that it would fall to her to placate Cook in the morning. "Well?" she said, when she judged he had had time to collect himself. "What's going on?"

"I'm running away."

"Again?"

"There you are, you see. I knew you'd make fun of me."

"In view of the fact that it's only a few weeks since you last ran away, I think it was an entirely reasonable reaction," India pointed out.

"If you say so," Bartram said with a studied politeness intended to convey that he didn't believe a word of it. "This time I'm serious."

"Are you telling me that last time you weren't?" India demanded. "I wish you'd let everyone know. We wouldn't have felt obliged to put ourselves to very considerable inconvenience to get you back. Do I take it you expect Richard to go with you again?''

"No, you don't. At least, I wouldn't mind if he did but I've a shrewd idea he'll tell me not to drag him into it."

"You've no idea how much that acknowledgement eases my mind," India told him. "Why try to wake him up, then?"

"I don't have any money left and I thought Richard would lend me some."

"Lend?"

"I intend to pay it back. Though I can't be sure when," he added honestly.

"Is this another attempt to join the navy?"

"Sort of—eventually. I decided that going in at the bottom, whether through impressment or volunteering, is probably not going to suit me very well. I'll have to buy myself in, but I've no money—and I don't expect Richard to help me with more than my coach fare to London. That's where I'm going and I'll find some work and save until I've enough to buy myself in as a midshipman."

"I think you'll find it takes you a very long time," India told him. "You won't earn much and you've got to live. Surely it would be more sensible to try to persuade your brother that you're really serious. He doesn't think you are, you know. He thinks you imagine it will be like one long cruise on his yacht."

"That's stupid," Bartram said scornfully. "I'll admit that's what gave me a taste for the sea, but I'm not a complete half-wit. I do realise that the navy won't be half so much fun. In fact, I don't think it'll even be very pleasant most of the time, but it's what I want to do."

"Then convince Lord Bardolph," India repeated. "He's the one who can find the money—and the contacts to get you on the right ship."

"I've tried, but he won't listen. I tried again this evening, but he just told me it was time I grew up and, anyway, he's already arranged for me to go to this old college and there's an end to it."

"He wants you to go into the church, I believe," India said.

"He always did—he said it was the best place for younger sons. Then when he realised I was set on the navy he changed his tune a bit and said I was to go to Cambridge first and then we'd see."

"That sounds a perfectly reasonable compromise to me," India told him. "I can't see that a few years at university can do anything other than good."

"You don't know Edward," Bartram said bitterly. "Not really know him, that is. All he's doing is buying time. He thinks I'll have changed my mind by then and he can push me into the church after all."

The more India saw of Bartram, the less suited she thought him for the career his brother was supposed to have planned for him and she was only surprised if Bardolph himself hadn't yet realised it. She was inclining to the view that, while she couldn't see what attraction the navy held for Bartram, it might be good tactics to suggest that he pursue his studies at Cambridge with the promise that then, if he still wanted the navy, no obstacles would be placed in his way. It was not, however, a suggestion that was best made by Bartram, so she kept it to herself.

"Be that as it may," she said, "I can't see that running away is the answer. I think you'll find life in London very different from what you imagine and your brother will worry about you."

Bartram snorted. "Edward? Worry about me? Rubbish! He'll be glad to be rid of me."

Correctly diagnosing the first hints of self-pity in this reply, India adopted a suitably bracing tone. "He was worried enough last time to set out after you—and to have his people scouring the countryside to find out where you'd gone."

"He was worried about his horses. If we hadn't taken them, we'd have been welcome to go. Well," he amended, "I would. I shouldn't think he cared much either way about Richard."

"You're forgetting that I was with him. I can assure you you're mistaken. I dare say we'll never agree on that so I think we'd better decide what to do for the best tonight. Richard, happily, is sound asleep and I'm not having him woken up just to lend you money. Nor am I lending you any at this time of night. It's extremely dangerous to wander about the countryside at night, as I'm sure you're very well aware, and you'll have to tramp into Wisbech to find a coach. I suggest you spend the night here and have a good breakfast and then the three of us will put our heads together and decide what to do for the best. How does that strike you?"

Aspects of it, notably the thought of a warm bed followed by a filling breakfast, were definitely appealing. "You won't send a servant over to the Hall to tell Edward where I am?"

"The servants are all sound asleep and I'm certainly not waking them up just to run over there with pointless messages—after all, Lord Bardolph presumably doesn't even know you've gone yet, so why wake him up to tell him?"

"But I'll wager you'll send someone over there first thing," Bartram insisted.

India had no intention of frightening him away from the safe haven of the Leigh household, nor did she want to wake up and find he'd gone from here, too. "I promise I won't let him know until after we've had a chance to discuss it thoroughly. Will that do?"

Even Bartram could see it was the best he could hope for, so he agreed, albeit grudgingly. India gave him one of Richard's nightshirts and showed him into a spare bedroom. She handed him bedlinen and blankets.

"Here you are," she said. "Have you ever made your own bed before? No? Well, you'll certainly have to do so in the navy, so you may as well get some practice in. I'll see you're called in the morning.''

She went out and closed the door behind her. As a hostess she felt quite guilty at such perfunctory hospitality but she had a shrewd idea that the last idea she needed to convey to Bartram was that he was in any way an honoured guest, and being obliged to make his own bed—which, if he'd never done it before, would be bound to be an uncomfortable one—was as good a way as any she could think of achieving that object.

India had closed his door behind her. She was about to close her own but thought better of it and left it half-open. She was a heavy sleeper but the landing and stairs creaked. If Bartram, upon reflection, decided he wasn't happy with the scheme he had grudgingly agreed to, at least there was a chance she might hear him tiptoeing past.

"DID YOU KNOW you slept with your door open?" Eliza demanded when she brought India's morning chocolate.

"Did I? Oh, yes. That's right. It was intentional."

"And Cook's in none too good a humour, either," Eliza went on, throwing back the curtains. "She says the cherry cake she made for today has had half of it eaten and since the back door was securely locked and bolted she supposes Master Richard felt hungry in the night and would you be so good as to have a word with him."

"Oh, dear, she's discovered it already, has she? It wasn't Richard, it was me."

"*Half* a cherry cake, madam? You've never been one to peck at your food, I know, but half a cake..."

"Was it as much as that? It didn't seem it. Give my apologies to Cook. Actually it wasn't me, precisely. It was my idea but the eater was Bartram Chelworth. He's in the blue room in Richard's nightshirt. Someone had better take him up some water and wake him. If he's still there," she added doubtfully.

"But the bed's not made up in there, madam. We weren't expecting anyone."

"Don't worry, I gave him the bedlinen and told him to make it himself."

"You told him to...? Dear God, anyone would think you'd been brought up in the gutter!"

"It was entirely calculated, I assure you. Now please be so good as to let Cook know there'll be a third for breakfast—after you've apologised about the cake, of course—and then see to it that both boys are down at about the same time. I don't want them putting their heads together before I've had a chance to talk to them both."

"Like a Dutch uncle?" Eliza suggested.

India grinned. "More like a spinster aunt, I think."

Her plan of waiting until the boys—and Bartram in particular—had been comfortably fed and were consequently in a favourable humour before discussing what to do for the best was destined to be thwarted. Bartram was tucking into his second helping of kedgeree when the sound of the heavy brass door-knocker reverberated down the hall and into the breakfast-room at the back of the house.

"Funny time to be calling," Richard remarked.

"It doesn't sound like someone paying a morning-call," India agreed, and her heart sank. If it were whom she thought it was, an unpleasant interview was likely to ensue.

Bartram went pale. "It's Bardolph," he said.

"Nonsense," India told him, even though she thought he was probably all too accurate. "How would he know where you were?"

"He has ways of finding things out," Bartram said darkly.

Their common suspicion was verified when Lord Bardolph entered the room on Eliza's heels, before the maid could announce him.

"I knew it!" he said. "I was right!"

"How gratifying for you," India said coldly. "That will be all, Eliza. You may leave us." She turned to her visitor.

"And you, my lord, will sit down like a civilised human being and take three deep breaths before you let your temper get the better of you."

"You're impertinent, madam," he retorted.

"Quite possibly, but very sensible. You've remarked upon it yourself. Nor am I a toad-eater. Do, please, sit down. It makes my neck ache to look up at you and Bartram here looks most uncomfortable."

"Not half as uncomfortable as he will when I've finished with him," his brother said grimly. "And no, Miss Leigh, I will not sit down. This isn't a social call."

"Do you know, somehow I didn't think it was?" It was an effort to speak equably but India was determined not to be pushed into answering him in kind.

"Would you be so kind as to explain to me what justifies your undermining my authority?" he demanded.

"In what way am I doing that?"

"By harbouring my very foolish brother," he said.

"'Harbouring'?" India repeated. "Isn't that what one does for criminals? I'm sorry, I didn't know. I thought I was just offering a bed to a friend of Richard's."

"With his own home less than a mile away, why should he need it?"

India smiled. "You have me there, sir, but I'm sure you're going to tell me."

"He ran away—again—as I'm sure you very well know. And you were stupid enough to take him in instead of sending him straight home."

"And how was I supposed to do that?" India turned to the boys. "Richard, take Bartram upstairs and stay there until I've had a chance to talk to Lord Bardolph. And I mean stay there—I expect you both to be there when I've finished. Is that clear?"

Richard, who had no idea what this was all about except what his intelligence suggested, agreed but Bartram became even more petulant.

"If you're going to discuss me, I've got a right to stay and listen," he said.

"Don't talk to me about your rights," his brother snapped.

"I really think it would be better if you weren't here," India suggested. "Now be a good boy, do, and go with Richard."

Bartram looked suspiciously from one to the other. "This is something you've cooked up between you, isn't it?" he said. "I reckon you sent a servant over to the Hall first thing. How else did he know where I was?"

"I made an intelligent guess," his brother said, exasperated. "It wasn't difficult. If you ever used such intelligence as you possess you'd have realised this was the first place I'd think of."

"This is getting us nowhere," India pointed out. "Bartram, I did not send a message to the Hall, though I have to say I'm not nearly so surprised as you seem to be to see your brother here. Now go with Richard. He has some Greek translation to do. You can help him with it."

This suggestion was greeted with a snort of good-humoured derision from Richard and an expression of incredulity from his friend, but they both went.

"And now, my lord," India said as the door closed behind them, "perhaps you will sit down after all, and let me pour you some coffee."

He hesitated as if seeking some hidden meaning in her offer, decided to take it at face value, and did as she bade.

"What time did he arrive?"

"I've no idea. I didn't look at a clock, but he woke me up. You may count yourself lucky that he mistook my room for Richard's, so it was at my window he threw handfuls of gravel." She chuckled. "I asked him if he wanted to elope for the sake of my fortune. I don't think I've ever seen such a look of pure horror on a man's face."

"I can imagine," he said grimly, totally unaware of how this reply might be interpreted by his audience. "You said I might count myself lucky. In what way?"

"His plan was to persuade Richard to lend him some money—enough for the coach to London. I gather that, after the last little escapade, you were unreasonable enough to keep the stables locked, so he had to walk."

"I wish I'd locked the bedroom door, too," Lord Bardolph said savagely.

"I thought of that," India said. "I decided if I did he'd only go by way of the window if he wanted to escape. Besides, what useful purpose would be served by keeping a boy of that age a virtual prisoner?"

"Peace of mind. Mine."

India hesitated. Disagreements within the Chelworth family were nothing to do with her. In so far as she had been dragged into them, it had not been at her instigation. Both prudence and good manners dictated that she should not get any further involved. That said, it seemed highly unlikely that Lord Bardolph and his brother were going to reach any accord without some kind of outside mediation and she was as well placed as anyone to be that mediator. Perhaps she shouldn't speak, but she would.

"My lord, I know you had your heart set on Bartram's going into the church and I dare say it's an idea of some standing. Perhaps it was originally your father's wish and you're simply anxious to see it fulfilled, but hasn't it struck you as the years have passed that he's really quite unsuited to such a career?"

Lord Bardolph's mouth set in a thin, humourless line. "You feel the navy would suit him better, do you?"

"Frankly, I can't see why anyone should want to join the navy—or the army, if it comes to that, but then, I've never understood the workings of the male mind."

"No, you haven't."

"It's not that I think he should join the navy, even though that seems to be what he's set his heart on. I simply don't think you should insist on his entering the church."

"I wasn't aware that I had insisted on it."

"Bartram seems to think you have."

"Much as it grieves me to call my own brother a liar, the fact remains that if that's what he's told you, then that's what he is. As a matter of fact, Miss Leigh, I had come to precisely your own opinion some time ago. I have suggested to him several times that he should go to Cambridge and then we'll think about his future again."

"He says you want him to go because you hope he'll have dropped the idea of the navy by the time he leaves."

"Then he's shrewder than I gave him credit for. His experience of life is quite limited. The Grand Tour, which would have put that right, is out of the question. University will educate more than his brain. It will enlarge both his circle of acquaintance and his understanding of life, if not of the world, and all without being under the disapproving eye of an elder brother. Yes, I hope the outcome of that would be a change in his ambition and I'd be lying if I said anything else."

"In short, the church."

"No, Miss Leigh. Not at all. It's most unlikely that he would come round to considering that as a possibility, but there are other choices, you know. I confess I can't quite see him as a scholar—unlike your own brother—but there's the law, there's farming, about which he's a great deal more knowledgeable than he chooses to admit. There's even business. If he displayed an aptitude, I can see no reason why he shouldn't go abroad—India is the obvious choice, of course—and see what sort of a success he can make of it."

"But you wouldn't want him going into business in this country?"

"I think the opportunities for success are greater elsewhere."

"To say nothing of the fact that a peer of the realm would prefer not to have to admit to a brother in trade."

"There is always that, I suppose."

This conversation was not going quite as India would have wished. In pursuing her well-intentioned goal of mediating between the brothers, she had now heard two things of which she would have preferred to remain in ignorance. She steered the converse back on course.

"Bartram thinks that you'll still try to insist on the church," she said.

"I'm well aware of that, Miss Leigh. I had a far from enjoyable evening yesterday being told so in a variety of intemperate ways. I have made it as clear as I possibly can to Bartram that such is not my intention but I can hardly force him to believe me. Now I'm telling you. You're an irritating female but you don't lack intelligence or common sense so I hope I can convince you that I mean precisely what I say."

India flushed. "Your compliments unman me, sir."

"Do they? Then make the most of them for they're likely to be the last you get—from this source, at least. I take leave to tell you that I resent your interference in the private affairs of my family and I'd be much obliged if you'd keep your meddling fingers in your own pies and leave mine alone."

India kept her temper with an effort. "I was only trying to be helpful," she said.

"Oh, I'm quite sure your intentions were of the best," he retorted scathingly. "That doesn't alter the fact that they were unnecessary and unrequested."

"This was the house to which Bartram came for help," India pointed out.

"No, this is the house he came to for money. And by your own admission it was from your brother he intended to ask it, not you. If you did anything at all, it should have been to send him straight back home."

"He wouldn't have gone."

"You have servants. One of them could have accompanied him."

"My servants need their sleep and, besides, they wouldn't have had any authority over him if he had decided to run off. I kept him here because I thought that after a good night's sleep—what was left of it—and a good breakfast, I could make him see sense and come home of his own accord this morning."

"My complaint exactly—you meddled."

"If you're determined to see it like that, my lord, there's nothing I can do about it. All I can say is that it was intended for the best. Obviously I erred."

"Obviously."

India stood up, knowing that by doing so she brought this difficult interview to an end. "How extremely pleasant to know that we agree on one thing," she said. "You'll want to take Bartram back with you, I imagine."

"I shall. I have to tell you, Miss Leigh, that, while he has never been a particularly easy boy, his behaviour and his attitude have deteriorated since the onset of his acquaintance with your brother. Richard's has not been a good influence. I wish them to have nothing more to do with each other."

"I'll be sure to pass your wish on to Richard as soon as you've gone."

"And you will forbid their meeting?"

"No, Lord Bardolph. I shall make it clear that *you* forbid it. I've no desire to spark off in my own family the sort of problems your high-handed demands have engendered in yours. Good day, my lord."

"Good day, Miss Leigh."

When the breakfast-room door had closed behind him, India sank back on to her chair, trembling with impotent anger at his unreasonableness. She had been trying to help. She had been hoping that the friendship so painfully established over the preceding weeks was sufficiently solid to permit her to step outside the bounds of conventional good manners in order to help. She had been mistaken and the direct consequence was that they were back where they had been after that first confrontation all those weeks ago.

In the course of their disagreement she had learned quite a lot, none of it to her liking. Lord Bardolph found her irritating, regarded her as a meddler and had, above all, made his views on those engaged in trade perfectly clear. It was acceptable only if it were done abroad and it was something with which a peer of the realm preferred not to be associated. That told her very clearly where she stood. The fact that she had previously worked it out for herself was no consolation. While it had been in her head, there was always a barely acknowledged possibility of error. But Bardolph had confirmed it. Very well. At least she had been careful never to let him guess that her feelings for him had gone deeper than was proper. That meant she could hold her head up and appear unmoved by the coldness that must now inevitably descend between them. She wondered briefly whether he would do as once before he had done, and come with an olive-branch. She decided not. This time the breach was both wider and deeper. She was left with the sole satisfaction of not having lost her temper. It was a very small consolation.

Richard burst into the breakfast-room. "Bartram's gone," he announced. "My, wasn't Bardolph in a fury? Did you and he have one of your battles?"

"We weren't entirely in agreement," India admitted.

"That's what I thought. He had a face like a thundercloud. I'd have guessed you'd fallen out even if we hadn't been able to hear you."

"You heard us?"

"Good grief, India, I should think the whole village heard you!"

"So you know what it was all about."

"Not exactly. I mean, we couldn't make out the actual words, though we tried—short of coming downstairs and putting our ears to the keyhole, that is. Bartram was all in favour of that but I told him it wasn't on."

"I'm relieved to hear it."

"He told me why he came here last night. What a hoot him catching the wrong room! Not that it would have done him much good if he'd got the right one because I'm out of funds till my next allowance is due. Well, not *entirely* out of funds," he added punctiliously, in case India thought he was about to touch her for more, always a sore point between them. "But too low to be able to lend him any, and certainly not the coach fare to London. Do you know what I think?"

"About Bartram? No, tell me."

"I think if he isn't very careful he's going to become a dashed loose screw. I'm not surprised Bardolph gets annoyed with him. I don't like Bardolph above half but give him his due, he's a gentleman through and through."

"I'm glad you can recognise that fact," India said and wondered whether the life stretching endlessly ahead of her might not have seemed so featureless had Bardolph been less of a gentleman.

"Did Lord Bardolph say anything to you before he left?"

Richard shook his head. "No. He seemed more concerned to get Bartram home. You know, if Bardolph let up a bit, I don't think Bartram would do half the silly things he does."

"Well, at least he left it to me to broach in my own way," India said.

"Broach what? No, don't tell me. Let me guess. He wants Bartram to stay away from my evil influence and since he doesn't seem able to stop Bart doing exactly what he wants he expects you to make me promise not to have anything to do with him. Right?"

"Masterly. I was going to try to phrase it more diplomatically. You've saved me the bother."

"So much for what Bardolph wants. Do you agree with him?"

"It seems to me that the bad influence, if there is any, is all on Bartram's side, but maybe I'm just as biased as Lord Bardolph. In any case, that isn't really the point, is it? There's no denying that the two of you do seem to have a genius for getting into mischief and perhaps it wouldn't be a bad idea not to see each other for a while."

Richard grinned. "Until Bardolph's calmed down, you mean."

"No, that's not what I meant, but it'll do to begin with."

"Are *you* forbidding it?"

India thought about that. "I suppose I ought to. It's certainly what Lord Bardolph expects me to do but, no, I think not. If it's not forbidden, there's no challenge to be taken up, is there? Let's say I'd prefer you not to see him for the sake of good relations with our neighbour."

Richard hooted. "What good relations? If Bardolph's the neighbour you're talking about, I shouldn't think relations could be much worse."

"You may be right. I'd rather not risk discovering that you're wrong. What do you say?"

He shrugged. "Why not? Bart's good company when he's in a good humour—and very knowledgeable about the countryside and horses, but he spends so much of his time grumbling about his brother and how nothing's fair that it really becomes a bit tedious. In any case, I think I'm better able to find my own way around now. The people know who I am. They don't treat me like one of them, the way they do with Bart, but they don't become all silent and stolid any more. In fact, old Micah, down by the estuary, offered to take me out plover-netting some time. I'd like that. I don't think it'll bother me, not for a while, anyway. Mind you, it could be a bit difficult if Bartram decides to disobey his brother, and he's very likely to."

"I'm afraid you're right. You'll just have to deal with that if and when it arises. Do you still want to be a farmer?"

"As a matter of fact, I do. Why? Afraid you're turning into a female Bardolph?"

"Nothing of the sort," India said indignantly, refusing to
admit that he had been disconcertingly accurate. She had
found herself wondering whether there was any great difference between the Viscount's refusal to sanction Bartram's ambition and her similar refusal to accept Richard's.
They went about it differently but the underlying principle
wasn't so different. "Would you rather do that and not go
to college?" she asked.

"Oh, no. I shall enjoy Cambridge. Besides, I can't see
that it hurts to be an educated farmer."

"Very true."

"Does this mean you've changed your mind?"

"It means I'm thinking about it. I'll certainly be a lot
happier at the prospect if you've had a good education
first."

"You sound like Papa," Richard commented.

"Is that so surprising? I'm trying to take his place—and
Mama's, too."

"I suppose you are. I've never thought of it quite like that
before." He slapped her on the back. "You're not doing too
bad a job of it, either."

"Thank you. I'll remind you of that some time."

"Well, you're making a better job of it than Bardolph,"
Richard said in qualification.

"I rather think that constitutes damning with faint
praise," his sister said wryly. "Now be off with you, I have
to make my peace with Cook."

India had no difficulty making her peace with Cook.
Making it with herself was another matter. She had handled the interview with Lord Bardolph badly. She must have
done or they would still be on friendly terms. Yet she was
uncertain what else she could have done. The only thing that
would have met with the Viscount's approval would have
been for her to drag Bartram back home in the middle of the
night, wake up the Viscount's household and hand him over.
Leaving aside the sheer physical difficulty of compelling an
unwilling sixteen-year-old to go a mile in one direction when

he was intent on going a hundred in the other, would any rational person really expect a woman to get dressed and traipse through the streets at dead of night? Of course not, as Lord Bardolph must surely recognise when his anger had subsided. She had done what she could by keeping Bartram there until morning and she had been entirely confident of her ability to persuade him to go home of his own accord. Lord Bardolph's arrival had pre-empted that plan. He had been angry that she had been meddling in his family's business, and India accepted that it would have been better had she not been, but it was his brother who had embroiled her in it and she couldn't for the life of her, think what else she could have done in the circumstances.

She had more than half hoped that the Viscount would seek her out when he had calmed down and, without necessarily apologising, make it clear that he knew he had been unjust. As the days passed and no such approach was made, India realised that his pride, or perhaps it was his family pride, was too offended. He neither came nor wrote. When they met in church, there was nothing more from him than an icily polite inclination of the head, to which she responded in kind. She might have her origins in trade, but she would see she could be every bit as high in the instep as he. The almost daily rides ceased. India told herself these would soon have come to an end anyway, with the onset of winter, but there was no denying she missed them. She wasn't sure whether it was rides themselves she missed the most, or the company in which she made them.

Some of the blame must surely lie with Lord Bardolph, who had apparently not known her well enough to realise that she had acted with the best of intentions. She had known him to be arrogant but perhaps she had underestimated his pride. It was at best a great pity things had turned out as they had but she must learn to live with it. They would stay here until the spring and then, if it was still too painful only to encounter the Viscount in this cold and distant manner, she would suggest to Richard that they would be happier elsewhere.

There was every sign that Richard was keeping his word and not seeing Bartram. India wasn't sure that this was altogether an improvement. He was acquiring a repertoire of skills of whose existence she had previously been totally ignorant and all of which seemed to necessitate crawling across mud-flats or wading in muddy dykes in the hours before dawn. He learned to set plover-nets and eel-nets, to go punt-gunning and ferreting, to catch moles and set rabbit-snares, all good Fenland pursuits that endeared him to the villagers if not to the servants who had to clean up the mud he trailed through the house. India sighed, said nothing except to suggest that he use the back door and wipe his feet before he came in, not afterwards and was quietly grateful that he also spent some time on his studies. It began to look as if he had been successfully weaned off his friendship with Bartram, and India hoped Lord Bardolph was observing the same change in his brother.

Her complacency was jolted when Richard announced that he had bumped into Bartram on his way back from the salt-marshes that morning.

India tried to appear unconcerned. "Indeed? It must be some time since you've met. Did he have anything much to say?"

Richard helped himself to three large slices of sirloin before answering. "Much as usual. Bardolph won't let him do anything. Bardolph keeps him on a short lead. That sort of thing."

"Not so short that he can't go to the salt-marshes in the early morning," India remarked drily.

"That's what I said, but you know Bartram—nothing's ever right and Bardolph's only out to do him down, though why he should want to I've never been able to make out."

"The sort of person who makes it feel as if the sun has just gone in," India suggested.

"That's it exactly. Half an hour with Bartram's enough to throw anyone into the doldrums. He's still going on about old Huggate and the smugglers, you know."

"Don't let yourself be lured into another escapade like the last one, I beg you," India said.

"I don't intend to. Not unless he can find rather more convincing proof. He's decided Bardolph's involved."

India's teacup halted halfway to her mouth. "Bardolph? Involved with smuggling? Nonsense." She thought about it. "I can't think of anyone less likely to be involved. For one thing, he's a magistrate."

"That's what I told Bart. He said there's plenty of magistrates who are, and a lot more who just turn a blind eye in return for the odd cask of brandy."

"That may be so," replied his sister, who had heard much the same herself. "I can't believe Lord Bardolph to be among their number."

"That's what I said, but Bartram won't have any of it. In fact, he says it's a lot more than just turning a blind eye. He says Bardolph's up to something. He says they've had some rum visitors from time to time who come to see the Viscount but who come and go through a side-door—not even the kitchen where they'd have to account for themselves."

"You don't think this could conceivably be a case of Bartram's imagination reading far more into it than is really there?"

"Probably—and fuelled by his dislike for his brother, as well, I don't doubt. All the same it *is* odd even if it's only half true. Old Huggate *was* up to something—still is, if Bart's to be believed—and Bardolph refused to take it seriously, or even to go through the motions of getting the authorities to look into it. It does make you wonder."

"Just so long as wondering doesn't lead you into more mischief," India said flatly. "Are you sure you've had enough? You wouldn't like me to send out for another side of beef?"

He grinned. "No, thank you, I'll have died of starvation before it's cooked. I've got some work to do. If it's all the same to you, I'll take a chunk of this Dundee cake to tide me over. You can send Cook my compliments, if you like."

He left India a prey to mixed thoughts. If ever there was a case of the devil finding work for idle hands, it was Bartram Chelworth, who seemed to spend his spare time—a time which appeared to constitute all his waking hours—developing grudges and then finding evidence on which to feed them. When it came to accusing his own brother of having something to do with the smuggling that Bartram alleged to be centred on Huggate's barn, he was being downright malicious, and malice was unforgivable.

Then the uncomfortable thought occurred to her that it might be malicious but that didn't necessarily make it untrue. She was able to discount the episode involving the boys and the barn. Lord Bardolph had been understandably angry and, while that might be due to the discovery that the boys were looking into something he preferred to see kept secret, it was much more likely that he was angry because, if Huggate was to be believed, they had been behaving in a thoroughly irresponsible way and because his pride couldn't tolerate having to apologise to the likes of Mr. Huggate.

The visit he had paid with India was much more puzzling. There was no denying his interest in the Dutch ketch's activities and they had ridden over to the farm presumably in order to see what was going on. Yet when she had reported some of the odd things she had seen, he had dismissed them and derided her theories. Had he gone to the farm because he didn't want her to think he was dismissive of activities that were possibly illegal? Or had he done so knowing full well that their open approach would result in any evidence—including the presence of foreign seamen—being hidden? There would have been plenty of time to do so. All Huggate had to do was to keep them talking—or, more accurately, to hold them captive to his own volubility—while the seamen got away to catch the tide. He did it very well. India had presumed Lord Bardolph found it tolerable only because he was accustomed to such effusiveness, but what if the real reason was that he knew very well its purpose and was perfectly willing to encourage it?

India shivered. She wouldn't have believed Lord Bardolph capable of such duplicity. It seemed totally out of character. She didn't *want* to believe it, and yet…and yet…

She slept restlessly that night and awoke miserable and depressed. Her friendship with Lord Bardolph might have regressed into nothing more than a cold and impersonal acquaintance but she found it very hard to believe his worst fault was anything more than pride and arrogance, reprehensible as those might be.

Perhaps she should advance her plans to move away from here; to dig up now the first slender roots of whose thickening and strengthening she had gradually become aware and to do so before it became too painful. She would have preferred to go with her conviction of Lord Bardolph's integrity intact but the seed of doubt had been sown and, so far as she could see, nothing now could totally eliminate it. The recollection of what had been, the dreams of what might have been, would always henceforth be marred by that small, insidious question mark.

CHAPTER EIGHT

"I CAN'T, BART. I promised India." Richard Leigh tried to sound as determined as he knew he ought to be but his friend caught the hint of doubt and worked on it.

"How old are you? Fourteen? Don't you think you ought to be out of leading-strings by now?"

"I am," Richard protested indignantly.

"No, you're not. You're just tied by longer ones. If your sister won't undo them, then cut them yourself. Or don't you want to grow up?"

"It's not that. It's just that she'd be furious if she knew what we—you—were planning. And I'm not very happy about it myself," he added frankly.

"Just because she's forbidden you to see me. Well, Edward's done the same, and how much notice do I take?" Bartram said with the triumphant air of one clinching an argument.

"As a matter of fact, the one thing she *hasn't* done is forbid me to see you. She said she'd prefer it if I didn't because it causes bad feelings between the families. That makes it much harder to go against her wishes, that's all."

"So your sister is a lot cleverer than my brother, isn't she? She realises it's much easier to disobey a flat prohibition than an appeal to one's better nature. I bet she'd be furious if she knew we met the other day."

"She does know, because I told her, and she wasn't, but what you propose is a horse of a very different colour."

"But there's got to be more than one of us." Bartram was almost pleading now. "It's a matter of safety. There's got to be one who can go for help in an emergency."

"Doesn't it occur to you that if it's potentially that dangerous—and I'll not deny it is—we'd be better advised to be sleeping soundly in our beds?"

"Where would be the fun in that?"

"It sounds to me as if it could be about as much fun as being taken by the press-gang. That may not have bothered you, but it did me and I'm not ashamed to admit it."

"It wasn't quite the way I'd intended to enter the navy, either. But this is quite different. No one's going to take us captive and ship us out to sea for a few years."

"No," Richard said bitterly. "This lot will just bundle us overboard in the German Sea with or without slitting our throats first."

"All the more reason for us to be very, very careful. And all the more reason to see them brought to justice," Bartram added altruistically.

"If you're right, one of them's your own brother."

"Yes, but I'm not sure he isn't clever enough to slide out of it at the end."

Richard shook his head. "I don't like it. It'll be exciting and I suppose you can argue that it's one's duty and all that, but I don't like it a bit."

"But you'll come?"

"Before I decide, I want to be quite clear about what we're going to do."

"We're going to spy on them, that's all. We're not going to tackle them or anything foolish like that. Just watch them so that we can each verify what the other says when we take the evidence to the revenue men in Wisbech."

"Wouldn't it be wiser to tell them our—your—suspicions and leave it to them?"

"They wouldn't take them seriously. They'd say it was too much imagination and send for Edward to take us home— and that's something I couldn't face."

Richard was inclined to agree with him on both counts.

"Can you get horses?" he asked.

"No. Edward keeps the stables and the tack-room locked. In any case, we want to be able to lie low and horses would get in the way of that. We'll have to walk."

"But it's miles!" Richard protested.

Bartram shrugged. "So we have to leave that much earlier."

It was Richard's bad luck that the enforced early departure coupled with his sister's troubled mind meant that she was only drifting on the outer edges of sleep when he closed his bedroom door and made for the stairs. He was as quiet as he possibly could be but, even so, the click of the bolt slipping back into its mortice was dismayingly loud. He comforted himself with the thought that all sounds seemed louder at night and probably no one had heard it, and prayed that the same should be true of the creaking board across the landing—which he had tried to avoid but miscalculated—and three creaking stairs in succession.

His prayer was unanswered, though he continued in blissful ignorance of that fact. India heard the click. To be more precise, a small, sharp sound penetrated her sleepy haze sufficiently deeply to make her wonder whether she had heard something. The creaking board told her she had, woke her up completely, and sent her mind racing over the possibilities, of which burglars headed the list. They were there only briefly. No one had been in her room—she hadn't been sufficiently soundly asleep for them not to have wakened her—and there was nothing in Richard's room worth stealing, and it must have been Richard's door she heard.

She listened briefly to the creaking stairs and guessed that Richard was on his way out of the house. But why? Quickly, she swung her legs out of bed and crept across to the window where, as on a previous occasion, she stood to one side and parted the curtains just enough to enable her to see down the garden path. She had already dismissed the idea that Richard might leave by the kitchen door: its locks and bolts were old and clattered heavily whenever they were moved, certainly enough to wake at least one servant. The front door had modern, well-oiled hinges and a smooth lock. Even the bolts slid more easily and almost silently.

India strained her ears, and even though she was listening for the sound of the front door, and even though it was immediately below her, she only just heard it. The slim figure that slipped out and along the muffling grass bordering the path was unmistakably Richard's.

She wasted no time assuming he was off fishing or wildfowling for the very simple reason that he always told her so that, if she heard him leave, she wouldn't worry. No, this was something else, and, since he had said nothing to her about it, it was reasonable to conclude that she'd disapprove.

Therefore it was something she ought to know about.

In that case, she'd better find out.

The only way to do that was to follow him—and quickly, while there was still a chance of picking up his trail.

She opened the wardrobe and reached inside for her habit and then had second thoughts. Richard had no access to a horse at this time of night and if she again borrowed some of his clothes she'd be able to move much more quickly. It wasn't as if there was anyone to see her. She guessed that Richard must be planning to be home before morning because otherwise he would surely have given her some story to account for his possible absence.

She snatched breeches and boots and tucked her voluminous night-chemise into the former. It wasn't comfortable but it was warm and, in any case, she didn't have time to fiddle with shirts. She grabbed a coat and was still pulling it on when she reached the stairs. Since she had no desire to draw to herself the attention of any of the neighbouring houses, she, too, closed the door as quietly as she could and kept to the grass beside the path, though this was as much to prevent the sound of her footsteps reaching Richard as for any other reason.

India slipped out of the gate and stood under the over-hanging branches of a laburnum so that she could have a good look in either direction with a minimal chance of being spotted herself. She was just in time to see Richard disappear round a corner at the far end of the village street, a corner that she knew led only to the marshes. She hastened after him, instinctively making what use she could of any trees, and found this was just as well, because when she was about halfway to the turning another young man came stealthily out of the cobbled street opposite, crossed the main road and followed Richard up the grassy track.

Bartram? Of course it was Bartram, she thought bitterly. Now what are they up to? Surely he hasn't persuaded Richard to run away with him again? No, said her common sense. Not on to the marshes. They're playing some other game.

LORD BARDOLPH dismounted and signalled to the men behind him to do the same. It had been a long and difficult ride, made worse by the need for concealment. They had set out in the darkness before the sliver of moon was in any position to cast even its thankfully inadequate light over a landscape which night rendered not only flat but also featureless. They had been obliged to avoid roads and habitations; their bridles had rubber bits and their horses' hoofs were muffled; all the men wore dark, enveloping greatcoats with buttons that matched rather than the fashionable mother-of-pearl or bone ones that such coats usually sported; they communicated by hand-signals instead of words—not easy to spot in the poor light and therefore requiring a part of each man's concentration to be on the dim shapes ahead, while another part watched the possibly treacherous saltmarsh underfoot.

There were fifteen of them, a paltry enough number but all that could be spared, and Lord Bardolph comforted himself with the knowledge that at least the fewer there were the less became their chances of being noticed. He and the riding surveyor beside him glanced seawards. They were unlikely to be spotted yet, even had there been a ship out there. If there was, it showed no lights and their keen eyes, accustomed to detecting objects far out to sea, could see nothing. It was a little early yet. The tide wasn't quite right.

The danger was greater from the landward side. They weren't going to be the only horsemen abroad tonight. It behoved them to find their cover before the others dispersed themselves along the creeks and runnels of the marshes. They needed to be sufficiently far back to remain unobserved until it suited them to move, yet sufficiently far forward to see what they wanted to see and to be able to cover the ground before the others could flee. It was a nice problem.

The riding officers knew the terrain, but only in a broad, general sort of way, far removed from the minuteness of Lord Bardolph's familiarity with it, and the surveyor knew that their success depended largely on his presence with them, allied to a large chunk of luck. They therefore moved inland, partially hidden by the banks of a muddy defile, at his signal and then took the necessary risk of leading their mounts over the sea-bank and quickly down the other side. There was less cover on the outmarshes, but they contained the remains of another bank, intended to hold back the sea in the old days before the systematic drainage of the Fens rendered it obsolete. It provided cover of a sort, albeit inadequate, but it had the advantage of being sufficiently far from the anticipated scene of operations for the horses to remain there with little likelihood of being detected. Stakes were driven into the soft, fertile soil; ropes were stretched between and each horse was tethered to it. Then the riders moved forward, crouching low so that they presented no recognisable shape should someone catch a glimpse of them against the sky. Even a moonless night wasn't totally dark. Even on a moonless night some things were a denser dark than others and this was no moonless night—it was cloudless and the thin sickle-blade of the moon was approaching its zenith. Very little remained hidden for long from those actively searching.

It was the riding surveyor who first spotted the ship, a lightless form moving softly, slowly against the lighter sky. He touched Lord Bardolph's sleeve and pointed. The Viscount nodded. Both men knew the master steered a dangerous course so close to land in channels that were deep enough but narrow. Both knew that a seaman must be taking soundings on each side of the bow and the captain must be praying that there had been no great shifting of the mud- and sand-banks since his last visit.

Without a sound, by touch and signal, the news passed along the attenuated line of riding officers that at least one part of their information had proved correct: a ship had come; a master had risked a channel that few would have chanced in daylight. No captain did that unless the rewards were worth the risk. And men prepared to take that sort of risk were unlikely to be too squeamish about the welfare of a few revenue men. It was a wonderful incentive to keep the senses alert.

BARTRAM, keener-eyed than his companion, spotted it, too. "Out there," he whispered fiercely. "I told you so."

Richard nodded, but with a sinking heart. He hadn't been altogether convinced by Bartram's story, which had seemed to him to have a strong element of imagination in it. He didn't think Bartram was lying; on the contrary, he was quite sure his friend had convinced himself of the truth of his imaginings. This reservation had been in his mind when he had agreed to join the older boy. Now it began to look as if Bartram might not be so fanciful, after all. Richard couldn't compete with him when it came to knowledge of ships and the sea, or with this stretch of water in particular, but he was intelligent, he had spent the last few weeks in the company of men who might be unlettered in a bookish sense but whose minds were packed with information about the Wash, its mudbanks, creeks and marshes, and even he now realised that no master in his right mind sailed his ship up that channel at the present state of the tide except for a very strong incentive. Such as money. Danger had hitherto been something to think of lightly because it was unlikely to happen. That had changed with the arrival of the Dutch ketch—for, although Richard didn't know enough to recognise it, he had no doubt that they were looking at the *Amelia*.

So intent were they that neither boy heard the rustle of sedge behind them and both spun round, wide-eyed with fear, when a discreet cough told them they weren't alone.

It was several seconds before they recognised the newcomer.

"India?" Disbelief permeated Richard's whisper.

"What on earth do you two think you're doing?" she asked, whispering, not because she thought there was any need to, but because it seemed entirely natural to answer one whisper with another.

"Go home," Richard said. "Go home and go back to bed. I thought you were sound asleep."

"I thought you probably did. You were mistaken, so I decided to see what you were up to. You know you're not supposed to meet, Lord Bardolph won't be pleased if he gets wind of this."

Bartram snorted. "I don't think we need worry unduly about what my dear brother thinks," he said. "Please go home, Miss Leigh. You could spoil everything."

"I have a feeling that spoiling everything might be the best thing to do. Tell me what it's all about. I can see that, whatever it is, it's both clandestine and secretive, otherwise why should we be whispering? So either you tell me, or I'll jump up and down singing 'Lillibullero.'"

Bartram stared at her, dismayed. "You wouldn't."

"Are you willing to take the risk?"

He shifted uncomfortably. "I think you're bluffing."

He could feel rather than see India's smile. "There's one way to find out," she said.

"She will," Richard broke in. "We'll have to tell her. You keep watch while I explain. It's Huggate and the smugglers, you see," he offered.

"Not entirely. You'd better elaborate."

"Bart says that Dutch ketch has been here several times, both during the day and at night. He reckoned they'd be due tonight—and he was right; she's out there now. So, in order to have a witness before telling Customs what's going on, he asked me to come along, too."

India decided against letting them know that at least one of the ketch's daytime visits had been seen. Better to play devil's advocate. "If it's been here during the day, why hasn't it been boarded and searched?"

"Those visits were just ruses so that tidesmen got used to seeing her in that channel."

"Don't you think that possibility has occurred to them?"

"If it has, they've done nothing about it," Richard said. "Bart wants to present them with evidence they can't refute." He hesitated. "And that's not all."

India groaned. "Go on."

"Well, since you're not friends any more, we can tell you. Bart's convinced his brother's one of them."

India felt her stomach lurch. This was not something she wanted to hear. "What? A Dutch smuggler?" she asked, deliberately obtuse.

"No, of course not. Involved at this end—not just turning a blind eye to what goes on but actively helping them."

"Aren't you forgetting he's a magistrate?"

"He wouldn't be the first," Bartram hissed over his shoulder. "Hurry up, you two. We shouldn't stay here much longer or we'll be too late."

"And just what evidence does your friend have to back up this bizarre story?" India demanded.

"He says that at first he didn't think it amounted to much more than turning a blind eye, but when he was forbidden to see me he was at a bit of a loose end so he started shadowing Bardolph, and he found he was meeting with some very rum coves—peculiar individuals," he amended hastily, knowing his sister's objection to cant.

"And all this time Bardolph never suspected he was being followed?" India asked sceptically.

"So Bart says—and he's very good at being unobtrusive when he wants to be," Richard added.

India resisted with difficulty a gibe about being sly, underhand and deceitful. Members of the same family often shared characteristics, and hadn't she already had a suspicion that Lord Bardolph was less than entirely open? It wasn't a reflection that gave her any comfort. She had no intention of letting either boy get wind of her feelings on that score and if there were any truth in Bartram's story they were putting themselves in an extremely dangerous position.

"This amounts to the biggest cock-and-bull story I've ever heard," she said finally. "Richard, you're coming home with me. Bartram may do as he pleases since he's not my responsibility, thank God. If he's got any sense at all, he'll come too. If he's right, you're running into considerable danger and if he's not you're going to make fools of yourselves."

"Well, I'm staying," Bartram said. "You can run home with your big sister if you want to be a baby. I keep forgetting you're only fourteen."

"It's about time you remembered it," India snapped. "Richard?"

"Do I have to? I don't want to. After all, if Bart's wrong the three of us are the only ones who'll know what fools we've been, and if he's right we'll be doing our public duty, and you can't object to that."

"Very noble," India told him. "I'm not convinced that in this case it's worth the risk."

"In any case," Richard said, ignoring the argument of common sense, "I don't quite see how you're going to drag me back if I don't want to go."

His point was unarguable but India knew she couldn't, having found out so much, go home and back to bed and leave them to get on with it, yet the last thing she wanted to do was to stay and take any part in the rest of this expedition. The choice was denied her.

Bartram turned his head towards them. "Come on, or we'll be too late. They've just launched the long-boat."

India glanced out to sea but could see nothing new. "How do you know?" she asked.

"I saw the white foam when it hit the water," he replied impatiently. "Come on. The gentlemen'll be waiting. We'll have to go cautiously."

Caught up in the excitement of things happening, Richard forgot his earlier misgivings and followed Bartram. India, after a brief hesitation during which she was sorely tempted to go home and leave them to it, followed close behind. She hadn't been able to stop them. At least she must stay with them. It was probably just as well that she didn't stop to ask herself what she could possibly do if they were caught because she wouldn't have had the slightest idea.

Bartram soon proved that he could move a great deal more quietly than either of his companions and India was forced grudgingly to admit that he might very well have been able to follow his brother without the latter's having any inkling of it. There were fields in which such skills might have their uses but she didn't think they were ones which a viscount would consider more acceptable for his younger brother than the navy.

A hand-signal from Bartram had them lying flat on their stomachs. He breathed an instruction to India to button her jacket to the neck, and she realised that the white of her chemise would be like a beacon to anyone who caught sight of it. She did as she was told.

"Over there," Bartram whispered, pointing to their left.

India's gaze followed the direction of his outstretched arm but at first she could see nothing. Then it was as if a denser part of the darkness stirred. People? Something about the movement made her think not. "Horses?" she whispered.

Bartram slithered back towards them from the tussock from behind which he had been peering. "It must be the pack-horses waiting to be loaded," he whispered. "If they are, their hoofs will be muffled and that can only work to our advantage. We'll have to keep on the alert for signs of the gentlemen. They can't be far and they could be very close indeed. What I propose we do is creep up behind them and take the horses. That leaves them with the problem of carrying away their contraband, while we have the evidence of the horses. Not only that, but all those horses must have owners so we indirectly identify others who are involved."

India had an uncomfortable suspicion that this was one of those ideas which sounded easier than it proved. "We're going to have to be very careful," she offered.

"Haven't I said as much? I can't see anyone placed to guard them but that doesn't mean there isn't someone and the moment they spot us..." Despite the dim light there was no mistaking Bartram's gesture of drawing his finger across his throat. India shivered and wished herself almost anywhere else.

They made slow, crouching progress towards the tethered horses and had covered half the distance when Bartram held out a hand to stop them again. This time he pointed away in front of them and when they had concentrated for several minutes on the dark landscape ahead his companions could make out the occasional movement that this time did resemble that of humans rather than horses.

"They're a good way from their animals," Bartram murmured. "If we don't run into a guard, it should be quite easy."

If...India thought, but it seemed that luck was with them. As they approached the stake-line there was no sign of anyone's having been left on watch.

The horses stirred restlessly as they came closer but this only served to reveal their muffled hoofs, firm evidence of the accuracy of Bartram's assumptions. Coiled ropes hung from their saddles, further evidence of their nefarious purpose. It was Richard who raised a brief objection.

"These aren't pack-ponies," he said. "And they're not carrying panniers. Are you sure you're right?"

"Of course they're not carrying panniers—that would give the game away to anyone who happened to see them on the way here," Bartram replied. "The ropes are more than enough to lash barrels alongside, and they're all of them pretty sturdy animals."

This was true enough. They might all be riding-horses but with one exception they weren't what any gentleman would want in his stables. It was the exception that attracted India's attention. She knew it well.

"Bartram," she whispered urgently. "Isn't this your brother's horse?"

"It is, by God! I knew he was involved! I knew it!" India had the distinct impression that if his life hadn't depended upon remaining concealed Bartram Chelworth would have danced a victory jig on the spot. She enjoyed neither the implications of the horse's presence here nor the light Bartram's reaction threw on his character. She wished more than ever that she had stayed in bed. There were suspicions she would have preferred to see allayed, not confirmed.

"Right," Bartram went on. "There's no time to waste. Let's take them—"

"Hold on a minute," Richard interrupted. "There's five or six horses each here. We can manage three each—one to ride and one led on either side, but how can we manage more?"

Bartram hesitated, but only briefly. "No good turning them loose—they'll be spotted before we've got far enough away. We'll have to tether each horse to the saddle rings of the one in front. If the reins aren't long enough, there's always the ropes."

The plan was sound enough. Unfortunately for their peace of mind, it was also a time-consuming one and the fear of being discovered conspired with the horses' restlessness to make fingers behave like thumbs and the task take twice as long as it might otherwise have done in broad daylight and without the sense of urgency.

It was accomplished at last and the trio by tacit agreement resisted the impulse to mount up immediately and get as far away as possible. Instead each led a string of horses away from the staking rope as stealthily as possible and only when several hundred yards had been covered without any alarm being raised did they pause to mount up.

It was difficult to believe their luck was holding and when faint but unmistakable sounds of distant uproar floated across the still night air towards them they knew with awful certainty that the horses had been missed. They also knew that, with four or five horses in train behind each of them, it was out of the question to increase the pace; time spent untangling the inevitable confusion of ropes and reins would use up more time than any increase in speed would save.

"They can't follow us on foot," India said, "but how quickly will they be able to find fresh horses?"

"Huggate might be willing to lend one or two," Bartram conceded. "Otherwise they'll have to go to the Hall, Edward's got enough in his stables. But there's no need to worry. They'll let us go."

Neither Richard nor India shared his complacency. "Not if they can be identified by their horses," Richard said bluntly. "And if India could recognise Bardolph's, other people won't have any difficulty either with that one or the others. They'll be after us and they won't waste their time. We need to get these to customs as soon as we can."

THE ATTENTION of Lord Bardolph, the riding surveyor and his officers was fixed so intently in front of them on the different shades of dark that the landscape had become that they simply didn't hear any sound from their horses even though the abduction was far from silent. They had concealed them a good way back, horses being larger and less biddable objects than men, and since they had seen no sign of their adversaries' ponies they assumed they had done the same.

Like Bartram, they spotted the spurt of white that signalled a boat hitting the water and they concentrated their attention in two directions: on the incoming boat, which they couldn't hear and could no longer see, and on any signs of movement on the marshes that might give them a clue as to the whereabouts of the receivers.

Only when the boat, with another close on its heels whose launching they had failed to spot, could be detected in the winding creek in front of them to the right did they also spot the first signs of movement on the landward side. Now every man's hand went instinctively to the pistol tucked into his belt and his grip tightened on the cudgel that was likely to prove the more useful weapon of the two.

All knew the importance of judging their assault with precision. Too soon, and the boats' crews would be able to push off and rejoin the ketch; too late and many of the receivers would be too widely scattered to be rounded up effectively. The success of this expenditure of men and horses would be judged on the number of smugglers and the quantity of contraband apprehended.

The first boat had come as far inshore as it safely could. The crew were in the shallow water of the small creek. The goods were being unloaded. Previously invisible figures grew out of the marshes and ran forward to help and soon the second boat was close behind the first and its crew, too, was overboard and at work.

Lord Bardolph's optimism leapt three notches higher. The first boat would be forced to wait until the second had unloaded before it could return to the mother-ship because the creek was too narrow to allow it to do anything other than follow the hindmost out. Their chances of catching both crews were greatly increased and that, in turn, meant

that any attempt by the ketch's captain to weigh anchor
would be handicapped by a shortage of seamen. A revenue
cutter should by now be approaching the channel where the
Amelia lay. That, however, was not Lord Bardolph's immediate concern. It was more important to concentrate on
the job in hand. It wasn't going to be easy. There must be all
of thirty or forty people out there now, and many of them
would be his own tenants and neighbours. That couldn't be
helped.

The right moment came. Lord Bardolph exchanged
glances with the riding surveyor and the latter nodded
briefly. It would be a gamble to wait for a better opportunity. A hand-signal passed down the line and the revenue
men ran forward, cudgels flailing, shouting and yelling to
create the impression of a much larger force. Some of them
spread out to the rear of the landsmen, thus further en-
hancing this illusion.

The ensuing uproar—which India and the boys heard and
misinterpreted—was proof that the smugglers were taken
totally by surprise.

Few shots were fired, the revenue men preferring to lay
about them with cudgels, weapons which had the advantage of not needing several seconds to reload after every use.
Only when a man's cudgel was struck from his hand did he
reach for a pistol and a cutlass. It no longer mattered if the
thin moonlight caught the blade.

Some of the landsmen deserted their comrades and fled
for their homes before retribution could identify them for
future punishment. This considerably reduced the opposi-
tion and by the time some five-and-twenty smugglers lay
clutching broken heads and slashed arms only two of the
revenue men were similarly out of action, one of them dead.

Lord Bardolph sent a man for the ropes while the others
rounded up the walking wounded and encircled them until
they could be brought to justice. The punishment for those
among them with sea-going experience would be impressment into His Majesty's Navy. The rest would be lucky to

escape with hard labour, especially since a customs official had been killed in the mêlée.

"They've gone!" came a shout from behind as the man sent to fetch ropes ran towards them, leaping tussocks as he came. "The horses have gone. All of them," he panted.

"You sure you looked in the right place?" the riding surveyor said sharply.

"He's a local man," Lord Bardolph interrupted. "He knew where they were."

"The stakes are still there—and the stake rope, but that's too thick for tying men. They've gone all right," the young man replied.

Lord Bardolph looked about him and frowned. He would have sworn their enterprise had been a complete surprise. How, then, had someone taken the horses? "You're sure they haven't just slipped their tethers?" he asked.

The man shook his head. "No, my lord. The tethers are all there. They've been unclipped. There aren't any horses wandering about, grazing, either. They've been stolen."

The Viscount could think of only one explanation. Someone—possibly someone arriving later than planned, had come up from the rear and, seeing the horses and guessing what they betokened, had simply abducted them. The horses would have told him the strength of the force was heavily outnumbered by the smugglers. That would mean its defeat and the loss of the horses would make it impossible for any survivors to escape either to sound the alarm or bear witness at a later date, and bodies were easily enough disposed of in these waters.

One man alone couldn't have done more than set the horses loose. Two would have had great difficulty leading them all away. Three could have managed it and four would have found it relatively easy.

"There must be three, maybe four horse-thieves, then," he said. "I want them, and when I get them they'll be prosecuted to the full extent of the law." He turned to one of the smugglers. "I know you, Coldham," he said. "I knew you were a fool but I never guessed you were such a big one. You've a wife and how many children? Seven? Eight?"

"Seven, me lord," the man said sulkily.

"Then do yourself and them a favour by telling me where the ponies are to shift these goods inland. You'll save your neck and I'll see the family doesn't starve."

The man hesitated only briefly. His sound arm pointed. "Over there, me lord. About three hundred yards back."

Lord Bardolph turned to the surveyor. "How many men can you spare?"

"We'll tie this lot with their own belts if there aren't any ropes on their ponies. That done, I can let you have four or five."

"Better than nothing. Let's get on with it. God alone knows how much of a start they've got."

THE HORSE-THIEVES found their escape fraught with anxiety because of the impossibility of making any speed. They guessed pursuit was inevitable and even a man on foot could catch up with a string of horses obliged to keep to a walk. If the smugglers got a couple of cobs from a helpful farmer—or even a plough-horse, for that matter—they would be overtaken very quickly. They were continually glancing back over their shoulders, a vain exercise in the darkness: any pursuer would be upon them before they spotted him.

"It isn't your eyes you need to use," Bartram scoffed as India looked fearfully back for the hundredth time. "It's your ears. You'll hear them long before you see them. Listen for the sound of hoofs. They won't be muffled."

"If they've got horses," Richard said. "We don't know that they will have. It'll be much more difficult to hear them if they're on foot."

"And it'll be much more difficult for them to catch us up," Bartram replied.

They were on the embankment now. It offered smoother going than the marshes and, while it was a longer route than riding across country, it wasn't intersected by dykes as the farmland was and therefore no time need be wasted riding along a dyke in the search for a bridge across it. A rider with only one horse to consider could jump the intersecting dykes, even at night. It was impossible when one was leading a string. It was worth the disadvantage of the extra distance, especially since the distance saved cross-country would probably have been consumed by the necessary detours. Less easy to accept was the fact that they were much more visible.

They were able to lead their retinues across the Westmere creek with no greater difficulty than that caused by the balking of one or other of the horses in each string and were on their way towards Cross Keys House. This stood at the junction of the track along the embankment and the road from Boston of which the treacherous Wash Way was an extension. They could just make out the chimneys of this landmark when Richard, the last of the three, called out, "Whoa!" and then, "Hush!"

"What is it?" Bartram called in a loud whisper.

"Horses, I think. Listen."

They did, straining their ears through the sighing wind to catch the thud, thud that Richard had detected.

"More than one," Bartram guessed. "Coming fast." He looked down at the estuary stretching away on their left. "It's a risk but we'll have to take it," he said. "They'll be just too far behind to chance following us."

"Are you suggesting we ford the estuary?" India demanded.

"Don't worry. I know the path. You've only got to follow me," Bartram told her. "I think we'll have to let the extra horses go, though. Saving our own skins is more important than evidence right now."

"But the tide's already turning!" she exclaimed.

"Then let's stop dithering," Bartram said with a decisiveness India had never heard before.

"We were going to Wisbech," Richard objected. "This way we'll find no customs officers before King's Lynn."

"Good God, man, if they catch up with us, we won't live to reach Wisbech, Customs or no Customs. Can't you hear them?"

"They can't have seen us yet," India protested. She didn't at all fancy another crossing at the most dangerous point of the tide. "Why not just turn the extra horses free and make for Wisbech at a good gallop?"

"If they haven't seen us, it works to our advantage," Bartram pointed out. "We'll be halfway across before they spot us and we'll have plenty of time to get to Lynn. Come on. Follow me and you'll be safe enough. We've wasted enough time."

Without looking to see whether they were following his lead, he released his string of lead horses and put the big bay he was riding into a canter that would bring him to the ford in minutes. His companions hesitated only briefly before following his example.

When they pushed their mounts into the river, their hoofs were already splashing in water just level with their iron shoes but India remembered how rapidly it deepened once it was on the move.

"We're too late, Bartram," she called out.

"Not if you keep at him," Bartram called back. "Use your heels. Drive him on. He'll do it."

It was easy for him, India thought, mounted on his brother's horse which had both size and stamina, neither, she suspected, strong points of the two she and Richard were riding. She glanced back. They could see their pursuers now. Maybe they'd drown. Perhaps that was a fate preferable to having one's throat slit. She and Richard drove their heels into their horses' sides and followed Bartram's lead as precisely as they could. It wasn't easy when water swirled over the hoofprints and wiped the mud clean.

Lord Bardolph and the riding officers drew rein at the ford and watched, aghast, as the three horses ahead of them ploughed through water that was already hock-high.

"The poor beggars'll drown," one of the customs men said.

"Serves them right," Lord Bardolph replied savagely.

"Isn't that your horse in the lead, my lord?" said one of the others.

The Viscount stared. Even in that dim light there was no mistaking the outline. It was well ahead of the other two. "It is," he said grimly. "And if any of them survives this crossing, it'll be that one—provided his rider doesn't lose his nerve."

The first grey hint of dawn was lightening the sky ahead of them now and when one of the riders glanced over his shoulder Lord Bardolph thought he caught a glimpse of a tail of hair. He stared intently into the distance and groaned.

"Oh, my God, no!" He rode his pony down to the water's edge and raised his voice. "India. For God's sake come back! You'll drown! India!"

India turned again at the sound of voices. She neither recognised the voice nor could she distinguish its words but she had a shrewd idea such urgent tones must be framing a warning and quite likely a request to turn back. She glanced down and her heart sank. They were already halfway across and it was at least as dangerous to return as to go on. She had very little faith in either being successful. Ahead of her, it looked as if Bartram on the strongest horse might very well make landfall. Richard was in the same boat as herself—and looked as frightened as she felt. The horse beneath her was increasingly unhappy, too. India knew all horses could swim, but not all were too willing to try, especially with a rider increasing their weight.

"Come on!" she shouted, urging him forward. "Come on! You can do it! You can!"

Back on the shore, Lord Bardolph leapt from the saddle, tore off his coat and his boots.

"We've made a terrible mistake," he shouted as he strode
into the water. "These aren't smugglers. Find a dinghy and
get the boy over there." He pointed towards Richard. "I'll
swim for the other one."

"And the third one, my lord?" someone called out.

"The horse will get him across, God willing."

Then he was striding into the water until a combination
of in-flowing current and the depth of water obliged him to
swim. It wasn't easy to maintain his course and keep an eye
on India, whose horse was now floundering badly.

He reached her at last and trod water as well as he could.
"Let go the reins," he commanded. "Give him his head.
Swing your leg over his neck so that you're in the water."

"I can't swim," India protested.

"Then it's a good thing I can. When I've caught you, do
as you're told and go quite limp. Don't struggle and don't
try to swim. Just relax. Do you understand?"

India didn't but she nodded just the same. She was conscious of two contradictory thoughts. One was the depressing one that here was her proof that Lord Bardolph was
involved with the smugglers; the other was a certainty that
at least in his hands she was unlikely to have her throat slit.
All the same, it took courage to relinquish her mount, the
only security she seemed to have in these terrifying waters,
and only the confidence in Lord Bardolph's ability to extract her from difficult situations that she had learned in the
past could have persuaded her to do so.

She was conscious of a moment of sheer panic as she relinquished all contact with the horse and felt him surge away
from her, free at last of her hindering weight and—to him—
confusing aids. Then she felt strong hands under her arms
and was dimly aware of the strong, rhythmic propulsion of
Lord Bardolph's legs through the water, fighting the current that would otherwise carry them both upstream until
they had to contend with the conflicting river currents
flowing in the opposite direction.

Long before they reached the bank, cold, fatigue and fear conspired to render her unconscious. She was oblivious to the fact that a dinghy had rescued Richard and then, having deposited him safely on shore, returned to take first her and then Lord Bardolph from the water.

"You'd better wake them in the house," the Viscount said when they were all ashore. "There's three of us at least in need of warm, dry clothes."

"You know them, my lord?" one of the riding officers ventured.

"I know them all right—and a constant source of trouble they are."

"The third one, too?"

"The third one, unless I'm very much mistaken, is my misguided younger brother."

"Then I hope he got across safe," the man said respectfully.

"Do you? Then you're a great deal kinder than I am. I hope the horse did, certainly. I've mixed feelings about Bartram."

One of the other men had been trying unsuccessfully to rouse India. He lifted his head and looked across at the magistrate. "My lord, I think this one's a lady."

Lord Bardolph smiled grimly. "A woman, certainly," he said. His tone did not invite clarification.

CHAPTER NINE

INDIA WAS only hazily aware of the next few days. She spent most of them in bed, warm and cosy and being cosseted by Eliza, whose motherly instincts came to the fore so that she not only looked after her employer's physical well-being but also defended her against the local gossip. In this respect, Eliza had the advantage of not being local and therefore not subject to conflicting loyalties.

It was hardly likely to have escaped remark that Miss Leigh had been brought back to the house in the early morning—but not early enough to have been unobserved—by his lordship and several of the hated revenue men. Nor did it escape the sharp eyes of those who saw her return that her hair was in its night-time pigtail and she was wearing men's boots; there was even a rumour that, when the greatcoat covering her had slipped to one side, she was seen to be wearing breeches, but this wasn't altogether believed.

Eliza, totally ignorant of the circumstances preceding her mistress's return, dealt roundly with the questions and speculation.

"And what would you expect her to do when her brother's off on one of his escapades except go after him and bring him back? It was just their good luck that there were revenue men on the river at the time or I don't think we'd have seen either of them alive again. What was Lord Bardolph doing there? How should I know? I doubt if Miss Leigh or Master Richard'll be bothered about the whys and wherefores. Just grateful he was is my guess."

So the villagers had to be satisfied with answers like this and speculate among themselves as to why Lord Bardolph and the riding officers, who had descended on an old-established smuggling route in such force and with such ferocity, also happened to be several miles away at the Nene at precisely the right time to haul the Leighs to safety. "Mark my words," they said to one another, "there's more to this than meets the eye."

India was oblivious to all this, her time being largely divided between sleeping interspersed with shorter bouts of eating the delicacies that Cook sent up to tempt an invalid appetite.

"Not that she's an invalid, exactly," Eliza commented to Cook as she relieved her of a tray bearing a coddled egg, wafer-thin slices of bread and butter, a *compote* of pears and two slices of walnut cake. "She's just totally worn out. Quite grey with fatigue, she is."

Cook nodded knowingly. "Needs her strength building up, I don't doubt. I'll get a nice bit of lamb's liver for her lunch tomorrow. That'll do her the world of good."

The household was less sympathetic towards Richard. Those who had joined the Leighs in London knew that it had been his propensity to get into undesirable company that had brought them to this dead-and-alive hole in the first place. They did not for one moment doubt that whatever had taken place had been for precisely the reason Eliza had put about—that India had been trying to get her brother out of some scrape or another—and it wouldn't have surprised them one little bit to have learned that Richard had got himself entangled with smugglers. Quite why the revenue men should have helped him home rather than carted him off to gaol was an interesting question but quite possibly Lord Bardolph's former friendship with Miss Leigh had something to do with it.

In any case, Richard's recovery was much swifter than his sister's. He had been in far worse case when he was brought home because he had been floundering in the water for some time before the dinghy reached him, whereas India had never been without some support, Lord Bardolph having provided it at the very moment that the horse began to be in difficulties. Richard had the resilience of youth and within twenty-four hours inactivity had become irksome and the walls of his bedroom a prison. Within forty-eight he was not only up and about but itching to be out and doing.

Since India was in no position to keep an eye on him, Eliza took it upon herself to exert an authority which she knew to be outside her normal power. Catching him on his way out of the house, she drew him to one side.

"Now I don't know where you're off to. Master Richard, and I dare say you'll tell me it's none of my business to enquire, but I'm enquiring all the same because your sister's far from well and, as far as I can see, it's largely your fault. She's in no condition to keep an eye on you so I'm doing it for her. I don't mind not knowing exactly where you're going or what you're going to be up to, but I want your word that it'll be nothing that would cause your sister one moment's anxiety."

"I only want some fresh air," Richard said. "I probably shan't go outside the village. Will that satisfy you?"

"Then keep a watch on your tongue. There's a lot of gossip running around and it's my guess they'll pounce on you to try to get at the truth. I've told them your sister went off to drag you out of some scrape. They've had no details and they've not dared ask me any. Not," she added in a burst of frankness, "that I had any to give them, but that's not the point. Miss Leigh's reputation hereabouts is what you might call teetering on the brink, whether she was gallivanting about the countryside with free-traders or with revenue men. You stick to my story if you're asked, and if they want to know how come his lordship and the customs men were there be vague. You don't know. It was just one of those happy coincidences."

Richard grinned. "That's no lie—I *don't* know. Don't worry, Eliza. I'll be discreet. I'll be very vague—I can be when it suits me, you know. I'll make sure I say nothing to harm India. That's a promise. And I'll not do anything that would worry her if she knew about it. All right?"

"I'll take your word on it," Eliza told him.

"Do you think I ought to go over to Old Fen Hall and thank Bardolph?" he asked.

"Not knowing all the circumstances, I can't say," the maid replied truthfully. "I think it might be safer to wait until your sister's fully recovered and ask her. Maybe she'll want the two of you to do it together."

He nodded thoughtfully and then smiled engagingly. "You can trust me, Eliza. Really you can."

"I'm depending on it but, just in case you waver, remember that if you break your promise the side of your face might just collide with the flat of my hand—one of those nasty, unforeseen accidents, you understand, but none the less painful for that."

EVEN WHEN THE overwhelming need to sleep had passed, India was disinclined to do anything more strenuous than lie back against her pillows and drift into a world which was half-thought, half-daydream. She reflected with wistful pleasure that this wasn't the first time Lord Bardolph had come to her rescue nor the first time she had felt his arms around her and known the comfort of their strength, even if on this occasion her consciousness of both facts had been short-lived.

At first, she thought he would call to see how she did or, at the very least, send a note wishing her well. When neither happened her disappointment was lessened by the thought that perhaps he had called when she was in the first depths of her exhaustion and unable to receive anyone. Perhaps, having learnt that, he was waiting until she was fully recovered. Eventually, unable to bear the uncertainty any longer, she tackled her maid about it.

"I don't suppose Lord Bardolph called in the first few days after he brought us home?" she said hopefully.

"No, Miss Leigh. Master Richard was wondering whether he ought to call on him and thank him, but I told him to wait until you were better. That you'd probably want anything of that sort to come from the both of you."

"Yes, of course, but I'm not up to it just yet. Eliza, if his lordship should call, you won't refuse me, will you? Even if he has to kick his heels in the morning-room while you make me presentable."

"No, madam, I'll not refuse you."

The gentleman didn't come, however, and India's recovery was slow enough to alarm even the sufferer. The doctor, a sensible, down-to-earth country physician with no fancy city ideas about leeching bad humours out with the blood, told her all she needed was time, rest and good food and gave his opinion that the occasional brandy would lift her spirits and do her no harm.

"Give it time," he said. "You young things are always in such a rush. Good heavens above, it's not all that long since you lost your parents and then you had all the upheaval of leaving India and then you decided to abandon London in favour of the Fens. It's no wonder one small adventure, whatever its explanation, should leave you worn out."

India listened to him, because he made sense, and reminded herself that he didn't know the half of it and the half he didn't know added still more weight to his advice.

But as the days passed and thought occupied more of her waking moments than unprofitable daydreams she became more and more depressed that there was still no word from the Viscount. No enquiry after her health, no request to be allowed to visit, not even a demand for explanations. Nothing. Then her common sense took over. The last thing he would want, as a landowner and more particularly as a magistrate, would be for India Leigh to lay information against him in connection with his smuggling activities. If he had thought she might not have known who had rescued her, that would be more explicable, but he must have realised the servants would have told her who brought her home. Therefore he was lying low in the hope that she would simply say nothing and, since whenever they met they ended up disagreeing with each other, he probably thought it wiser not to risk provoking her into a retaliation more severe than a mere tongue-lashing.

With that realisation she spent some almost pleasant hours devising plans whereby she would be able to convince him that, although she thoroughly disapproved of his activities, they were none the less his business, not hers, and he could depend on her discretion. If she suspected that she was only able to take this view, even in the privacy of her thoughts, because deep down she still had difficulty believing he was actively involved in smuggling, she refused to let that interfere with her mental plans.

Those plans were knocked sideways when Richard came into her room one afternoon.

"Am I disturbing you?" he whispered as he crept in, anxious not to wake her if she should be asleep.

"Not at all," she said. "I'm quite glad to see you. You seem to have recovered from the effects of that awful night more quickly than I."

"Oh, goodness me, yes. I don't let a little thing like getting my feet wet keep me out of commission for long. I did promise Eliza to behave myself and not to do anything that would worry you if you knew about it," he added anxiously.

"I'm sure you kept your word. To what do I owe the present honour?"

"I bumped into Bartram Chelworth this morning. Actually, he was on his way to find me." Richard hesitated. "I know it's not a friendship you're very happy about and I know you think he's been a bad influence—except that his brother thinks the influence has been the other way around . . ."

"With some cause on both sides, don't you think?"

"Well, yes, I suppose you could look at it like that."

"I rather think we both do," India said drily.

"Then you'll be glad to know you're not going to have to worry much more," Richard told her. "Guess what? Bardolph's given in!"

India sat up, her interest suddenly sharpened. "What do you mean, he's given in?" she asked. Had the strain been too much for him? Had he gone to whoever magistrates went to when they wanted to confess to wrongdoing? Or did they just resign the Bench?

"To Bartram. He's decided to let Bart join the navy after all. He's bought Bart in and he was coming to say goodbye—he's off to London tomorrow and then Bardolph's taking him down to Portsmouth to join his ship." Richard chuckled. "I never thought he'd cave in as easily as that."

"I doubt if he found it all that easy," India said shrewdly. "Or maybe he was buying his silence."

Richard was genuinely puzzled. "Why should he want to do that?"

"To stop Bartram telling anyone of his involvement with smuggling."

"Oh, that." Richard was scornful. "The whole county knows about that. They don't love him any the more for it, of course, but they certainly respect him."

India was silent. It was, she thought, a strange comment on a society more corrupt than she had thought. The subject was uncomfortable mainly because of Lord Bardolph's involvement so she hastened to shift the conversation sideways. "I suppose this means you expect me to let you start farming straight away," she suggested.

"Heavens above, no! I don't know a quarter of what I need to know. Besides, I'm not so dead set on it that I don't want to go to Cambridge first. Mind you," he warned, in case she was getting quite the wrong idea, "I still intend to farm. I just intend to do it intelligently."

"No one can complain about that," India told him. "If anything else had been your goal, I'm afraid I'd have told you you were still too young."

"I know that, silly. Bartram would like to say goodbye to you. I told him you were probably asleep. Do you want to see him?"

India hesitated. She ought to and the fact that she had never liked Bartram meant that she really should be punctilious in the observance of all the courtesies. Nevertheless, she didn't want to and at least she had a good excuse.

"I don't think so," she said. "You can tell him I was asleep if you like, or you can say I'm not receiving visitors yet but I wish him well."

"It'll have to be that, then, or he'll wonder why I was so long. You'd better go back to sleep."

Sleep was a long way off when India was alone once more. So Bartram was being quite literally shipped out of the way. It might well be true that "the whole county" knew about Bardolph's illegal activities. It was much more likely that he wanted to eliminate the chance of positive information, as opposed to mere local rumour, reaching the ears of those with the power to do something about it. She wondered what he could do to keep her quiet. Richard posed less of a problem because of his age; it would be easy to convince someone that a fourteen-year-old boy's story was as much the product of his imagination as of his experience. India could not be so easily dismissed. Perhaps that was why he hadn't been near her: he hadn't let her drown—which would have solved the problem for good; perhaps he was regretting the rash decision to save her life and hoped by avoiding her to avoid the questions that she might reasonably be expected to ask and thereby lessen the chances of making some sort of representations to the relevant authorities. Lord Bardolph, after all, wasn't to know that she hadn't the slightest idea who were those relevant authorities, nor that, regardless of his more nefarious activities, she loved him.

For there lay the nub of it. It was no good pretending that she enjoyed his company, that she appreciated his sardonic humour, that she liked arguing with a man who argued back

on equal terms and never, ever, wriggled out of a superio
argument on her part by dismissing it as "feminine logic"
All these were true but the real reason she would never in
form on him, the real reason she was miserable, was quit
simply that she loved him.

In India her choice had been between fortune-hunter
whom she had had no hesitation in sending about thei
business and thoroughly worthy men, her rejection of whon
no one else could understand. She had returned to Englan
more or less resigned to remaining an old maid and had in
comprehensibly fallen head over heels in love with a ma
whom she had designated—with some justification—arro
gant, haughty and overbearing. Indeed, she had dislike
him intensely. That dislike had gradually changed into
mixture of respect and gratitude. How long had she love
him? She found it impossible to pin down the precise mo
ment. It might have been the moment when his tongu
slipped and he used her given name; it might have bee
when he held her before him on his horse; when his finge
casually flicked her cheek or tilted her chin. None of thes
was sufficient in itself to make a woman fall in love but i
conjunction and over a period of time...

She knew now that when he had lifted her down from he
horse and she had not wanted him to let go of her it hadn
been just his hands on her waist that she'd wanted. That wa
the closest he had ever come to holding her in his arms an
she now realised that just now she would give a good part o
her fortune for precisely that. She longed for the closene
of lovers and her heart responded even to the thought o
what might have been with all the ardour of one encounte
ing true love for the first time.

She knew—she supposed she had always known—tha
anything more than the little she had had was all she coul
expect. Smuggler or not, he was still a viscount with a wel
developed sense of his own standing in the order of thing
He had never made the slightest pretence of regarding he
as anything other than what she was—the wealthy heiress

a fortune made in trade. She couldn't fairly complain of that, of course, because it was the case. What hurt was that her origins made her quite unacceptable to a man of his sort on any level other than that of purely social intercourse. If he had needed her money, he might have overcome his scruples, but India was honest enough to acknowledge that, had she suspected him to be in that position, she would have taken very good care not to let herself be led into the sort of feelings she was now experiencing.

Lord Bardolph might quite possibly believe that she had an interest in his title. He must, after all, have come across as many women thus inspired as she had fortune-hunters. She knew she had no particular desire to be a viscountess and she hoped she'd never behaved in a manner that suggested otherwise. If he had ever done or said anything that thoughtful reflection suggested could justifiably be interpreted as serious interest, she might have tried assuring him of the truth. However, any softening of his attitude towards her had not been sufficiently pointed for her to be able to delude herself for long that it had any particular significance, and even if it had, she thought in a sudden burst of uncomfortable candour, her attempt would probably have been self-defeating.

No. She was, and would always be, trade. Pert and unbecomingly forward trade, at that. For whatever reason, Lord Bardolph had clearly decided to end the acquaintance and that was probably just as well. It confirmed her former idea that the best thing for her to do was to move well away from here. She would notify the London agent through whom she had found this house that she wished to discontinue her tenure and ask him to engage a house in London for a short time, while he found something equally quiet in a more congenial part of the country. Near Bath, perhaps. Richard wouldn't like Bath, of course, but there was no denying it was ideal for a spinster sister. He could still go to Cambridge if he wished—or perhaps he might change his mind and settle for Oxford.

Since India was not a woman to dilly-dally once her mind had been made up, instructions to this effect went off next morning and the day after that she told the staff of her plans. Those that wished to come with her were welcome to do so; if not, their employment would cease at the end of the month.

"If a place is found before then, I'll of course make up your wages to the full month," she told them.

Richard was more displeased than she had anticipated. "How could you, India?" he protested. "Just when I've got to know the place and the people and decided I want to farm round here, you decide to up sticks and go somewhere else. It's not fair."

"That's what you said when I told you we were leaving London," India pointed out. "I don't think you've had many regrets. I'm sure you'll find any other rural area just as good for your purpose."

"Yes, and just as soon as I find my feet you'll decide it no longer suits and we'll have to go somewhere else," he retorted bitterly, and stomped out of the house, giving the front door a hearty and expressive slam as he went.

LORD BARDOLPH heard the news almost as soon as he returned from seeing his brother safely on the first rung of his naval career.

"I gather Mr. Chelworth's young friend is leaving the neighbourhood," Folksworth told his master as he laid out clothes suitable for an informal dinner at home.

"You don't waste much time catching up on the gossip," Lord Bardolph replied, amused. "Which friend is that?"

"Young Master Leigh. I gather he and his sister are relinquishing the house by the end of the month. Miss Leigh's been most generous, by all accounts. Those of her household who don't wish to go with them will still be paid to the end of the month even if she goes before."

Lord Bardolph's face betrayed nothing though it seemed to his valet that he selected a diamond pin for his cravat with more than his usual care.

"I don't believe I've ever heard anyone complain that Miss Leigh was tight-fisted," he said.

"No, my lord. By all accounts she strikes a nice balance between keeping a judicious eye on the household expenses and undue prodigality."

Gidding, too, had wasted no time in catching up on local gossip.

"It looks as if the lady's saddle can be put aside for the foreseeable future, my lord," he said next morning, apropos of nothing in particular.

"I wasn't aware that you had been anticipating its immediate re-use, anyway," Lord Bardolph told him.

"No? Well, you never can tell, can you, my lord? Nice woman, that Miss Leigh, if you don't mind me saying so. Enjoyed riding and handles a horse well. Much liked in the village, too, by all accounts."

"Indeed? I'm glad to hear it."

"Far be it from me to speak out of turn, my lord, but it does seem a pity to let a woman like that go away without clearing the air, so to speak."

The Viscount's lips twitched. "Far be it, indeed," he murmured.

"Not been at all well, by all accounts," the groom went on, undeterred by a comment he had no difficulty pretending he hadn't heard. "The boy, now, he was up and about in a couple of days, but the sister's been confined to her room most of the time. Gone into quite a deep melancholy, so they say."

"You seem to have access to a hitherto unsuspected store of private information about the Leighs," his employer commented.

"As to that I couldn't say, I'm sure, my lord. It's just that my sister-in-law's cousin's boy, Will, helps out in the garden there and you know what youngsters are, my lord. Devil of a job to stop them gossiping.''

"Quite so."

Gidding wisely judged that he had said enough for now, possibly even enough, full stop. Let his lordship mull that little lot over and hope he didn't mull for too long. He'd been like a bear with a sore head since that business at the river, not that Gidding had been there, but fortunately young Mr. Chelworth was never one to hold his tongue when he was in a sulk and he hadn't liked being dragged back home for the umpteenth time. Between the two of them, there wasn't much that Gidding and Folksworth hadn't deduced with reasonable accuracy even if they were content to let the lesser household mortals speculate without feeling any need to put them right.

INDIA EASED the cushion behind her back, put her book aside and reached for her tambour frame. She was deriving no particular pleasure from either activity but couldn't bear to be totally idle. If she were really honest, she thought, she'd amend that to not being able to bear to be *seen* to be totally idle, because idleness was all she felt good for. A letter lay on the little work-table beside her. It contained the news that Mr. Risinghurst had found a house in the capital that was, in his estimation, ideal for her needs. It also urged her to authorise him to settle on her behalf without delay because he happened to know that the owner's statement that two other parties were interested in it was absolutely true and not just a ruse to obtain a tenant quickly.

She had no reason to doubt Mr. Risinghurst's word, yet her heart had sunk when she had read his letter. The house he described was admirably situated and had all she required. There was absolutely no reason for not writing to him immediately with instructions to take it on her behalf. Yet she delayed. Not only that, but she found herself unwilling to reread his letter, as if by ignoring it the letter would go away and the house remain unfound. She looked round the drawing-room. It was comfortable enough, but it wasn't the house of her dreams. She felt no ties to it. It was just a house.

She looked across to the window where the late after-noon sun could be seen already trailing clouds of red and gold. The sunsets were one of the glories of the Fens. In India the sun simply went down. Here it made a festival of it. She had at first assumed this was characteristic of England and it had been Lord Bardolph who had told her that the Fenland skies were nature's compensation for the flat land-scape. She had looked at them with a new awareness after that and told herself she would be more loath to leave the skyscape than the house. It was not a calculation likely to raise her spirits or encourage her to write that letter to Mr. Risinghurst.

Her melancholy reverie was interrupted by an apologetic Eliza. "It's Lord Bardolph, Miss Leigh. He says he knows it's not the right time to come calling but hopes you'll for-give him."

India started. "Lord Bardolph? Are you sure?"

"Of course the woman's sure—do you take her for a fool?" Lord Bardolph appeared behind the maid. "That will be all, Eliza. If you're needed, Miss Leigh will ring for you."

The maid hesitated and looked at her mistress.

"Yes, Eliza, that will be all right," India said and, as the door closed behind her, went on, "That was remarkably high-handed of you, my lord."

"Yes, wasn't it?" he agreed affably. "It made it impos-sible for you to refuse me, however."

India flushed. "Did you think I would?"

"It crossed my mind as a distinct possibility. May I sit down?"

Flustered because he shouldn't have had to ask, India re-plied, "Yes, of course," and was even further taken aback when, instead of taking one of the chairs with which the room was amply provided, he sat on the sofa beside her, unceremoniously pushing her legs out of the way so that he had enough room. "There are chairs, my lord," she pointed out icily.

He glanced around. "So there are, and very comfortable they look, too. I prefer to be here, however. Do you object to my being close enough for us to speak without shouting or would you prefer us to have to shout at each other across the room?"

"The room is quite small enough for neither of us to have to raise our voice."

"Perhaps, but not small enough to enable us to talk sufficiently quietly to prevent those outside from hearing."

"Are you suggesting that my servants listen at keyholes, sir?" India asked indignantly.

"If they don't, they must be unique."

"If that's your experience at the Hall, I can only conclude you don't give them enough work to occupy their time," India told him.

"I dare say you're right. I imagine they're sadly mismanaged. They lack the firm guiding hand of a mistress, you see."

Suspecting that here lay a baited hook which she would do well to ignore, India shifted the focus of the conversation. "In any case, I can't imagine that we have anything to say that we wouldn't want them to hear."

"Can't you? Dear me, and I'd always thought your imagination was almost as vivid as your brother's."

India blushed, uncertain how to respond, but he relieved her of the need to do so by picking up the letter that had slipped between her leg and the back of the sofa. He flicked open the folded sheet and saw the embossed address at the top. "Ah, Risinghurst. I see you employ the best," he said and began reading.

India snatched it from his hand. "Do you always read private letters, my lord?" she said angrily.

"Very rarely, as a matter of fact," he replied, unperturbed. "So rumour doesn't lie?"

"What rumour would that be?"

"That you're leaving here. Or is it supposed to be a secret?"

"It can hardly be that as I've told the servants."

He held up the letter. "And will you take this house?"

"I haven't made up my mind."

"It sounds ideal and, from what Risinghurst says, you'd be unwise to delay too long."

"My lord, I've no desire to be offensive, but I am capable of reading and correctly interpreting a letter for myself," India said stiffly.

"That's entirely true," he said and, as she opened her mouth to protest, held up a staying hand. "You had every desire to be offensive. It seems to come over you whenever we meet, yet other people say it's a side of you they've never seen."

"So you discuss me with all and sundry?"

He grinned. "It was an educated guess but I'll wager it's true."

Enough of this, India thought. When he had entered the room, it had been as if a dream had been answered. Now she was beginning to wonder how she could possibly have imagined herself in love with so provoking a man. The sooner she and Richard were gone the better.

"If you came here to find out whether the rumours were true, my lord, you've succeeded. You don't have to put yourself to the trouble of being sufficiently unpleasant to ensure that I don't change my mind. There isn't the least chance of that. We're going, so you may as well waste no more of your valuable time but be on your way, too. And to put your mind entirely at rest by answering the question you probably dare not ask, I can assure you that you need have no fear; your secret's safe with me. I shall tell no one."

If her intention had been to disconcert him, she could only be gratified by her success. He stared at her in blank astonishment.

"My secret? You'll tell no one?" he echoed. "Tell no one what? What secret?"

"Come, my lord—don't pretend to be obtuse when we both know you're not. I shan't inform on you."

"I'm relieved to hear it but I'm still completely mystified as to what I've done that might require me to be informed upon."

His bewilderment seemed so genuine that India began to doubt even her own certainty. Hadn't she led away the horses? Hadn't she seen him with her own eyes? Hadn't he chased them to the river? The only mystery was why he hadn't let them all drown. All the same, the seeds of doubt had been sown.

"Do you deny that you've been involved in smuggling?"

For the first time there was a gleam of comprehension in his eye but it was swiftly extinguished. "No, I don't deny that."

"Do you deny you're a magistrate?"

"No, of course not."

"Doesn't it strike you that the one activity is just a shade incompatible with the other?"

"No, not at all, given the particular circumstances."

"I don't see how particular circumstances can alter it."

"No? Perhaps that's because you're unaware of them." He let the letter fall to the floor and caught both her hands and when he spoke there was a warmth and a tenderness she had longed to hear. "My dearest India. I don't believe you have the smallest notion how much trouble you and the boys caused that night on the marshes. Yes, I was involved in smuggling—but in much the same way as the revenue men who were my companions. I was there in my capacity as a magistrate. You took away our horses, not—as Bartram seemed to believe—the smugglers'. The three of you came within yards of scuppering a plan which had taken months of careful observation and meticulous planning to set up. We wanted more than just the impoverished peasants using a pound of smuggled tea or a cask of geneva to provide the

PLAY
ONE MILLION
BIG BUCK$
ONE MILLION
AND YOU COULD WIN THE
$1,000,000.00
PLUS JACKPOT!
YOUR PERSONAL GAME CARD INSIDE...
HARLEQUIN

IT'S FUN! IT'S FREE!

BIG BUCKS

HOW TO PLAY

It's so easy...grab a lucky coin, and go right to your BIG BUCKS game card. Scratch off silver squares in a STRAIGHT LINE (across, down, or diagonal) until 5 dollar signs are revealed. BINGO!...Doing this makes you eligible for a chance to win $1,000,000.00 in lifetime income ($33,333.33 each year for 30 years)! Also scratch all 4 corners to reveal the dollar signs. This entitles you to a chance to win the $50,000.00 Extra Bonus Prize! Void if more than 9 squares scratched off.

Your EXCLUSIVE PRIZE NUMBER is in the upper right corner of your game card. Return your game card and we'll activate your unique Sweepstakes Number, so it's important that your name and address section is completed correctly. This will permit us to identify you and match you with any cash prize rightfully yours! (SEE BACK OF BOOK FOR DETAILS.)

FREE BOOKS PLUS FREE GIFTS!

At the same time you play your BIG BUCKS game card for BIG CASH PRIZES...scratch the Lucky Charm to receive FOUR FREE

Harlequin Historical™ novels, and a FREE GIFT, TOO! They're totally free, absolutely free with no obligation to buy anything!

These books have a cover price of $4.50 each. But THEY ARE TOTALLY FREE; even the shipping will be at our expense! The Harlequin Reader Service® is not like some book clubs. You don't have to buy any minimum number of purchases–not even one!

The fact is, thousands of readers look forward to receiving four of the best new romance novels each month and they love our discount prices!

Of course you may play BIG BUCKS for cash prizes alone by not scratching off your Lucky Charm, but why not get everything that we are offering and that you are entitled to! You'll be glad you did.

TWO WAYS TO WIN BIG BUCKS!

1. Uncover 5 $ signs in a row...BINGO! You're eligible to win the $1,000,000.00 SWEEPSTAKES!

2. Uncover 5 $ signs in a row AND uncover $ signs in all 4 corners...BINGO! You're also eligible for the $50,000.00 EXTRA BONUS PRIZE!

LUCKY CHARM GAME!

Claim 4 FREE books AND a FREE Mystery Gift!

HURRY! This Jack pot must be claimed! Scratch here ↴

YES! I have played my BIG BUCKS game card as instructed. Enter my Big Bucks Prize number in the MILLION DOLLAR Sweepstakes III and also enter me for the Extra Bonus Prize. When winners are selected, tell me if I've won. If the Lucky Charm is scratched off, I will also receive everything revealed, as explained on the back and on the opposite page.

247 CIH AS2J
(U-RG-03/95)

NAME _____

ADDRESS _____ **APT.** _____

CITY _____ **STATE** _____ **ZIP** _____

NO PURCHASE OR OBLIGATION NECESSARY TO ENTER SWEEPSTAKES.

© 1993 HARLEQUIN ENTERPRISES LTD.

PRINTED IN U.S.A.

EXCLUSIVE PRIZE # 9C 620892

BIG BUCK$

$

wherewithal to feed their families. We wanted the master of the *Amelia* and the man who co-ordinated the distribution from here."

"Mr. Huggate?"

"Who else?"

"Is he in gaol?"

"No. So far as we know, he's in London, but it's only a matter of time before he's caught and enough men have saved their own necks by offering to turn King's Evidence to convict him. Had some of us not had to make off after the "smugglers" who stole our horses, we'd have had sufficient men to catch him there and then."

"But we took your horses—not the smugglers," India protested, baffled.

"As I soon discovered. At the time, however, we assumed that one of their look-outs had appropriated them. When I recognised Bartram—and then you—I knew we were wrong though I was completely mystified as to your real purpose. Bartram explained it all, of course."

"I wish someone had explained it to me," India said with some feeling.

"I know Bartram said something about it to Richard. I assumed your brother would have told you."

India thought back. "He did say something about everything being sorted out. There wasn't any detail. I suppose it didn't occur to him that I still didn't know."

He raised her hands to his lips and kissed them one after the other. They were not the cursory kisses of social convention. "What your brother needs is the constraining influence of a man, rather than that of a household of women."

India's eyes flashed. "So that he might turn out like Bartram, you mean?"

She saw the momentary anger in his eyes but it was swiftly replaced by rueful laughter. "*Touché,*" he said. "Perhaps not. I wonder what other reason I can offer you?"

"Reason for what?"

"I'm trying to find an unanswerable reason for suggesting you should marry me."

"Marry you?" India repeated.

"Is it so unappealing an idea?"

"Not unappealing, exactly," India said with perfect truth, and was startled by his sudden laugh.

"I must thank you for so effusive a compliment," he said sardonically.

She blushed with confusion. "It's just that . . . well, my family is trade; I'm vulgar—you've often commented to that effect. Why on earth should you want to marry such a woman?"

"I've often asked myself the same question," he said and then caught her to him. "No, India, I don't mean it quite like that; it's just that you provoke me into saying the most outrageous things. Haven't you realised that I only say such things when I'm losing an argument?"

India cast her mind back and realised that it was indeed so. A slow smile lit up her face. "Then we're going to have a sad marriage for, if I'm to believe you, I have either to let you win every argument or risk having my lack of breeding thrown in my face. Not a recipe for fairy-tale happiness."

"True—if there is such a thing, which I take leave to doubt. On the other hand, it isn't a recipe for a boring marriage, either, and I know which I'd prefer."

"But you can't think of a reason why I should marry you?"

"You don't need my fortune any more than I need yours, and I don't think you care two hoots about the title. We've already established that I'm not the ideal person to exert a sort of paternal influence over your brother. What other reason can I think of?"

"You don't think that perhaps loving you might be reason enough?"

His grey eyes looked down into her brown ones. "It's the only really unarguable reason," he said. "I just didn't think . . . I never imagined . . ."

"Then why on earth did you ask me?" India replied softly.

"Good God, woman, hasn't it dawned on you? Why do you think you make me so angry? It's because I love you. I haven't been willing to admit it, even to myself, but I think it's been so ever since you answered me back when I brought Richard home that time."

India's heart clutched at his words though her mind had difficulty grasping them. "Is anger the way you always express your love?" she asked, bemused.

"Yes... no... How should I know? I've thought myself in love before but none of those ladies provoked in me any of the feelings you do."

India dropped her gaze demurely. "Perhaps that was because they were... ladies," she suggested.

"Quite possibly that's the difference," he agreed, "and it's just as well you reminded me of it, or I might have made the mistake of treating you like one. As it is, I don't have to be so circumspect."

So saying, his hitherto gentle hold became almost savage as he crushed her to him and his mouth descended on hers in a ruthless, demanding kiss to which her whole body responded as if this was what it had been yearning for since womanhood dawned. Nor was there any simpering, maidenly withdrawal when his embrace went far beyond the bounds of gentlemanly conduct. Her whole body told him that here, at last, he had found a woman whose passion equalled his own and for whom it would be the greatest pleasure in the world to open one by one the doors of pleasure through which their mutual desire would lead them. The fast-fading light created the fitting backdrop to the urgent, demanding consummation of passions so long held in check by misunderstandings and convention.

And when the thrusting surge that made them one had eased and India lay relaxed and secure within the strong circle of his arms, she sighed and snuggled closer to him. "So much time wasted," she murmured.

He lightly kissed the top of her head. "We've plenty of time before us. Let's waste none on regrets."

India's glance fell on the letter that had slipped unnoticed to the floor. She bent over and picked it up, holding it out between two fingers. "Do you think I should write to Mr. Risinghurst?" she asked.

"Immediately—and preferably to tell him you've changed your mind."

India turned in his arms and looked up at him. "You sound as if you think I might be having second thoughts about marrying you," she said.

"You wouldn't be the first," he reminded her.

She kissed him. "You won't be so easily rid of me, my lord."

"'My lord'?"

"Edward."

He chuckled. "I knew you'd see it my way in the end," he said, and neither of them noticed when the last glimmerings of light drifted from the sky.

About the Author

Petra Nash is the author of several Regency
romances, most of which have been published by
Mills & Boon in England. She is now beginning to
attract a strong North American following, as well,
and we're sure you'll enjoy her latest book.

HEIR APPARENT

Petra Nash

CHAPTER ONE

"I AM AFRAID it is true. Our poor brother is dead."

Georgina, Lady Tarrant, touched the corners of her eyes with a wisp of violet-scented cambric, and cast a hopeful look at her sister, who disappointed her by neither fainting, nor falling into strong hysterics. Her heart-shaped face lost no jot of its delicate colour, no tremor shook the head of chestnut brown hair that was arranged so neatly and smoothly in its simple knot, nor did she raise her brown eyes from her work. Mary Hadfield continued to stitch composedly at the prosaic mending of something that her ladyship recognised as one of her daughter's torn pinafores.

"Surely you must be mistaken, Georgie. Giles was perfectly well only two days since. You know how my father exaggerates."

"But this letter is not from Papa! It is always the same with you, Mary! I am not clever, I know, but I am nine years older than you, and I think that I should know when a message is to be believed!"

Irritation brought a flush to her plump cheeks, and sent two genuine tears coursing down them. Mary set down her work, and went to her sister. Though taller than her sister, she moved so lightly and gracefully that her greater height gave no suggestion of an awkward tallness, and she was slim as a willow wand. The present fashion for simple, straight-skirted gowns flowing from a high waist suited her to admiration.

"I beg your pardon, Georgie! You are quite right, and it is bad of me. Now do not, pray, upset yourself! It is not good for you at such a time, and I should never forgive myself if you should come to any harm." She took Lady Tarrant's plump hand in her own slender one, and drew her to the sofa, into which she sank, with some care, breathing a little sigh as her heavily pregnant body sank into the cushions.

"I am afraid I was irritable, dearest," said Lady Tarrant, leaning into the carefully arranged pillows and submitting to having her feet lifted on to the sofa. "Oh, that is better! I do think that the Almighty might have arranged for some simpler method of producing babies! It is all very well for Tarrant to be so pleased, and say that he would like another four or five, but when I think what I have to endure... Eggs, for instance."

"Eggs?" Mary was arranging a shawl round her sister's shoulders, but looked up in puzzlement. "I am sure that you need not endure eggs, if you do not want to. You have only to speak to Cook, after all! But they are so light, and nourishing, that it seems a pity."

"No, I mean eggs, for babies to hatch out of. I should not even mind sitting on them, if I had to. I am sure it could not be so inconvenient and undignified as this."

"Oh, I am sure Sir Anthony would arrange a broody for you. So much easier than finding a wet-nurse. Not that he does that, of course."

"No, indeed! I should not at all care to leave such a choice to him! I always make sure to see them myself, and enquire very particularly into their histories."

Mary, satisfied that her sister was now calm again, ventured to return to the alarming news.

"About Giles, Georgie..."

"Oh, what a shocking thing! To think that I had forgotten, for a moment, the death of my only brother! How I could be so callous, so heartless..."

A few more tears were shed, and Mary comforted her.

"Not heartless at all, but very sensible. You must remember what Dr. Black said about being calm, and avoiding any upsets. I wonder, would I be wise to send for him?"

"No, no, do not do so. I shall be quite well. But this news is so sudden!"

"It is indeed, and that is why I ventured to doubt it. Are you able to tell me more? Who sent the news; *was* it Papa?"

"No. It was the rector."

"The rector? Good heavens, I see what you mean." No more than her sister would Mary have dared to doubt any message sent by the redoubtable churchman who was married to their eldest sister. While they might, on occasion and in the strictest privacy, giggle together at his pompous manner and his banal, if worthy sermons, they would no more doubt his veracity than they would question the evidence of their own eyes.

"Poor Papa! How he must be feeling! I must return to him at once, Georgie."

"Yes, I know. Of course your place is with him. Only, he is not alone at home, after all, and it does seem hard that you should have to go away just now! I am sure the children mind you far better than they do me, or even Nurse, and I was relying on you!" She spoke with the petulance natural to one who had been indulged all her happily married life, and Mary was in no way put out.

"You know I would not wish to leave you, when I am so happy here. This is quite a holiday for me!"

Even Georgina's complacent selfishness was not proof against this.

"A holiday! I wish I might see you take one! I know full well that when you are not keeping me company you are up in the nursery letting the children romp with you, and tear their clothes, so that you are obliged to mend them. And no one coming to call but a few old tabbies of neighbours! No society! No parties! Nothing!"

Her nervous irritation brought on more tears, and Mary was obliged to administer some of Dr. Black's cordial. As she held it to her sister's trembling lips, Mary spoke calmly.

"If the society of my sister and her family were not sufficient to amuse me, then I should not have come. Your children are delightful, and since you are my sister I do not scruple to tell you that even at their naughtiest they are far, far easier to care for than poor Papa."

Lady Tarrant, though it was many years since marriage had taken her from Hadfield Priory, could not deny the justice of this remark, but confined herself to a speaking look and a sympathetic pressure on the hand that held her own.

"I do not want parties or society," Mary continued. "I wish you would believe that I am perfectly content to be here."

"I do believe it, and that is just the trouble. You should not be content with such a life, as young as you are!"

"Twenty-five is not so very young. I know that you think you should be finding me a husband, but I can assure you I do not require your assistance in that department."

Georgina's butterfly mind was easily distracted.

"Do you mean...? Oh, Mary, is it true? I had heard from my godmother that our cousin danced with you several times, and seemed quite particular in his attentions. Oh, I am so pleased! Nothing could be more suitable, particularly now! Tell me, is he as good-looking as everybody says?"

A faint blush stained the creamy skin of Mary's cheeks.

"Really, Georgie, how you do take one up! It is true that Mr. Hadfield danced with me three times, at the Fordcombes' ball last month. But so he did with several others; he is a good dancer and much sought after as a partner. He is pleasant, and friendly, but there is nothing between us that might not be found between one distant cousin and another."

Mary felt no scruple in thus concealing from her sister that Mr. Jason Hadfield had, indeed, been very attentive at the ball, and that his manner had, of recent weeks, assumed that kind of bantering familiarity that implied a particular intimacy. Though he had not, in fact, spoken words of absolute love, yet there had passed between them such innuendoes of looks, and sighs, and half-formed phrases, that she had little doubt that he would soon declare himself.

As to her own feelings, she could not honestly say that she loved him above all others, but certainly to be singled out, at an age when she had begun to fear that she would end her days in spinsterhood, by a man as handsome and charming as Mr. Hadfield, was both flattering and exciting. When he was not there she could think of him quite coolly, but in his presence she found herself fascinated by him, almost mesmerised by his handsome face and charismatic personality.

"And now, with poor Giles gone, nothing could be more suitable! Oh, my dearest, it really does seem that it was meant!"

Mary frowned. This aspect of the case had not occurred to her.

"You mean—the entail?"

"Of course I mean the entail! You cannot have forgotten that his father is the next heir! And he, I believe, is several years older than Papa. Though really we know so little of them, it is quite ridiculous. Our own cousins, and complete strangers to us all, until now. The wonder of it is that Papa permitted you to meet him at all."

"I suppose he would not have done, if he had known. But you know he never goes to parties, though he does not object if Mrs. McLaren takes me with Emily. It was the purest chance, I suppose, that he should happen to be staying in the neighbourhood at that time, and that I should be introduced to him. And that, he told me, was only because he heard someone mention my name, and found it to be the same as his, though he is known as Mr. Hallfield locally, except to his particular friends, who are all sworn to secrecy. In order not to upset Papa, you know. For as you say, we know so little of them, and probably they know just as little of us. And all because of the entail."

Lady Tarrant sighed.

"The entail! You would not remember it, of course, for you and Martha were only babies when Giles was born, but when I was a child I sometimes thought that Papa never spoke of anything else! It was an obsession with him. Of course, he did not discuss it with me or Caroline, but nevertheless we were always aware of it. I can remember, when I was very small, having nightmares and crying out to Nurse that the entail was coming to get me. Heaven knows what I thought it was. I believe I imagined it as some kind of monstrous serpent.''

''Poor little Georgie! But surely, then, they explained it to you?''

''Yes, but I do not know but what that was not even more frightening. All I knew was that we should all be turned out of doors to starve, because of the entail.''

''Hardly to starve—surely there was always poor Mama's money.''

''Yes, but you know Papa! You said only just now how he exaggerates.''

Mary fell silent. It was true that she did not remember those distant days, before Giles was born, but she knew only too well how large a share of her father's heart her brother had occupied, how painfully interested, even obsessed, he was about Giles. She had heard more times than she cared to remember how they had celebrated Giles's birth, how there had been bonfires, and a feast for the tenants.

Such rejoicing was not unnatural. The elder Giles Hadfield, married at twenty-one to the heiress of his choice, had been only slightly disappointed by the birth of Caroline, his eldest child. Of course a boy would have been better, but the child was healthy, and the mother well, and there seemed then no fear that the longed-for heir would not soon make his appearance. A stillborn son the following year was much mourned, but the renewed hopes of the next pregnancy were dashed by the birth of Georgina. Two more daughters followed in quick succession, both dying in infancy, unmourned by their father, and then it seemed as though poor Charlotte Hadfield had exhausted her childbearing capabilities.

This was the time that Georgina so vividly recalled, when her father could think of nothing but that his house and his estate would pass on his death into the hands of a distant cousin. Hadfield Priory was not, as the name implied, an ancient foundation, and the family had been settled there for only three generations. The original Giles Hatfield, newly rich from sources he preferred not to reveal, and discovering with disgust that the town which bore his name was already blessed with a great house, had changed a letter in his surname and moved to Sussex. There, in Hadfield, he had built himself a magnificent house, complete with a brand-new ruin, and settled down to live the life of a country gentleman. In his anxiety to do so, he had arranged matters so that the property must always pass to the nearest male heir, as was commonly the practice in the great families, and from his pride had come his great-grandson's fall, in knowing he must leave the Priory to his cousin.

This gentleman, much the same age as Mr. Hadfield, was descended from a great-uncle, and since the family resided in Yorkshire there was not even the barest acquaintanceship between them. Of this man, his heir, Mr. Hadfield knew nothing but that he had property of his own, not large, which he farmed himself, and that he had not just one, but three sons. This last put the final seal on the hatred and envy that he felt, and Mr. Hadfield never permitted the existence of his relatives to be acknowledged or mentioned in his presence.

Then, nearly a decade after the birth of Georgina, her mother again found herself with child. Great was her joy and relief, and greater still when the midwife declared that her swollen belly bore not one, but two babies in its straining rotundity. Surely, she thought, one of them must this time be a boy! But it was not to be, and with the birth of Mary and Martha it seemed, for a while, that her husband would run mad. For several months he refused even to look at his daughters, nor would he permit them to be baptised though one of them, Martha, had spinal problems and appeared, for a while, unlikely to live.

After so many years of childlessness, and the exhausting pregnancy and birth, Charlotte Hadfield could scarcely believe that she might be pregnant again. When her natural cycle was not renewed she thought no more than that her body was worn out with child-bearing, and it was not until the other signs were borne out by the unmistakable feeling of a child quickening within her that she dared to mention her hopes. Even then she said little, and had little hope, but, as if the birth of twin children had opened some hitherto unfound door, it was followed almost exactly a year later by the arrival of Giles the younger. That she herself survived the birth by only a few days seemed a matter of little interest to her bereaved husband, who appeared to mourn her only as the mother of his son. Her daughters wept for her, and comforted one another, but he would not allow the arrangements for celebrating this august occasion to be marred by any thought of loss.

And now Giles, so long awaited, was dead, and his father was left to mourn the end of his hopes, the end of what he saw as his family dynasty. Mary, his only surviving unmarried daughter, wondered what she would find, and how she could possibly comfort him for such a loss. Though naturally shocked by the news of her brother's sudden death, she could not pretend to any profound sorrow. Her brother's spiteful ways had made her childhood miserable, the more so since he had employed them most against her much loved twin, who was usually too weak to withstand him. Since he had reached young manhood he had been little at home, and when he had returned it was usually because he was in want of money. On those occasions he had treated Mary with the careless churlishness that he habitually used towards the servants.

"Forgive me, Georgie, but I must know. Does the rector say how Giles died? I suppose it must have been an accident?"

"It is so very strange, he does not say! You may see for yourself; his letter is here in my reticule."

Mary ran her eyes down the rector's firm handwriting, which covered no less than three pages. The first two, however, she did not bother to read carefully, since they served merely to prepare the reader's mind for a coming shock, the rector being the kind of man who assumed that women were unable to bear any unpleasant news that was not approached by the most circumspect route.

"If he would but be brief! It is like a game of Grandmother's footsteps—every time he gets within sight of a bare fact, he stops! If I were hearing this, instead of reading it, I should have gone mad with fear by now!"

On the third page, however, the rector was obliged to reveal himself, and to state baldly that Giles was dead. And there, quite suddenly, he stopped, with none of the verbiage Mary would have expected, and finished with no more than a paragraph of pious hopes for his sister Tarrant's continuing good health.

The entrance of Sir Anthony Tarrant put an end to Mary's reading. A genial, hearty man, he had taken care to absent himself during the first shock of disclosure, knowing that in moments of stress whatever he might do or say would annoy his wife.

"Well, my dears," he said, tiptoeing with elephantine care across the room, as if he feared a heavier tread might break their composure, "this is a bad business. A very sorry business indeed."

"And now poor Mary must leave us, and go to Papa! I do not know how it will be," mourned Georgina.

"Nor I. It is a sad loss for him. He will feel it very greatly."

"For him, and for the family, Anthony! Our only brother, and so young! And then, he was so gifted!"

"Ah, yes. Indeed." Sir Anthony spoke with his usual agreeable good humour, though he had always thought of the poetic effusions of his young brother-in-law as something to be pitied rather than admired. A dedicated sportsman, he had regarded with tolerant astonishment a man who not only did not hunt three days a week during the season, or shoot his own birds, but who unashamedly professed a dislike for such pastimes. Mary, who loved to read, had always privately thought that her brother's vaunted genius amounted to little more than a superficial facility, and therefore maintained a discreet silence on the subject.

Having disposed of these tepid eulogies, they were free to plan for Mary's departure. Her father, who could not bear solitude, had reluctantly agreed to stay with his eldest daughter, in the rectorial residence in a village just outside Lewes, while Mary made herself useful with Lady Tarrant. Knowing him as she did, Mary thought that he would be in a frenzy to return to Hadfield Priory, since even in his better moments he found the rector's pompous voice and overbearing manner hard to bear.

"I must be there as quickly as possible, and take Papa home, if he is well enough to travel."

"Of course you must. You shall take the carriage, and Sam Coachman. I have already sent orders to the stables that you will leave first thing in the morning."

For the first time Mary felt inclined to shed tears.

"You are too good to me, Anthony! I cannot deprive you of your carriage and coachman, however! I can travel post just as well."

"Aye, at three times the expense! It is not to be heard of. As if I would let you do so, Mary, or Georgie allow me to! And you must use the carriage to convey Mr. Hadfield to the Priory, since it is almost on the way home. I would not, for the world, inconvenience the rector." Sir Anthony had a simple man's reverence for the cloth, and would not dream of mentioning his relative by marriage's well-known tendency to clutch-fistedness. Mary could only thank him, with genuine affection and gratitude, before she took herself off to see to her packing.

They spent a quiet evening, and in the short time alone after dinner, before Sir Anthony left his solitary table and joined them in the drawing-room, Georgina again reverted to questioning her sister about what she insisted on calling her conquest.

"What age is he? And what does he do? Are they really farmers, as Papa once said?"

"If they are, I saw no sign of it. He neither had straws in his hair, nor much on his boots, and he certainly did not confine his conversation to turnips. He is twenty-seven, he told me."

"You asked him his age? That implies a certain degree of intimacy."

"Not really. It was part of a general discussion."

"I hope you did not tell him yours?"

"Why should I not? You know I have never cared for that kind of deception. If a man will not like me, because I am twenty-five rather than twenty, then what should I care for him?"

"Never mind that now. Tell me more of him." Georgina, bored with inactivity, longed for romance.

"There is little to tell. He is a gentleman, I suppose, and that is all that is to be said of him."

"How provoking you are! Does he still stay in Sussex? Shall you see him, when you return?"

"How should I know? I think he was intending to stay with his friends until April, but men, you know, may change their plans, and flit round the countryside, in a way that we women are never permitted to do."

"Now, if ever, would be the time for him to declare himself," mused Georgina. "Situated as you are, what could be more proper? You might then continue to live at the Priory, and Papa with you, as if nothing had changed!"

"I hardly think Papa would like to hear you say that," said Mary drily.

"Well, you know what I mean! For though I am sorry he is dead, naturally, I cannot say that I truly loved Giles as a sister should. I expect it was my own fault, but he was so... so very..."

"Yes, he was, wasn't he?" agreed Mary equably. "And of course it is not your fault, but his. I did not love him, either. Indeed, it is hard to see how anyone could, except Papa, of course. A more spoiled, selfish, spiteful child never lived, and he grew up to be a spoiled, selfish, spiteful man."

"Mary!" Georgina was shocked. "With our brother not yet in his grave!"

"I say no more than I said when he was alive, and to his face, too. You know I have always held him responsible for Martha's accident. The fact that he is dead does not change what he was in life. Of course I am sorry for his death, as I hope I would be for any human creature, but I reserve the main part of my sympathy for poor Papa." And, she added silently, for herself, who would have the sole care and company of poor Papa.

It was still dark when Mary left the following morning. She had refused to allow either of her relatives to see her off, and in truth was glad to be spared Georgina's lamentations at her departure. She was glad of the company of her maid, a woman who had been nurserymaid in her own childhood and with whom she had a close relationship, for it was a bleak start to an unpleasant journey. The previous winter would long be remembered for its prolonged spell of icy weather, when the Thames actually froze over and a frost fair was held on its rock-hard surface. Mary had not seen it, of course, but she had listened a little wistfully to tales of stalls set up on the ice, of entertainments and amusements that were only an introduction to the festivities later in the year, when the Regent celebrated the visit of the allied heads of state that marked the end of the wars with Napoleon with his usual gusto and vulgarity. Mary had not seen that, either, and when she questioned Giles about the firework displays, and the great fête at Carlton House, he had been able to tell her only that he had been so drunk that he could remember nothing of it, though to be sure he had enjoyed himself.

The Great Frost of 1814 had been followed by a deep fall of snow throughout the country that had persisted for six weeks. Villages and towns had been isolated from one another, and Mary remembered the period as an endless battle to keep the Priory warm, to care for the poor of the village, and to attempt to beguile her father's boredom, and distract him from his restless irritability because he could have no news of his beloved Giles. To venture on even so comparatively short a journey as this, if it should snow like that again, was a risk, but one that she felt that she could not refuse to take.

The roads were frozen hard, but dry, and they made good time to London, arriving before the heat had dissipated from the hot bricks placed at their feet. A hurried meal in a private parlour was as welcome as the fire, but when they went down to the yard Sam Coachman greeted them with a long face.

"I don't like it, miss, and that's a fact," he said, with the confident familiarity of an old and trusted servant. "If those clouds don't mean snow, then I'm a Dutchman. Coming to Lunnon, that's bad enough, but at least the roads is getting better, the nearer we come. But going down to Lewes...that's different altogether. Meaning no disrespect, miss, but we all do know what the roads be like in Sussex, and that's bad. Come it snows, we'd be benighted sure as eggs, and frozen to death by morning, most like. And what would Master say then?"

"Well, nothing that could bother us, surely," said Mary impatiently, but repented at the expression on the old man's face. "I'm sorry, Sam. You are quite right to be worried, and you should not risk yourself, or your master's horses. But you know that I must try to reach the rectory today, and all the more so if it is going to snow, for then who knows when I may be able to set forth? But I will hire a post-chaise, so you may be easy. I shall do very well, you will see."

Sam chose to be affronted.

"Go off, and leave you to traipse around the country in the post-chaise, me that knew you when you was no more than knee-high? I'd like to see it! Post-chaise, indeed! The very idea! What would Master have to say to that, I'd like to know?"

"You are very good, Sam, but I do not care to put you into danger."

"Ar, danger'd be what I would be in, if so be as I went home and told Master as I'd let you go off in a post-chaise!

Now give over, do, and get in this carriage, and let's be off, if we're going!''

"Very well, but, if there should be any mishap, on my own head be the blame. You must be sure to tell your master that, as I shall."

Sam's pessimism was soon seen to be justified. The air, which during the morning had been hard and ringing as steel, now turned heavy and damp, though there was no appreciable diminution of the cold. By the time they reached Godstone the snow was falling: fat white flakes that blotted out such a view that was to be had through the steamy windows, and covered the outside world with a rapidity that was both astonishing and alarming.

As they approached East Grinstead the roads took on, for Mary, the familiarity of home, and she was not sorry to break the journey there, where the landlord of the Dorset Arms greeted her with acclaim that turned to dismay when he learned the sad reason for her journey. When he learned that she was not, in fact, merely going home to the Priory, he was horrified.

"Carry on to Lewes, in this weather, Miss Mary? Across the Forest, and all? You'd do better to put up here, and let my good wife give you a meal, and a bed for the night. With the Priory shut up, you'd not be wanting to go there alone, and you know you can trust my girls to have the beds well aired, and everything just as you'd like it."

"I know it, and do not think me ungrateful, but I am so anxious for my father! I fear for his reason, if not for his life, and even if there was nothing I could do to help him I must do my best. But I should not say no to a cup of tea, and some bread and butter."

He shook his head, but knew that it was no use to be arguing with her. Sam, having been reluctant to continue the journey, was even more reluctant to abandon it when the ostlers told him that he should do so. His pride as a Hertfordshire man would not allow him to concede that he feared to continue. So, after a break, they carried on, Mary peering through the window as they passed down the hill, and through the village of Forest Row, until the turning to Hadfield was passed. Then she sat back, and sighed.

"I hope I have not put us all in danger, Sarah," she said to her maid, who had preferred not to look.

"So do I, miss," was the comfortless reply. There were times, thought Mary wearily, when it was less than encouraging to be with servants who had known one in the cradle, and been in a position of authority over one's nursery days.

The road that wound up the hill out of Forest Row had never seemed so long, or so steep. Though it was only just after half-past two the gathering clouds had hidden the sun to such a degree that it might almost have been dusk. Mary could hear Sam's voice as he encouraged the horses, and her heart went out to the patient beasts. Through the window of the carriage, heavily obscured now with driving snow, she could dimly see the great beeches that lined the road, their branches already thickly caked, and their height and thickness added to the darkness.

At length the summit of the hill was reached, but though there was an appreciable addition of light this was of little advantage since it served only to show how very much deeper was the snow on the more exposed plateau of the forest. There could be no going back, however: climbing the hill had been bad enough; to attempt to descend it would be suicidal, with the snow already freezing on to the icy ground.

Two or three more miles were passed in silence. Outside the snow deadened even their own sounds like a blanket of wet wool, and it was thus all the more shocking when a great creaking, groaning noise was followed, so quickly that they seemed one, by a tearing crash. Mary had no time to be aware of it happening, for in the same moment the lead horses reared at the sight of the rotten branch of oak that had fallen so close in front of them that it only just missed them. In that moment of shock Sam was helpless to control them, and their movement sent the carriage skidding across the slippery road to end, half on its side, wheels in the ditch and body against a tree.

His shout of alarm was echoed by another shout, and a mounted figure loomed out of the snow. In some relief he heard the accents of authority.

"Get to the horses. I will see to the carriage," said the newcomer crisply, dismounting in haste and looping his horse's reins over its head. Sam went to his charges, quieter now but shivering and twitching with shock, and ran anxious hands down their legs, watching out of the corner of his eye as the stranger wrenched at the door of the carriage and climbed inside.

Mary opened her eyes. She seemed to be lying very uncomfortably, with some heavy weight across her legs that was causing her great discomfort. It seemed to be rather dark, and very cold, and she was relieved when a face appeared in front of her, though it was that of a man quite unknown to her. She blinked at him, at the white line of scar that ran down a suntanned cheek and gave what some might consider a ruffianly appearance to what was otherwise a handsome, if rugged face.

"What is happening?" she asked. Her head was spinning; she could not remember where she might be.

"There has been an accident to your carriage, Miss...?"

"Oh." She seemed about to drift off, and his eyes were anxious. In the cold it would be fatal to allow her to fall unconscious, and he needed to know if she were injured before he attempted to move her.

"Come now, wake up! What is your name?"

She answered obediently, as if a child, "Mary."

"Have you much pain? Can you move your limbs?"

She experimented, and gave a little gasp.

"Yes, but it hurts. My leg hurts. Oh, dear, I must be Martha, then, not Mary at all."

He did not attempt to unravel this confused statement. With impersonal gentleness he ran his hands down her, finding nothing that indicated serious injury.

"Who are you?" she asked vaguely.

"Well, if you are Martha or Mary, I suppose I must be Lazarus," he said with grim humour. "Now, I am going to lift you." But even as he spoke, he saw that she had fainted once more.

CHAPTER TWO

MARY'S SECOND, and more complete, return to consciousness occurred some little while later, and this time she broke through the dream-state meniscus that had held her submerged, and came right to the surface of reality. The last thing she remembered was that hideous, crackling crash, and she was not altogether surprised to find herself across the knees and saddle of a rider, held firmly in his arms.

"Sam? Sam Coachman?"

"No." The voice was deep and steady, slightly familiar and yet oddly accented. Instinct told her to struggle, but common sense reasserted itself before she had time to make more than a feeble movement, and she was still again, though watchful, before he spoke.

"Good girl," he said approvingly. "I had feared you would go into hysterics, like your maid."

"Sarah? Oh, is she all right? Where is she?"

"She's well enough. I found her weeping over you, moping and mowing and screeching that you were dead. I fear I spoke roughly to her, but she was bent on lifting you, and I wanted to be sure you had no broken bones before moving you. You can feel your feet and your hands, can you not? I know you can move."

"I can feel that they are very cold," she said, conscious for the first time of her discomfort. "Where are we going? And where is Sarah?"

"There was a farm cottage not far from where your carriage came to grief, but it was not a place fit for you. They have, however, consented to lend a donkey cart, and your Sarah is to follow us in that, while the coachman brings his horses. There is an inn not far away, about a mile off the road. I have been staying there myself, the last few days, and it seemed best to convey you thither. We are nearly there."

He said no more and she, conscious that she was aching in every part of her body, was glad to be silent, biting her lip to keep back the gasp of pain when the horse stumbled on some unseen obstacle, and sent a jolt of agony through her head, and set flashing lights dancing before her eyes. He felt her quiver, and tightened his grip, wishing with all his heart that he had not been returning by that road, on that day. A visit to Brighton, at the light-hearted invitation of a chance acquaintance, had been no more than a way of filling in a few days' leisure. Since he must return to London, the urge to gratify a mild curiosity to see the countryside round Hadfield and perhaps the house itself had seemed perfectly reasonable. But now what had he tumbled into? The very last thing that he wanted, now or ever, was an encounter with the girl he now held cradled in his arms.

Nevertheless, the harm was done, and the dim glow from the windows of the inn were doubly welcome since he had taken off his caped great-coat and wrapped it around Mary's form. He rode right to the front door and shouted, until the landlord came bursting out to seek the cause of the commotion.

"Mercy on us, Mr. Smith! I never thought you'd be back with us today, with the weather so fierce! I said to Missus, I said, 'Mr. Smith'll be sure to put up elsewhere, since he's not back by now!' And she said to me . . ."

"Save it for later, Runforth. This young lady has had an accident in her carriage, and has been hurt. We must get her inside at once."

"To be sure, to be sure, the poor thing! Do you hand her down to me, Mr. Smith, and we'll have her adin doors directly."

The rider was not sorry to relinquish his burden. Mary, protesting weakly that she was quite fit to walk, found herself carried indoors by the talkative landlord, who bellowed for his wife, for fires to be lit in the second-best bedroom, for Jim to take Mr. Smith's horse, and for everyone to do everything as soon as possible, if not sooner. Floating on a tide of words, Mary allowed herself to be taken into the landlady's private parlour, where a bright fire promised warmth and comfort, and laid on a couch with as much care as if she were made of blown glass.

"Now, then, Runforth, what are you thinking of, to leave Miss all wrapped in this wet coat? She'll catch hurt for sure, if she's left in it. Help me to undo it."

Mrs. Runforth, who looked to be only half the size of her hearty spouse, spoke in the gentle voice of one who was used to being obeyed without question.

"Quite right, my dear, quite right, as usual. And what of the fire in the bedroom, and airing the bed?"

"Adone-do with your fussing. I've already sent Jenny to see to it. The gentleman told me he would give up the best room for the young lady, so the fire's already set there, and the bed aired, only needing fresh sheets. There, that's better, and I'll just take your bonnet off, miss. Tch, it's nigh ruined with this wet, and so handsomely trimmed, too! What are you standing there, for, Job?"

"Shall I sent for Doctor, Missus? Is the young lady hurt bad? It's a wicked day, out there, but I'll send Jim on the cob, if you but say the word. I'd not have it said that Miss didn't have every care we could give her, and she do look a shade particular, that she do!"

"Give over talking and go away, you great lummox! How can I find how bad hurt she is, with you standing there, and your tongue flapping like it was hinged at both ends?"

"Ah, you've the right of it there, Missus," he said admiringly, no whit abashed by her words. "Runforth by name, Runforth by nature, that's me, and I knows as I do run on a bit! Just you call me, come you need for anything!"

He strode from the room, closing the door behind him with a crash that made Mary quiver from head to foot.

"He means well, Miss Hadfield, but he don't know how to behave with gentlefolk."

"You know my name?" Mary pressed one cold hand to her throbbing head, and winced at the swelling she felt on her temple.

"Yes, indeed, miss, I recognised you at once, soon as I had your bonnet off. My sister's youngest is in service at the Priory and my sister pointed you out to me, many a time, driving through Forest Row. Now, tell me, miss, where does it hurt? You've had a nasty knock on the head, that I can see, but is there anything else?"

"I don't think so." Once again, Mary moved experimentally. She was stiff and sore all over, but there were no sudden pains, and now that her own pelisse had been removed it could plainly be seen that there was no blood on the fine wool of her gown.

"Then I'll get some arnica for your head, and we'll have you in a warm bed in a shake of a lamb's tail." Mrs. Runforth bustled off, and Mary lay back, her eyes fixed bemusedly on the leaping flames of the fire. For the first time since her emergence from the nursery she felt the luxury of having all decisions made for her, and, worried though she was for her father, there was a relief in knowing that for one night, at least, she was to be spared his lamentations and his general apportioning of blame to everyone for his son's shortcomings.

Mrs. Runforth returned, with such remedies as seemed good to her, and obliged Mary to swallow a peculiarly disgusting concoction which she assured Mary would make her feel much better. Having choked it down, and successfully kept herself from vomiting it straight back up, Mary was thankful to lie still with her eyes closed, while a soothing pad of dampened linen was tenderly bound round her aching head. She was concentrating on controlling her nausea, and did not hear the door open, or the approach of gentle footsteps.

"I should never have said it," she murmured to herself. "On my own head be it! And now, of course, it is!"

There was the sound of a low laugh, and her eyes flew open. Her rescuer, swiftly changed from his wet clothes, stood over her, the light from candles and fire illuminating the white slash of scar that seamed his cheek, and striking sparks in the grey eyes. Now that he was bare-headed, his hair was seen to be dark brown, very thick and unruly, and in need of the attentions of a good barber. Mary's brow furrowed.

"Oh!" she exclaimed. "You said you were Lazarus! How very odd! I had forgotten it, until this moment."

"A connection of ideas," he apologised, "since I have recently returned to this country from a prolonged absence abroad. Have you decided what your name is yet? You seemed to be in some confusion, before, as to whether you were Mary, or Martha."

"This is Miss Hadfield, Mr. Smith," said the landlady repressively.

"Yes, I know. That she is Miss Hadfield, I mean. The coachman told me. Is she much hurt? Should I ride for the doctor?"

"No need, sir, and if there were then Jim could go. But I doubt there's worse wrong with Miss than a good night's sleep will cure."

"But her head? She was unconscious, you know, and quite out of her senses for a while."

"I wish you would let me speak for myself, and not talk across me like this," said Mary crossly. "Of course," she added in softer tones, "I am very grateful to you for rescuing me, and I don't know what I should have done if you hadn't happened to come at the right time..."

"Well, you wouldn't have done anything, being dead to the world," he pointed out, "but there is no need for gratitude. Why, it is a young man's dream come to life, to rescue a beautiful girl in the nick of time. What a pity there was not a highwayman, as well, whom I could have fought single-handed."

"Yes, indeed, but why stop at one? Why not two, or three?"

"Oh, I would not like to appear greedy. And, to be honest, I think I could not have managed more than two. I am not such a warrior as my appearance might suggest, you know."

"I beg your pardon," Mary apologised. "I am afraid that my tongue never knows when to stop joking. I did not mean to imply—"

"Of course you did not! And in any case, you are in no state to cast aspersions. Unless I am very much mistaken, you are going to have a real shiner tomorrow morning that will put my paltry scar right in the shade!"

"Not if she's let lie quiet, and I put plenty of arnica on it, she won't," hinted Mrs. Runforth. "That room should be ready by now, and I'll call Runforth to carry Miss upstairs."

"No need, when I am here, and already in practice," he said, and, wasting no time, stooped and lifted her once more in his arms. Mary felt her cheeks flame at finding herself so suddenly clasped to his chest, and she stiffened protestingly.

"But I don't even know your name!"

"Of course you do. Lazarus—Lazarus Smith." He was already through the door that Mrs. Runforth, obedient to his masterful nod, had hurried to open.

"But that was no more than a joke, surely?"

"Then would you prefer plain John Smith?"

"I would not! Of all the unimaginative names to choose!"

"Then Lazarus must do. I own I prefer it to John, in any case. And, after all, ours is but a recent acquaintanceship, and doomed to be but a short one, I fear, since I must leave tomorrow morning."

"And I, too! Poor Papa, he will be so upset!"

"Shall I send a message to the Priory, miss?" The helpful Runforth was waiting in the hall to see them upstairs. "It's not so far, and we might get someone through, if he should leave at once."

"No, thank you, for there is nobody there. My father is with my sister, at Lewes."

"At the rector's? Then he'll be well cared for there, miss, and they'll not be worrying. We'll see how things are in the morning. Your maid's arrived, Miss Hadfield, and she's up in your room now, unpacking your bags. I hopes as you will find everything to your satisfaction, miss, and as you'll feel better in the morning."

Whether from the blow to her head, or general exhaustion, or the effects of Mrs. Runforth's potion, Mary slept deeply and long, awakening in the middle of the morning to the news that the snowfall had been so heavy and prolonged that they were, to all intents and purposes, marooned.

"Stay here? But we cannot! What about poor Papa?"

"There's no good to be done by fretting, Miss Mary," said Sarah sensibly, revelling in a return of nursery tyranny. "What Master don't know, won't harm him. He'll think you in London, or at least at the Priory, where any person of sense would have stayed."

"I know, I know," sighed Mary. "I am well served for that piece of folly. And at least it will give my face time to settle down." For Mr. Smith's prognostications had proved only too correct, and the glass showed her, this morning, a pale face disfigured, to her way of thinking, by the rich plum shades of a fine black eye.

Refreshed by her long sleep, and by the hot bath that Sarah prepared for her before the fire, Mary found herself ready for the plentiful breakfast carried up by the bashful Jenny, who had never had occasion to serve anyone half so grand as Sarah, let alone Miss Hadfield of Hadfield Priory. A short battle as to whether or not she should dress and go downstairs ended in victory for Sarah, who controlled the wardrobe, but the victor kindly conceded to the extent of allowing her mistress to sit up, in a dressing-gown, in a chair by the fire, instead of returning to bed. Mary had to admit that her knees still felt wobbly, and her head was inclined to throb if she moved it suddenly, or bent over, and she was not unwilling to stay as quiet as she was bid.

A gentle knock at the door sent Sarah bustling to repel boarders.

"Don't worry, I will not ask to come in," said Mr. Smith in a low voice. "I merely wished to ask how Miss Hadfield is today."

"A little better, thank you, sir," said Sarah. Surprisingly, she seemed to bear him no ill will for his brusque treatment the day before, but on the contrary seemed to respect his show of force. Mary, who would have been only too quick to deny him entrance if he should have asked for it, now felt a contrary wish to call him in, since he did not seem to want to.

"Please *do* come in, Mr. Smith," she said in a pleasant tone. "I am well enough to be out of bed, if not downstairs, and certainly well enough for a little conversation."

"Conversation? I'm not very good at that, having lived so much abroad, you know, and in such rough places. I fear I'm more at home in the stable than in the drawing-room."

"Well, this is neither. And I cannot believe you have never felt at home in a lady's bedchamber!"

"Miss Mary!" Sarah was scandalised, but he only laughed, and came in.

"I will neither confirm nor deny your belief. How do you do, Miss Hadfield? I believe we have not been introduced."

"Nor we have. How very shocking." She held out her hand and he shook it with a little bow of great correctness, his eyes fixed in admiration on her face. The admiration was, she feared, not for any beauty he might find there.

"As I had thought—and I don't know that I ever saw a finer one! Not even on Saturday night in the...well, never mind about that."

"The Hadfields pride themselves on never doing anything by halves," she informed him grandly. "Did I thank you for helping me? I don't remember."

"You certainly did, and there is no need to refer to the matter again. It was simply chance that led me to be in the right place at the right time." He sounded as though chance had much to answer for, as in his opinion it had, and glanced hopefully at the door behind him. Mary, contrary as her name, gestured him to sit and he did so, without enthusiasm but without visible unwillingness.

"Do you make a long stay in Sussex, Mr. Smith?" she enquired with stately politeness.

"I have not yet decided. Probably not."

"You have no acquaintance in these parts, I suppose, since you are staying here. Perhaps you are here on business?"

"I know nobody here, and as to business . . . I do not expect to find anything to concern me over much. I am merely a traveller, who has been so long away from his native land that it is all equally unfamiliar."

Mary studied him consideringly. His clothes were of good cloth, but poorly cut and in an outmoded style. His face, with its all too visible scar, was bland and uninformative. It crossed her mind that he might well be a smuggler, or worse, and for the first time she felt a shiver of apprehension.

"And what might your business be?" she asked boldly. His grey eyes looked into hers.

"Oh, different things, in different countries," he said with affable vagueness. "For instance, I have been a merchant in India—not a very successful one, I fear—and a cattle farmer in America. That was more successful, for a while, but I got bored with it. Then I have been a sailor in the Pacific, and an explorer in the Antipodes." He smiled at her expression. "Well, you did ask!"

"Is all that really true?" He nodded. "Goodness, what a chequered career. And now you are come home to the bosom of your family, to settle down and be respectable?"

"Whatever gives you that idea?"

"But surely. . .if you have returned to England, it is to see your relations . . ."

"I have none," he said, and closed his mouth like a trap. Mary felt rebuffed.

"I am sorry. I did not mean to be vulgarly inquisitive."

He shook his head, both in a negative and as one shaking off unhappy memories.

"It is I who apologise. I spoke very abruptly. The fact is, Miss Hadfield, that my family washed their hands of me, many years ago. I am dead to them, literally and metaphorically, and so they are to me."

"Then you do not intend to be Lazarus at all?"

"No. I do not need anything that they might feel obliged, or even willing, to give me."

"You are fortunate," she sighed. He raised his eyebrows. "Oh, not that I should wish to separate myself from my family! I am very fond of them. But, even did I wish to, an unmarried woman, you know, cannot hope to have the kind of independence that you enjoy."

"It is unfair, of course. Have you always wanted to be an explorer?"

She laughed. "Who hasn't? But, seriously, you must agree that a young woman's life, if she is of gentle birth, is in general much trammelled and confined."

"A few escape. Haven't I heard of Lady Hester Stanhope, for instance?"

"Yes, poor creature, but she was in love with Sir John Moore, and only went away after he died. No, in general, the only way for a young woman to enjoy such excitements is to marry a man as adventurous as herself." His assent was guarded, and she laughed. "Do not be afraid, this is not a leap year!" Sarah tutted in the background, where she was sitting in a window-seat and mending a tear in Mary's gown of the day before, and he gave a rueful laugh.

"Alas! For a moment, I dared to hope . . ."

"Dared to fear, more like! I can assure you that while I may speak of adventure I have no great expectations in that direction. I am not likely to marry such a man." Somewhat embarrassed at the levity she had betrayed, she was almost anxious for him to know that her affections were on the way to being fixed on another, so she cast down her eyes modestly, and let a little smile cross her lips.

"Have you then, perhaps, an idea in mind of the kind of man you are likely to marry?"

Her smile broadened. "You should know that a young woman never speaks of such things, until there is a formal arrangement."

"But there is . . . someone?"

Mary nodded. To his surprise he felt, not relief, but a spasm of irritation. He conceived an instant and irrational dislike of the unknown gentleman, deciding in that moment that he was probably some milksop of a dandy, all high starched collars and scented snuff, fit only to strike attitudes in a lady's drawing-room.

"Who is Martha?" he asked, changing the subject abruptly.

"Martha was my sister. My twin sister. She died, oh, six years ago. Why do you ask?"

"I am sorry—perhaps I should not have done. But when you were in the carriage you seemed to think that you were Martha, because your legs hurt."

"Did I? I don't remember that. Martha was born with a deformity in her spine; we never knew why, unless the midwife damaged her when we were born. She was never strong, and when she was tired she had dreadful pains in her legs. She was always very brave, but I always knew when she was in pain, and then I would rub her back for her, and that helped a little."

"I have heard that twins can sometimes sense one another's feelings. Was it like that with you?"

"No, I don't think so. Only that we loved one another very much. Our sisters were many years older, and then our mother died when we were only babies, so it was natural that we should be close."

"You must miss her greatly."

The firelight sparkled on the tears that came to her eyes.

"Oh, I do, so very much! She was so good, so patient, and always so cheerful. We could always find something to laugh at together. I think that is what I miss the most. None of the rest of my family understands my jokes."

She fell silent, and he respected her quietness and sat, the only sound coming from the hiss and murmur of the flames in the fireplace. Even the click of Sarah's thimble against her needle was stilled, for Sarah had succumbed to the effects of a night sitting up watching over her mistress, and had fallen asleep with her head pillowed against the thick curtains of the window-seat where she had sat to have the best of the light for her work. She gave a little snore, and Mary exchanged a glance and a smile with her companion. His voice was low when he spoke.

"She was very weak, I suppose, to have died so young?"

Mary's tones matched his, the suppressed anger in them all the more powerful in the murmur she used.

"Not so very weak. We had always thought—hoped—that she would live for many years; for a normal lifespan, in fact. But my brother would insist on her accompanying him, when he had my father's phaeton out to prove that he was able to drive his new pair of horses. Of course, he was not—he was only eighteen, after all—and the horses bolted. They were heading straight for the ha-ha, and Giles, my brother, jumped out into the soft long grass. She tried to turn them, but of course she was not strong enough, and the phaeton rolled right over. She only lived for an hour."

Mary's voice was bitter, in spite of her care.

"It is not unusual for a boy of that age to panic, and act on impulse like that. Your brother must have felt very badly about it," he suggested.

"He was very angry," said Mary drily. "He blamed her, that she did not jump when he did—as if she could have done, with her back! And he blamed the groom, that the horses were too high-spirited, and my father, that he bought them at all. But never himself. He was brought up, you see, in the belief that he could do no wrong, that he could do and have whatever he wanted. Oh, dear, I should not be telling you all this! It is very wrong of me to do so."

"You need not fear to speak openly," he said. "Have you not noticed that often it is much easier to talk about things with complete strangers than those who are near to us? And situated as we are, isolated in this inn by a chance encounter that no one could have foreseen, there can be no harm in

it. You may be sure that I am not likely to repeat anything
that you may choose to tell me, the more so since I know no
one, in Sussex, to whom I might tell them.''

She was a little comforted, but ashamed that she should
so lightly reveal her inmost thoughts to this strange, rough
man. The warm, firelit room, her own *déshabillée*, and the
conspiratorial nature of their lowered voices, had conspired to create a curious sense of intimacy between them.
She could only hope that he spoke the truth, when he said
that he would be discreet.

He saw the trouble in her face, and sought to dispel it.

''I, too, have—had—a brother, and I do not scruple to say
that he cared for me as little as I cared for him. Certainly I
have never missed him, since I was cast off by my family.''

''Cast you off!'' She could not but be intrigued. ''That is
a dreadful thing to do. Whatever had you... ? I beg your
pardon, I should not ask.''

''Whatever had I done? It was not, I now think, so terrible. I fell in love with one of the maids.''

''But surely... many young men do the same! I remember the housekeeper complaining to Papa...'' She stopped,
and bit her lip in embarrassed vexation.

''Kissed the maids as well, did he? Well, I did more than
kiss them. At least, it is not what you think! I truly believed that I loved this girl, and I was quite set on marrying
her. Young fool that I was, for she was at least five years
older than I, and of course nothing could have been more
unsuitable, but she said that she loved me, and naturally I
believed her!''

''How old were you?''

''Seventeen.''

''So young? Poor boy! Your father's anger I can understand, I suppose, but surely your mama... ?''

''She was dead, died when I was born. She was my father's first wife, and I have since come to believe that he
married her only to oblige his family, because she was rich.
Only a few months after her death he married again, and it
was my stepmother who brought me up, and was mother to

the brother I spoke of, and a younger brother besides. She never cared for me, nor I for her.'' He spoke with cheerful callousness, but Mary shivered at the thought of that little boy growing up in so loveless a household. She, at least, had had two older sisters to care for her as she grew, and Martha to love and be loved by.

"But I still cannot believe that they would send you away merely for that! After all, you could not have married her, young as you were, without your father's consent, so he had but to dismiss the maid, or pay her off, and be done with it.''

"So you would suppose. But in my madness I chose to defy my father, and arranged to elope with her, that very night. Of course, she had been sent away but I was to meet her in the road, outside the lodge gates. God knows what I thought we would do, where we would go, what we would live on! But when I went she was not there, only two of my father's gamekeepers who took hold of me and dragged me back to the house. My father was waiting for me, sitting in his study for me to be brought before him like a prisoner before a judge. There and then he went for me, in front of the servants. That was what hurt me, more than anything—the sight of them grinning to see the young master in trouble, so of course I lost my temper, too. My father had the goodness to inform me that he had arranged a marriage for me, that in view of the disgrace I would be lucky if the girl's father still consented to ally his family with ours, and that I was to go, the very next day to propose to a girl—woman, rather—nearly ten years older than me, whom I scarcely knew!''

"He cannot have expected you to agree? Was he always so high-handed?''

"Always, but our wills had never crossed on anything that mattered before, so it never occurred to him that I would not obey. My prospective bride was rich, and well connected, and in worldly terms I could hardly have expected to have done better for myself. Poor thing! She was very meek, and had buck teeth. I often wondered what became of her.''

"I am sure her wealth and birth were not left to go to waste," responded Mary drily. "Was that when your father cast you off?"

"More or less. He told me that if I would not obey him I should no more be his son, that I should be given a sum of money and must take myself away, never to return. I suppose he thought I would be cowed by the threat, and he probably never intended it to happen, but I was so furiously hurt and angry that I told him I would live without his charity, and flung out of the house. It was headstrong, of course, and later when my blood had cooled I wrote to him, apologising for my disobedience and saying that while I could not marry his choice I would in other respects be his dutiful son, and not marry to disoblige him. But he did not reply, and I never wrote again."

"But...that is dreadful. And what of the girl, the maid?"

He shrugged, with a little smile.

"He had offered her money to go, and she took it. Of course, she did not love me, and no doubt I should soon have learned that I did not really love her, if I had had the chance. He was right, at any rate, to forbid our marriage!"

"But you have not forgiven him?"

He looked surprised.

"Forgiven him? I suppose so. The truth is I have enjoyed my life, far more than I would otherwise have done. So I suppose I should be grateful to him, really. During the first few years after I left I wrote two or three times, merely to say that I was alive, and well. My father never answered. I believe that I am no more part of his family, and I cannot say that it grieves me over much."

"But—your inheritance? You are the eldest son?"

"Yes, but there was no entail. I suppose it was always expected that I should inherit, but my father always preferred my brother, so perhaps I should not have done even had I stayed. I sometimes wonder..."

"What?"

"How my father knew of my intentions. My stepmother was away from home with my youngest brother, who was no more than a child at the time. I could have sworn that no one knew, and my father was the last person to notice anything to do with me."

"You mean it was your brother who betrayed you? How base. And should he now take your inheritance also?"

"Why not, since he cares for it and I do not? It may be that I wrong him. We were not friends, but I was not aware of any enmity between us. If he noticed anything, said anything, it could have been no more than an accident. He was only fourteen. What could I say, after so long a time? Accuse him, with no atom of proof? You, after all, have presumably never denounced your own brother, whose crime is far greater? Yet you could do so, tomorrow, if you chose."

"No, I couldn't. Not now."

"Your father would not believe you?"

"No, but even if he did it would make no difference. I suppose I assumed that you knew why I was making this journey, in such weather. My brother is dead."

"What?" He jumped to his feet, almost shouting the word, his chair toppling backwards with a crash that made Mary wince. "Your brother is dead? My God, I had no idea!"

CHAPTER THREE

"MR. SMITH! Whatever can be the matter?"

The sleeping maid also started awake at the sound, and jumped to her feet, ready to seize the poker, if necessary, and defend her charge. Mary's look and astonished words seemed to recall him to himself. With a muttered apology he righted his chair but did not re-seat himself, remaining on his feet with his hands gripping the chair-back as if for support, or as if it provided a defence.

"I beg your pardon! I scarcely know...I had no idea that your brother..." He drew a breath. "I am afraid that I might have spoken in a fashion that would have given you pain. Naturally, if I had known the reason for your journey, I would never have mentioned your brother in the same breath as mine."

"There is no need to apologise, Mr. Smith. I have never pretended that my feelings for my brother were anything more than duty required of me. My sole concern is with my father."

"Yes, of course. Your father. He will be very unhappy, having been so fond of the young man."

"Fond is scarcely an adequate word. He doted on him. That was only natural, since he waited for so long to have a son. Why, my oldest sister is more than twelve years his senior, and my father had almost given up hope of an heir."

With an effort he sat down, and composed himself to behave naturally.

"All men of property want an heir, of course." His words sounded inane in his own ears, but Mary only nodded.

"Of course, but in my father's case the need was extreme. The house and the estate are entailed."

"Ah. Entailed. I see."

"So you may understand how very precious my brother was, and why he was indulged as unwisely as I consider him to have been. My father placed great pride in being Hadfield of Hadfield Priory, and in passing it on to his son. All his disposable income, since Giles was born, has been devoted to the estate, to enlarging and beautifying the house, improving the land, planting trees. And now, of course, it goes for nothing."

"I can understand your anxiety for your father."

"Yes. Otherwise, of course, I would not have attempted so imprudent a journey. But for the past few years, ever since my second sister, Lady Tarrant, was married, I have been the mistress of Hadfield, my father's companion. He has recently been subject to fits of melancholy, and now...I do not know how he will bear it."

"He is lucky in his daughter."

She shook her head with a small smile. Impossible to explain to this stranger that to her parent she was a convenience, a captive audience, a whipping-boy, even. Only her pleasure in caring for a house such as Hadfield, and the boon of pleasant society nearby, had made her life even tolerable. Now, when they might no longer entertain and she could not pay any but the most formal of visits to neighbours while she was in mourning, she wondered how she was to bear it, knowing that she had no choice.

"But you—what shall you do? If your father should die, where will you go? To your sisters? Or will the heir permit you to stay at the Priory?"

She wondered at his concern, but answered quite freely.

"Either of my sisters would, I am sure, offer me a home. But I believe... I hope... it would not be necessary for me to accept, or at least not for very long."

"Aah." He breathed out a long sigh, and sat down again. "I had forgotten. There is someone, is there not...?"

"Yes, someone..." Again she smiled that small, secret smile. Sarah gave a little indignant snort, indicating that she thought Mary was speaking too freely. Irritated, Mary glared at her, and rather pointedly sent her out of the room to fetch some tea. The maid went with a suspicion of a flounce, and pointedly did not quite close the door. They listened to her retreating footsteps, and Mr. Smith continued.

"And then you will have your own home..."

This time she laughed out loud.

"Yes, indeed! My own home!" She stilled her mirth, which, truth to tell, was slightly hysterical. The air in the room was so full of tension that it seemed to cackle, like static on a frosty morning. "Oh, dear, I should not be laughing like this. But the truth is so strange... you see, for all of my life my father has hated and resented his cousin, who is now his heir. We have never had anything to do with him or his family. But recently, and quite by chance, I made the acquaintance of his son..."

He stared at her, frowning.

"His son?" he repeated stupidly. "Your cousin's son? What is his name?"

"Why, Hadfield, of course! Jason Hadfield. And he is... is someone!"

"You are telling me," he said slowly and carefully, "that you are to marry the son of your father's new heir? That you will continue to be mistress of your old home?"

"Yes! Is it not the strangest, most providential thing?"

"Oh, quite. Very providential." He stood up once again, quietly this time. His face was hard as a rock. "I should not be tiring you with talk, Miss Hadfield. As I said before, I shall be leaving as soon as the snow permits. If I should not have the opportunity to bid you farewell, please accept my congratulations on your good fortune." With a stiff little bow he turned and left the room, almost colliding with Sarah as she returned from her errand, and closing the door behind him with delicate care.

"Well, really!" said Mary crossly. "He is a most peculiar man."

"Handsome is as handsome does," uttered Sarah.

"Oh, did you think him handsome?" Mary asked.

"Perhaps not, but he's a good, dependable kind of gentleman all the same," said Sarah with irrational crossness. "But you've no business to go blabbing your business to him, all the same."

"Oh, dear, I know it," admitted Mary. "But he seemed so interested in the family."

"Mark my words, no good will come of it. And as for boasting about your conquests, I don't know when I was so shamed! Counting your chickens, that is! Why, he ain't even asked you, that I know of, and who'd know better'n me?"

"But I think he will, Sarah, I truly do. He has hinted, you know, and I believe that if it had not been that I went away so soon after we met he would have spoken."

"That's as may be. But how many times have you met him? You hardly know him yet. Marry in haste, repent at leisure. Yes, that makes you laugh, but it's no less true for that. And you don't want to go a-marrying him, just because he's a handsome man, and all the other girls are after him. No sense that I can see in that."

Mary wondered what her maid would have said if she had known the identity of her lover, which she had not dared to confide to her.

"Beggars can't be choosers," she said, taking up her opponent's weapon.

"A beggar you'll never need to be, Miss Mary, with your poor ma's money and all. You don't want to go marrying someone you don't care for, that's all."

"But I do care for him! At least, I think I do. He is so very handsome, Sarah, and such a good dancer!"

"That's no great thing in a husband, Miss Mary. A good dancer, indeed! Whatever next?"

"I beg your pardon, Sarah," said her charge with feigned meekness. "But I thought you would like me to be married."

"So I would," said her servant with maddening inconsistency, "if I could be sure it's what you want."

"Well, I can't be sure of that myself, yet," said Mary sensibly. "And there is poor Papa to consider, after all. We must try to get away tomorrow, if we possibly can."

Meanwhile John Smith, as he had named himself to the Runforths, having closed the bedroom door as if it were made of eggshells, took himself downstairs at a speed that brought his host running, in fear that the house was on fire. Pausing only to snatch up his great-coat, he flung out of the door and out into the snow, which now came up to the height of his top-boots and soon slowed his rapid progress. Nevertheless, he continued doggedly on, trying by dint of exhausting his body to quiet the turmoil of his mind. In this laudable aim he partially succeeded, so that on his return an hour later, in what was now full darkness, he was so far recovered that he was able to reply quite civilly to Job Runforth's remarks and even, with a little pressure, choose the dishes for his dinner.

This meal, over which Mrs. Runforth had exercised such anxious care, he ate without so much as tasting a single bite, chewing and swallowing with stubborn perseverance in the lonely state of the downstairs parlour. Miss Hadfield, he learned, had taken some soup, and some fowl with bread sauce, and had returned to her bed. For perhaps the fiftieth time he cursed the fell hand of providence, then sat drinking Runforth's best—smuggled—brandy, and wondering what, if anything, he should do. Neither the brandy, nor the fire into which he stared, provided any answer, and his dreams were nightmares of flight and pursuit, in which he never knew if he was the chaser, or the chased.

The following morning brought no comfort to him. The snow was as impassible as ever, and he had a fierce headache from his over-indulgence the night before. It was scant comfort to learn that Miss Hadfield had passed an excellent night, and that her own headache was so well abated that she proposed to dress, and even come downstairs later in the day. When, during the middle of the morning, he heard a little bustle above stairs, he abandoned the lonely game of cards he had been playing, left hand against right hand, with a greasy pack the landlord had produced, and made his way out to the stable. There he found Sam, who was if possible even more gloomy than he to find himself trapped, so far from home, and with his master's horses to care for in such indifferent surroundings.

From there he took himself on another solitary walk, returning only when he was so cold that he could scarcely feel his feet and hands at all. Since he had been blessed with abundant energy, his life had accustomed him to solving his difficulties by action, whether violent or otherwise, and nothing could be more irksome to him than to be forced to be still and quiet. Coming back to the inn, he tried to creep upstairs, but Runforth called out to him in his genial, roaring voice, and at once Mary's gentler tones summoned him from the private parlour that led off the hall.

"How d'you do, Miss Hadfield? You must excuse me; I am very wet, and must go directly to change my clothes."

"Of course you must! Why, you are soaked! How very imprudent, Mr. Smith. But perhaps, having lived for so long in hot climates, you enjoy the novelty of the snow?"

His room, since he had perforce given up the principal bedroom to Mary, was small and incommodious, with a fireplace that smoked no matter what was done to it, and a piercing draught through the ill-fitting casement window. He bore it as long as he could, but at length the discomfort drove him back downstairs.

"I hope you have not caught a cold, Mr. Smith," Mary said politely, seeing him wipe his watering eyes.

"Not at all, Miss Hadfield. I never catch colds. Merely, the confounded fire in my room smokes like the devil. Oh, I beg your pardon."

"There is no need. I have been quite used to language far worse than that! I should think my vocabulary would amaze you."

He thought it unlikely, but let it pass. There was silence between them for a while. It had been a long time since he had been in the company of a well-bred young lady, and as he was still undecided on his future course of action it seemed to him impossible to start any conversation, however inconsequential, without revealing to her such things as he wished to keep to himself, or displaying a knowledge that he should not, in fact, possess.

"I am afraid that, situated as we are, we have nothing but our own wits to divert us, Mr. Smith. If there were a piano, I could play for you, but as it is, will you not play cards with me? I see that you were playing earlier, and I often played with Martha, when she was in pain and had to keep to her sofa."

He was thankful to agree, and under the influence of a game of picquet his discomfort thawed. They played for imaginary stakes, cheerfully writing out vowels for fabulous sums and signing them with fictitious names, until by the time dinner was announced they were both laughing uproariously.

"I am afraid Mrs. Runforth is very shocked," whispered Mary when the good lady had served them and withdrawn. "I should not be laughing like this, with my brother so recently dead. The truth is, it seems so unreal to me that I find myself forgetting that he is no more. I do not even know how he died!"

"Your being cheerful cannot harm him, any more than sitting with a long face can bring him back."

"Very true. And I shall have enough of that, later, to make up for it." She spoke without complaint, but he found himself moved by her stoic acceptance of the discomforts of home. Over dinner he told her stories of his travels, several of them quite true, and she listened with shining eyes. He found himself no longer noticing the bruising on her face, when her brown eyes were lit up with the pleasure of his tales.

At the end of the evening she gave him her hand with unaffected friendship.

"It has been such a pleasant evening," she said. "One of the most pleasant I have ever spent, I think."

A certain hardness, which she had noticed from time to time in his grey eyes, softened as he looked down at her, his hand still clasping hers.

"If there should ever come a time..." he began, and she looked up at him in frank enquiry. "Miss Hadfield, I know that you have the protection of your family, of your father, and sisters, of wealth and connections. But if there should ever come a time when you need a friend, then I hope that you would call on me."

She looked at him in perplexity.

"It is unlikely, I know. But I should like you to remember that, for the next few weeks at any rate, I shall probably be here, at this inn, or at least if I go away I shall undoubtedly leave a forwarding address, so that any message sent here would find me."

She thanked him, with her doubts ill concealed. He found himself wondering whether Jason Hadfield had yet tasted the sweetness of those soft lips, had held that slender form in his arms. He remembered, achingly, the feel of her as she lay against him, how lightly he had lifted her to carry her upstairs, and how perforce her head had lain against his shoulder, her soft hair tickling his chin and smelling faintly of flowers. Abruptly he raised her hand to his lips, and let it go. With a murmured farewell she was gone, and he groaned aloud.

"I must be gone tomorrow, even if I perish in a snow-drift," he said to himself. "This is a game too deep for me."

Mary, for her part, still felt the heat of his lips against her hand as she ran lightly up the stairs. Jason Hadfield, an accomplished drawing-room flirt, had never yet attempted even so chaste a kiss, and she told herself that she should be angry that this man, who might be a gentleman by birth, if his story was to be believed, but was sometimes so uncouth in his manners, should dare to take such a liberty. Anger, however, she could not find within her. There was something refreshing in such directness, and as for his peculiar request... Mary could not imagine any circumstance which might induce her to take advantage of it, but nevertheless there was something so frank and manly in his offer of help that she could not help being warmed and cheered by it.

Once again she slept deeply, and in her fire-warmed room was not aware that the temperature was rising, nor did she hear the rush of softened snow as it slithered down the roof, or the dripping of water from twigs and eaves. In the morning she woke late to the sound of water gurgling in the gutters, and knew at once that there was a thaw.

With the entry of Sarah and Jenny, carrying the ewer of hot water, came the news that the snow was indeed half gone, that Jim had been sent to inspect the road and reported that it was slushy, but passable.

"Then we must go at once," decided Mary. "There must be no more time lost in reaching the rector's, and my father."

"I've already spoke to Sam, Miss Mary, and the horses will be put to as soon as you're ready to leave." In a fever of haste, Mary dressed in her travelling clothes and swallowed a quick breakfast. None knew better than she how difficult the roads of her home country could become in wet weather. While they were still half frozen it would be possible to move, but should the thaw continue even the better cared for toll-roads were liable to become quagmires of sticky clay.

In all the rush, it was not until she was bidding farewell to the innkeeper and his wife that she thought to ask after Mr. Smith, to be told that he had been up early, almost before it was light, and had left long before she had woken.

"He did ask me to ask your pardon, miss, for not bidding you farewell. Left his best wishes for your safe journey, he did."

"Please thank him for his kindness, if you should see him again." Mary was half ashamed of her duplicity, but she could not bring herself to ask straight out whether he intended to return to the inn, as he had said he would.

"Oh, I will, miss!" responded the innocent Runforth. "He'll be back in a day or two! Left half his luggage here with us, he has."

Mrs. Runforth insisted on pressing a bottle of her sovereign cordial into Sarah's hands, "for fear Miss should be took swimmy, like, in the carriage," and then they were moving. Mary was surprised into a pang of sadness as she watched the disappearance of that small, ancient building that seemed to huddle close to the ground in its little clearing in the great forest trees. Then she straightened her spine, lifted her head, and prepared herself for whatever reception she should meet at the Grange, where her sister Caroline lived in childless state with the rector.

In the event, her coming had not been looked for so soon. Her family, aware that she would have set off immediately on receipt of the message, had assumed that the bad weather would have kept her in London, and that she would not arrive for several hours, if at all. In the hallway of the Grange, with its cold, gloomy air of ecclesiastical grandeur, she was met by Caroline, thinner than ever, who squeaked in horror at the sight of her eye, the purple of which was now streaked with dirty orange.

"Mary! Whatever have you been doing? Are you all right?"

"Yes, of course, merely the carriage met with a small accident on the way. It looks worse than it is. But tell me, how is Papa?"

Caroline glanced round her, as if suspecting that some critical presence lurked in the chilly shadows.

"My poor father has not left his bed since the news came to us. Oh, Mary, I fear for his reason! He will not speak, even to the rector! All he does is moan, and sigh, and hide his face in the pillows!"

Mary was not altogether astonished to hear this, since it was her father's invariable habit to refuse to confront anything that he did not like.

"It was bound to be so, Caroline," she soothed. "You know how he is. My father does not easily bear sorrow."

"The rector has been very good," said her sister in an even lower voice. "Very good indeed! He has sought to pray with him, and has often exhorted to bear his trials like a man, and a Christian, but to no avail! I fear that he is displeased, very displeased!''

"I shall take Papa home, if he is well enough," promised Mary. "But how was it that Giles came to die? The last news I had of him, not a week since, he was in good health. Was there an accident?"

"Oh, hush!" Caroline's slightly protruding eyes filled with tears. "I do not know what happened, but it must be very terrible, for the rector said it was not fit for a lady's ears!"

"But you are his wife, and Giles's sister! Surely you must be told how he died?" Even as she spoke, Mary knew that her sister would never stand up to her husband's decree. With no children to fill her mind or her heart she had devoted the whole of her energies to her husband, whose every pronouncement she accepted with as much awe as if it had been carried down from the mountain by Moses himself. In her eyes he was perfect, and, if at times she was fearful of him, she expected no less from such a godlike being.

"Well, I shall ask him myself. But first I must see poor Papa."

"Yes, I shall take you up directly. But I must warn you that you will find him sadly, sadly changed."

Before she could do so, however, the door of the rector's study opened and the master of the house appeared.

"My dear sister! I have just this moment been apprised of your presence. God be thanked, dear sister, for your safe arrival." He pressed a moist kiss to her forehead, eyeing in some horror her disfigured face, to which he doubtless felt it would be improper to allude.

"Thank you, Rector. I am certainly relieved to be here, and as you can see my journey has not been without mishap."

"I am sorry to hear of it. Very sorry to hear of it. Later, you shall tell me of it, unburden your soul. But for now—"

"For now I should like to see Papa," said Mary firmly. It was not unknown for the rector to hold an impromptu prayer meeting to celebrate, if such was the word, an arrival, a departure, or other unusual event.

"To see Mr. Hadfield. Ah, yes. Yes. To see your father. I do not know that I would consider that a wise thing. Not a wise thing, no."

"He is well enough to see his daughter, I trust?"

"As to that, I do not know that it will make a difference either way. Your father... does not bear his affliction lightly."

"He never has," said Mary.

"Ah, you speak with the quick, thoughtless tongue of youth," he said pompously, rocking back on his heels and running his fingers lovingly along the heavy gold watch-chain that adorned the curve of his equally heavy stomach. "But you must see him, doubtless, you must see him. It is your duty, my dear sister. Your duty."

"Yes, that is why I am here." Mary suppressed her irritation at these needless repetitions. "Shall I go up to him now, Caroline? Will you take me?"

Her sister sought permission with a quick glance, and, receiving a portentous nod, led the way up the stairs, glancing back once or twice to check that she was behaving correctly. At the door of the room she paused.

"The housekeeper is sitting with him," she whispered. "The rector thought it better that he should not be alone, and she is a very good, sensible sort of woman." If it occurred to Mary that the properest person to sit with Mr. Hadfield was his eldest daughter, she did not allow herself to show it, merely nodded, and went in.

The room was very dark. The heavy brocade curtains were tightly shut over the windows, excluding any light, and though a small fire burned in the grate the room was not particularly warm, though the air was close and musty. An unlit candle stood beside the dark cavern of the canopied bed, and a small, shaded lamp illuminated one corner of the room, where the housekeeper occupied herself with darning some linen. There was no sound of motion from the bed, and as Mary stepped forward she nodded to the house-keeper, and looked a question.

"I think he's asleep, Miss Mary," was the whispered reply, "but it's hard to tell. He don't say nothing, hour after hour, only sighs. Poor old gentleman, I feel that sorry for him. Shall I leave you with him, miss? Maybe he'll talk to you."

"Yes, thank you." When the housekeeper had gone Mary crept to the bed. Nothing was to be seen but the mound of the bedclothes, and a tousled grey head buried in the pillows. She took the candle, lit it with a spill at the fireplace, and carried it back to the bedside table.

"Papa!" she said gently. "Papa!"

There was no movement, but the sound of his breathing hesitated, then resumed.

"Papa, it is I, Mary. How are you, Papa?"

Beneath the bedclothes he seemed to shrink into a small compass, and even his breathing appeared to stop.

"I am so sorry, Papa. So very, very sorry." She put out a hand and laid it where his shoulder must be. "Will you not turn, and look at me, Papa? I should so like to comfort you, if I might." She felt his body tremble beneath her touch. "Please, Papa!"

At last, with infinite slowness, he turned. His unshaven face was gaunt as she had never seen it, the flesh fallen from his bones, and she was shocked by the fragility of the hand that came out, wavering as if palsied, from beneath the sheet, and groped for her own. She took it in her warm grasp, and it felt as bony and lifeless as if he had already died. His eyes were still closed, but from beneath the lids two tears trickled down, finding their way through deep furrows that had not been there before. Mary took out her handkerchief, and wiped them away.

At last his eyes opened, and fixed on her. They seemed to regard her with a kind of horror, and he shrank back from her as she leaned to embrace him. Mary, hoping to rouse him, essayed a more cheering tone.

"Do not look so frightened, Papa! Indeed, it is only I, though I am afraid this black eye makes me look quite outlandish! You need not be alarmed. It was merely a slight accident, caused by the bad weather."

Slowly, he shook his head. Pleased to have even so small a response, Mary sat down on a chair at the bedside, keeping his hand in hers.

"I came as quickly as I could, Papa. Sir Anthony was so kind, and sent me in his own carriage, with his coachman to look after me, so I was quite safe. Georgie would have come with me, of course, if her condition did not forbid it. So you shall have another grandchild soon, to comfort you, Papa!" She knew how much pleasure he had in the Tarrant children, particularly the two little boys, but he only shook his head again in hopeless grief.

"I am afraid you are making yourself very unwell, Papa," she said. "Now that I am here, will you not take a little wine? There is some set ready on the table, and a dish of broth keeping warm by the fire. That would do you good."

Ignoring his negative, she poured a glass of wine, slipping her arm beneath his shoulders to raise him a little, and obliged him to drink some. She was pleased to see a tinge of colour return to his cheeks, and at last he spoke.

"No more," he said.

"Very well, if you will take some broth later. Oh, Papa, I know what a terrible loss this is to you, but you must not give way to it! Hadfield is still yours, after all! Does that mean nothing to you? You are still Hadfield of Hadfield Priory."

This appeal to his ancient pride sent his eyes glancing sideways towards her. If she had not thought it impossible, she would have thought that his face betrayed, not just grief, but a look of guilty dismay. He was still reluctant to fix his eyes on her face: they kept sliding away from her, as if he could not bear to have her in view, yet returning as though fascinated as a rabbit by a snake.

"Do you want to go home, Papa? You must be well, if you want to travel back to Hadfield."

"Go home!" His voice was no more than a croak. "Yes! I must go home! I shall be better there, if anywhere. Take me home, Martha!"

"I am Mary," she reminded him, quite accustomed to his inability to remember which of his twin daughters was which, but hurt none the less that he should make the mistake at such a moment.

"Mary, then!" he replied with a flash of his old irritation. "What does it matter, so that you take me home?"

"What indeed?" she answered, but low, and went to fetch the broth.

CHAPTER FOUR

AFTER HE HAD swallowed a bowlful of broth, spoonful by spoonful as his daughter fed it to him, Mr. Hadfield confessed himself tired.

"Nights without sleep! You cannot imagine how it has been. No one who has not known such misery can possibly understand how I felt. The rector is heartless! Quite heartless!"

"You must try to sleep, if you want to be well enough to go home," Mary pointed out.

"I think I might manage a few moments' slumber now. But not alone! I cannot abide to be left alone! And do not send servants to sit with me, if you please! Not the rector's servants, at any rate. They are all as heartless as he, I am convinced of it. You shall stay, and watch by my bed. It will not be for long, I can assure you. I never sleep for any more than a few minutes together."

Mary assented, though she was tired from her journey and her head was aching. Her father, still mumbling complaints, sank into a doze, and was soon deeply asleep. After about an hour there the door opened softly, and Sarah looked in.

"I thought as much," she hissed. "Now you come away this instant, Miss Mary, and lie down!"

"I cannot leave Papa. He does not like to have the rector's servants with him, and if he should wake, and find himself alone..."

"He won't wake for hours! But I will come back and sit with him myself, as soon as I've seen you settled. It's barely three hours till dinner, and if you don't have an hour or two of rest you'll be knocked up worse than he is. And don't try to tell me you haven't a headache, because I know better!''

Mary owned meekly that it was true, and submitted without much argument to having her forehead bathed with aromatic vinegar, and to lying down in a newly warmed bed. She woke two hours later, somewhat refreshed, and was pleased to learn that her father had showed no signs of waking. This encouraged her to change her dress, and re-arrange her hair, a task which she was perfectly capable of managing for herself, though Sarah generally did it for her. Just as she was finishing tying the ribbons of her gown, a demure garment of white muslin, cut high in deference to the rector's frequently expressed views on female apparel, her sister came in.

"Are you all right, Mary? The rector was very shocked by your appearance."

"Then I beg his pardon and yours."

"Oh, he is not angry with you!" Caroline spoke as though this implied a rare virtue. "But he is very put out. He wishes to know whether Papa has spoken to you."

"Only to say that he would like to go home," said Mary diplomatically. "I do think, you know, that Hadfield is the best place for him just now. If anything can distract him from his grief, it will be his love of the place."

"But will it not also remind him of what he has lost? That it will no longer pass to his descendants?" said Caroline, with more shrewishness than Mary had given her credit for possessing.

"It is bound to, but he will remember that wherever he is. In any case, he wishes to go, and under the circumstances it is scarcely possible to deny him. I am sure the rector will be relieved!''

Unable to admit that her spouse could have so un-Christian a thought, but unwilling to lie, Caroline took refuge in a few tears. Then she wiped her eyes.

"Are you quite ready to go down, dear?"

"Yes, perfectly ready. But surely we do not dine for some while yet?"

"No, but the rector sent me to ask you to join him. He is in his study." Mary's heart sank, but she could do no more than acquiesce as gracefully as she might, remembering as she did so that the rector's study, at least, was well warmed. The heavy silk shawl she had put out to protect her from the draughty dining-room would not be needed just yet.

Entering the hallowed room, it was difficult not to think of herself as a naughty child, summoned to receive justice. The rector's well-padded body stood directly in front of the good fire, legs apart, and, since the only other lighting in the room came from branches of candles on the mantelshelf, the effect was to make him seem huge, even threatening. At Mary's entrance, however, he came forward affably enough, and took her hands. She stood with lowered eyelids, suffering him to kiss her forehead once again, a form of salute she particularly disliked. He smelt of singed cloth, and soap, and clean linen, by no means unpleasant except by association. He led her to a chair, then took up his fireside stance again.

At first, the interview followed very much the pattern Mary had expected. After offering up a long prayer, during which Mary was thankful not to be obliged to kneel, he informed his sister-in-law, at great length, how very unhappy she must be feeling, and how her only hope of future happiness lay in doing her duty by her father, devoting herself to his care, and attempting to distract his melancholy. It was no more than Mary had told herself, but it was very dispiriting, all the same.

"Of course, my dear sister, your poor father is not a young man! Not a young man at all! It is scarcely to be expected that he will be spared to us for many more years, particularly after this fearful shock! And in the light of this unhappy event, this sad loss of his heir, I should like you to know, my dear sister, that you must never consider that you have no home, no resting place for your head. When that much to be lamented event occurs, and you are an orphan, you must not hesitate to come to us!"

"You are very kind, Rector," murmured Mary, "but I hardly think..."

"No, no, it will be no trouble to us! No trouble at all! And as to the expense, you are not to be thinking of it! Of course, with your dear mother's money, you will be quite an heiress—thirty thousand, is it not?—so you might always make some little contribution to the expenses of the household, just to make things feel quite comfortable between us!"

He beamed on her, clearly feeling that he had arranged matters very well, and that she must be grateful. Mary thought privately that not even in the direst penury could she spend the rest of her days living in this house. Polite usage, however, forbade her to say so, and once again she expressed her gratitude with the greatest warmth she could muster, though without committing herself. She could not help wondering how welcome she would be if, instead of bringing with her the income of thirty thousand pounds, she were penniless. That shelter would be offered, she had no doubt, but that she would earn her keep she was similarly certain.

At this point she would have risen to leave, thinking that the interview was over.

"One moment, my dear sister," said the rector. "One moment." Mary sank back into her chair. "There is something else I am constrained to tell you. Something that, I am afraid, will make you very unhappy. Something...in short, something that no lady should be called upon to know. I think that a brief prayer, asking that strength be granted to you to bear this affliction, and that the purity of your girlish mind should not be sullied by what I have to impart..." Obediently Mary folded her hands and bowed her head. Behind her closed eyelids scenes of horror unfolded. What, she wondered, was to be told her?

The prayer finished, the rector seemed at a loss to know where to start. He swayed backwards and forwards on his widespread legs, rising to his toes and rocking backwards on to his heels until Mary feared he might actually fall into the fire. She waited with what patience she could muster, and at last he made an attempt at speech.

"What I have to tell you, my dear sister, has to do with the death of your brother, Giles," he added, presumably in case she might have some confusion as to whom he was referring.

"I am glad to hear it," she said. "It has seemed to be that there is some mystery connected with his death, for nobody has been able to tell me why or how he died."

"Why, or how? Ah, yes. Yes, indeed. That is precisely the problem. My dear, dear Mary, you must prepare your mind for a dreadful shock. You must be strong. Remember your poor father. Remember your duty to him. Remember, in short, that you must be...be strong." Mary could have screamed with irritation, but she pressed her hands tightly together, and her lips, and was silent. "I very much regret, my dear Mary, that I shall be unable—yes, actually unable—to officiate at the funeral of your poor brother, Giles."

This, so far removed from her fevered imaginings, was such an anticlimax that Mary could only stare at him while she fought down her laughter.

"That...that is certainly a pity," she managed at last. "Of course I am very sorry to hear it, and so will Papa be. But of course, in this weather, you would not wish to travel...the vicar in the village, however, has known us all for many years..."

"You misunderstand me, Mary." His voice was very solemn. "It is not the *weather* that prevents me. I hope that I should never be kept from doing my duty by the *weather*. It is my own conscience that prevents me. That voice of God that speaks within us all, when we will listen to it, tells me that I may not, must not, be there."

"But...but why? I am at a loss to understand you, Rector."

Agitation made him leave the fireplace, and take a quick turn around the room. Mary was astonished at the waft of heat that the absence of his large frame released, and almost shrank back from it. On his return her eyes were dazzled by the brightness of the flames, and she could only blink up at him.

"I fear, indeed I believe it to be true, that your brother did not die in a state of grace."

"But if he died suddenly, that is not so surprising, is it? I mean, which of us is? I am sure if I were to die tonight, there would be many sins and mistakes that I should regret not having put right. But, Rector, you are not, in general, an advocate of the confessional, are you? I am sure I have heard you refer to the giving of absolution as quite beyond the ability of any cleric."

"You misunderstand me, Mary. He died in sin. He committed—how I shudder to say it!—the vilest sin, perhaps, that a man can commit!"

He stood looking at her, his eyes so round that she could see the whites, a little bloodshot by good living, clearly all round the irises. To what could he refer? Murder? Incest—with whom? Treason? Atheism? Her mind reeled as she searched it for possible sins. She shook her head, wordlessly.

"You force me to say the words. On your own head be it." Mary winced, and half unconsciously put up her hand to the tender place on her forehead. "Your brother, Giles, has taken it upon himself to arrogate the power that only God possesses, to decide, to choose, the hour of his own death."

It took a moment for Mary to decode his words, but then she shook her head again, more violently.

"You mean, he killed himself?" she said baldly. "Oh, no, he would never do that. Giles was far too fond of himself, you know. I am sure you must be misinformed."

The rector looked pained.

"You do not know what you are saying, my dear sister. You are overwrought. Nothing else could induce you to speak with such callous levity."

"I beg your pardon, I did not mean to be so. But truly, sir, it was not in Giles's nature to behave so. You must not forget that we were almost of an age. Martha and I spent the first years of our lives with him, in the nursery. I do not think that I could be so deceived in him."

He frowned.

"I am afraid you must accept, my dear Mary, that there are many things in which a woman must be guided by her male relatives. In this case I must desire you to submit to my judgement, both as a brother and as a cleric, and accept what I say. You are aware, of course, that your poor, misguided brother had pretentions of a poetical nature?" Mary nodded. It would have been difficult, she thought, for her to have been ignorant of it. "You, whom I have always regarded as an example of pure-minded young womanhood," he bowed, and Mary gravely inclined her head in thanks, "can have no idea, no idea at all, of the way of life such men sometimes lead. Of his abilities I say nothing. I am not fitted to judge. Though I must admit that with his sentiments, however expressed, I found myself frequently out of tune, and on occasion quite disgusted. But I digress. Your poor brother, Giles, thinking that in order to produce great poetry he must experience all the varied excitements and experiences of life, had begun to mix with what I can only describe as a very wild set, a very wild set of people indeed. People whose names I would not soil my lips by repeating. Their manners, their habits, their morals were all of them such as to disgust any right-thinking person, and among these habits was that of taking laudanum."

"But I have taken that myself, when I had the toothache!"

"Yes, indeed, and so have I. But when I say taking, I should more properly say over-indulging! You know, I suppose, of the extract opium, that gives laudanum its power? In small doses what a boon, what a gift to suffering mankind. But when taken to excess . . . a poison. Your poor brother had acquired this habit, seeking the strange and exotic visions that it is said to bring. And then some misfortune befell him—I know not precisely what. At his age, one may suspect that he was crossed in love. Whatever the cause, he was heard to speak very wildly, very wildly indeed. And the very next morning he was found, dead, with the empty phial of laudanum by his side!"

He paused, in triumph. Clearly he considered that his case was so complete that it would brook no argument.

"Are you saying, Rector, that it is accepted belief that my brother committed suicide? That he may not be buried in hallowed ground?" Mary spoke out bluntly, in her shock.

"Accepted belief? Certainly not. Naturally, his friends saw to it that the death was seen as no more than an accident. But I, having heard the full details, had no doubt, no doubt at all." Clearly, he expected Mary to share his certainty. She rose to her feet.

"You will excuse me, Rector, if I continue to differ with you. I find it impossible to believe that Giles would kill himself for love of any woman, or indeed for any other reason. It seems to me only too likely that Giles, who had a weak head for drink and probably for this drug also, merely took a second dose by accident, being fuddled with the first. It would be just like him!" she finished bitterly.

"You are, of course, entitled to think as you choose," he responded stiffly, clearly without any sincerity. "You are to be congratulated, I suppose, on your loyalty to your brother."

He was obviously deeply affronted, and Mary was relieved to hear the sound of the dinner gong. He offered her his arm, as she rose, with much correctness, but the meal was a very silent one, with only as much conversation as was necessary to keep up appearances before the servants. Mary ate little of the food set before her, though the rector was famed for the excellence of his table, and as soon as was possible excused herself, and returned to her father.

Mr. Hadfield woke soon afterwards, protesting that he had hardly slept more than a few moments at a stretch, and had merely been lying with his eyes closed, in obedience to his daughter. Too used to this kind of behaviour to remonstrate, Mary persuaded him to eat a light supper, and drink two glasses of wine. He agreed, reluctantly, to her going to her own bed, on the understanding that she was to be called at once if he should need her.

The following day seemed very long. Sitting in her father's room, Mary could not help recalling the cheerful afternoon and evening she had spent with the man she still, in her own mind, called Lazarus. That time in the inn seemed, in retrospect, like an interval in another world, a period of halcyon peace that was all the more unreal since no one but Sarah knew of it. Caroline, informed by the rector that her sister had chosen to disagree with him, naturally displayed a subdued and anxious face on her rare encounters with the recalcitrant one, and Mary found herself longing for the morrow, when she might take her father back to Hadfield.

Once again the carriage left early, and such stilted farewells as were given had taken place the night before. The journey, though slow, was as comfortable as the weather and the time of year would allow, and Mary felt a rise in her spirits as Sam Coachman turned the horses on to the public highway, and headed for Uckfield. When, later on, they passed the place where the track to the inn branched off through the trees, Mary kept her eyes studiously trained forward, and did not permit herself so much as a glance out of the window.

Never had Hadfield Priory looked so imposing to her eyes as it did that day, never so welcoming, so much like home. The knowledge that she might never, on the death of her father, live there again, or that in other circumstances she might find herself its mistress in truth, gave it a kind of luminous aura in her eyes, gilding every famous stone, every tile and timber and window, with its own radiance.

Mr. Hadfield, however, could do no more than weep, and Mary was obliged to use her best efforts to comfort him as they crossed the threshold. He glanced around the well-appointed hall with a depreciating look.

"Alas, alas," he wailed theatrically. "The last of the Hadfields looks on his own, but for how long? My dear, I very much fear that my days on this earth are numbered."

"Come, now, Papa, you are tired, and overwrought. Things will not look so bad tomorrow, I hope."

"How can one night possibly improve things?" he snapped. "A thousand nights cannot do that. My son is dead, and..." He paused, and once again his eyes met hers with an expression of guilty dread. "What did the rector say to you?" he asked suddenly, in sharp tones.

"Oh, nothing that you need concern yourself about," she prevaricated.

"Nothing? You are quite sure?"

"Well, he may not be able to be here for the funeral," she mentioned carefully.

He appeared relieved, but said only, "Heartless! Quite heartless!" As this was his usual term of opprobrium for anyone who chose to disagree with him, Mary was not particularly worried.

The funeral was held two days later, and fortunately the weather provided quite sufficient reason for the absence of the rest of the family. The tenants, as duty bound, attended, but those of their neighbours who did so came, as Mary knew, to comfort and support the living rather than out of any sorrow or respect for the dead. Giles had not been popular in the area.

"My dearest Mary!" Emily McLaren, Mary's particular friend, embraced her warmly. She and her mother had come to the Priory early in the day, assuming that Mary would not attend the actual ceremony, and intending to bear her company. "You are surely not meaning to go out?" She gestured to the pelisse and bonnet, complete with thick black veil, that lay ready for use.

"Yes, I think I must. Neither the rector nor Sir Anthony is able to be here, you know, and I cannot leave poor Papa to go through such an ordeal on his own."

"In the general way of things, I should consider it most improper for a young lady to go to the actual graveside, but under the circumstances, my dear child, I cannot blame you." Mrs. McLaren also kissed Mary. A widow, with no more than a respectable competence to support herself and her only child, she had come to Hadfield many years since.

She was a woman of much good sense, and Mary had frequently been grateful for her advice in the past. Emily, though two years younger than she, was her closest friend, and possessed the same cheerful and practical nature that made her mother so universally popular in the neighbourhood.

"Can you bear it, Mary? There will be no other women there, but the tenants, I suppose."

"I can, because I must. And I need not pretend to you, I know, that I feel any deep grief."

"I know, but still…it is a solemn thing. Mama, may I not go with Mary? She should not be alone at such a time."

"I would not hear of it, Emily. I shall do very well with Papa."

"Emily is right, my dear. Though I should prefer that she remain here; will you allow me to accompany you? I shall not do so, if you do not like it, but my age and situation make me a most suitable person to be with you, I think."

Mary was grateful, and said so. In the event she was very glad of the silent support of her friend's mother, for even behind the thickness of her veil she felt very conspicuous at the graveside, though most of her mind was set on supporting her father. A light drizzle was falling on ground where the snow still lay in sheltered pockets, and the small church was thronged with black cloaks and coats, beneath which it was almost impossible to distinguish individuals.

After the last words had been spoken, the company began to disperse. Mr. Hadfield was led away, but Mary lingered for a moment. An opulent wreath of flowers and foliage had been laid on the coffin itself, but she carried a small posy of sweet violets, picked that morning in the glasshouse.

"I should like to put these on Martha's grave," she said in low tones to Mrs. McLaren. "Pray do not wait in the cold; I shall not be long."

"Of course, my dear. I shall wait for you in the carriage."

Mary was grateful for her companion's sensitivity in allowing her these few moments of solitude and peace. She laid her flowers on the quiet grave, and stood there quietly for some minutes, not in prayer, but simply breathing in the clean, cold air, which seemed so welcome after the heavy atmosphere of home, and the almost overpowering scent of the hothouse flowers that had pervaded the church. Turning, she saw a solitary figure watching her from the far side of the graveyard. As she looked towards him in some surprise and anger, he lifted his hat and she recognised the rugged face and dark hair of her newest acquaintance. Glancing round, she saw that she was screened from sight of the carriages, and walked swiftly towards the waiting figure, raising her damp, clammy veil to see him better.

"Mr. Smith! What are you doing here?"

"Paying my respects, I suppose. All the countryside was aware that the funeral was for today. I did not hope to see you here, but, as I do, may I ask how you are?"

She found herself amazingly cheered by the sound of his voice, after the hushed and reverent tones of other visitors to the Priory.

"I am well, thank you. My poor father feels his loss very greatly, I fear. And you? Have you yet found any business in these parts?"

"I think I might have done. I am not yet sure." His eyes were fixed on her face, noting its pallor, unmarked now except for a faint yellow shadow on her eyelid, and the fact that she was thinner. "Are you sure you are well? You do not look it."

"Why, thank you, sir! You are not very gallant!"

"Well, it is the company I keep," he said with a twinkle.

"Of course. I know I should not ask, but are you a smuggler?"

"A smuggler?" He looked amazed, and flung back his head to laugh, recollecting just in time where he was, and in what circumstances. "I have been many things, but not a smuggler, as yet. Why on earth should you think so?"

She felt herself grow warm with embarrassment.

"Oh, merely that you are a stranger, yet you have some mysterious business that you will not tell me of. There are many smugglers in Sussex, you know."

"Should you mind, if I were?" he asked curiously.

"No! At least, I don't know, but I don't think so. I believe that many perfectly respectable people are connected with them. I suppose there is hardly a house of note in the county that does not have a barrel or two of brandy in its cellars that has had no duty paid on it. No one thinks any the worse for it. Of course, if you had had anything to do with that robbery of the Blue Coach at Handcross—but no, that was three years ago. I suppose you were not in England at that time?"

"I was not," he answered, his repressive tones belied by the twinkle of amusement in his grey eyes. "Do I really look like a highwayman?"

"Well ... I have never been acquainted with one, that I knew of. But this was no mere highway robbery, but a coach of the Brighton Union Bank. I believe as much as eight thousand pounds was taken, and they have never recovered it, or caught those responsible. Yet."

"I see that you still harbour a suspicion that I might be the guilty party. Shall you inform on me?"

"Oh, dear, I suppose I could not do so, when I owe you my safety. But I should inform you, sir, that I am making a considerable sacrifice, for there was a reward of eight hundred pounds offered! But I must not stay here talking, though it is so agreeable to have a conversation that is not connected with my brother."

"I am glad to be that much of service to you, at any rate. You must not remain here, however. Tell me only that you have not forgotten what I said."

"I have not, though I cannot imagine— Oh, there is Mrs. McLaren coming to look for me. Goodbye!" She put down her veil, and he bowed, making no attempt to detain her and indeed seeming quite anxious to be gone.

"Who was that, my dear? Some friend of Giles's. I suppose, who knows no better than to keep you talking in the

cold and the wet. Come, we must get back to the Priory.
Your father will be wanting you."

Mary was glad that she was not called upon to answer her
first question, and meekly followed her friend back to their
carriage.

Later, when the visitors had departed and her father had
been settled, exhausted with emotion, in his bed, Mary sat
with a sigh of relief in the little upstairs sitting-room that
had once been the schoolroom, and was now regarded as
particularly her own. Emily had begged to stay, and her
mother had given permission, seeing that the company of
one her own age would be the best comfort for Mary, stip-
ulating only that her daughter should not keep her friend up
talking half the night.

"My poor dear! Was it so very dreadful?"

"It seemed very long, certainly. But my father has borne
it better than I had feared."

"Poor Mr. Hadfield! I am so sorry for him!"

"Let us not talk of it now. Tell me what has been happening here, since I went away. There must be a great deal
of news. Have there been many parties? And has Miss
Fordcombe become engaged yet? I was sure there would
soon be an announcement."

Nothing loath, Emily chattered of the numerous small
doings of their set, confirming that the gentleman who had
showed so marked an interest in Miss Fordcombe had indeed come up to expectations.

"I am so pleased! She is a thoroughly nice girl, and I
think it a most suitable match. And, with three daughters to
settle, I imagine her parents must be happy?"

"Oh, beyond anything. And, since we are speaking of
suitable matches, a certain gentleman has been most assid-
uous in asking for news of you."

Mary frowned, blushed, and laughed.

"I cannot think what you are talking about," she lied.

"Of course you cannot! Perhaps I should remind you of
a relative of yours, who may not be in possession of the

Golden Fleece of his namesake, but certainly has hair to rival it! Does that give you the clue?''

"I suppose you mean Mr. Hadfield," said Mary. "You must be careful how you mention his name in this house, Emily. You know how Papa has always felt about the family, and now, in particular..."

"Of course! Of course! But he has been most discreet, I can assure you. I do not think that many people are aware of the connection. He is actually calling himself Hallfield, as you know, so as not to cause any awkwardness."

"It would never do for word of his presence to reach Papa, at the moment, and you know how people talk..."

"If that is to my address, you need have no fear. I am far too careful of your comfort for that. He does not even visit in the village, but keeps to the neighbourhood of the Fordcombes, so I have only seen him there. I believe they have hopes of him for Miss Celia Fordcombe, the second girl, but I have not seen him take any particular notice of her. But in *you* he is always interested."

"I should not listen to you, when you talk like this."

"Admit that it is not unpleasant to do so, at any rate! I must say, Mary, that if I thought he liked me at all, other than as your friend, I should not be displeased. He is so *very* good-looking!"

It was true that Jason Hadfield, with his head of golden hair that was so beautifully cut and arranged, his classic features and his sparkling hazel eyes, presented a picture of manly beauty that would gladden the heart of any young woman, and Mary could not say that she was indifferent to his charms. To hear that he had not forgotten her in her absence, that he asked for news of her, was flattering in the extreme, and she allowed herself to fall into a little reverie that her friend, with her mother's sensitivity, did not attempt to interrupt.

CHAPTER FIVE

IF MARY HAD HOPED that the passage of time would bring
some improvement in her father's state of mind and body,
she was sadly disappointed. The passing of the weeks, instead of dulling the pain of his misery, only seemed to enhance it. He had always been inclined to be irritable,
querulous and demanding, but now his spirits were so vol-
atile that Mary sometimes despaired.

The day after the funeral his man of business, who had as
a matter of course attended the obsequies, was closeted with
Mr. Hadfield for several hours. When he finally left, his face
was grim, and Mary was not surprised, on entering the library, to find her father livid with emotion. Such was his
anger that he could only rail against her, and against the
now departed Mr. Camden. Mary bore it with what patience she could muster, but when her father turned on her
and informed her, in tones of fury unbridled, that it was all
her fault, she could not forbear to ask why.

"Why? Why? You should have been a boy! What's the
use of girls? I never wanted 'em. Useless things, always demanding settlements, and dowries, and I know not what!"

Mary was too used to his ways to feel more than a momentary pang at this, nor did she think it worth her while to
protest that she could not be held responsible for her sex.

"Well, I am sorry for it," she said cheerfully, "and I shall
try not to ask you for a settlement or a dowry, at least for a
while." She spoke lightly, meaning it as a pleasantry, but her
father gave her a hunted look, and almost collapsed into a
chair.

"I did not mean it!" he said, almost whining. Mary looked at him in astonishment.

"Of course not, Papa! If you think I can be upset by the intemperate things you say when you are angry... now, do not be distressed!" She went as if to comfort him, but he shrank from her as if in terror, and she drew back her hand.

"What is it, Papa? Are you ill?"

He was trembling, his hand quivering as he raised it to cover his lips.

"Ill? Ill? Yes, yes, I am ill. That is it, I am ill. God knows, I have enough trouble to make me ill. Who could have foreseen...? But he was at fault! He was much at fault!"

"Who, Papa?"

"Why, Camden, of course. Who else should be at fault?"

"I thought—maybe—poor Giles?" She spoke in hesitant accents.

"Giles?" he sounded as though she had uttered the vilest blasphemy. "Giles, at fault?" Then he fell to weeping, and proclaimed that Camden had behaved like a villain, and poor Giles, poor dear Giles, had been quite deceived.

"Papa?" While he was in this softened mood, Mary thought that she might risk the question. "The rector hinted that Giles's death was not... not altogether natural. Is it true?"

"Natural? How can it be natural for a young man of twenty-four to die so suddenly? He was murdered! Murdered!"

"Papa! Can it be so? But by whom?"

He looked at her. For a moment the wildness left his eyes, and she beheld a depth of suffering that was terrible to see. When he spoke, it was almost calmly, and it was this quiet certainty that convinced her where his former violent accusations had not.

"I am sure that it is so. Giles would never have destroyed himself by his own hand." It was what she had said herself to the rector, and she acknowledged the truth of it.

"What can be done? His murderer must be brought to justice!"

"What could I do? I am only a weak old man, fit for nothing but to live but his few remaining days in misery. I tell you, Martha—Mary, I mean, there is no justice in the world. No justice at all. Men are heartless creatures, at the best of times; I have always known it. There is nothing to be done. I cannot speak of it any more."

"But Papa—"

"Enough!" he almost shouted, all the former excitability of his manner returning. "I have said I cannot speak of it! Do not torment me with questions! Nothing can bring him back to me!" He snivelled in a welter of self-pity, and Mary stared at him in horror. Up until then, she had not wanted to question him about the rector's allegations, fearing that they might turn out to be only too true, and not wishing to cause any problem about the impending funeral. Now, with Giles safely buried in hallowed ground, she had asked, and her answer had been even worse than she had feared.

That night, when her father had moaned and snuffled himself into sleep, she paced her room for a while before opening her writing desk, at which she sat, pen in hand, with the ink drying on the nib before finally scribbling the request for help that she had never thought she would need to make. Surely Lazarus, whoever or whatever he might be, would be able to untangle this knot for her? She entrusted her note to Sarah, with instructions that it was to be sent at once, and without any undue fuss being made. Sarah sniffed a little, but made no other complaint, which would have surprised Mary had she bothered to think about it.

A week went by, and she received no reply. She could not help acknowledging to herself that she was disappointed, but as the days passed and no answer came she told herself that he had spoken idly, perhaps meaning what he said at the time but soon forgetting it. Probably he had left Sussex, left England even, without giving her another thought. She should, she knew, be glad of it. What could he be to her, after all? So lacking in polish, almost rough in his ways, really barely a gentleman! And if not the smuggler she had once thought him, then certainly up to no good, and if his name was really Smith she would eat her best bonnet. Lazarus, indeed!

Meanwhile, the house must be run, her father cared for, and somehow an appearance of normality must be kept up. Emily visited her nearly every day, and Mary was thankful for her company, though even to her friend she hesitated to confide her fears for her father. His behaviour was erratic in the extreme. For some of the time he was so sunk in lethargic misery that he could not be brought to leave his bed, lying for days on end in a darkened room, refusing to speak. Then, quite suddenly, he would become seized with a kind of frantic activity. With the energy of a man half his age he would be out on his horse, inspecting every foot of ground, every tree, every crop and beast and hedge. The account would be checked and counter-checked, letters fired off to his man of business, even the household expenditure examined and, where possible, cut down. Mary would find herself justifying the cost of employing a second laundry maid, or the size of the bill for candles and lamp oil.

"Surely, Papa, you need not concern yourself with such things, when you are not well?"

"But I must, I must!" he answered feverishly. "I must do something..."

Mary hoped that his busyness signified a return to a more normal life, but she soon learned that it led only to exhaustion, to a return to his sickroom habits, which in their turn restored him only to a further bout of activity. She herself he regarded with a mixture of resentment, dependence, and something that she would, if she could have seen a reason for it, have called guilt.

The third such episode had just finished, and her father was lying once more in his bed, with his head turned away from the closely curtained window, when Emily made her accustomed visit.

"I do not ask how you are," she said when she had kissed her friend and taken off bonnet and pelisse, "for I would not like to have your perjury on my conscience. I can see for myself that you are far from well."

"Thank you," murmured Mary drily. "I knew I could rely on you to raise my spirits."

"Do not try to pretend to me that I have hurt your feelings, for I know you too well for that!"

"Yes, and, besides, I have only to look in the mirror, have I not? It is only that I am a little tired. And the time of year, you know, is not one of my favourites. No one can look their best at the end of winter, when spring seems so long in arriving."

"I will admit all of these excuses, but truly I am worried for your health, Mary. Spending all day and every day in your father's sickroom, as you do, will make you ill yourself, and then what will he do?"

"Nonsense! You know I am never ill."

"Can you look me in the eye, and tell me that your head does not ache? No, I thought not."

"I admit it, you are too clever a diagnostician for me. I am not used to being so much indoors, that is all, but that is soon cured. Put back your bonnet, and we shall have a walk in the garden. The clouds are heavy, but it does not rain or snow yet, and the paths should be quite dry."

Emily agreed, and for a while they walked briskly down the gravel paths that wound so invitingly through a pretty shrubbery that, even at this time of year, had the interest of variegated leaves, and a promise of spring in the appearance of small buds, to please them. This, however, was far from fulfilling Emily's wishes.

"This is all very well, and better than nothing, but I wish you would go out more. I believe you have been no further than to church on Sunday, and to visit in the village, since you came home."

"No, I have not. I hardly like to go too far, with Papa as he is, and besides, how should I go? Papa does not care for me to use the carriage just at present, and I cannot be seen riding round the countryside, as I used to do. It would be quite unseemly, in my situation."

"Yes, but you might surely ride on your own land? To go further might cause remark, but within the park and the estate, who would be the wiser?"

For the first time Mary looked embarrassed.

"I am afraid that it would not be possible. My father has... our stable is rather depleted, just now."

"You mean he has sold your lovely mare? Oh, Mary, why should he do such a thing?"

"I don't know. He has sold nearly all the horses, except a pair for the carriage, and his own cob that he uses to ride round the land. When I asked him why, he just... well, he is so unhappy, Emily."

"Yes, much must be allowed, much forgiven to a man in his circumstances. But it does seem hard! I had hoped we might ride together, as we used to. What a pity I have no second mount that I might lend you!"

"Well, I am sure Papa will be better soon, and then perhaps I shall have a new mare. But now tell me all the news! I am starved for it!"

"I am afraid you must go hungry, for I have none. We are all very dull just now, for the Fordcombes have gone to London." She glanced at Mary, who kept her eyes demurely lowered. "They did not, however, take all their visitors in their train. Is that what you wanted to know?"

"I cannot imagine what you might mean."

"No, of course you cannot. So I need not scruple to ask you to visit us tomorrow afternoon, need I? If we should happen to have any callers, they would be of no interest to you at all."

"Anyone who likes you must be of interest to me, Emily." Her friend smiled, and said no more, nor did Mary ask any questions, for fear that the answers might not suit her. The following day, having ascertained that her father did not need her, she set off to walk into the village, and was thankful that the lanes, though dirty, were not in such a state as to preclude a journey of more than a mile on foot. She would not admit, even to herself, that she had dressed with more than usual care, nor that she was being particularly fussy about keeping her petticoat and skirt clean, and her hair neatly arranged. Her gown, though of the utmost simplicity of cut, was of the finest muslin, printed with a delicate tracery of leaves and flowers in pale grey, and ornamented with deeper grey ribbons, as befitted her mourning state. Her pelisse, bonnet and mantle, of a green so dark that they were almost black, were in the Russian style made fashionable the previous year, and ornamented with bands of fur that matched the large muff that protected her hands.

Her welcome was a warm one, but to her surprise she found only Emily and her mother present. It was not long before more visitors were announced, bringing with them news from London of the most startling kind.

"Buonaparte—escaped? I cannot believe it!"

"It is no more than the truth, I can assure you. I had it from my sister, whose husband is well acquainted with Creevey."

"With Creevey? Then you need say no more. I believe you. But how can this be? I had thought him safe on Elba."

"Nevertheless, he has made his escape, and now I suppose it will all be to do again. God send, at least, that it should not go on for as long as before."

"And that we can defeat him," put in Mary. Her companion cried her down.

"The Duke will do that, you may be sure! I have met him you know. He is charming, quite charming, in spite of that nose. And his eyes! So bright! So expressive!"

Mary acknowledged that with these attributes he could not fail to defeat the Monster of Corsica, and was deep in conversation with another friend when a small bustle at the door made her look up, and she saw her cousin in the doorway, his eyes searching the room. He found her just as she lifted her eyes to him, and there was no mistaking his pleasure. His manners were too good, however, to allow him to make his way at once to her side, and she was able to study him covertly as he made his greeting to his hostess, and to Emily, who wore a conscious look and was careful not to glance in the direction of her friend.

Mary found herself thinking that she had forgotten how very handsome he was: even more handsome than memory had painted him. Tall, slimly but strongly built, he carried himself well and with a kind of presence, so that he appeared larger than he actually was. His hair was of a gold that any society beauty might have given her eyes for, curling a little, and beautifully cut so that it always looked well arranged but not over carefully. It was the same with his clothes, so well tailored that they verged on dandyism, and yet worn with an air of unconcern that could only enhance the beautiful arrangement of the snowy necktie, the height of the starched collar, the glowing shine of the top-boots.

As if this were not enough, his face, particularly in profile, could almost have stood as a model for a Greek God, Apollo perhaps. He was fortunate that the eyebrows and lashes above his fine hazel eyes were of a darker shade than his hair, and his only flaw, if such a thing could be admitted, was in a certain lack of animation in the features, as if too wide a smile might mar the smoothness of the carefully shaved cheeks, or break the symmetry of the face. Nevertheless, he was generally admitted by men to be a dashed good fellow, since he rode well and had a couple of good hunters, while in the eyes of the ladies he was a paragon.

With easy assurance he made his way to Mary's side, and her erstwhile companion melted away, leaving the seat next to her empty for him to take. As he approached she felt a tingle run through her entire body, as if at some physical shock. She could hardly keep her eyes from his face—he seemed almost ringed with light, with a kind of supernatural radiance that held her spellbound. She held out her hand to him, and, if he kept it in his own for longer than a mere greeting necessitated, it could be seen as no more than an accompaniment to the words that naturally were the first that came to his lips.

"Miss Hadfield, you must allow me to express my deep sympathy at your recent sad loss."

His words were formal, but his voice was warmer and while his lips framed her surname his eyes called her Mary.

"Thank you, sir. It was naturally a shock, particularly to my poor father."

"Of course." Again, his look expressed to a nicety what his words could not acknowledge, which was the peculiarly awkward situation in which they were both placed. As the son of the next heir, the death of her brother could do him nothing but good. While he had never, perhaps, expected to be in such a position, it could not be denied that the future, for him, had taken a turn for the better as dramatically as her father's had done for the worse.

"What an impossible thing this is!" he exclaimed. "I cannot express my sorrow, without sounding completely insincere!"

"It is awkward," she admitted, pleased with his openness, "but less so than if we were meeting for the first time. That, indeed, would have been uncomfortable. But since we are already acquainted—"

"Acquainted!" His look spoke of a kind of playful hurt. "Acquainted! That is a very cold word, a very distant kind of word to use. I had hoped..."

He paused, looking at her warmly. Mary felt a pleasurable heat suffuse her face, an agreeable flutter of her spirits, and dropped her eyes.

"We have known each other for so short a time, Mr... Hallfield. What had you hoped?"

He glanced around, and spoke with a lowered voice.

"I had hoped that there was something warmer between us, than a mere acquaintanceship."

"Well, we are cousins, of course... though you do not choose to acknowledge it just now."

"Do you blame me for that? It is true that I feared to let the relationship be generally known, for your father has always been so very... but it is only natural that he should dislike me and my father, of course. I cannot blame him for that. I should not, perhaps, have come here at all. If it were not for one thing, I should say that I regret having done so. It was whim that led me here, and dare I say a certain curiosity? And now I am punished for it."

"Because you find yourself in an embarrassing position?"

"Because I have lost something, something very necessary to my happiness. Shall I tell you what I have lost, M... Miss Hadfield?"

This was moving rather more quickly than Mary had expected. She glanced round the room, to see if anyone marked them, and he was quick to interpret her look.

"I beg your pardon. I spoke more warmly than is allowable in an acquaintance." He gave her a quick sidelong glance, and she could not help smiling.

"How you do harp on that word! Of course, if we had been brought up knowing one another, as cousins, I should think of you as such, but, since we were not, it is difficult to know what our relationship is."

"Yet I am not the less your cousin, because our fathers were not friends. Indeed, one could say that it is our duty to heal the breach between them. There is, after all, a goodly precedent. What do you say to that?"

His manner was half playful, half serious. Mary hardly knew how to reply. If she should take up his allusion, as perhaps he intended, then she would be acknowledging that there might be, between them, a love that was more than cousinly. A few weeks ago she would not have hesitated, but would laughingly have hoped that she would come to a happier end than Shakespeare's star-crossed pair. Now, with the death of her brother having so unexpectedly changed their situations, she would do nothing that might appear to encourage him, to lead him into an outright declaration. If he had been merely an unknown and very attractive cousin, she might have done so. But as he was the next heir, after his father, to her own father's estate, her pride would not allow it.

"I would say that I hope I should always be ready to do my duty, sir," she said sedately, and as they were then interrupted he had perforce to be satisfied.

Though the days were beginning to draw out, the winter afternoons were still short, and Mary rose to take her leave not much more than twenty minutes later. Her father's strange behaviour regarding the sale of most of their horses had meant that she was very reluctant to ask for the carriage to be put to merely to bring her home, and she was resolved on walking. Since she was known to be an energetic person this occasioned little surprise to her hostess, and she was able to slip from the room without any fuss. She knew that her sisters, and their husbands, would frown to know that she intended to walk such a distance in the dusk, unattended, but comforted herself that nobody would know, and that she could hardly be in any danger in a place where every stone, almost, was a familiar friend.

Nevertheless, she walked briskly, a little concerned to find that the sky was less light than she had thought, and that a young moon was already clearly visible in the lucent blue. When she heard footsteps coming behind her, quite fast and heavy, she was a little alarmed, but determined not to show it. Without looking round she quickened her own pace, her anxious ears straining, and finding to her dismay that the other was also hurrying, and gaining on her. She cast a glance to either side. The road, no more than a small country lane, was quite deserted, and she knew only too well that she would pass no human habitation for at least half a mile, when she would come to the lodge gates of the Priory. She had no riding crop or stick with which to protect herself, and she doubted whether she had time to find anything by the roadside that would be strong enough to be a weapon.

She could feel her heart pounding in her throat. She found herself thinking of her new acquaintance, Lazarus Smith. How happy she would be to see his tall, broad-shouldered figure appear through the trees. How she would welcome the sound of his voice, uncouth though it might have appeared in a lady's drawing-room. The footsteps behind her were very close. She drew her breath to scream, determined at least that she would not give in quietly to her assailant, but before she could utter a sound heard her name called, urgently.

"Miss Hadfield! Cousin Mary! Do not be alarmed!"

She whirled around, the indrawn breath leaving her with a rush that made her head swim, for a moment. She gripped her hands together, waiting as he came up to her.

"Did I frighten you? I beg your pardon. I had no idea you would walk so fast! I wanted to accompany you home, at least to the gates. Surely you do not usually walk through the dark like this, alone?"

"Not as a general rule. I must admit I did not think it was as late or as dark as this. I—I did not wish to ask for the carriage, for Papa has sold most of the horses and I have nothing to ride or drive, just at present. But I often walk into the village on my own. I think nothing of it."

"It is hardly right, but I do not complain, since it gives me a chance to speak to you." He stood beside her, head elegantly bent, neither his dress nor his hair at all disturbed by his haste, and offered his arm with a courtly gesture. She laid the tips of her gloved fingers on it, and could have laughed at the difference from the protector she had been imagining. Mr. Smith, if that was indeed his name, would have been more likely to scoop her up on to his horse, she thought, or grasp her under his arm.

Her cousin Jason, however, did neither, but paced decorously beside her. She cast a sideways glance at him. His handsome profile, seen to great advantage against the glowing sky, was thoughtful.

"I beg your pardon if I frightened you just now," he repeated.

"Oh, I was not very much alarmed," she prevaricated. "It was merely the surprise. If I had known you intended to walk with me, I should have waited."

"I thought it better," he said confidentially. "I thought you would prefer not to make any kind of talk. I know how these country villages are: the slightest rumour flies round like the wind."

"Thank you," she responded dubiously. "Though I think my credit is good enough for me not to be compromised by walking with the guest of my sister's godmother, for so short a time."

"Of course, of course!" he hastened to say. "Of your reputation there can be no doubt! But your situation, and indeed mine, is one of such peculiar delicacy. And nothing, to me, can be more important than your happiness and peace of mind!" He gave her a glowing look, and just pressed the fingers that lay on his arm with his other hand. If the look in his eyes was a shade calculating, Mary was not aware of it. Her eyes were bedazzled, her spirit englamoured by his presence.

"You are very kind," she said. "My fear is not of talk among my friends, who I am sure would say no harm of me, but of my father coming to hear of it. I know you are only too well aware of his unfortunate prejudice against your family. He is so—unwell at present that I should not wish to cause him further distress."

He looked serious.

"Ah, yes, your father. Not for the world would I want to give him cause to be vexed with you! If I thought that I might be the instrument of harming you, through him, I should leave here immediately, at whatever cost to my own feelings!"

She was bewildered.

"My father would be angry, certainly, but he would not harm me! I am past the age for nursery punishments, Cousin, and poor Papa would not think of lifting his hand against me!"

"Of course, of course, but you misunderstand me, Cousin Mary. I was referring to your future prospects!"

Mary was at a loss to comprehend him.

"My future prospects? What can you mean, Mr. Hadfield?"

He gave a little laugh.

"You are so delightfully innocent, my dear cousin! I mean, with regard to money! I know that you should receive a not inconsiderable sum, on your father's death. If he should be so angry with you as to deny you this security, I should never forgive myself. Never!"

Mary, who seldom gave much thought to such matters, laughed back to him.

"Then you may be easy! It is quite beyond his power to punish me in that way, even if he wanted to. The sum you refer to is settled on me by my mother's will. No, my fear is on his behalf, that I do not wish to add to his present misery."

He pressed her hand again, more warmly.

"My dear cousin," he sighed. "You are too good, too noble! Your duty to your father, of course, transcends all other duties, but can it be right to blight, perhaps for ever, the happiness of another? You must be aware—it cannot have escaped your notice—that my feelings towards you are very warm, very warm indeed? And I have dared to hope that you are not indifferent to me?"

Quite suddenly the conversation, which though personal had before seemed rather circumspect, had taken a direction that could lead to but one end. Mary knew that she should be flustered, that her heart should be thumping and full of joyful anticipation, and she was a little disappointed to find that she could listen quite calmly, and respond in an even voice. It was as if she were living a fairy-tale, and her life of late had been so prosaic that magic and romance seemed far removed from it.

"I could not be indifferent to my newly found cousin."

"Oh, Mary!" He stopped, and stood facing her. "If I could think that I might be more than a cousin to you! I can be silent no longer! Will you not make me the happiest of men, by saying that you will be mine?"

Mary looked up at him. The handsome face expressed everything that was proper to the moment: ardent affection, and hope, and perhaps a kind of certainty that her answer would be in the affirmative. Though this was not unexpected, and she had no grounds for maidenly dismay even had she been given to such coy behaviour, she felt a sudden reluctance to appear over-eager, as if the spell he cast over her might be broken by too close a contact.

"I do not wish to upset my father," she temporised. "Perhaps in a while..."

"In a while! My dearest Mary, can you find nothing kinder to say to me than that? Your father cannot harm you, and why should this news make him unhappy? Is it not the best thing that could have happened? His daughter, at least, will live in his ancestral home, his grandchildren will continue the Hadfield line! Surely, when his first shock is over, he will gain comfort from this?"

"You would think so, but Papa does not always see things as others do."

"Forget Papa. You have not yet given me your answer. Will you be my wife?"

Her pride made her wish to refuse him, the fear of looking as though she married him so that she would not lose her home, but the glamour of his presence was stronger than pride, and she could not say no. She nodded her assent.

"My dearest!" He raised her hand to his lips, but through her kid glove she felt only the pressure of his lips, not their warmth. She gave a little shiver, and he was all contrition.

"You are cold! I am much at fault, keeping you standing here in the dark! God forbid that you should take any harm from it! Come, we will walk on. I can hardly find words to tell you how happy I am! Of course, we can scarcely be married for some months yet. Such a wedding as this will need careful planning, and there is your father to placate. Besides your mourning, of course. You would not wish to be married while you are in mourning."

Mary thought that her groom was not in a hurry to claim her, but reflected that it was just as well. It would give her time, at least, to try to teach her father to accept her marriage.

As they reached the lodge gates, he stopped again.

"It is better, perhaps, that I should not come to the house just yet. You are not afraid to go alone, from here?" He kissed her hand again and, when she raised her face, her brow, a chaste salute that she accepted with meekness.

"Farewell, dearest Mary. You have made me the happiest of men, and I know that I shall be the happiest of husbands. I shall call, the day after tomorrow, to speak to your father, unless you send word that you do not think it advisable. Farewell!"

He was gone, his footsteps hurrying away down the darkening lane. Mary stood watching him for a moment, then turned to walk down the long drive. She was, she told herself, very happy. Her future was settled in the best, the most appropriate way possible. Her betrothed had expressed himself becomingly, had been fond without attempting to take advantage of their solitude, which showed that he was truly the gentleman, she decided firmly. And if, in his raptures, he had referred only to his own present and future happiness, and made no mention of hers, it was merely an oversight. The building was in view now, bulking huge and dark against the sky. Her home, past, present, and future. And it was merely because she was cold, and tired, that it assumed for a moment the appearance of a prison.

CHAPTER SIX

THE ELDERLY BUTLER was on the watch for her, and the front door was opened before Mary had so much as raised her hand to it. She would have given anything she possessed to have been able to creep in unseen through a side-door, to have made her way quietly to her own room and spend a solitary hour there, putting her thoughts in order. But she knew that Hampton would have been mortally offended had she done such a thing. It was his job, and his pride, to let her in, to exchange the sedate words that his exalted position in the household permitted, and she could not deprive him of this, particularly now when there were so few visitors to the house. She had been in charge of running the Priory for many years, and since her brother's death it seemed that the servants turned to her for orders and advice more, rather than less.

Now she laid aside bonnet and pelisse, and went straight to her father's room. As usual he lay curled up, turned away from the door, either asleep or feigning it. She tiptoed to the bedside.

"Papa? Are you awake, Papa?" She spoke low, in a voice that could not have disturbed him had he been truly asleep, and he gave a little moan.

"Now you have woken me! If you knew how I lay, night after night, never closing my eyes, you would not treat me so! But it is always the same. The young and healthy have no idea, no idea at all, of the sufferings that such a one as I must endure!"

"I beg your pardon, Papa. I did not mean to disturb you. Shall I go away?"

"And leave me all alone again? No one to talk to all afternoon, and now you cannot even spend a few minutes with your poor old father? Well, you must do as you please."

"So I shall," she said with an assumption of calm cheerfulness. "And what pleases me most is to sit here with you, and tell you all the village news, if you would like to hear it? And there is still some while before dinner, so perhaps we might drink a cup of tea together? It is so cold outside."

He grumbled a little at this, but when she had poured his tea just as he liked it, and plumped his pillows comfortably so that he might sit up to drink, he was a little less fractious. Mary told him such items of local news as she hoped might interest him, exerting herself to make them amusing. He would not laugh, but once or twice she thought he almost smiled, though he quickly hid behind his cup.

"Hmph. Servants' gossip," was all he said, but he did not stop her when she continued. The news of Buonaparte's escape interested him little. The wars, to him, had meant almost nothing, since they had never been a family with connections in the military or naval world, and his only worry was whether the price of corn would be affected. Mary knew an insane desire to blurt out the only real piece of news she had. What, she wondered, would be his reaction if she were boldly to announce that she had betrothed herself, not half an hour since, to the son of the man he hated most in the world? She looked at his face, which had grown so pale and bony, and thought that the shock might actually kill him. And yet he had to be told. He, of all people, must know of this change in her fortune. But how, and when? In which of his alternating states of mind would he best be able to hear her? The thought was so impossible that she half smiled to herself and shook her head a little.

"You're looking very cheerful, very pleased with yourself," her father grumbled. "Glad to have got away from me, to go out and enjoy yourself, I suppose."

As she protested against these unfair words, Mary thought how typical it was of him, who so rarely noticed anything about her state of mind or appearance at all that she could have grown a second head without exciting much remark from him, that he should see that little smile.

"I suppose I do feel more cheerful tonight, Papa," she admitted carefully. "Not that I want to be away from you, but it is pleasant to visit, and meet other people."

"Old tabbies in the village, and pert young chits! If that's your idea of visiting..."

"And gentlemen, too, Papa," she said carefully. He looked at her sharply.

"Gentlemen? The vicar, I suppose. And the general, perhaps? Pair of old fools."

She persevered.

"Younger gentlemen as well, Papa. Visitors, you know, from the houses."

He went white, and his voice was almost a scream.

"Young gentlemen? What do you mean, young gentlemen? Flirting, I suppose? Whispering and giggling and pressing hands! I won't have it! I won't have it, hear me? Hear me?"

"I do, Papa. Probably, the servants do. And possibly the village does, also."

"Don't be pert with me, miss. There's your poor brother, your poor dear brother, hardly cold in his grave, and you're carrying on like a... Well..." He paused, a little deterred by the flashing look she gave him. "Well, I do not find it proper, that is all."

"No, indeed, and nor should I, if I had in truth been behaving as you imply. But surely, Papa, you do not think I would be so lost to all sense of my position, as to be a vulgar flirt, now, or at any other time?"

"But you have just told me there were gentlemen there, have you not?"

"I certainly have, but I hope I am old enough, and sensible enough, to be able to carry on a rational conversation with any person, female or otherwise, without flirting."

He was soothed, and while it was not in him to apologise his anger subsided.

"Perhaps so. Perhaps so. You are not in your first season, after all," he murmured to himself.

"But not quite at my last prayers I hope, Papa," she teased him, hoping to cheer him. He scowled at her. "Come, Papa," she said coaxingly. "You would wish to see me suitably married, would you not? I thought that was every parent's wish?"

He looked at her in horror, as if she had proposed some vile act.

"Married? No. It cannot be. I will not permit it."

"But Papa—"

"Not another word." He was gabbling, almost cowering against the pillows. "I am ill," he gasped. "You have made me ill, with all this talk of marriage. I shall die, and yours will be the blame! Selfish, heartless girl!"

He did indeed look ill, his lips blue and trembling, his face livid. Mary started towards him.

"Keep back! Keep back!" he almost screeched, lifting the sheet to his face as if seeking its frail protection.

"But Papa, your cordial! Let me give you some of your cordial! Pray, Papa, do not look at me so! I do not want to hurt you!"

He was breathing in tearing, ragged gasps.

"No, no! Get away! Where is that man of mine? He will see to it. Ring the bell, and go!"

Puzzled and dismayed, Mary did as she was bidden. She waited outside his door, and was comforted when her father's servant came out a few minutes later to tell her that he had taken the cordial, was calmer, and a better colour.

"Leave him to me, Miss Mary," he said gently. "He'll soon be right, come you leave him be."

It was with relief that she approached the door of her apartment. It was, in fact, a self-contained suite of rooms at one end of the old wing, with an antechamber leading to two large rooms, connected by a smaller. In the past she and Martha had slept in the two bedrooms, for Martha's frequent attacks of pain had made her a restless sleeper, and she had been resolute in refusing to allow Mary's sleep to be broken by sharing a bed, or even a room. When Martha had died her sister had, at first, been unable to bring herself to alter her room, but after some months her habitual common sense had asserted itself, with the thought of how much Martha would have disliked to have her chambers kept as a shrine to her memory.

With some tears Mary had caused the bed to be removed, and with the addition of a small piano and a good-sized work table to the existing furniture had made herself a little sitting-room, where their books sat side by side on a broad bookshelf, some of their better attempts at water-colour sketching enlivened the walls, and their old dolls sat in a friendly row on the window-sill. It was in this peaceful haven that she was in the habit of passing her quiet hours, and now she breathed a little sigh of relief as she opened the door and saw the firelight gleaming on the familiar, if battered furniture.

Then a tall figure unfolded itself from the fireside chair, and the sigh caught in her throat as she stifled an involuntary scream. Never before had any man, even her brother or her father, made himself at home in this private sanctuary, and for half a minute she thought she had surprised a burglar. Then the figure turned his head, and she saw the silvery gleam of his scarred cheek. The relief was so great that her knees trembled, and she felt sharp needles of burning cold shoot up her back, and down her limbs so that she gave a shudder. At once he was beside her, one warm hand grasping hers and the other slipping round her waist to support her.

"I beg your pardon! I have startled you!"

"Well, yes, a little!" she admitted. "I had no idea...so few people ever come up here. I suppose Sarah brought you up? Where is she?"

"Looking for you, I imagine, to warn you of my presence. She must have missed you, and it is not difficult to see why. I never was in such a rabbit warren!"

"Yes, I know, it is a little—overweening." Mary became aware that her hand was still clasped in his, and that he held her in a warm, if passionless embrace. In confusion she almost snatched herself away, then tried to cover her abruptness by going to light the candles. She hoped that the warmth of the fire as she stooped to light a spill would account for the burning of her cheeks. "I cannot understand why she should have done so—brought you here, I mean. What was to stop you from calling, in the usual fashion, and having yourself announced?" Her voice sounded peevish to her own ears, and she was not altogether surprised when he replied with wry irony.

"Surely you have not forgotten that I have picked up the habit, abroad, of visiting ladies in their bedrooms? It was you yourself remarked on it, I believe. Of course, this is not quite your bedroom, but I do retain some vestige of correct behaviour, whatever you might think!"

Mary had been moving towards a chair, about to sit and invite him to do likewise, but this unwise speech brought her upright and bristling.

"How very unfair of you to throw my ill-considered words back at me! I think my brains must have been addled when I asked for your help!"

He saw that he had overstepped the mark, and was instantly contrite.

"Forgive me—I am afraid that I have lived too long out of civilised society and am become quite boorish. I meant no more than a jest, and I hope very much that you will still permit me to help you. It is my earnest wish to do so, if I may."

So handsome an apology made her ashamed, in her turn.

"No, no, it is you who must forgive me, for I knew very well that you were only joking. The truth is that I have had rather a difficult day." She suppressed a hysterical giggle at this choice of words. "Pray sit down, and let me ring for some refreshment."

He did as she asked, but lifted his hand in firm refusal of anything to drink.

"No, do not ring. Only your maid knows that I am here, and it might occasion some comment were the other servants to find out. For reasons which I cannot, at the moment, divulge, I feel that your father would not welcome me under his roof.''

"My father keeps to his room, and would not have been aware of your presence if you had been admitted and asked to speak to me.''

"I know, and for that reason I could not do so. I could not take advantage of his state of health by being accepted as an accredited visitor to this house.''

It seemed odd, to Mary, that his scruples did not appear to include his surreptitious entry into her private sitting-room, but long experience of the ways of gentlemen enabled her to be silent. It was, she reflected, one of those mysterious matters of honour, like duelling, or the sacred necessity to honour gaming debts, however dubious, that seemed to most women more akin to the barbaric superstitions of prehistoric tribes.

At that moment Sarah burst into the room, panting.

"Oh, Miss Mary! And to think I've been seeking you all over the house, and you in here already!''

"As you see, Sarah. I gather I have you to thank for Mr. Smith's presence in here?''

Her maid flushed a little, and bridled indignantly.

"Well, miss, I knew as you'd been worrying, the last few days, when you didn't get no answer to that letter you sent, so when he sent me in a message, private like, I thought it were for the best to bring him up here. For you'd not be wanting to go out in the dark and cold to talk to him, nor you wouldn't expect a gentleman to wait outside till morning, would you?''

"I wasn't worried, exactly,'' began Mary. "But never mind that now,'' she added hastily, seeing that Sarah was ready to argue the point, and noticing the gleam of amusement in her companion's eye. "Since he is here, it is better that no one should know. Will you make sure we are not interrupted?''

"Don't you worry, miss,'' was the hearty rejoinder. "I'll be in your room, and I'll keep the door open, so I'll hear if anyone comes. Or if you should need me," she added, with an admonishing glance at the gentleman that Mary, for one, thought rather belated.

"She makes a splendid conspirator, doesn't she?" he said as the door closed. "You are most fortunate in your maid."

"Yes." Now that he was here, lounging at his ease by her fireside, she hardly knew how to frame her request, and she wondered at her own temerity in writing to him. Of course, if she had known that her cousin was about to propose to her, she would not have done so. She could have asked Jason instead; after all, to whom should she turn if not to her intended husband? From him, at least, she should have no secrets, and he who would one day promise to love and to cherish her was surely the most proper person to help her now. And yet the thought of talking to him of her brother and his death was somehow distasteful, almost unthinkable, and she knew that she could never have asked him to find out the truth. The man now with her, uncouth though he might appear, whose true name she did not even know, still gave her a feeling of safety, of a security that was not stifling or over-protective, but made her feel at peace with the world.

She saw that he was smiling at her, with a warm look of kindly amusement and something else that made her blush and lower her eyes with the awareness that he had a tolerably good idea of what she was thinking.

"I should not have written to you," she murmured.

"Perhaps. But you did, and here I am. So you might as well tell me what is troubling you, and see if I can do anything about it. I make no promises, mind, but you know I'll do my best."

She knew that it was true. Haltingly at first, then with greater ease as her narrative progressed and he displayed neither surprise nor disgust, she recounted what she had been told of her brother's life and death, both by the rector and by her father. He listened intently, without interruption or exclamation.

"And so, you see, it seems possible, even likely, that his death was not natural. I never pretended to love him, any more than he did me, but he was my brother, after all, and his death has caused so much misery to my father! If it is true that he died by his own hand, I would rather know the truth than not, and if he were murdered..."

"Yes, what then? You wish the murderer brought to justice?"

"Yes, I suppose so," she said dubiously. "That is, of course such a person should not go unpunished. But there would have to be a trial, and I do not know if my poor father could bear it. I... oh, dear, I just don't know. But I want the truth."

"The truth can be an uncomfortable bedfellow," he said gently. "Your brother is in his grave, and no amount of knowledge of the manner of his death will bring him back. Would it not be easier and pleasanter to leave things as they are?"

"Yes, it would be. But I cannot do it, you see. Could you?"

"I think you know I could not, just as I knew you could not. But I had to ask, to be sure."

"Yes." There was a companionable silence, as the fire hissed and murmured in the grate. Presently he stirred.

"Well, if I am to find anything out I will not do it by sitting here. I had best be going."

"Just like that? Do you not want to know where he was living, who were his friends, those sort of things?"

"Do you know them?"

"Where he was living, of course. And some of his friends, although I think he only brought the more respectable of them here."

"Give me the address, then. The rest I can find for myself." He spoke with careless certainty, and Mary looked at him in wonder.

"You make it seem so easy. Have you, perhaps, done this kind of thing before?"

"Not precisely. But there have been times when I have needed to learn things, find things out, look for people..."

"And you will tell me what you discover? Whatever it might be?"

"You have my word on it," he promised soberly, rising to his feet. She followed suit, looking up at him in some embarrassment.

"You may be put to some considerable expense. Will you allow me—"

"No, I will not," he broke in roughly. "My dear girl," he continued in gentler tones, "there is no need. I am not a poor man. Many would say that I am rich. I dress like this, and stay at Runforth's inn, because it suits me to do so, not because I cannot afford anything better. And before you ask," he added with rough good humour, "it was *not* by stealing the Brighton bank's eight thousand pounds that I made my fortune!"

Scarlet in the face, Mary muttered an apology.

"No need to look so upset," he rallied her. "It takes more than that to offend me. Yet another example of the deplorable effects of living in the wilds, I'm afraid. Talking of money does not embarrass me at all these days."

"Well, why should it? I ought to be accustomed to it also, for my father speaks of scarcely anything else, on the days when he is well and gets up. He is for ever quizzing me over the household accounts."

His unorthodox entry into the house had given him a glimpse of the stables, empty and cold, and of rooms shrouded in holland covers, and tell-tale marks where pictures had vanished from the walls.

"Turned a shade miserly, has he?" he asked easily.

"I'm afraid he has. I think it is the shock of losing Giles."

"Very likely," he agreed, keeping his own counsel.

She held out her hand and he took it, drawing her nearer. In the dim light his eyes examined her face.

"You are very pale," he said abruptly, "and I believe that if I were to lift you up now there would be no weight to you at all, you are so thin. Have you been ill?"

He released her hand, and showed signs of intending to test his theory by putting it into practice, and Mary stepped back and took hold of his hands to prevent him.

"No! Yes!" she said disjointedly. "That is, no, I have not been ill, but, yes, I am thinner. I do not seem to have much appetite just now, and I have been worried about Papa."

"You should get out more, take more exercise."

"Yes, Doctor," she murmured meekly.

"I am not joking. It can be of no possible help to your father if you yourself fall ill. You must take more care of yourself." He spoke roughly, for he had been alarmed by what he had seen in her face. A little frown, more of perplexity than annoyance, creased her brow, and he put out gentle fingers and smoothed it away. Her lips trembled until she firmed them resolutely, and her eyes glistened with tears, but she would not lower her gaze. She blinked a few times, then gave a little smile.

"Good girl," he said encouragingly. It seemed only natural, then, to kiss her, and since she neither screamed nor repulsed him he bent and touched her lips with his own. It was a quick, passionless embrace such as he might have given to a child, but her lips were sweet and soft so he kissed her again, more firmly, and would have continued if her eyes had not suddenly flown open, while the hands that had, he was sure, been creeping up to his neck, turned and pushed him away.

"Oh!" Her eyes were round with horror. "How dreadful!"

"Was it? Not to me, I assure you."

"No, no, I mean how dreadful of me!"

"I don't think so. I should say the fault was entirely mine. I'm afraid I was carried away."

"Yes, that's the trouble, so was I. I have never been kissed before, and it was very...that is to say, I was taken by surprise!"

His eyes danced at this artless admission, but he managed to keep his expression becomingly sober, even contrite.

"Of course you were! Think no more about it. And if I should ever be inclined to do it again, I promise to warn you first."

"But you must not! Oh, you don't understand. I have behaved so very wrongly!"

He frowned.

"Surely you are being unnecessarily missish. What harm is there in so brief an embrace? Who has been hurt by it?"

"My—my betrothed!"

He looked at her, thunderstruck.

"Your betrothed? You are engaged, then? I had no idea."

She was annoyed by his surprise.

"Well, how should you? I have not seen you for more than a few minutes since I left the inn."

"I mean, it is not generally known? I think I must have heard of it otherwise. The marriage of Miss Hadfield of Hadfield Priory would be a fine piece of news round here. When did this happen?"

"This afternoon. And nobody knows, not even Papa. I should not really have told you, and I would not have done, if you had not kissed me."

"But you were with your father just now."

"Yes, I should have told him," she admitted. "But he finds the thought of my marriage very distressing. When I only said that I hoped to marry one day, he was so angry and upset that I was quite worried for him."

"Well, you have been his only remaining daughter for some while now. It is natural that he should wish to keep you with him." He spoke absently, not really thinking much of it, and Mary kept to herself the thought that her father's behaviour was far from that of a possessive, fond parent. "So, who is the fortunate man?"

"Why, the one of whom I spoke to you. My cousin, Jason Hadfield."

He had known it must be so, but his mind had not wished to draw the inference. Somehow, he had hoped that she had managed to meet some other eligible man, or even a wildly ineligible one, come to that. Anyone, rather than the man she meant.

"Yet you still ask me to run your errands for you? I suppose he is too fine for such work. Mr. Hadfield of Hadfield must not go grubbing around after the skeleton in the family closet." He spoke bitterly, out of a hurt that he scarcely comprehended.

"No, no! How can you say such a thing? It is only that when I wrote to you I had not seen him, did not know he was near or that I should ever even see him again. Then, when you were actually here, it seemed silly not to ask you."

"No wonder you wanted to pay me."

She only stared at him, astonished by his attack.

"You said . . . I thought you were my friend," she said at last, in a low, shaking voice that pierced through his anger and pain.

"Yes, I am. I am. Forgive me, I spoke harshly. Of course you were right to ask me. I had no right to question your actions or motives, no right at all. And it is much better that he should not know of it, if there should be any scandal. You may rely on me to hush it up."

"But . . . if it should prove to be murder?"

"You may safely leave me to deal with the murderer." He gave a wolfish grin, and she shivered. He looked at her, unsure whether he wanted to throttle the life out of her or snatch her up and carry her off with him by force. With an effort he made a formal bow.

"I will take my leave of you, madam. Accept my congratulations on your good fortune. You will have to change neither your name, nor your abode, I presume. A happy outcome, indeed."

His voice was cold and distant. Like a puppet whose strings had been suddenly relaxed, Mary bobbed an automatic curtsy in response to his bow.

"Thank you, Mr. Smith. I am very grateful for your help. You are angry with me, I know, but I turned to you as the one person who had offered to assist me. If I had had another brother—"

"Do not," he said between gritted teeth, "say that you will be a sister to me. A sister! Hah!" And with that he turned on his heel and left the room. While Sarah took him out of the building, Mary locked herself in her room, and celebrated the happy event of her engagement with a hearty burst of tears.

John "Lazarus" Smith rode off into the darkness of the winter night at a reckless speed which took no account of his own neck, or his horse's legs. He was furiously angry with Mary, and still more angry with himself, but he reserved the bitterest of his feelings for Jason Hadfield, the man who had once called him his brother. In his mind's eye he saw him as he had known him: a golden-haired child, so beautiful that it had been scarcely surprising that few people noticed the calculating look in those clear hazel eyes. The little events of their nursery days came back to him: spiteful, secret words and deeds that were never noticed or discovered. And this was the man to whom she had given her heart and hand.

Or had she? As his blood cooled, he reined in the horse and set his mind to work. That she would marry out of pure self-interest he could not believe, but it had to be admitted that, since the opportunity had presented itself, it was a most appropriate match. That she might be dazzled by his looks, as people had always been, was only too likely, and who should know better than his half-brother how much charm Jason Hadfield could put forth?

At the same time, it was unlikely that their relationship had progressed beyond the superficial level possible when all their meetings must, of necessity, be conducted beneath the public eye. That Jason had not kissed her she had herself confessed, and surely that was strange in a newly affianced couple? Nor had she discussed her problems with her lover, or asked for his help.

A little smile crossed his lips, and his anger drained away like dry sand through the fingers of a child. He acknowledged to himself, for the first time, that he had fallen irrevocably in love with his little cousin, and now he allowed himself to believe that she was not altogether lost to him.

Whether he should follow his biblical precedent, and return from the dead to claim his undoubted rights as the inheritor of Hadfield Priory, or whether he should keep to his original intention of allowing his family to think him dead, he had no idea. But come what might, he would do his best to win the daughter, if not the house.

CHAPTER SEVEN

MARY ATE her dinner in solitary state. She was thankful for
the dim lighting in the gloomy dining-room, where the
gleam of the candles seemed all but extinguished by the
dark, heavy curtains against the dark panelling. Her eyes felt
hot and prickly, her nose swollen and tender, and she pushed
the food round her plate without interest, making no more
than a show of eating. Her father, she was told, had refused all offers of food with loathing, and when she went to
his room afterwards she found him fallen into a restless
doze, which she thought a good thing. She sat with him for
a while, but since he did not wake she went thankfully to her
own bed.

Once there, however, tired though she felt, sleep evaded
her. Her whole body ached and that, coupled with the continuing congestion in her head brought on by weeping, made
her fear she might be coming down with a cold. In vain she
tried to fix her thoughts on cheerful subjects. Her wedding
day, which any young woman might be permitted to dream
of as a happy and exciting prospect, could scarcely be en-
visaged without a pang. How could she picture herself
floating up the aisle to a waiting Jason Hadfield, when cus-
tom decreed that she be accompanied on that triumphant
walk by her father? And, looking further ahead, the idea of
spending the rest of her life as the chatelaine of the Priory
seemed, that night at least, like a sentence of penal servi-
tude.

Then she tried to take her mind back to that happy moment when Jason Hadfield had proposed to her, but somehow the memory was overlaid by her more recent interview

with Mr. Smith, and its shocking conclusion. Try as she might, she could not summon up her beloved's face, and, though she could recall individual features such as hair, eyes, nose and mouth, she knew that were she to attempt a sketch of his face, as a heroine was required to do, she would be unable to produce any kind of recognisable likeness. Instead, Mr. Smith's sardonic face, cold and distant as she had seen it last, kept obtruding itself in her mind's eye, and the memory of his kiss, which should have been hateful, brought instead a kind of delightful shiver that made her feel that even her own body was betraying her.

At last she fell into a heavy, dreamless sleep, from which she dragged herself the following morning with as much difficulty as if it had been quicksand. The morning was grey, damp, and cold, and Sarah greeted her with a sniff and the unwelcome news that the kitchen range, always temperamental when the wind was in the east, had this morning refused to do more than smoulder, with the result that her washing water was tepid, and her breakfast very late. She paused outside her father's room, and his manservant came out to her, his pale face worried.

"He's passed a bad night, I fear," he said in response to her enquiry. "I'm not happy about him, Miss Mary."

"Should I send for the doctor?"

He frowned. "I don't know as it would help. He's not been eating or sleeping properly, but though that weakens him it's not really the problem, to my way of thinking. It seems to me he's something on his mind, something bothering him."

"Oh, dear, yes. Shall I come in and sit with him?"

He looked doubtful.

"I suppose so, miss. He's in a strange sort of mood, though. Not like usual, not at all, and that's what worries me."

"I shall send for the doctor, then," said Mary decisively. "He may at least be able to prescribe something to quiet him. Then I'll come and see him." She correctly interpreted the servant's look. "Don't worry, I shall do my best not to upset him, and if it worries him to have me there I shall go."

She found her father, as often before, huddled in his bed with his face firmly turned away, as if denying the reality of the world around him.

"Papa?" she whispered. "How are you today, Papa? I hope you are better?"

"I shall never be better," he muttered. "Never, in this world." The fact that he did not rail, or complain, or shout at her, was worrying and made her thankful that she had sent for the doctor.

"Come now, Papa," she said in rallying tones, "you must not speak like this. If you will only take some nourishment, and perhaps let the doctor give you something to soothe you, so that you can sleep..."

"Nothing can soothe an unquiet mind," he said, so low that she had to strain to hear him.

"I know," she said sadly. She stroked his hand where it lay on the sheet, but he took it away, as if her touch was painful to him.

"I have not been a good father to you," he said at last, after a long silence. Mary looked at him in amazement. Never, in all her years, had she known her father to blame himself for anything. Other people, often. His wife, his children—not including Giles, of course—the servants, the King and his court, everybody she knew had at some time or other been held responsible for some ill or slight, real or imaginary. But that he himself—and his son—was without fault was the *sine qua non* of his existence.

"Papa, how can you say so? I have always had every comfort, every luxury, even! My friends have often envied your liberality." And she had envied them, too, for the affection their parents showed them, though she never blamed him for that. She had had her sisters, and especially Martha, and though she had missed a mother's love she had never expected to be loved by her father, who had never shown more than tepid approval for any of his daughters. It was useless, however, to blame him for a lack that he was constitutionally unable to remedy, and, though she had often been saddened by it, it had not embittered her.

"Not a good father," he repeated dismally, shaking his head.

"But we all understood, Papa," she said earnestly. "My sisters and I, we knew that you could not love us as well as Giles. Perhaps, if he had been born first...but you must not blame yourself."

He looked at her blankly, as if she spoke in some unfamiliar language that had no meaning for him. Then he turned away from her, with a gesture of dismissal. She waited for a while in silence, but he had closed his eyes and was either asleep or wishing to be thought so. Worried and distressed, she left the room.

Outside, on the landing, she found the butler hovering. If she had not had so much on her mind she would have wondered why he had come himself, instead of sending a footman, but as it was she even failed to notice his air of scarcely veiled excitement.

"A gentleman to see you, Miss Mary. A Mr. Smith. I've put him in the morning-room, as there's no fire lit in the library."

"Mr. Smith? How very odd, I thought that he...that is, thank you, Hampton. I shall be down directly."

"Shall I bring the Madeira, miss?"

He was, she saw, delighted by this small return to the old days when the house was often full of visitors.

"Oh, yes. Thank you, Hampton."

"I shall bring it myself, miss," he said with a conspiratorial smile. It seemed strange, for not only had Mr. Smith declared that he would not call formally in a house where he had reason to think that he would not be welcomed by his host, but his appearance and even his manners did not seem of a kind to endear him to the old-fashioned butler. However, she supposed that the servant hoped for some little romance to brighten the house and bring a little pleasurable excitement to the servants' hall, though of course nothing could have been further from the truth.

Nevertheless, she took the time to return to her room. Her gown of white cambric had seen better days and was limp with much washing, but there was no time to change it, so it would have to do, and it was at least clean and neat. Her hair she had arranged herself in a simple knot, and she smoothed it hastily, before dabbing her eyes and nose with cold water in an attempt to tone down their puffy appearance. She tried out several expressions in the glass, but the smile looked toothy and a little mad, while the severe look only made her look bad-tempered. She rubbed her cheeks and bit her lips, to get rid of some of the pallor he had complained of, and ran downstairs.

As she opened the door of the morning-room her visitor was standing with his back to her, looking out into the garden. The room was very dark, for the ivy that grew over the back of the house had been allowed to encroach over the outside of the window, and no candles had been lit to counteract the greyness of the day. She could scarcely see more of him than a dark silhouette.

"Mr. Smith! I did not think to see you today!"

He turned, and displayed, not the scarred and sardonic face of last night's visitor, but the handsome aquiline features of her betrothed. At once she wondered why she had not realised before. It was true that, with the grey light dimming the gold of his hair, his figure from the back did have a disturbing similarity to "Lazarus's," perhaps in the set of the head, or even just the stance. Now, of course, she saw that he was shorter by several inches, dressed with his usual exquisite care, and could not have been more unlike him.

"Not see me today? How could you say such a thing, when you made me the happiest of men only yesterday!" He came forward and saluted her gracefully, bowing over her hand as he kissed it, then pressing his lips to her brow. If it was not the most passionate of embraces it was certainly performed with elegance and propriety, and since Hampton entered only a moment later with the Madeira she thought it fortunate that he had not attempted anything more lover-like. After all, she scolded herself, he could not possibly know how much she disliked to be kissed thus, nor that it reminded her unpleasantly of the rector.

Any further conversation was restricted to conventional inanities until the wine had been lovingly poured, the plate of biscuits and the more old-fashioned cake had been offered and partaken of. Mary saw, now, why Hampton had displayed such avuncular approval of her visitor, and she stifled a smile to see the older man's pleasure that she had so personable and fashionable a gentleman calling on her. At last he withdrew, closing the door with discreet firmness behind him, and she felt quite sure that he would station himself near by, far enough away that he could not be suspected of eavesdropping, but near enough to be of use if needed, and to prevent the entry of any less exalted servants into their privacy.

"How clever of you to guess that it was I," remarked Jason Hadfield easily when they were alone. "It was not, I fear, an imaginative choice of name, but I thought that to call myself even Hallfield might raise some conjecture or suspicion among the servants."

"Oh . . . yes, that was very wise," she responded disjointedly. "Of course, Smith is the name one always thinks of, when disguising oneself. Not that I have ever done so, naturally, but still...it is rather awkward for you, coming here when Papa is so...but I am very pleased to see you. Delighted," she added, fearing that her former phrase had sounded a little tepid.

"And I you." He turned his glass slowly in his hand, and the tawny liquid caught red sparks from the fire. "You have not told your father of our intentions?"

"No. I should have done, of course, but I knew how angry he would be."

"It is a pity he is so set against my family. It is not my fault, I think, that my father is his heir! And then, surely our marriage is a very suitable one. After all, you will be able to stay in your home, your money will stay in the family—one would have expected him to be delighted. And from your point of view you are better off, for if your brother had married you might very well have taken a dislike to his wife, or she to you! These things happen, you know.''

''Yes.'' It all sounded very depressing, but true. She could not imagine feeling happy with any girl mercenary enough, or silly enough, to have married Giles.

''I hope you do not think,'' she said in some discomfort, ''that I would marry you for such reasons? I could never marry someone I did not love, merely out of self-interest.''

''Of course, of course, it goes without saying.'' He waved his hand dismissively. ''All I mean is that our match ought to please your father. Otherwise, what is to be done? Will he ever give his consent, or must we wait until he dies?''

''He will never give his consent.'' She could not bring herself to mention the other choice. It seemed too much like wishing her father dead.

''Then what are we to do? If we may not marry, may not even let our engagement be known...''

''I do not know,'' she said miserably. ''We must wait, I suppose. My father is not well, at present. The shock of my brother's death has been too much for him.''

''But he may well recover.''

''So I hope. That is what I meant—that he might be well enough to see things in a more reasonable light, or at least so that I need not fear that a second shock might kill him.''

''Of course, of course. But meanwhile, must we be condemned to use our youth in waiting? My dear Mary, another course is open to us. We are both of age, after all. You may marry without your parent's consent. A special licence is not so hard to procure.''

''You mean... elope?'' Shocked, she stared at him.

''Do not be imagining anything too terrible! I do not speak of a flight to Scotland through snow and hail, with your outraged relatives in hot pursuit, so that we may take part in some barbaric ritual over the anvil! Merely, that I could procure a special licence in London, and that we might be married there, quite quietly and respectably. It is not so far away; after all, you need only leave him for a few

days, and say that you need to see the dentist, or your mo-
diste, or something.''

"But my father! The shock would be even greater than if
I were to tell him we are engaged! I could not do it.''

"You need not tell him.''

"Not tell him? Whatever can you mean? I cannot disappear without leaving him word!''

He rose to his feet and came to her, kneeling gracefully
beside her and taking her hand into his own. His handsome
face was raised to hers, his hazel eyes clear as water as they
looked earnestly into her own. The familiar glamour of his
presence stole over her, she was dazzled by him, her mind
distracted from other memories and thoughts. She could
smell the delicate scent of his pomade, and his handsome
face was shaved to such perfection that his skin looked as
smooth and soft as her own. Without knowing what she did
she raised her free hand to her lips, feeling the slight sore-
ness round them from the rougher skin that she had felt the
night before.

"I want to know that you are mine.'' His voice was low
and impassioned. "I want to be sure of you, and what other
way is there than this? I will not take you away from your
father: once we are safely wed, you may return here and stay
with him as if nothing has happened. He need never know,
you see. His last days may be peaceful and happy with you
at his side. And when he dies, then I will claim you for my
own!''

"You mean we should not live together?'' She blushed a
little as she spoke.

"Oh, not all the time. But I could visit you, in secret! This
is a huge place, and there seem to be very few servants.
Surely we could find a way!''

"But if I should become . . . oh, it is not possible. Only
think of the scandal! I should never be forgiven.''

"As the mistress of Hadfield Priory, I think you would
find that much would be forgiven you that would not be allowable in lesser women,'' he said, shrewdly cynical. "But

it would perhaps be better if we did not…stay together. But we must still be wed! You must be my own wife!''

"It seems very strange.'' Mary looked at him dubiously, not knowing how to express what she felt. "I mean, forgive me, but I hardly see the point of it! We should be husband and wife in name only, surely. What difference would it make? We could just as well wait, and then be married properly.''

He half turned from her, his handsome profile like a Roman coin against the dim light of the window. His voice was severe, wounded.

"Of course, I know that all girls want to have a lot of fuss at their wedding. Fine clothes, and a bevy of bridesmaids, and a breakfast. You must not think that I do not want that for you, also, but in the circumstances I had not thought that you would set so much store by such trumpery.''

"No, no!'' she cried, stung by his unfairness. "It is no such thing! That kind of display holds no pleasures for me, and I would willingly forgo them even if it were possible to have a big society wedding just now! You must not think it is that.''

"What else can I think?'' he asked in wounded tones. "You do not want a quiet, simple, private wedding. You just said that you could not see the point of it.''

"Oh, dear!'' Mary put her hand tentatively on his arm but, feeling his lack of response, withdrew it again. "Please, Jason, let us not quarrel over this! Of course I want to be married to you, as soon as possible! How can you doubt it? If you think it best that we should do as you suggest, then so be it. I am afraid that I sometimes worry too much about what others may think, but what does it matter, after all?''

She was rewarded with a brilliant smile, and he turned back to her once again.

"I knew you would see it my way, once you had thought about it! Dear Mary, it is only that I want to know that you are mine! An engagement that is known only to us two is after all scarcely binding.''

Mary was so relieved that all was well again between them that she did not allow herself to dwell on the fact that he did not appear to trust her. She did think fleetingly that she would have considered herself bound to him just as firmly by her word, once given, as if she had a diamond ring and a paragraph in the *Gazette*, but decided that it was really very flattering that her cousin was so eager to tie the knot between them.

"I cannot leave my father just at present," she said. "I have already sent for the doctor, and I do not think he will be well enough to be left for some days. You would not wish me, I am sure, to excite too much comment in the neighbourhood by taking myself on a shopping expedition when my father is ill! In any case, I suppose it will take some time to get the special licence, and make the arrangements. I am afraid I do not know much about such things."

"Nor I—believe it or not! But I shall make it my business to find out. I shall do myself the honour of calling on you tomorrow morning, for I may not leave my hosts too abruptly, but when I have done that I shall go to London directly. I suppose I may write to you here? Send me word when you think you may safely leave the Priory, and I shall be waiting for you."

Rather breathlessly Mary agreed, and her lover rose to take his leave. Once again he bowed over her hand, and this time Mary, blushing a little to find herself so forward, raised her face to his kiss. He seemed a little disconcerted, having expected to salute her brow again, to find her offering her lips, and there was a small, but perceptible hesitation before he touched his lips to hers. Scarcely had she felt their pressure than they were gone, but Mary would not allow herself to acknowledge any disappointment. His manners were most correct, and it was surely only uncouth men like Mr. Smith who seized one in their arms and almost crushed one with the strength of their embrace.

Mary rang the bell, and when Hampton appeared she bade her caller farewell with great correctness under his beaming and avuncular regard, then took herself up to her apartments in the hope of finding a few moments of solitude in which to explore her feelings, and enjoy the happiness which she knew she should be experiencing, and which surely would well up in her when she had freedom to give it rein. Sarah, however, was waiting for her, and insisted on knowing the identity of the visitor.

"Mr. Hallfield? That danced with you at the Fordcombes' ball? What ever did he want?"

"Why should he want anything? It was merely a visit of form," prevaricated Mary.

"That's as may be. You want to be careful, Miss Mary. A girl like you, in your position, with no brother and her father too ill to protect her; it doesn't do to make talk."

"Sarah! When you yourself brought Mr. Smith up here, to my own private sitting-room, only last night! If that wouldn't make talk, I should like to know what would!" Mary was well aware of the relative merits of attack and defence, and knew also that she would need a good strategy to mislead someone who knew her, probably, better than anyone else in the world.

"That was different," dismissed her maid loftily. "You asked him to help you, didn't you? Besides, you know you can trust him, though he may go round the countryside calling himself Smith. I know a gentleman when I see one."

"Merely because he happened to be handy when our coach overturned! Granted, I suppose he could have ridden off in the opposite direction, or stolen my jewels and ravished us both, but the fact that he helped us then does not turn him into an angel!"

"Did I say it did? I hope I should have more respect than to compare a mortal man to one of God's holy messengers," responded Sarah sanctimoniously. "All I say is, he's a good man."

"But I didn't say he wasn't!" Not for the first time, Mary was finding her maid exasperating. "Only why should you think Mr. Hallfield is not?"

"Why should he come calling, and give his name as Smith?" asked Sarah suspiciously. "You can't tell me that's the conduct of a gentleman."

"He had an excellent reason for that, which I do not propose to discuss with you," Mary said with an attempt at firmness. "You may take it from me that Mr. Hallfield is a perfect gentleman, and I suggest that if you cannot find anything good to say about him you keep your own counsel. Better still, try to get accustomed to the idea of liking him."

In her irritation she had said more than she had intended, and Sarah stared at her round-eyed.

"Oh, never say he's spoken! Never say that, my chick!"

"Well, I didn't say it," Mary pointed out reasonably.

"Oh, my lamb! To think that there I was thinking...well, no more of that, though you did write him a letter! My dear, dear child! I'm sure I hope he's the finest gentleman in the kingdom, for you certainly deserve it!" Sarah gathered her nurseling to her bosom, and shed tears, while Mary resigned herself. "But what do you know of him? Not that I mean to speak a word against him, and I'm sure any friend of the Fordcombes...but still, you've known him such a short time! What of his family! Is he rich?"

"I really do not know how rich he is, but I do know that he has...expectations."

"Well, so I should hope. I'd not see you tied to a fortune-hunter, if I had any say in the matter."

"I am not that rich, Sarah."

"But not that poor either," responded her maid shrewdly. "And now you have poor dear Miss Martha's money as well, it's a tidy sum, when all's said and done. There's many a man would think himself lucky to line his pockets with that."

"I think you may take it from me that Mr. Hallfield is in a position that precludes any mercenary interest. Oh, Sarah, I wish you would stop carping! I have no one else in the world to tell, for my father is unwell and finds the thought of my marrying so distressing that I may not even tell him!"

"Ah, my poor little love! Of course I am happy for you, as happy as you are for yourself! And I ask your pardon if I seemed to say otherwise. Oh, what fun we'll have, planning your wedding! That'll brighten the house up, and no mistake! Surely Mr. Hadfield will be better soon, and then he'll be happy, too!"

Mary agreed, but her maid's speech banished any pleasure she might have been feeling and her doubts, which she had succeeded in banishing, returned. Her spirits were not raised by the doctor's visit, for after examining the patient he came out of the bedroom and shook his head at the waiting Mary.

"I can't say that I'm easy about him," he said in low tones. "There's no single condition that I can put my finger on. His pulse is moderately even and strong, his temperature normal, but I am not happy. There is a debility, a degree of depression, that worries me. I fear that he could think himself into death, if that does not sound too fanciful."

Mary sighed.

"I know just what you mean. He has always been liable to periods of melancholy, but this is not the same. He is so quiet, so gentle! I do not wish to sound undutiful, but it is so unlike him! I do not know what to do."

"I have left some stimulant cordial, but other than that we can only trust to time that he will become more cheerful. Try to see that he eats, of course, and takes a little exercise, if he will. I will call again tomorrow."

He did so, and was encouraged to find his patient no worse, if no better. Mary listened to him only half distracted, for Jason had not yet paid his promised visit, and she was listening all the time for his arrival. At last Hampton came to her, but instead of announcing a caller he handed her a letter, offering it carefully on a silver salver.

"This has just arrived for you, miss," he said.

The handwriting was unfamiliar, and once alone in her sitting-room Mary skimmed it quickly, her heart sinking as

she did so. It was from Jason himself, informing her that
news had reached him of his own father's illness. He wrote:

It may be that it is no more than a false alarm, for he
has always been as strong as an ox, but I think it best
to go and see. My dear Mary will, I know, understand
and forgive my haste, for, the sooner I am gone, the
sooner I may return to London and pursue the matter
we spoke of. Therefore I will not do myself the honour
of calling on you today, as I had intended, but will, by
the time you read these words, be already on my way
home.

He finished with protestations that were very gratifying
to read, and seemed warmer than his behaviour the day before had been. Mary decided that in spite of his handsome
face he was perhaps a little shy, and her heart warmed at the
thought. She could not answer the letter, since he had omitted to give the address of his home and she knew only that
it was in Yorkshire, but the loving words that she soon knew
by heart cheered and comforted her through the days that
followed, when her father was querulous, irritable and
melancholic by turns, giving her tearful apologies and un-
merited scoldings almost in the same breath. To her anxious eyes he was thinner than ever, and his colour so bad at
times when he slept she could hardly tell whether he still
lived or not.

Nevertheless, he continued in life, and it was not he but
his hated heir, the man as strong as an ox, who breathed his
last barely a week later. Mary received a short letter informing her of the fact, and that her betrothed must therefore stay in Yorkshire to see to the obsequies. She went to
her bed that night knowing that she would, indeed, be marrying the next master of Hadfield Priory. The thought,
however, gave her little comfort or pleasure.

CHAPTER EIGHT

THE LETTER announcing the death of Jason's father was the culmination of a truly dismal week. Mary's worry over her father's health was exacerbated by loneliness, for Emily had a bad cold, and her prudent mother had confined her strictly to bed lest it turn to a putrid throat or, worse, a congestion in her lungs. The late Mr. McLaren had died of consumption, and his widow was in constant fear of the appearance of the dread disease in her only child. Mary longed for someone with whom to be able to discuss her doubts and fears, and never had the ills of her motherless state been so apparent to her.

With Jason so far away, and without the pleasure of his polished manners and handsome person, she found herself wondering whether she had not acted hastily in betrothing herself to a man she scarcely knew. That such doubts were normal in a prospective bride she knew, but it had to be admitted that even by the standards of a more formal age she had spent very little time in his company, and when she thought of their conversations it seemed to her that although she knew that he danced gracefully, and paid the most elegant compliments, his opinions and feelings about more serious and important subjects were a closed book to her.

Only one thing occurred to lighten the gloom of the passing days, but that was enough to afford her great pleasure. During the day after Jason's departure she had a message from the stables that was mysterious enough to send her hurrying there as soon as she was at liberty to leave her father. The groom, an elderly man with a face wrinkled like a

walnut and just as brown, led her in silence past a sad row
of empty stalls to one that was newly filled. A pretty chestnut mare turned her head from the manger of hay she was
lipping, and regarded them with an expression of gentle
pleasure in her liquid eyes. A good horse blanket, quite new,
was draped over the partition of the stall, plain but for the
letter "J" embroidered in one corner. Mary stepped forward and stroked the glossy neck, smooth and warm to the
touch, and the mare nuzzled at her hand, hoping for a tit-
bit.

"There, now, my pretty, if I had known you were here I
should not have come empty-handed! She is lovely, Studeley. Where has she come from? I did not know my father
had bought her."

"No more he did, Miss Mary," said the groom, his wiz-
ened face scowling, which was his way of expressing pleasure. "Master don't know nothing of her. Brought here this
very morning early, she was, and all the man would say was
that she was a gift for the young lady, from a friend, and
that you was to be sure to take her out every day, if the
weather allowed."

"A gift? But I cannot possibly accept anything so valuable!"

"Don't know as how you can refuse, 'less you know who
give you her."

"Of course I do not! At least..." She paused, blushing
slightly.

"Thought you might," said Studeley laconically. "Well,
miss, you know the saying about gift horses. Not that you'd
need to look in her mouth, with this one, for anyone with
half an eye can see she's a prime one, just what I'd have
picked myself for you."

"Yes, indeed, and so gentle. I know I ought not to, but
after all I do not really *know* who has given her to me, so I
cannot send her back, can I? I shall take her out today, after my father has taken his luncheon. He usually sleeps then
for an hour or two."

"I'll have her ready for you, miss."

"I think, perhaps, I shall not mention to my father that I have been given the mare. It might . . . worry him."

"That's right, Miss Mary. Time enough to tell him when he's up and about again. I shan't say nothing."

The mare proved to be as delightful to ride as she was to behold, with easy paces, a soft mouth, yet with a spark of fire in her that was often lacking in horses considered to be a suitable ride for a lady. Mary relished the freedom of being once more on horseback, the more so when she rode to visit a newly recovered Emily and found her and her mother busy with preparations to go to the seaside.

"I am quite well now, but Mama is still not easy in her mind, and I own I am excited at the prospect."

"Brighton, at this time of year? You will die of exposure, surely?"

"We are assured that the rooms are very warm, and sea air has always agreed with me. It will be like a holiday, only I shall be sorry to be away from you."

"And I! How I shall miss you! It is the greatest misfortune, just when I have the means to visit you more often!"

"The mare? She is very pretty, isn't she? A gift from your father?"

"A gift, yes, but not from my father. No, do not tease me! I may not tell you anything, and if you knew how I long to do so!"

Her friend contented herself with a speaking look, and a kiss. Now, as she cantered down a ride in the woods, Mary's thoughts were full of gratitude to the giver, whom she had longed to name to Emily. It was not, she thought, so difficult to guess who he was, for very few people knew of the state of the Priory stables. Mrs. McLaren, though she had frequently mourned the loss of her young friend's mount, and regretted the lack of such healthful exercise, could never have afforded such a generous gift, nor would she have made it in so secretive a fashion. No, the mare must of course have come from Jason, whose initial was on the blanket, and her heart warmed with this evidence of his kindness and thoughtfulness. He had remembered what she

had mentioned about the selling of the horses, and had sent
her a betrothal gift that she valued ten times more than the
more conventional jewels.

"And now I know what I shall call you," she said aloud
when she had slowed the mare to a walk. "You shall be
Jewel. Then you have your very own initial on the blanket.
How do you like that, Jewel?" The mare twitched one ear
back, and Mary gave the first spontaneous laugh that she
had given for days.

Thereafter she rode every day, usually at the same time
when her father had less need of her, and found that both
her health and her spirits benefited from the exercise, and
that she was better able to withstand the debilitating effects
of long hours with her demanding father in the stuffy air of
the sickroom.

The day after the arrival of Jason's letter she went out as
usual. The day was fine and mild, and Mary went further
than she generally did, through the new plantations and into
the older, wilder part where last year's bracken, dry and
brown, would soon be pushed aside by the tight-curled
fronds of this year's growth. Her father had seemed a little
stronger that morning, had eaten more breakfast than usual,
and she had been emboldened to tell him the news of his
heir's demise. Not much to her surprise, this had acted on
him like a tonic, so that he had sat up in his bed with a brisk
air, eyes sparkling with malicious pleasure, and talked with
something as near cheerfulness as one of his disposition
could achieve.

"So, he is dead! Older than I, of course, but I always
heard he was a coarse, robust sort of fellow. Always the
same, these tough yokel types! Think they're as strong as
horses, then pouff! The slightest thing knocks them down.
No resilience, do you see? No real fibre. All bluster and hot
air. And there's an end of all his bragging and boasting! Saw
himself as Hadfield of Hadfield Priory, but what is he now?
Cold clay."

"Now, Papa, you are unfair. I am sure he never expected
to inherit, or gave it the slightest thought."

"That's all you know, my girl. Wrote to me, he did, after your poor brother... Damned impudence. Cruel, heartless impudence."

"He wrote? I did not know."

"Not worth mentioning. Hypocritical stuff anyway, had the nerve to send his condolences! Said he was sorry to hear about Giles! Then, as if that wasn't enough, he had the audacity to suggest that since he would be inheriting the estate he should come and see it! Get to know the place! Coming to gloat, more like. I soon set him right, told him if he so much as set foot on my land before I was cold in my coffin I'd have him shot for trespass. Meant it, too!"

"But surely it would have been sensible, Papa? You could have taught him about the way you do things, introduced him to our people. I know it is hard to think of a stranger coming to make this his home, but then he would not have been so much of a stranger, would he? Still, as the poor man is dead now I suppose it would hardly have made any difference."

"Now I think of it, it wasn't he who wrote, but the son. Not the first one—he was hanged or transported or something disgraceful; he's been dead for years. No, this was the next one. Had some fanciful name—Ulysses or something."

"I fancy it is Jason that you mean, Papa. I have heard that is his name. Oh, then it is not too late! You might still write to him, and invite him to visit."

Her father glared at her as though she were proposing to wrap a large and venomous snake round his neck as a cravat.

"Invite him! Have him sniffing round here, pricing everything up, snooping into matters that don't concern him? Never! Over my dead... yes, well, suffice it to say that I utterly forbid it. He shall never set foot on my land while I am here to prevent him!"

Mary thought guiltily that the feet to which her father objected had not only pressed his land, but actually trodden across his threshold, and been made welcome in the morning-room. Certainly, she thought with a little sigh, this was hardly the moment to broach the subject of her engagement.

Her father, at least, appeared highly refreshed by this passage, and announced his intention of getting up for a while, and sitting in a chair. He spent what was, for him, a pleasant morning musing on the fact that justice had, for once, removed her blindfold and given his opponent what he deserved, and retired to bed after his luncheon, spiritually refreshed if physically tired. Once she was sure he was asleep Mary slipped to her room to change into her habit, then ran down to the stables where Studeley had Jewel saddled and ready for her. He deplored her habit of riding out alone, but since she had done so for many years he knew that there was no point in offering to accompany her, so he merely begged her not to go too far, and not to be putting the mare at every gate she came to.

It was therefore with more than her usual relief that Mary found herself alone in the forest. She should not, she was guiltily aware, have been riding there, for she was outside her father's land, but the chances of meeting anyone were so slight that she did not scruple to go against convention. She knew the paths and tracks as well as she did her own garden, and had no fear of losing her way, or of being troubled by footpads or gypsies, who would be unlikely to venture so far from roads or villages.

It was all the more of a shock, then, when a figure on a large black horse, muffled in a cloak and with a hat pulled well down over his face, stepped out into her tracks and stood blocking the way. She was moving at a brisk canter, so that she was obliged to rein in sharply to avoid colliding with him, and there was no time to pull up her mare short of him, while the path was too narrow for her to be able to turn quickly. So she made the best of a bad job, raised her chin, and spoke as imperiously as she knew how.

"Who are you? What do you want? Kindly move over, for my groom is behind me and will be here directly, and you are in our way."

At once he removed his hat, and the thin winter sunshine glinted on his dark hair. He smiled approvingly, the thin line of scar creasing his cheek.

"Bravo! Bravely spoken!"

"I might have known it would be you," she said bitterly.

"Well, yes, you might. Surely you want to hear whether I have learned anything, and what? I cannot forever be creeping up to your boudoir."

"It is not a boudoir, it is a sitting-room! You make it sound as though it were full of yapping pugs and lace cushions. And of course I do not want you in it. But nor do I want to be frightened half out of my wits when I take myself out for a solitary ride!"

"Solitary? What about your groom, or is he so far beneath you that he does not count as company? Where is he, by the way?"

"Nowhere, as you very well know. That was merely a pretence, when I thought you were dangerous."

"Not quite out of your wits, then. I should not care to meet you when you are fully in them."

"I hope I usually am. But you must stop this habit of appearing so suddenly, when I least expect it. I could have fainted, and broken my neck falling from my horse! You should be thankful that I have not even fallen into the vapours."

"Oh, I am, I am, believe me. But you have done neither, have you? Nor did you jab at your mare's mouth, which would have been almost as bad. I congratulate you; you are an excellent horsewoman."

"A compliment! I thank you, sir."

"Yes, and when you come to think of it, two compliments, for I took it for granted that you would behave as you did, like a woman of sense."

"I am overwhelmed."

"So I see. Now, if we have finished this delightful exchange, shall we ride on? You would not want your new mount to take cold, would you?"

"By no means. She is lovely, isn't she? I am so delighted with her. Her name is Jewel."

"An unexceptionable name. Why did you call her that?"

"Because she is a betrothal gift," she said with pretty modesty. "I had mentioned to—to Jason that my father had cleared the stables, and he must have remembered it, for the day after he left she arrived. Is that not delightful? So much more welcome than a pair of earrings, or a brooch, or even a ring, though I suppose I will have that by and by."

He looked grimly amused.

"Very possibly. And what did he say when you thanked him?"

"Nothing, for I have not been able to do so. I have not seen him since he was called away, naturally, and I foolishly never thought to ask his address, so I was not able to write to him. Then, when I did write in reply to his letter, it seemed hardly appropriate to mention it, for he had sent me sad news. You will not be aware of it, but his father has died, only a few days ago."

"I had heard." His voice was blank, almost dismissive, but she sensed that he was not as unmoved as he appeared.

"How strange! I myself only received the letter yesterday, and I would not have thought he was sufficiently well known for his death to be common knowledge in London. How did you come to learn of it?"

"Need you ask?" He raised a sardonic eyebrow. "Everything that concerns you, or your family, is of concern to me, since it might have some bearing on the matter you asked me to investigate. Naturally I have made it my business to find out as much as I could."

"Oh, my goodness, I was so distracted that I had quite forgotten! Tell me, have you learned anything? About my brother's death, I mean?"

"Yes." He looked down at her. They rode side by side, the narrowness of the path making it necessary that they should be almost touching, but his horse's height carried him far above her. His eyes were unreadable, fixed on her face. "Are you sure you want to hear what I have learned?"

"Yes. Quite sure." She wasted no time on protestations, but returned his look as steadily as she could, though her heart seemed to be beating in her throat. "Was he murdered?"

"No. At least...not murdered, in the sense that someone forced a fatal draught down his throat. That he did indeed kill himself, I have come to be as certain as one may be. But you yourself said that he was not the type of young man to commit such a deed, and everything that I have learned from those who knew him confirms your statement."

"Then what are you saying? He was not murdered, he was a suicide, but did not kill himself? I do not understand."

"I am sorry. I am not making myself at all clear. I am afraid there are matters here that are not easy to speak of to one of your sex, and gentle upbringing. I should say that, though your brother poisoned himself with opium by his own hand, and even with the knowledge of what he was doing, he was driven to that desperate act by someone else, on whose head the guilt of the death lies as firmly, to my way of thinking, as if he had stabbed him with a stiletto."

"But who? Who is this man?"

"That, I am afraid, I cannot tell you. I have not been able to learn his name, or anything about him."

"But how can this be? Surely my brother's friends must have known him, seen him, met him?"

"It seems not."

She reined in, and looked him earnestly in the face.

"Is this true? You are not saying it just to protect me? Or him?"

His eyes were unwontedly serious, devoid of their usual impudent twinkle.

"Quite true."

"But you said it was something difficult to explain to me. I wish you would try. I am not stupid, you know, and I do have some knowledge of the ways of the world. Also, you know that I had no love for my brother, nor any respect for him. It pains me to say it, but I do not think that I would be surprised by anything that you could tell me about him, though I might be shocked."

He continued to look at her, a questioning stare that she returned without flinching, then he sighed.

"Very well. But it is not a pretty tale, and I should have preferred not to sully your ears with it. I know that you had cause to dislike your brother, but still...I will tell you about it, as I learned it."

He encouraged his horse into a walk, and she followed suit, all her senses concentrated on what he would say.

"First of all I went, naturally, to your brother's friends, and talked to them, asking them everything I could think of. And then...I hunted for his lodgings," he said slowly.

"His lodgings? But surely Papa had opened the town house for him? I thought he was living there?"

"He had been, but some months ago he moved out, to all intents and purposes, returning to the house only occasionally, holding a card party there, entertainments of that sort. At first he would be away only for the night, and the servants thought little of it that a young man of his wealth and tastes should be absent once in a while. Then the disappearances became longer, until at last he had his things moved to these lodgings, the address of which he kept secret from your father's servants. When he returned to the house, it was on the day before he died, and it was the first time he had visited it for weeks. He only came back, I think, to die there. I do not suppose your father knew that he had moved out."

"No. He would surely have mentioned it. But I do not think he would have minded very much. I suppose he had a—a *chère amie*? And kept her there? Papa would not have been worried about that. He would probably have thought it a great joke."

"Possibly. That was certainly what I assumed to have been the case, but I was a little surprised when I found that none of your brother's friends knew of the address either, until I thought that perhaps the lady was not a...not a professional, but some respectably married woman whose identity had to be kept secret from her husband and from society.''

"That would be just like Giles," said Mary bitterly. "He was never in the slightest bit interested in the kind of girl who would have made a suitable wife for him, though Papa was almost desperate to see him married, with a nursery of his own."

"Understandably. It is a pity the young man was not more biddable, and there is not a little Giles to take the place that his father has left vacant. However, all I could then learn was that he would not be seen, sometimes for as much as a week at a time, and then only in gambling hells."

"Gambling? I did not know he cared for that. What of his poetry? Surely he was still writing?"

"It seems not. And during the last few months of his life he seems to have been betting heavily. Drinking heavily, too, and those of his friends who saw him said he was almost frantic with excitement, laughing to excess, secretive. I am afraid—" he glanced apologetically at her "—that none of them were sufficiently interested to find out what his secret was. He was no longer good company, you see."

"I knew some of those friends. Toadies, most of them, flattering him because he was rich. He was never any good at making friends, even at school."

"More than that I could not learn. And yet I was sure that if I could find the lodgings I must be able to discover more. I asked among all my acquaintance—some of them rather dubious, I am afraid—"

"I always said you were a smuggler!" Mary exclaimed with satisfaction.

"Well, I do know some, as surely you do, too, living in Sussex! And one of them gave me the name of a man he had heard of. A gentleman, as I suppose, but one who makes it his business to seek out information. He is known in all the best circles—you might meet him any evening at Almack's, or even at Carlton House—but he must have led a strange, chequered life, for what he does not know about the affairs of the underworld is nobody's business. He must have friends and spies everywhere, I should think. An interesting man; I liked him. Anyway, not to make too long a story of it, this man Forester agreed to find out what he could, for a fee, and I agreed.''

"For a fee? I thought you said he was a gentleman?''

He gave her an ironic look.

"Aye, so I did. But maybe I am not the best judge! To my way of thinking he was. He is educated, speaks well and with some wit, and I take him to be a man of honour. If he is not rich, how many gentlemen cannot say the same? He remedies it with the only skill he has, and all credit to him, say I!''

"I beg your pardon! I did not mean to criticise this paragon! And, I assume, he found the answer?''

"He did.'' He fell silent, staring at the ground. Mary waited in patience, aware that he did not want to continue and that no urging of hers would make him do so if he decided against it. "It was not a pretty tale,'' he said at last, low and reluctant. "Your brother had become entangled with a man—no one could say where they met, but it was almost certainly at the card tables somewhere. He...fascinated Giles. Under his influence he gambled more and more recklessly, losing money hand over fist, often to his new friend. He led your brother to drink more heavily, and to experiment with opium, not just in laudanum, but in other forms. Giles left the London house to be with this man, and took the lodgings, which I visited. The landlord was a surly fellow, who cared for nothing so long as his rent was paid regularly, but his wife had talked with your brother's friend. She, it was plain, had adored him, been fascinated by him almost as your brother was. She did not know his name, or rather she referred to him as 'Mr. Smith'...yes, I know,'' he added as she gave him an expressive glance. "There are altogether too many Mr. Smiths in our world, just at present.''

"More than you know,'' she murmured, "and I don't believe any of them were born to the name.''

He disregarded the dig, and continued, "Mr. Smith, she said was a fine young gentleman, a very fine gentleman indeed. Friendly and pleasant, and handsome as a god, as an angel, she said. That, of course, did not surprise me."

"Why?"

He looked down at her with exasperation tinged with pity.

"You have not understood, have you? When I said that our brother was obsessed with this man, that they stayed at the lodgings together, I meant that your original guess was not so far out. But it was not a *chère amie*, nor a well-born wife of another man, that was the secret he was hiding, but a more unnatural lover. A catamite, in fact."

"You mean that they...that he...? But how?" In her shock she spoke without thinking, and a flood of fiery red flowed over her face and body so that her very fingertips prickled with embarrassment at his amused glance. "No, no, pray do not tell me! I was merely... Good God, no wonder he kept it hidden! I did not know that such things happened! The ancient Greeks, of course, but that was then, not now, and I had always thought it no more than a kind of extreme form of friendship, not an actual..." The flood of words with which she attempted to cover her feelings dried up, and she turned her flaming face away from him.

"You see why I would have preferred not to tell you! Forgive me, my dear girl, and do not be distressed. I can imagine only too well what your feelings must be, and how you must be wishing me a thousand miles away! But if there be shame in such things, it is not for you to feel it, and I can assure you that I am very hard to shock! Such things happen in most societies, and often far worse. Young ladies like you are brought up to be pure and virtuous in thought and deed, and that is right for young girls. But you are old enough to be aware that our bodies may not always be ruled by our minds, and that there are in all of us darker feelings and passions that cannot always be denied. Your own purity is not sullied by speaking of such things."

The blood ebbed slowly from her face, and she drew a little hiccuping breath that was half a sob.

"Yes. I am afraid I am being missish. But it was a shock, you know. I could never have imagined that Giles...I mean, he never seemed at all...and then there were the housemaids!"

"It was not, probably, a settled inclination. Given time, no doubt he would have given up his illegal affair, and settled into a suitable marriage. From what I can learn of him, he was a seeker after novelty, after the pleasures of new sensations."

"Yes. My father denied him nothing, and from an early age his every whim was gratified. He loved excitement, and danger. I can see how he could have been tempted by so new and titillating an experience. But I cannot understand how he could have continued with it, and why he should have killed himself."

"As you say, such a young man would find it more and more difficult to satisfy his quest for a new pleasure. And this other man, with whom he became embroiled, obviously had the kind of charm that is almost irresistible to others. Your brother was certainly completely enthralled by him, and I imagine that if, later on, Giles had been rebuffed or taunted by him, it might have been enough to drive him to suicide. Such a thing, after all, had never happened to him before. And if, as I understand, he had been losing heavily at cards, it would be all the more reason."

Mary shivered. She still could not imagine the Giles that she had always known desperate and miserable enough to do so fearful a thing as to take his own life.

"It is pitiful," she said, low.

"Yes, it is. A weak character, led into darkness by one who appears to have been altogether callous and heartless."

His final word recalled Mary to herself, and to her duties. She glanced up at the band of sky that showed between the trees on either side of them.

"Good heavens, it must be very late! It will soon be dark. I must hurry back, or they will be sending out search par ties for me, and even alarming my father, if he should hear of it." She turned her horse, and he did likewise.

"I will accompany you to the border of your land." She did not answer, but kicked her horse to a canter, and heard the thud of hoofs as he rode after her. She reached the gate at a gallop and, knowing the ground well, put Jewel to it, exulting in the effortless surge as the mare responded and jumped, landing neatly. Glancing behind, she saw that he had not copied her, but sat like a statue on the further side, so that she was obliged to turn and trot back.

"I cannot stay! Will you not come back to the house?"

"No." It was a flat refusal that brooked no argument. "No, I will return to London."

"To London?" She was dismayed. "I thought you would stay at the inn for a few days. I wanted to... that is to say, surely I should reimburse you for the money you have spent on my behalf."

He grinned.

"Oh, I shall expect a full accounting, never fear. But my task is not finished yet. Only half the tale is told. I mean to find this man."

"Oh. Of course. I suppose you must."

"Do you not want to know who he is, why he did it, call him to account?"

"Yes, I suppose I do. Yes. Yes, of course it must be so. If he is guilty, he should not go unpunished. But... shall I see you again?"

"Of course. Did I not just say there must be an accounting between us?" He looked at her, the little frown of perplexity between her brows, underlip caught unthinkingly between her teeth. His voice was gentler.

"Do not distress yourself. Even if you had not wanted me to continue, I should have done so. It is not in my nature to leave such a thing half done. Go back to your home, Mistress of Hadfield. Maybe—who knows?—it may all be happily resolved. And if not, are we wrong to try? Trust me."

His hand stretched across the gate, and she leaned forward and put her own into it. Even through the leather of her glove she felt the warmth of his clasp, and the firm strength of his fingers comforted her. She smiled tremulously, withdrew her hand, and turned towards the Priory.

CHAPTER NINE

IT WAS with a feeling of unreality that Mary sat with her father, later that same day. Refreshed by his sleep, he was unwontedly alive, almost cheerful. His eyes, which had been as lifeless as those of a fish, snapped and sparkled, his thin wrinkled face seemed already fuller, the glow of the fire casting a spurious lustre of health over the yellowed parchment skin. He spoke of Giles, recounted tales of his childhood and school-days, as if he were not dead but away on some extended holiday, and Mary repressed a shudder. She tried to concentrate her mind on that little boy, but her memories of him at that time were so much at variance with those of her parent that she could think of nothing to say that would please him, and contented herself with smiles and nods.

This, however, was enough, and such was his flow of spirits that he ate a good dinner, taking a large portion of buttered crab and, when Mary was unwise enough to protest, demanding another spoonful.

"I do not know why you order such dishes, if I am not to be allowed to eat it! Since you know it is one of my favourites, I had assumed it to be a kind thought on your part, but I dare say that you had forgotten my partiality for crab! You will not grudge me so small a pleasure, I hope."

Mary forbode to mention that the last time he had been offered crab he had refused it with disgust, saying that shellfish in any form was far too indigestible, and asking whether she was trying to poison him. The crab, one of her own favourites, had in fact been sent up by Cook as a small treat for her, as had been the dish of damson tarts that was to follow.

"I am so glad that you have a good appetite this evening, Papa, and that you are enjoying the crab. I was only worried that it might be too rich for you, especially at this time of day."

"Nonsense," he said through a mouthful, a dribble of butter slipping down his chin in an unlovely manner. "I do not know why you must treat me like a baby. You will be feeding me pap out of a boat, if I am not careful." Another forkful went into his mouth, the pink-white shreds gleaming richly and fragrant with nutmeg. "Besides, the doctor said I was to eat anything that I could fancy."

There was no point in mentioning that the doctor had also prescribed a light, nourishing diet. Nor, later on, did Mary have any more success in preventing her father from taking his port.

"A good wine never hurt anyone," he pronounced, "and port is particularly strengthening. My father drank a bottle a day, as I have always done, and he lived to a ripe old age."

An attempt to dissuade him made him almost incoherent with rage, and Mary soon abandoned it, contenting herself with staying with him rather than withdrawing, as she usually did, to keep up the illusion of a formal dinner although he was eating it in bed. Over the wine he was increasingly loquacious, with a kind of frantic energy that began to frighten her. His words grew more and more wild, until it seemed that he was moving into some kind of fantasy landscape, woven out of his wishes and longings and desperation, a world where his son, still living, was dutiful and fond, where a golden future stretched ahead for all of them. Mary, lost in a blend of pity and distress, did all she could to calm him, and at length, to her relief, his wild speech became slower, and slurred, finally ceasing altogether as he sank into sleep.

She stood at his bedside, waiting to be sure that he would not jerk himself awake as he sometimes did. A snail track of spittle wound its way from the corner of his mouth, even in his sleep his face twitched, the lips moving convulsively round half-formed words, his breath moaning a little in his throat. With a kind of horror she thought of what she had learned, only a few hours before, about the last weeks and months of his adored son's life, and she prayed with a fervour she had not felt since Martha's final illness that the old man before her would never learn of it. Better, she now realised, that he should believe his son foully murdered than that he should know that the heir from whom he had hoped so much had died for love of a male whore.

Longing for solitude, she sent an unwilling Sarah to bed, saying that she would sit and read for a while. Alone, she laid down the book she had been sightlessly looking at, and pressed her fingers to throbbing temples. She wished, fleetingly, that she had not asked her unlikely acquaintance to make his enquiries. If only, she thought, she had been sensible and delayed her journey at East Grinstead, she would never have met him at all, and there would have been no one to ask. Or, which might have been worse, she would perhaps have asked Jason Hadfield, and then it would have been he, not Lazarus, who would have made the discoveries and reported them to her. Even alone, she felt her whole body flame with embarrassed horror at the thought of discussing such matters with the elegant beau who was her betrothed.

Exhausted, she dozed, waking with a start to find that the fire had died down and she was cold in her dress of fine white muslin. Sighing, she bent to untie the ribbons of her kid slippers, feeling the ache of tension in the muscles of her shoulder and neck. As quickly as tired limbs and mind would allow she slipped off gown, petticoats, chemise and stockings, and pulled on the lace-trimmed nightgown that Sarah had left warming by the fender. The bed was cold, but soft and welcoming, and Mary was just tying the strings of her nightcap before blowing out her candle when she heard rapid footsteps coming to her door, and a low, insistent rapping.

Huddling a shawl round her shoulders, she climbed wearily out of bed, calling an answer as she did so. The round, florid face of the housekeeper appeared in the opening, incongruously framed in voluminous goffered frills. Her habitual placid calm was overlaid with concern.

"Oh, miss, Johnson sent me to tell you he doesn't like the look of Master. He thinks Doctor should be sent for. Will you come and see?"

"Yes, of course." Her tiredness forgotten. Mary quickly put a warm robe over her nightgown, and thrust her feet into slippers. "But let us waste no time! Send someone for the doctor at once. If Johnson thinks it is necessary, then I am sure he is right, and every moment may be precious."

"Very good, Miss Mary."

"Don't wait for me. I have my candle already lit. Oh, I knew I should never have let him eat the crab, and take all that port!"

"Nobody could blame you for that, miss," retorted the housekeeper robustly. "Nobody that knew the master, that is."

"Thank you, but please do go and send one of the grooms for the doctor!" Mary kept her voice equable, but she could have screamed at the sight of the large figure in its ballooning night attire still hovering in the doorway.

"Yes, miss. At once, Miss Mary."

Johnson did not open the door to her hurried knock, and when she did so herself she could see why. He lifted worried eyes to her in muted appeal, and continued to hold down the writhing, thrashing figure of his master. With an exclamation of horror Mary ran forward and pulled the bell for help, then went swiftly to his side and added her own strength to his.

She would not have believed that her father's frail limbs could have so much strength. He fought to be free, mumbling incoherently, the only distinguishable words being "No, no," uttered in tones of such anguished pleading that Mary felt her throat tighten.

"Papa! Papa!" she cried out, and his eyes turned to her, but there was no recognition in their depths, and when a moment later his arm slipped from her grasp she received a buffet on the side of her head that made her skull seem to ring like a bell.

"Don't take on, miss." Johnson was breathless with exertion, but soothing. "He's dreaming, miss. I've seen him like this before, when he got over-excited or ate too much rich food. It's like a bad dream that he can't come out of."

"That crab!" she exclaimed in remorse. "I knew I should have stopped him."

"That, and the other news. But you've sent for the doctor, Miss Mary? He's never been as bad as this before. I feared he'd do himself some hurt, and when he does wake he'll be exhausted, as like as not."

"Can we do nothing to waken him? Cold water, perhaps, or smelling salts?"

"I daren't let go to fetch them, miss. When Mrs. Turvey comes back . . . ah, here she is." For all his attempt at calm, his voice betrayed relief at the sight of the housekeeper. "The smelling salts on the table there, if you please, ma'am, and then a towel dipped in cold water. Yes, hold them under his nose. That's the way. Now then, sir! Master! Mr. Hadfield!"

The ammonia salts were waved before the head that tossed feverishly from side to side. Mary could feel the fumes making her eyes water, and watched in hope to see her father come back to himself. The breath caught in his throat, and he coughed convulsively. Mary feared that he would choke.

"Mercy on us! He was never this bad when you first called me, Mr. Johnson!"

"No, or I should have asked you to stay. Now, the wet towel to his brow, and I hope that will calm him."

Certainly the body was quieter now, and Mary dared to relinquish her hold and take the towel from the housekeeper. Her father lay still, his eyes closed, with only the occasional shudder to show how his body had been racked before.

Then his hand came up, and weakly pushed at the cold towel that was dabbing his face. Mary dropped the towel on the floor, and took the hand in her own.

"Papa! Are you awake, Papa?"

His eyes opened slowly, looking at her first blankly, and then with recognition.

"Mary." His voice was fine as a thread.

"Yes, Papa, here I am. How do you feel, Papa? You have had a bad dream, I am afraid, and frightened us all."

"I am very ill, Mary. I am afraid I shall not be with you long."

"Come now, Papa!" Mary spoke in rallying tones, as she had so often done in the past when he had spoken these self-same words, but her heart misgave her at the look on his face. He turned away from her look.

"I am sorry, my child. Forgive me."

Now indeed a pang of terror shot through her.

"There is nothing to forgive, Papa," she said gently. He shook his head, but did not speak again, only sighing a few times. His hand was cold and still within hers, so cold and still that when the shallow breaths slowed and then ceased she could feel no difference, and she was still holding it when the doctor came into the room, interpreting at a glance the stricken faces of the servants, and the still form on the bed that Mary still watched in anxiety, though no ill could come to it now.

Later, in her room, Mary lay sleepless in her bed. Sarah had fussed over her, had brought warm drinks, and cold, a hot brick for the bed, sympathy, even tears. Now, to Mary's relief, she had gone, driven away by her charge's silence and her determined pretence of sleep. After the door closed behind her Mary let her eyes open, the effort of keeping them closed having been as great as the reverse effort required to keep open eyes that wanted to sleep.

She should, she knew, feel something. A dutiful daughter should feel, or at the very least show some semblance of, grief. Tears should be shed, quiet, broken words uttered. Poor Papa. So sudden. Such a shock. Not strong, of course. And then the distress of poor Giles ... The morning would come, and in the days to follow such phrases would be murmured, by her and others, as they moved through the prescribed patterns. But for now she need not pretend a grief she could not feel, and could even admit, guiltily, that her strongest emotion was simple relief.

Not that she would have wished her father dead. On the contrary, she would have gone to any lengths, braved any discomfort, if any effort of hers could have prolonged his life. But since it was not to be, how simple things now appeared! All her difficulties seemed to be melting like snow. Free of her father's prejudices, she might announce her betrothal to her cousin, knowing that her friends would be no more than pleased by so suitable a marriage. They must postpone the wedding, of course, for some months, but surely she would be able to continue living here, at the Priory, as she had always done? Even the revelations about her brother seemed less terrible than before. Her father could no longer be hurt by them, and if Lazarus did discover the name of the guilty man he would surely be able to devise some form of justice that would not involve them in scandal.

The following week was just as bad as she had known it would be. In hushed-voiced, mourning-clad huddles her relatives arrived. The only mitigating circumstance was the presence of Georgina and her new son, only a few weeks old but proclaiming his health lustily to all within earshot. His voice was loud, his utterances prolonged, but not so prolonged as those of his uncle the rector, who rendered the hours hideous with his pious platitudes and endless prayers, so that Mary was driven to hiding in her bedchamber and feigning indisposition. Once again the funeral cortège set out, with even more pomp than before and with slightly more sincerity among the mourners. Once again Mary insisted on being present, though her sisters stayed obediently at home, and was treated with offended forbearance by her priestly relative, who had a profound disapproval of any of the women connected with him behaving in so outlandish a fashion.

It seemed to Mary that the interval between Giles's funeral and her father's had shrunk to no more than moments when, as before, she slipped away from the rest of the party to lay her posy of flowers on Martha's grave. She could not help glancing at the churchyard wall, and it was without much surprise that she saw a dark figure waiting there. With so many people present, and feeling the rector's eyes fixed on her, she did not dare to approach him, but bent to rearrange, quite needlessly, the flowers she had brought.

He made her a slight, formal bow which she answered with an inclination of her head. He made no attempt to draw nearer, or to speak to her, but made a gesture of greeting and farewell, and turned to stride away. It was not much, but she felt both warmed and comforted that he had come. It would have been quite improper, of course, for Jason to have been present, as well as shockingly ill bred, but at least she felt that she had one friend to support her.

On her return to the Priory, she was drawn aside by an agitated Hampton. Refreshments were being served, and already a hum of the kind of relieved conversation that invariably followed a funeral was issuing from the saloon. Mary, bracing herself for some domestic crisis, like a burned cake or insufficient quantities of Madeira, found that her presence was requested by her father's man of business.

"Mr. Camden? Now? But surely that sort of thing is for later, when the guests have gone? I cannot leave them now."

"He was very insistent, miss. He says it is important that he should speak to you now, alone."

"Well, I suppose I could see him for a few minutes. My sisters are with the guests; I will not be missed. Where is he, in the library?"

"Begging your pardon, miss, but I have taken him up to your sitting-room. He said he must be quite private with you." Mary raised her eyebrows. Mr. Camden must indeed have been insistent if he had induced Hampton to take him to her private room, where only one other male visitor had ever set foot.

Upstairs, Mr. Camden greeted her with grave courtesy. She had known him all her life, though never well, and was surprised by his attitude of avuncular anxiety. Although he had been eager to speak to her, now that she was there he seemed to be at a loss to know what to say. Restraining her wish to be gone, Mary sat down with as much serenity as she could muster, and asked him to do likewise. He did so, but continued to utter platitudes.

"Mr. Camden, I understood that you had something very particular to say to me? If I am absent for too long my family and our guests will be offended. Pray tell me what it is you wish to say."

"You are in the right of it, Miss Hadfield. I am wrong to prevaricate, and yet…how hard it is to speak! I cannot hide from you that I have news to impart of the utmost seriousness. Indeed, I fear you must prepare yourself to hear something that I fear can only cause you distress! Miss Hadfield, are you aware of your brother's activities in the last months of his life?"

"Am I aware of—? Yes, Mr. Camden. I am sorry to say that I am." Mary stared at him in horror. Surely this dry, precise man, old enough to be her father, and with whom she had never exchanged more than the most formal of civilities, was not about to discuss with her Giles's unfortunate love-affair? If so, she could only be relieved that she knew of it already, and would be able to cut him short before his explanations went beyond the bounds of supportable embarrassment. She saw that he looked relieved.

"Then you will know, I suppose, that he had lost considerable sums at the gambling tables. Very considerable sums indeed! I do not know what led him to this—" Mary, at this point, relaxed a little "—for he had become so very secretive, and I learned only the other day that he had no longer been living in the London house, but had taken lodgings somewhere!"

"So I had heard," murmured Mary. Obviously the disclosures she had feared were not to be made.

"Then it seems that you know as much as, or more than I. But were you aware, Miss Hadfield, that his debts of honour were such that I was no longer able to find the money to cover them? That he came to your father for help?"

"No." Mary was puzzled now. "It must have been while I was staying with my sister, Lady Tarrant. I have not seen Giles for months."

He sprang to his feet as if unable to remain still, and commenced pacing up and down, his eyes on the floor. With an air of violent distress he said,

"Miss Hadfield—Miss Mary, the debts to which I allude were monstrous! What he could have been thinking of... But there is no good speaking this way. I must tell you, Miss Hadfield, that in order to meet them your father was forced to raise every penny he could muster. All the available funds, everything that was not strictly part of the entail, even a parcel of land that had been bought some years since—all disposed of. I was not, I need hardly say, a party to it. I was not consulted, though, in fairness, if I had been, it is difficult to know what I could have done."

"Good heavens! No wonder my father was in such distress, and behaved so oddly, after Giles died! I had no idea why he should sell all the horses, and be so quibbling about the household accounts. If only he had told me, I should not have minded his economics. I could have helped him, perhaps."

"If he did not mention it to you, it was because he was ashamed."

"Ashamed? Papa? Why should he be ashamed? His was not the fault, though I know he hated to think any ill of Giles. Was that why?"

The man of business gave a little groan, and ceased his pacing, coming to stand before her.

"You have not understood me, my poor dear child! When I said everything went that was not entailed, I meant absolutely everything. Including, of course, the money your mother left. The money that should have come to you. There is nothing left...nothing! You are—God help me that I must say it to you—you are penniless. And, unless the heir consents to help you, homeless as well."

There were actually tears in his eyes, and so strong was her urge to comfort him that Mary could scarcely take in what he had told her.

"You are kind to be so concerned for me, but please do not distress yourself! I am sure I shall be all right. There are my mother's jewels, after all. I should be loath to sell them, but they are of great value, and if need be..." Her voice tailed off as she saw that he was shaking his head sadly. "You mean...my father sold those, as well?" She was silent for a moment at this final blow, which hurt her more than the loss of the actual money. "No wonder he asked me to forgive him," she said bitterly.

"I begged him to warn you, when I came before, but he refused to speak to you of it, or to allow me to do so. My dear Miss Hadfield, you must believe that if I had known of his intentions I would have done everything in my power to prevent him. Everything!"

"I know. You are very kind. Dear Mr. Camden, your kindness induces me to confide in you that I am not quite friendless. Oh, I have my sisters, of course, and I know that they would offer me a home, reluctant though I would be to subsist on their charity. But I have hopes in another direction. Nothing has been announced, and I had not even mentioned it to my father, but there is a gentleman who has asked me to marry him. So you see I shall be well-provided for, and you need have no fears for me."

He looked at her sadly, then seated himself at her side and took her hand in his.

"I would be only too glad to know it, but my dear child—forgive me—you are young and perhaps not as wise in the ways of the world as you might be. It pains me to say it, but a man, and his family, may not view marriage to a young woman in your position in quite the same light as a connection formed with a young lady in possession of thirty thousand pounds. I hope, for your sake, that the gentleman is above such mercenary considerations, or at least that he is a man of honour who will stand by his word.''

"I should not dream of holding him to it, should he be reluctant," said Mary proudly.

"I know you would not. And if, as you say, nothing has been announced and nobody knows of this betrothal, it would scarcely be possible for you to do so. Ah, you think me cynical, but such things are not unknown."

Mary was not as worried as he. It did not seem to her that the heir to Hadfield Priory would need to marry money. However, she was as yet reluctant to let the name of her suitor be known, and she contented herself with vague and soothing protestations. He appeared somewhat comforted, and at last left her alone with her thoughts.

"I expect you will prefer to be by yourself for a while. I must, of course, go down and read the will—not that it is of any moment now, since there is no money to fulfil any of the bequests. I shall explain matters, with your permission, to Sir Anthony, and the rector."

The thought of the result of such an explanation made her shudder.

"Oh, yes, please do. And perhaps you would tell them that I would like to be alone, for a while? I shall stay up here, if they will make my apologies."

He assured her that, if he could do nothing else for her, he would see that she was left in peace. After he had gone Mary allowed herself the luxury of a few tears, not so much for the sake of what she had lost as for her father's betrayal.

When the door opened a few moments later she said, with an averted head, "I should like to be alone, if you please. I thought I had made that clear."

"Well, not to me. But I will go away if you want."

She whirled round, handkerchief still to the nose which she had been blowing.

"Mr. Smith! What on earth...? How did you get up here?"

"There are so many people around, it was not very difficult. And of course I knew the way already. I've been here for some time, waiting for you, but when I heard someone coming up, wheezing like a grampus, my needle-sharp mind told me it was not you, so I took myself off."

"Where were you?"

He had the grace to look abashed.

"In your bedchamber, as a matter of fact. No need to look so shocked! I can assure you I have seen far more shocking things in my time. I would, naturally, have waited in the dressing-room, but I found that the voices carried too clearly. I am not," he declared virtuously, "an eavesdropper, so I removed myself beyond another door. And now, the grampus having departed, I am here. Do you want me to leave you alone?"

"Yes! No. Oh, I don't know." She gave her nose a final scrub and raised her eyes to his, knowing that they were red-rimmed and puffy, and that her face was blotched and shiny with tears.

"Forgive me." His voice was gentle. "This is a sad day for you. I had not thought you would mourn your father so deeply. I will leave."

"No, no, it is not that. At least, of course I am sorry for him, but I am afraid I would be more likely to weep for his shortcomings than for his death. The truth is, I have just been told some distressing news, and it has overset me for the moment. I shall be quite all right presently."

"The grampus?" She nodded mutely, her eyes filling once again so that she rubbed them crossly with the damp handkerchief. "What did he say to make you unhappy?"

He looked so angry that she was driven to protest.

"It is not his fault! Indeed, he was in the greatest distress himself. But it seems that my brother's gambling debts were far greater than we had realised, and my father has sold everything to pay them. My mother's money, that should have come to me. And her jewels. Everything. And I wouldn't mind so much, only he didn't tell me." Her voice wobbled, and she firmed her lips, blinking hard and sniffing.

For about three seconds he successfully subdued the urge to take her in his arms, then he pulled her towards him and held her in an embrace that he told himself was no more than brotherly, while she leant thankfully against him and wept comfortably into his chest. His hands were warm and strong as he stroked her back, his voice tender as he murmured the little, loving words that he had not heard since his early childhood. When her sobs had subsided to the occasional hiccup he took out his handkerchief, and tactfully withdrew his arms while she mopped and blew again.

"Better now?" he enquired, as to a three-year-old.

"Yes, thank you." Her smile was tremulous, but unforced. "You are very kind. I am afraid you must think me very weak, and silly."

"It is bound to be a shock, learning that you are penniless. And then, of course, there is your betrothed to consider, and his feelings on the matter. Will he mind, do you suppose?"

"Of course not," she said stoutly, but her eyes did not meet his.

"Well, if he does, you had better marry me instead." His voice was so prosaic that she hardly knew whether she had heard him aright.

"Marry you? Are you proposing to me?"

"Oh, only as second-best, of course. I could not hope to compete with the handsome Mr. Jason Hadfield. But you did say, early in our acquaintance, that you would like to have adventures."

"And to be married to you would be an adventure?"

"I think so," he said with becoming modesty. "Of course, I would not dream of putting any pressure on you, but I would not like you to think you had no other alternative than living with your sisters, or being a governess, or some such nonsense."

"You are sorry for me." It was an accusation.

"No, no. At least, yes, but that is not why I asked you."

"Then why did you?" Her face, raised to his, was the reverse of flirtatious. She looked suspicious, even worried, and the little frown was back.

"I do not think I am going to tell you, just now," he said. Then he bent and kissed, not her lips, but the furrow between her brows, and was gone.

CHAPTER TEN

MARY MANAGED to avoid seeing any of her relatives that night, but she could not hide from them for ever. The following morning she steeled herself to go down to breakfast, where she found her two brothers-in-law and her sister Caroline. Georgina, of course, was still upstairs with her baby. There was a short, charged pause in the conversation when she entered, and, though both the rector and Sir Anthony rose to their feet and set her chair, neither of them met her glance, or looked at the other. Caroline busied herself feverishly at the urn.

"My dear Mary—" began the rector.

"Mary, my dear—" said Sir Anthony at the same moment. They glared at one another and Mary stifled a giggle. Both of them, obviously, felt the right and the need to settle her future for her, and neither would agree to give the other precedence. In most things, Sir Anthony would have given way to the claims of the Church, but his wife had not made the journey to Sussex with a new baby, she had informed him in the course of the night, so that poor Mary should be made into some kind of unpaid female curate in Caroline's chilly house.

Mary decided to follow both her inclination and the forms of precedence.

"I must thank you all for your support and assistance yesterday. Your address was most—most comforting, Rector. Sir Anthony, I hope you slept well? You wished to say something to me?"

"Yes, I did. As to sleep, I should have been all right if it were not for the confounded...that is to say, I do not know why Georgie must keep the little fellow in the dressing-room, and not in the nursery! However, that is by the way. I need hardly tell you how very shocked I was, Mary, by what Camden told us last evening. It is altogether disgraceful, and what my father-in-law was thinking of... however, *de mortuis* and all that. Anyway, I feel, and Georgie with me, of course, that it is up to the family to make some kind of reparation to you. I can't promise to make you as rich as you should have been, but a few thousand, at least, would give you some security." He blew his nose violently. "So there it is, and I don't know that we need speak of it again."

"Or at all! My dear brother," replied Mary in moved tones, "you are too good, too generous, but it is not to be thought of. That you, with all your dear family to bring up and establish in the world, should make such a sacrifice! No, it is not to be borne."

"I am bound to say," put in the rector, "that I think this offer, generous and Christian as it undoubtedly is, has been made too hastily, and without proper forethought. No one, my dear Mary, could esteem you more highly than I. My home is always open to you..." He paused, and Mary murmured her gratification. "And nothing could please me more than to see you find a refuge beneath my roof. But as to money... it is all very well, Sir Anthony, to speak of finding a few thousand, as if it were no more than a handful of sovereigns. You have your estates, your revenues..."

"As you have your tithes," put in Sir Anthony with a show of belligerence.

"Indeed I do, but I have expenses, my dear sir, expenses! A man in my position must uphold the honour of the Church, and the tithes I receive are for that purpose, not for me to give away to a relative, however deserving! If Mary came to us, she would want for nothing, as I hope she knows, and she would have the satisfaction of using her hands and her time in the service of her Creator. No godly household could do less, or, I think, more."

"If you can't spare her any money, fair enough, but what's to stop me doing it? And offering her a home, too, of course. I'll take another cup of coffee if you please, sister."

"Oh! Oh, yes!" Caroline had been watching the menfolk with an expression of avid horror, and since she regarded herself as no more than a spectator it was alarming to be addressed directly. However, since she had been noticed, she ventured to remark,

"If my brother Tarrant wishes to do this, Rector, and we in our turn give Mary a home, does that not make everything right?"

Sir Anthony gave a snort of derision or amusement, and Mary, who had continued calmly to eat her bread and butter, lifted her napkin to her lips to hide a smile. Though her sister might not see it, the world in general would certainly have something to say about so uneven a providing. While the rector was reluctant to part with money, he was equally reluctant to have it seen to be so.

"Really, my dear, you speak of things you do not understand." Caroline flushed, and shrank beneath the rector's look.

"It would be acceptable to me," interrupted Sir Anthony, "if it pleased Mary. But I should be still happier if she would make her home with us."

"You are both very kind." Mary thought it time that she brought their bickering to an end. "But I will say once and for all that I will not accept any money from either of you. As for where I am to live, it is too soon to make any such decision. We do not yet know the intentions of the heir."

Three faces were turned to her in silent amazement.

"The heir?" boomed the rector. "What has the heir to do with it? You can scarcely expect him to give you a home. Of course, if there had been a dower house . . . but there is not, and as for staying here with him, it is not to be thought of! Most improper! I know that you have always thought of the Priory as your home, but you must learn to see that its doors must forever be closed to you now."

"Nevertheless—" began Mary, but she was interrupted by Hampton, who trod to her side with a note on a salver.

"This has just arrived for you, miss. The boy is waiting, but I am to tell you that it is not necessary for you to reply."

"Thank you, Hampton." Mary perused the few short lines, and passed it to the rector, whose hand was already outstretched to receive it.

"Mr. Jason Hadfield! Presenting his compliments, and trusting that it will be convenient...hm...eleven o'clock this morning! He certainly does not mean to waste any time. Strange that he should address it to you, but perhaps he does not know we are here. Well, he is within his rights, and this is a perfectly proper message. I suppose we should be glad to be given any warning at all, rather than thrown out of doors. I imagine you will scarcely wish to receive the fellow, Mary. You may safely leave it to me. And Sir Anthony," he added.

"On the contrary," said Mary gently, holding out her cup to Caroline for more tea, "I certainly wish to be present. I am still the mistress of this house, for the moment at least. If you would like to be there, I shall be happy to have your company. And, of course," she gave a warm smile, "that of my brother Anthony."

"Your bereaved state makes it impossible for me to remonstrate with you," said the rector heavily, "but I have a copy, which I shall lend you, of a sermon that I once gave on the sin of pride. I say no more, at this time. But you may rest assured that I shall certainly not permit a young and inexperienced lady to meet with this man, of whom we know nothing, alone and unsupported by the male members of her family. If you have finished, Caroline?"

He rose and his wife, who was still eating, hurriedly swallowed and set down the cup she had been about to lift to her lips.

"Oh, yes! Quite finished, thank you, Rector!"

The door closed behind him with what, in a lesser man, might have been called a bang, and Mary met Sir Anthony's eyes in a moment of shared amusement.

"I am afraid the rector is vexed," said Mary remorsefully.

"No more than I am," he said, with mock anger. "How can you be so stiff-necked, my dear girl? It would be no hardship to me to settle some money on you, and, as for living with that skinflint, just you dare! I own I never cared for him so greatly, but I respected his position of course. Now, however, I find I want to do nothing so much as to kick him downstairs!"

"Then I had better keep you out of his way," said Mary. "Come, Anthony, don't tease me to take your money. If I should be homeless, you may be sure that I shall fly to you for aid, and eat you out of house and home if it will make you feel any happier. Now take me to see Georgie, and that delicious nephew of mine! I did not see him all yesterday and feel severely deprived."

It was not difficult to distract him, and keep him talking of this and his other children. Georgina was more difficult to evade, but fortunately the baby set up a loud wailing and Mary had an excuse to leave them. In her room she inspected herself from head to foot. The funeral over, she had not felt obliged to wear black, but her morning gown of white muslin was very plain, adorned only with a small ruffle at the hem that was embroidered with a design of ivy leaves in black, with a similar band of embroidery on the little frill that encircled her neck. Her chestnut hair was arranged in a simple knot, from which a few soft wisps had escaped to frame her face, which looked pale and anxious. Hastily, with her ears straining for the bustle of an arrival, she rubbed her cheeks to bring a little colour to them, and pinched her pale lips. Then, with her heart beating so hard that she thought it should have been visible through the white muslin bodice of her gown, she went downstairs.

Her timing was perfect. As she reached the foot of the stairs Hampton was opening the door, and holding out his hand for the visitor's hat and gloves. At the sight of the unforgettable golden head and handsome face he paused, and opened his mouth to speak. Mary stepped forward.

"Thank you, Hampton," she said firmly, fixing him with her eye. He looked at her, read the unmistakable message in her glance, and turned impassively back to Jason.

"It is Hampton, is it?" he enquired with easy charm.

"Yes, sir."

"And you have been here many years?"

"Oh, yes, sir. Very many years."

"Then I hope you will stay for many more. Perhaps you would be kind enough to inform the staff that, while I may need to make a few changes, I should like to know that as many of them as feel able to stay will do so."

"Thank you, Mr. Hadfield. That is very gratifying news."

Mary had remained at the foot of the stairs while this interchange took place. Now, Jason came towards her, his face expressing just the right blend of polite concern and pleasure. Even in the dim light of the panelled hall he seemed to glow with a kind of radiance, and as always in his presence she felt the pull of his attraction, the glamour of his presence fall over her like a spell.

"Miss Hadfield! Cousin Mary! I am very pleased to see you." He bowed punctiliously over her hand.

"I must speak to you in private," she whispered, adding more loudly, "Welcome to the Priory, Cousin. My brothers-in-law are waiting in the library to greet you."

"They do me much honour. You must allow me, Cousin, to express my regret at the loss of your esteemed father. I wish that it had been possible for me to have met him. It is dreadful to think that I do not even know what he looked like."

Mary looked at him with approval.

"There is a portrait of him in his study, which was thought to be a very good likeness. Should you like to see it?" She led the way as she spoke, moving quickly, and closing the study door firmly behind them as soon as she might, in case the rector took it upon himself to follow.

"There is something I must tell you," she said baldly. "I have heard some bad news, which may affect our plans. The plans for our marriage, that is."

His eyes had been roaming round the room, passing indifferently over the portrait that hung above the fireplace, taking in the fine panelling, the buhl table against the wall, the air of luxury throughout. Now his gaze sharpened and he fixed it on her.

"Bad news? Concerning what? Your brother?"

"Yes, in a way." An expression of anger crossed his face, instantly banished. "Only indirectly, however. It seems that he lost so much money, gambling, that all my fortune is gone."

"Gone? The thirty thousand, gone?"

"Yes, I had to tell you. If you no longer wish...if it is not now possible for us to marry, you have only to speak. I would never hold you to your word, now that I am penniless."

"Your family would, however."

"They do not know. I have not spoken of it. That was why I wanted to speak to you, first, so that you should be warned."

His expression was unreadable; he was as aloof and beautiful as the statue of an ancient god.

"Do you wish to withdraw from our engagement?" He was neither hopeful, nor angry.

"I? No. But I will not tie you to me. I should tell you that there may be—are—some unpleasant and even scandalous circumstances surrounding my brother's death, which it may not be possible to hide."

"How do you know?" His voice was light, cool.

"Someone—a friend—told me. I had heard something from my father, you see, that worried me, and I asked him to find out what he could."

"You should have asked me." His tone was silken now, a caress. "In fact, you may leave it all to me. After all, I shall be your husband, shall I not?"

Something within her relaxed.

"You still want . . . ?"

"Of course I do! How could you doubt me, my dear Mary? Surely you did not think me a fortune-hunter, did you?"

"Of course not. But the estate has been so impoverished. My father has sold off everything that he could, to pay the debts. I do not know anything of your own circumstances. It might have been necessary for you to marry a rich wife, so that things might be put to rights."

He gave an odd little laugh.

"I have plenty of money, my dear. I can take care of you, and the estate, in every respect. And who is this friend who has been helping you? Somebody I know? Should I, perhaps, be jealous?"

"No, no, not at all!" Was her reply perhaps a little too hasty? She tried to speak calmly, to dismiss from her mind that strange proposal—surely not meant?—and, above all, those kisses. "An acquaintance, merely, someone quite chance-met, a gentleman fallen on hard times who will undertake, for a fee, to solve other people's problems." Impossible to explain about Lazarus—or John—whose true surname name she did not even know!

"A strange occupation for a gentleman. Now, of course, you will tell him that you have no further need of his services? If he is working for his hire, I do not suppose he will mind, so long as he is paid. You must allow me to give you the money for that. It shall be my first gift to you, but not the last, I hope."

"And not the first, surely? You are forgetting the lovely mare you sent me! So generous a gift, to forget so lightly, and one above all others that I am grateful for."

"The mare?"

"Yes, that you sent me just after you left. I wrote to thank you, of course, after you sent me the news of your father's death!"

"Of course, the mare! You must think me quite about in the head! I have been so preoccupied, since my father's death, that it had quite slipped my mind. And you are pleased with her? I am delighted to hear it. Now, I think I have paid my respects to the old gentleman for long enough, don't you? We had better rejoin your brothers-in-law.''

Rather shyly she drew near to him, laying one hand on his chest and raising her face to his. His hesitation was infinitesimal, then he bent and touched his lips to her own. The touch was so light and fleeting that she had no time to respond, but the sight of his hazel eyes looking so warmly down into hers was enough to quell any disappointment she might feel.

"Come, my dear. We must tell your family our happy news! Will they be pleased, do you think?''

"Oh, undoubtedly! But very surprised. You must not mind if the rector breaks out into a prayer.''

"Will he be *that* pleased? I shall have to take care not to please him too often." His light, bantering tone carried just the right nuance of cheerful amusement, but Mary had the feeling that his thoughts were elsewhere. But then, she thought, he must have a great deal on his mind.

Neither Caroline nor Georgina had felt equal to supporting this encounter with the young man who was to deprive them of their ancestral home, so it was to an audience of only two that Jason and Mary confided their secret. Sir Anthony, in his kindly way, at once expressed his pleasure, kissing Mary warmly and shaking Jason by the hand with his firm, sportsman's grip, and never thinking to ask how it was that the couple had so swiftly learned to love one another. The rector, frowning a little, was not so blinkered.

"It is a sudden start! Am I to take it, sir, that you have just this instant proposed to Mary, at your very first meeting? And she has accepted you, a stranger—though a cousin? And are you aware, sir, that she will have nothing, nothing at all, coming to her?''

"I am aware of it, sir." Jason spoke with the modest look of one who had done something worthy of praise. "Mary has told me so herself. That fact alone, Rector, would have been enough to have induced me to offer her such protection as a cousin might give—had I not already offered her my heart."

"Very prettily spoken! Charming, indeed!" Sir Anthony was delighted with this fairy-tale ending. "Love at first sight, I suppose?"

"Yes, sir. The very first time I set eyes on Mary—not knowing, then, that she was my cousin—I knew that she was the one woman in the world who could make me happy."

Sir Anthony beamed, but the rector was looking dour.

"Am I to understand," he asked in an offended tone, "that you were acquainted with my sister before today? That you have, in fact, known one another for some time?"

"Of course! I had the pleasure of meeting my cousin at a ball given by the Fordcombes, when I was staying with friends in the neighbourhood some months ago."

"And you have been carrying on this clandestine court-ship since then? For I suppose I need hardly enquire whether my father-in-law was aware of it, Mary?"

"Yes, I have," she answered boldly. "And knowing my father's unreasonable prejudices as you do, Rector, I do not think it is anything to wonder at! Surely, as a man of God, you cannot object to the healing of so unnecessary a breach within the family?"

He huffed a little, but could find little to say beyond,

"Naturally, my dear child, nothing could be more of a Christian duty than to make peace between members of our family! Indeed, when poor Giles was taken from us so un-timely, I suggested that very possibility to your father, but I am afraid that he was unwilling to listen to me. But what is proper in a man, my dear Mary, is not quite to be equated with what is proper, and dutiful, in a daughter."

"Well, I am afraid that I was always a source of dissat-isfaction to my father. But you must agree, Rector, that, left as I have been, such a marriage is both desirable and ap-propriate."

He saw that she was not to be put down, and, knowing the strength of her character, sighed, but said no more, merely offering with ponderous goodwill to perform the actual ceremony.

"Of course, it cannot take place for six months, at the very least. Anything sooner would be most improper. Most."

Mary was glad to be able to agree with him, for, irritating though she found the rector, she had no wish for a falling out between them. Jason, she thought, looked less than satisfied, and she felt a little glow of pleasure in knowing that he was so eager to make her his bride.

"In the meantime, my dear Mary, where are you to live?" queried Sir Anthony. "Surely you will come to us, now? We will be going to London soon, for the start of the season, and only think what fun you and Georgie might have, choosing your bride clothes! And I dare say Mr. Hadfield will come and visit, as often as he can!"

Mary was about to accept this invitation, when Jason stepped in.

"I confess that I had hoped, Sir Anthony, that Mary would stay here, at least for the next month or two. You are aware, of course, that my own father died not more than two weeks before hers, and as his eldest son I am naturally very occupied with his affairs, as well as those of the Priory. Much of my time must be taken up by the lawyers, and it will be impossible for me to spend any time here, other than for occasional visits, for a long while. A house like this needs a mistress, you know, and who more fitted to care for it on my behalf than its past and future one? She knows the people, the routines, the neighbours. In her hands, Hadfield Priory must be safe."

"Stay here, alone? Most improper." The rector was in his most contentious mood, and unable to see any of the advantages.

"I had thought of proposing my mother as a suitable companion," countered Jason. "She is, of course, much distressed by the loss of my father, and a visit to Hadfield would be of great benefit both to her health, and her spirits."

"That would, of course, be perfectly proper," conceded the rector. "A new mother for one, a daughter for the other, uniting in their grief and in their joy. I could see no possible objection to such an arrangement."

Sir Anthony, however, was indignant.

"Could you not? And what of Mary, who has just passed so many anxious weeks shut up in this dismal place—forgive me, my dear, but it is a little gloomy, you know!—with one sad old parent, and must now endure the same again? Does she not deserve a little gaiety, a little pleasure? Mrs. Turvey does not need help in running the house, and the estate steward has always seemed perfectly competent."

"Of course," said Jason gracefully. "I would not dream of depriving Mary of pleasure, merely to be of assistance to me."

At this, Mary was driven to exclamation.

"As if I should not wish to be here! This is my home, and will be in the future. Where else should I be but here, and if Mrs. Hadfield will give me her company I should be more than happy." She sternly repressed a slight pang at the loss of some of the pleasures of London, and shopping with Georgina. "Maybe, later on, we could both come to London? But truly, Anthony, though I do thank you for your kindness, I should not be able to go to parties or anything, so soon after Papa's death, and I should be no more than a nuisance to you and Georgie."

Sir Anthony was far from happy, but there seemed to be little more that he could say. The rector plainly considered the whole matter to be satisfactorily settled, and, since Mary looked both pleased and determined, he gave in.

Hampton arrived with wine and cake, and after a quick interrogative glance at Jason Mary quietly told him of the engagement. His delight was plain to see, and there were actually tears in his eyes when he offered his congratulations, and begged leave to inform the rest of the staff.

"No question of any of them leaving *now*, it seems," Jason remarked cheerfully when he had gone. "I can see that you are a treasure beyond price, my dear." Mary blushed at the compliment, and it was a pleasantly cheerful group that finally made its farewells, since Jason said that he must return to London almost at once.

After a nudge from Sir Anthony, the rector reluctantly agreed to withdraw so that the young couple might say goodbye in private. The stern glance that he fixed on them before going through the door was quite unnecessary, however, since the gentleman showed no sign of giving way to his baser passions, and their conversation was more practical than lover-like.

"I shall write to my mother at once, of course. I hope she will be able to join you here within a week."

"That will be very nice. Naturally I will write to her, too. Will she like me, do you think?" Her voice was wistful, but he seemed not to notice her need of reassurance.

"I am sure she will like anyone I have chosen," he said. "And you will be pleased to have the company, I imagine." Mary banished the thought that company was only a pleasure if it was congenial. Surely Jason's mother must be that, after all. "And you will write to your—acquaintance?" he continued.

"My acquaintance? Oh, you mean the one who was finding out about my brother?"

"Yes, the very same. Let me know what he charges you; I will send a draft on my bank."

"And you will try to find out the truth yourself? I am afraid that my brother was under the influence of a . . . of a person of unpleasant character and habits. Oh, dear, it is very difficult. I wanted to find out this person's name, for I believe that he is, to a large extent, responsible for my brother's death. It is not a pleasant story."

"Then do not soil your lips with it, or bother your head with such thoughts, I shall see to it all."

"But how can you, if I have not told you what we have already learned?"

"My dear, I have a large circle of friends in London. I am known everywhere, I believe. You may be quite sure that I can discover whatever you need to know. The best thing you can do is to forget all about it."

In all her life, Mary had invariably taken much of the responsibility for the running of her day-to-day affairs. Her father, of course, had housed her, clothed and fed her, given her pin-money, and required her services as the mistress of the house. While he had governed her movements, he had never shown any interest in her thoughts and feelings, or even appeared aware that she might have any. The choice of her friends, her books, and within certain bounds her occupations, was hers alone. Her problems, when she had any, she solved for herself, and it would never have occurred to her to take them to him. It seemed strange, just at first, to have someone not only able, but willing, to take on these responsibilities. In time, she was sure, she would come to appreciate it, but just at first it did seem a tiny bit irksome.

"Thank you, Jason," she said with tolerable meekness.

"And you will write tonight?"

He was very insistent, and there seemed no reason why she should not humour him.

"I shall write tonight," she agreed, and they parted amicably, with another of his graceful compliments and an equally graceful embrace.

Her letter, when she wrote it, was carefully worded.

My fiancé, Mr. Hadfield, wishes you to cease your enquiries on my behalf, and I have promised to write to you accordingly.

She finished with thanks and good wishes, but nowhere did she say that she, Mary, also wished him to stop. Knowing, of course, that he would not do so anyway.

CHAPTER ELEVEN

THE REST OF THE DAY passed in a glow of congratulations. If the rector was inclined to be shocked by Mary's behaviour in engaging herself to the son of her father's most hated rival, only his wife seemed to support him, and even she took the opportunity, when he was not by, of whispering her pleasure at this happy outcome. Georgina, of course, was almost wild with excitement, and loud in her lamentations that Mary was not to come to London with her.

"You are not saying no because you have no money to buy your bride clothes, are you?" she asked the next day, suddenly struck by this awful possibility. "Because, if you are, you must not give it another thought, but let us give them to you as a wedding gift. No, really! You know Anthony would gladly have done much more than that, and I shall be quite offended if you refuse me now."

"I am so lost to shame that I will not do so, for I own that my last quarter's allowance is all but gone! I shall not buy a great deal, however, for I may just as well buy things after I am married, when I suppose Jason will give me pin-money. I know he is generous—look at my lovely mare!—and he says he has plenty of money."

"How fortunate. And strange, too, for I had always heard that they were not wealthy, but scarcely more than farmers."

"That was probably Papa talking, and you know how he always exaggerated. He could not bear to think that the other branch of the family might be successful, or happy, and so he determined that they were not."

"Oh, dear, yes, poor Papa! Perhaps we had better not speak of him any more."

"No, I would much rather talk of dear little Giles. I have not seen him yet this morning, but I hear that he is in fine form." The baby, named with what Mary considered an excess of family feeling, had rendered the early part of the morning hideous with his yells.

"Yes, I am sorry. He does make such a noise, one can hardly call it crying, for he is not unhappy, only cross! He hates to be undressed and dressed, you see. I had him in here with me, but he is such an active little fellow, he is only happy if he is moving about, so I have wrapped him up and sent him outside. Nurse is walking him around the garden, as the day is so mild."

"Yes, spring is definitely here. The daffodils are quite out in the orchard, and in the old field. I thought of riding out to see them, later on, and perhaps going on into the forest. I love it when the buds are about to break on the trees."

"I do not care to ride just yet, but you should go. I am afraid you will go quite distracted if you have to spend the whole day with the rector and poor Caroline. Anthony has ridden off to look at the farms, and doesn't mean to return before nightfall. Thank heaven the rector's church duties require him to return tomorrow!"

"But if I go out you will be left to listen to him on your own. It seems hardly fair."

"Ah, but I have an infallible method of getting rid of him. I have only to send for Nurse to bring little Giles, and he is out of the door the next instant!"

In the end Mary decided against riding, which the rector seemed to consider indecorous so soon after the funeral, but she was determined on having some exercise, so arrayed herself in a warm pelisse and a pair of stout boots, and set off to see the daffodils on foot. The field was not much more than a mile beyond the immediate confines of the garden, and she strode briskly out, not heeding or minding that the path was very muddy, or that a few ominous clouds had gathered to spoil the clear blue skies of the morning.

The air was honey-sweet with the smell of the poplars in
the hedgerow, knots of primroses decked the bank beneath
the vivid green of the new hawthorn leaves. Mary, a child of
the country, gathered and nibbled at the hawthorn buds as
she went, and promised herself that she would bring back a
posy of the primroses for Georgina, as well as the armful of
daffodils for which she had brought a basket. Alone, like
this, she could admit that a shadow had lifted from her life,
and that her future shone ahead of her almost as brightly as
the spring day.

The daffodils grew thickly in one corner of the field. Mary
had always marvelled at them, for the place had been
ploughed up, to her certain knowledge, at least twice. The
second time had been by a whim of her brother's, and she
had pleaded with him not to have it done, until she saw that
he was all the more wishful to destroy the place because she
cared for it. Then she feigned indifference, but it was too
late, and the plough had come, furrowing the soil and cutting up bulbs and roots. The following year only a few poor
clumps had shown, but now, three years later, the leaves and
flowers were as thick as ever they had been, giving Mary the
promise that spite and malice could not, in the end, have
their way.

The flowers were double, their hearts frilly and crisp, the
outer petals thin, fine and pale. She was carefully picking
buds, hunting for those that showed a good gleam of gold
through the protective green that would burst open when put
in water. Her gloves she had long since discarded, since there
was no point in soaking them with sticky sap, and she was
humming contentedly, sliding cold wet fingers down the
satin-smooth stems to snap them crisply at the base. She
thought herself alone, and when a shadow fell across her
where she crouched in the grass she jumped, and would have
fallen inelegantly backwards if he had not put a supporting
hand on her arm, and held her up.

"Proserpina, I suppose?" He held out his own offering,
a fistful of fully opened flowers picked rather short. "Mine
are prettier than yours."

"Not tomorrow they won't be, but thank you. I hope you are not 'gloomie Dis'?"

"Come to ravish you away to the underworld? Well, I will if you like; in fact it was rather on my mind. But perhaps I am Orpheus, though. It accords better with my other name, don't you think? Returning from the realms of death, and all that?" Lazarus smiled at her, and she felt herself responding with genuine pleasure.

"I thought you had gone straight back to London, but perhaps it is as well you did not. Why are you still here?"

"Because you have not given me an answer, of course."

"An answer?" She continued to pick, and did not look up at him.

"Yes, to my proposal."

"But... surely that was a joke? You know that I am engaged to my cousin."

"Perhaps I thought that was a joke, too?"

"If it is, not many people will laugh at it. I can assure you it is quite serious. He called yesterday, and I told him that I would have no money at all. And it made not a scrap of difference! In fact, we have told my family, and the servants, so you see it is all quite official."

"Ah. He can afford to marry you, in spite of the great losses to the estate? I had not thought his family so rich."

Mary was puzzled.

"Surely you do not know anything about them? He told me himself that he has a good deal of money, and will be able to restore things as they should be, so I suppose his father must have left him well off."

"I had heard otherwise, but no matter. What about your answer?"

"But I have just told you, I am engaged to Jason Hadfield! What other answer is necessary?"

"You are quite sure about this, Mary? It is not just that he will inherit the Priory? No, don't take offence at my question! I put it badly. I know you are not mercenary, that you would not tie yourself to anyone merely for worldly gain. But this is your home, and you love it. It offers a strong temptation, the chance to stay here for ever, which might be enough to blind you to other things. Are you sure that you truly love him?''

His voice was unwontedly serious. Mary stood, idly moving the daffodils in her basket so that each stem lay neatly ranged side by side, separating those fat buds that still pointed guardsman-straight from those that had already turned to the horizontal, and laying these last carefully so that they all faced in the same direction. She hardly knew how to answer.

"I do. I am sure I do." She could not put her feelings into words, describe the sensation that came over her when in Jason's presence, how her eyes were drawn irresistibly to him, how he seemed more brightly coloured, more shining than anyone else in the room, how her skin tingled at his nearness, and the breath caught in her throat. He had never kissed her roughly, with passion, as this man before her had done, but that also seemed right to her. It seemed all of a part with his finesse, his perfection of behaviour.

Lazarus, whose mother had called him John, studied her downbent profile and cursed himself, and fate, and his brother. She had loosened the strings of her bonnet and let it fall back, wanting the feel of soft spring air on head and neck, and the chestnut of her hair caught fire from the sun as it lay in a soft curve against the smooth cusp of cheek, and fell in coiling wisps against the white skin of her neck. Any trace of coquetry was completely absent as she gnawed at the fullness of her lower lip with two white teeth, and he knew that the little frown would be between her brows that always made him want to snatch her in his arms, and protect her from the world and its dragons.

Now he was riven with anguish for her, wanting desperately that she should be happy, and fearing that she would not. It was true that his brother had been no more than a child when he had known him, with the cruelty and selfishness of an over-indulged infancy. That it had been Jason who had revealed his love-affair and his subsequent plans to his father he had never really doubted, but he was sadly aware that even without such interference his father would soon have found some reason for anger with him. It was inevitable, he thought, that he and his father would have crossed swords sooner or later, and the final outcome would doubtless have been the same. Though saddened to think that his father was now beyond any hope of making peace with his eldest son, he did not really regret that he had left home, and would almost have been grateful to Jason for making it happen.

Where Mary was concerned, however, it was not so easy. He wanted to doubt that she really loved his brother, and he could not believe that Jason loved her, though he had been shaken by the news that he was still prepared not only to hold to a secret engagement, but to announce it publicly, knowing that the marriage would bring in no money. The Jason he had known would not have behaved thus. Nor had the family circumstances, in the past, been such as would permit Jason to marry a penniless girl, however much he might love her. His own mother's fortune, he knew, had been swallowed up by debts. Still, he himself had made his own fortune, and perhaps his brother had been able to do the same.

How easy it would be simply to declare himself! That would be a test indeed, for both of them. But if he did so, he must inevitably take on the rights and duties of primogeniture, and deny his brother the Priory. And she, of course, would be deprived also. For if Jason had stood by his engagement when he had learned that his betrothed would have no portion, how much more would she stand by hers, though it should take her away from her home?

Becoming aware of his scrutiny, she blushed, and turned away to crouch once again among the clumps of daffodils. She picked slowly, choosing each stem with exaggerated care. He waited long enough to show her that he would not pester her with more questions, and to let her embarrassment subside. When she spoke, it was in a friendly, conversational tone, and only one who knew every nuance of her voice could have detected, as he did, the reserve beneath it.

"Have you received my letter? I sent it to the inn, yesterday. I suppose that is where you have been staying?"

"Yes. That is another reason why I came to meet you. It grieves me to say it, but I am afraid I have no intention of leaving this investigation until I am in full possession of the facts."

At once she abandoned her picking and rose to face him.

"But you must! You must stop, if I ask you. You only began it at my behest, after all. You do not have to continue now."

"I am acting of my own free will," he pointed out gently. "I am not a servant, or an employee, that you may hire and dismiss at will."

It was unfair, and he knew it.

"I never said you were! I am asking, not demanding!"

"Yes. I am sorry. But I have my reasons for wanting to find out, reasons that concern you, and others that do not. If you like, I will keep my findings to myself and not tell you, if they distress you."

"It is not that! Only Jason has said that he will do it himself. He was . . . a little displeased to hear that I have asked somebody else."

"Did you tell him who you had asked?" He kept his voice casual.

"How could I? I do not know your name! Lazarus is, after all, rather fanciful, and I could hardly say, merely, 'thou shalt call his name John,' as if he were Zacharias in the Temple. It was very foolish of me to ask you in the first place, I see that now. Of course, I did not know that I would be marrying him, then, but now I do not want to hurt his feelings, by letting him think I turned to another, and not to him."

"Jealous, was he? So what did you tell him?"

"Well, I remembered that other person, who helped you. The gentleman, who finds things out. I said that I was paying him to help me, and he offered to pay his fee, so that he would not have to do it any more. And of course he would expect him to stop, because that kind of man would, wouldn't he?"

Effortlessly disentangling this confused speech, he smiled reassuringly.

"I quite understand, and I think you did exactly the right thing. After all, when you are married, you will be able to tell him the whole story, won't you?"

"Yes," she replied dubiously. "But you do see why you must stop?"

"I do. Don't worry about it any more." She looked relieved, and did not notice that he had not, in fact, agreed to anything. That a newly betrothed man might be jealous of his bride's friendship with another was understandable, but he was not quite clear why Jason should be so very insistent that no one but himself should continue the investigation. Knowing Jason as he did, it gave him the best reason in the world to wish to carry on.

Now that her mind was relieved of that worry, Mary had time to remember something else that had bothered her.

"You said that you came to meet me. How did you know that I would be here?"

He grinned, no whit abashed.

"Aha, I have my sources, you know."

"It is from Sarah, I suppose. She certainly knew I was intending to come here, for I spoke of it to her this morning. You have certainly charmed her, anyway! I do not know how she can be so indiscreet!"

"She is a woman of great intelligence, and since you have turned me down I shall probably console myself with marrying her instead."

"An excellent idea," she responded at once. "I shall find you a little cottage. Or are you proposing to carry her off to the wilds of—where was it? Australia? If that is the case, I warn you I shall put a spoke in your wheel if I can. I could not bear to part with her."

A puff of air blew across the field, sending a ripple of silver over the new grass and shivering the daffodils. As they walked the clouds to the west had built up, and now they were perceptibly moving to cover the sky. The breeze came again, more strongly, and Mary shivered, putting down her basket to lift her bonnet back on to her head.

"You must hurry back. It looks as though there is rain coming, and you have a fair distance to walk back. What a pity you came on foot, instead of on horseback. Is Juno well?"

"Juno? You mean Jewel, surely?"

"Of course. I had mistaken her name. She is not lame, is she? I expected you to ride."

"My brother-in-law the rector thought it wrong, and I did not care to upset him, since he is already displeased with me for carrying on what he calls a clandestine courtship. But the mare is very well, and I hope to be riding soon. The rector goes home tomorrow."

The sun was gone, and with it the illusion of arriving summer. Suddenly the air that had been fresh was now cold and damp. The clouds were boiling up, the wind gusting more strongly. He made up his mind.

"Wait, I have my own horse tethered nearby. You will never reach home in time, and will be soaked to the skin." Before Mary could protest he was gone, and she knew him well enough to know that any protest she might make would be ignored. She contented herself, therefore, with tying a large handkerchief, from the pocket of her pelisse, across the basket, to keep the daffodils in place. The primroses, she knew, must wait for another day.

She saw Lazarus lead his horse along the side of the hedge, and made her way down the field to the stile, beyond which was the narrow lane, more of a track than a road, by which she had come. By the time she reached him he was mounted, and bending to reach for her. Gripping the basket in one hand, and climbing on the topmost step of the stile, she allowed him to lift her up before him so that she was seated, not very comfortably, across the pommel of his saddle in front of him.

"I suppose you must bring the flowers with you? Very well, then. At least you are awake, this time."

He kicked the horse to a trot, which was rather painful, since she had no way to rise to the movement, but could only cling round his waist with her free arm and hope that his firm grasp of her would keep her from slipping. After a few jolts the horse was cantering, and with the easier stride she slackened her grip though he, she noticed, did not. Plashy mud flew out from the horse's hoofs as they hurried along, and if it had not been so uncomfortable Mary would have found it rather exhilarating. Her bonnet, insecurely tied, had slipped back again, and she lifted her face to the rush of cold air and laughed, hearing and feeling that he was laughing, too.

There was a little gate set in the wall of the park, which led into a small plantation and thence, by a gravel path, to the house. At this gate he reined in. Mary raised her eyebrows.

"You know your way around very well, sir! Not many people are aware of this gate."

"No time to bandy words now, girl! You must run to the house!" In spite of his words he did not relax his hold round her waist, and though she would have let go her hold of him she was unable, without pushing at him, to bring her own arm back, so she left it where it was.

"This is one of the things I must not make a habit of, I suppose, like visiting you in your sitting-room! Still, third time pays for all, they say, so I shall not promise not to do it at least once more! Stay there; I'll lift you down."

His arm was gone, and suddenly the cold was biting again, and she was shivering. He dismounted, took and laid aside her basket, then held up his hands to catch her as she slid inelegantly down into his receiving arms.

"Thank you," she said, breathless. "I suppose...now that my father is dead, there is nothing to prevent you from coming up to the house, is there?"

"But the new owner may object to me just as strongly. In fact, I am quite sure he would! Not just yet, and maybe not at all. But you may be sure that I shall see you again. Now, run!"

He opened the gate, turned her round with his hands on her shoulders, and sent her on her way with a gentle slap as if, she thought indignantly, she had been a horse, or a small child. However, a few heavy drops of rain were already falling, so she did not wait to upbraid him, but snatched up her basket and ran towards the house, reaching it just as the full cloudburst started. Glancing back, there was nothing to be seen through the driving rain, but she had a sudden complete certainty that he had followed her to the edge of the plantation, and watched her safely home. Glowing with the warmth of exertion, and perhaps another inner warmth that she did not care to examine, she took off her muddy boots and pelisse and ran upstairs in her stockinged feet, greatly scandalising Caroline, who met her on the stairs, and upbraided her as a hoyden. Mary only laughed, and gave her a handful of daffodils.

It was no hardship to say goodbye to the rector and her eldest sister the following day, and for almost a week Mary and Georgina lived a carefree life. Sir Anthony, an active man, was happy looking over his father-in-law's coverts, and discussing new farming methods with the tenants, so Mary and her sister were left in full enjoyment of the baby and one another, taking little strolling walks in the garden when the sun shone, and discussing the latest fashions, a subject on which Lady Tarrant could talk for hours. Jason did not visit, but wrote a charming letter saying that he would be bringing his mother down quite soon, and Mrs. Hadfield also wrote in reply to Mary's letter, expressing herself delighted with her son's matrimonial plans, and equally pleased to be coming to the Priory.

The Tarrants had intended to remain until her arrival, but the news that the governess, in whose charge the older children had been left, had slipped on the stairs and broken her leg put Georgina into a fever of anxiety. Convinced that without Miss Elstead's firm hand her children would be running amok and putting themselves into all kinds of danger, she packed in haste, kissed her sister a hasty but affectionate goodbye, and was gone the following morning. The house seemed empty after she had left, and Mary was pleased when she heard from Jason that he and his mother would be arriving the day after next.

Mary dressed with especial care that morning. She would, naturally, have done so for her betrothed in any case, but his mother, being a woman, might be expected to have a still sharper and more critical eye for the niceties of female adornment. Though her gown was of necessity one from the previous year, it was still in the first style of elegance, and of fine silk rather than her usual white muslin. Promptly at eleven the carriage drove up to the door, and Mary went out to meet her future Mama as Jason stepped down and turned to hand his companion down the steps. She stooped a little, as was natural, to come through the carriage door, but when she reached the ground and stood straight Mary found herself looking down, for Jason's mother was scarcely bigger than a child, with the slender proportions and build of a young girl. The hair beneath her decidedly fashionable bonnet was the same gold as her son's, her eyes a clear, pale blue, very widely opened and with dark lashes that Mary instantly decided were artificially blackened.

She held out a hand, tiny in its kid glove.

"So this is Mary! You may kiss me, my dear, but gently, for travelling always gives me the headache. I am afraid I am ridiculously delicate!"

She tilted a porcelain cheek towards Mary, who bent and brushed it carefully with her lips, feeling suddenly like a lumbering giant against this doll-like creature. It seemed that she had not been careful enough, for Mrs. Hadfield closed her eyes for a moment with an air of exquisite anguish, then smiled bravely.

"How do you do, ma'am?" Mary began, moderating her voice almost to a whisper when she saw her guest flinch delicately. "I am sorry you are unwell. Should you like to lie down? I will take you up directly, and Mrs. Turvey will send you up some tea."

"No tea, thank you. I find it too stimulating to my nerves, after a journey. My woman will make me up a tisane, and I dare say that if I lie down for an hour, in a darkened room, I might be able to sleep a little, and then I could bring myself to take a little dry toast. Jason, my dear, where is my travelling case?"

"Your maid has it, Mama." His voice held a trace of impatience, and he greeted Mary absently. "I regret that I shall not be able to stay beyond one night. The lawyers are damned exiguous, and I must leave in the morning."

Mary, used as she was to hear her father and Giles, did not blink at his speech, though she was glad that the rector was not there to hear it. She began to express her disappointment, but was interrupted by the sweetly plaintive voice of her visitor.

"I am afraid that the air is a little cold out here. I am so susceptible to chills!"

Mary apologised, and took her diminutive guest indoors, where the staff had collected to greet their new master and his mother. Mrs. Hadfield smiled wanly at them all, and drifted to the stairs with Mary in attendance. She commented favourably on the proportions of hall and staircase, ran a finger absently along the carved balustrade and gave a disapproving look at the resultant dust, and in her room kept both Mary and her maid busy hunting for her vinaigrette, her handkerchief, her pastilles, her tisane mixture, and her lavender drops, before commencing the dispiriting regime that she had outlined earlier, leaving Mary to creep from the room while the maid dabbed her brow and chafed her hands.

The sleep, the tisane, and the dry toast seemed to revive her, however, and when she came down to dinner later she was vivacious, complimenting Mary on her toilette, her cook, and her great good fortune in making so excellent a match. When they left Jason to his solitary wine-drinking, she treated Mary to a minute description of her late husband's last days, and the splendours of his funeral, delicately touching a lace-trimmed handkerchief to her eyes from time to time, blotting away any moisture before it had time to form, and avoiding her lashes. Her gown was of purple silk trimmed with quantities of black lace, and she wore some very fine amethysts. Mary, in her white tarlatan, began to feel dowdy as well as elephantine, and she was glad when the tea-tray arrived, and Jason rejoined them.

He left straight after breakfast the following day, long before his mother had left her room, and Mary was glad she had come down early, for that meal was their only chance of exchanging a few words in private. There was a subtle pleasure in pouring his coffee, and learning that he liked rolls, not toast or bread, and cut all the fat off his ham before eating it. He seemed preoccupied, and when he replied in monosyllables to her tentative attempts at conversation she decided that he was a man who preferred silence at his breakfast table. Since her father had been the same she was neither surprised nor distressed, but sipped her tea and took pleasure in watching him surreptitiously, admiring the perfection of his travelling clothes and the way that his hair, even at this hour, fell into place with careful naturalness.

"Did you dismiss that fellow?" His question was so abrupt that she jumped, and had to think what he was talking about.

"Dismiss...? Oh, yes, Jason. I told him that he need not continue."

"And you paid him? How much?"

"Oh, nothing. That is, he did not require payment, I suppose because he had not finished the work."

He frowned.

"Strange, if that's how he's paying his way. And you are quite sure that he is not still prying into your brother's affairs?"

Mary hid her misgivings.

"Yes, Jason. I certainly told him he must not carry on." He seemed satisfied, and lapsed back into silence. Afterwards, as if recollecting himself, he began to express his sorrow at having to leave her.

"Yes, it is a shame. I am so looking forward to showing you the estate, and the house, and everything! But of course your business must be attended to. Still, we shall both be busy, I suppose, and the months of waiting will soon pass.''

''Yes. Though I should prefer...never mind. I must be gone. I shall hope to visit soon, and then...we shall see.'' He kissed her brow and, when she offered them, her lips, and was gone.

Mary did her best to amuse Mrs. Hadfield. She did not care for riding, but was fond of driving out in the carriage. Not, unfortunately, the open curricle, which she found too draughty, so Mary found herself spending afternoons shut in the stuffy coach, being driven very slowly round the countryside, without even the distraction of paying calls, since it was too soon for any but their nearest neighbours to have visited. As the days passed she learned that Jason's mother's fragile appearance concealed a will of iron, and that she was adept at gaining her own way with the use of sighs, little frowns, sweet little disclaimers and, if necessary, the big guns of headache, palpitations and moments of faintness.

It began to seem to Mary that she had exchanged one domestic tyrant for another, though she had to admit that so long as she was never disagreed with, or refused anything, her guest was perfectly cheerful, amiable and conversable. Nevertheless, she was pleased to learn that Mrs. Hadfield was not intending to make her permanent home at the Priory.

''No, no, my dear. Nothing would please me more than to be here with you, to help you with your little duties and give you my company, but I fear that, in my delicate state of health, I would not be able to bear the discomforts of the country. The air in Sussex is not what I am used to—I fancy it is a trifle heavy—and now that I have found a doctor who so exactly understands my constitution I think that I could not do better than to make my home in Bath. I went several times, you know, with Mr. Hadfield, in the hope that a course of hot baths might help him, and never have I felt so well!''

The joys of Bath—its shops, its assemblies, its concerts and the delightful company to be found there—occupied her conversation for some time, and Mary found it a useful distraction whenever other matters palled, and on the whole she thought that the visit could be counted a moderate success.

It was three weeks before Jason visited, though he wrote as regularly and delightfully as before. When he did come, it was without warning. Mary and Mrs. Hadfield were sitting after dinner, Mary reading aloud and her companion knotting a fringe, when the sound of wheels on the drive made them look up in surprise. As Mary laid aside her book they heard Hampton's voice in the hall, and a few moments later Jason walked in, laughing at their amazed pleasure.

"Well, my dear Mary! And Mama, how do you do? I need not ask; I can see that you have been enjoying yourselves together, not heeding my absence!"

They both cried out at this, and Mary protested that she wanted nothing more than to be with him every day.

"In that case, I have something that will make you happy, I hope!" He patted his pocket. "I am as weary as you, my love, of our enforced separation, and I have determined that it is no longer to be borne. I have a special licence in my pocket, and propose that we should be married at once. What do you have to say to that?"

CHAPTER TWELVE

MARY STOOD where she was, as unable to move as if she had been sheathed in ice.

"Married at once?" she heard herself repeating stupidly.

Mrs. Hadfield had also risen, or rather jumped, to her feet, and now danced across the room, her little hands uplifted and the fine French lace on her cap fluttering like butterflies' wings in the breeze of her movement.

"How charming! How delightful! How romantic!" She darted between one and the other, bestowing little scented kisses as if they had been bonbons. "It is so exciting, I declare I am quite about in my head! To think that I should live to see this happy day!" As far as Mary could tell, there was no reason why she should not have lived to see it even had it taken place six months or six years hence, but her mind was numb with shock.

"But... the arrangements?" Her lips felt dead and cold, and she had to frame the words carefully to be understood.

"Now, my dear daughter—I may call you that now, mayn't I?—you are surely not going to make a great fuss about a wedding gown, and bride clothes, and such like? Of course I know most girls like to have such things, but I had thought you above such mundane considerations. Besides, you have no money, you know, and once you are married you will be able to shop, and have everything nice!"

"My dear Mary looks beautiful to me in whatever she chooses to wear." Jason was beside her, lifting her hand to his lips. Mary gazed at him, almost hypnotised. As she watched him he put his other hand inside his coat, and drew something out of his waistcoat pocket. It was a ring, a large ruby set with diamonds. It glowed against the white of his fingers like a hot ember, and when he slid it on her unresisting finger it was warm from the heat of his body.

"Oh, what a fortunate girl! Such a beautiful ruby! And so very big! You will be the envy of all, my dear Mary."

The ring was heavy on her finger, the shank a little loose so that she had to crook her finger to keep it from sliding over her knuckle. The stone was cabochon cut, smooth and round, and reminded her rather horribly of a large drop of blood.

"I didn't mean clothes," she said, feeling the need to explain herself more clearly. "Of course I don't mind about them, though my brother and sister Tarrant were going to give them to me. I meant—oh, I don't know. The vicar. And telling our friends and family. That sort of thing."

"My dear, you might trust me to have thought of all that. Impatient though I am to call you mine, I am not quite so lost to the proprieties as that! Merely, I had been thinking that even by waiting six months, we will still only be able to have a quiet sort of wedding, since we have recently been bereaved not only of your father, but of your brother, and my father also. It must have been a sad, dismal sort of affair, the kind of thing that is quite repugnant to me. Not worthy of my Mary! What I should have liked for you is a wedding that would be talked of for years to come! Bonfires! Fireworks! A feast for the village and the tenants! The world and his wife here, the church overflowing! But that would mean waiting so long, and neither of us wants that, do we? So I thought something quite sudden, private and dignified, with no guests but my mother, who is with us anyway, and then we might slip away to the Continent! Boney's posturings need not bother us, I am sure, with the Duke taking command of the allied forces, and all ready to take him on. Brussels, they say, is very gay just now. We might go there, what do you think? We may travel around for six months or so, and when we come back we can plan a proper celebration. Who knows but there might not be another, still more auspicious event to celebrate in a certain number of months from now!" He gave her a burning look, which made Mary blush and drop her eyes. He had never spoken to her in such warm terms before, and she did not know how to respond to him.

"My dear! To visit the Continent! You could not then complain of missing your bride clothes, for you might buy them in Brussels, which is as good as to say Paris! I do not know how you can stand there so calmly, Mary!" Mrs. Hadfield made a playful tap at Mary's hand with her furled fan. It caught Mary across the knuckles quite painfully.

"I am sorry. You must think me very stupid. It is just that it is so sudden."

"Missish, my dear? Or perhaps—" Jason's tone dropped to one of earnest melancholy "—perhaps you doubt your love for me? You cannot doubt mine for you, for I believe I have given ample enough proof of it, but maybe you cannot do without all the frills and furbelows of a fashionable wedding? Does it mean so much to you, my dear Mary? If it is so, I shall naturally wait. God forbid that I should cause you a moment's pain."

"Ah, cruel girl! You would not play with my boy's heart, would you, Mary?"

"No, no!" Mary turned from one to the other, the hazel eyes and the blue eyes of mother and son seeming, at that moment, equally sharp and yet, at the same time, equally reflective betraying nothing of the mind beneath. "You are quite misunderstanding me! I doubt neither you, nor myself, and, as for clothes, I would be married in rags and not give it another thought! But you must be aware of the problems that would arise! Even with a special licence, the vicar will think it very strange, and I think he would be quite hurt to think that he was not able to read the banns for us! And then my sisters! They must be offended, to say the least, to feel that I did not want them to be with me. The neighbours, too! We should be universally vilified and in the country, you know, that will not do! I do not see how it may be done, without causing a scandal."

"What a clever little girl she is!" exclaimed Mrs. Hadfield, looking up at Mary who seemed in that moment to tower over her petite figure. "She thinks of everything! I do wonder, Jason, whether she may not be right. Six months is not so very long, after all, and then you might have a very pretty wedding, and go abroad after that. Might it not be better?"

Her son gave her no more than a look, his face turned away from Mary, and Mrs. Hadfield paled. When he spoke, however, his voice was gentle, smooth as silk.

"No, Mother. On the whole, I think it would not be."

"Then, of course, there is no more to be said." She fluttered to Mary's side, putting a cozening arm round her waist, and leaning against her like a confiding child. "It must be for the best, my dear, if Jason thinks so."

Jason Hadfield drew them both back towards the fire, and obliged them to sit.

"I have been too sudden, I perceive! In the impatience of my love, my longing to be with you, I have been too precipitate. But I am not blind to the problems you, with your quick mind, have perceived, my dear. Do not think that I wish to upset your sisters, or the neighbours among whom we shall live. Nor, of course, the good vicar. For that reason I propose that we go at once to London, and have the actual ceremony performed there. No one there will wonder at us, or be surprised. We could almost invite your sister Lady Tarrant, since she and Sir Anthony are in town, but I suppose we had better not, or we shall upset the rector and his wife. So, a quick, quiet, private ceremony, and then straight to Dover! I have our passages booked already!"

"Already? But when—?"

"We leave at first light tomorrow morning. You would not wish, I know, to stay at a common hotel, so we shall drive straight to the Church, and then set off for Dover. I have arranged for us to sleep on board, and we sail with the tide the following morning. In two days' time, we shall be in Belgium, as man and wife!"

It was all settled, all decided. Mary could think of nothing to say, no protest that she could make without bringing down the reproaches of Mrs. Hadfield, or the more subtly expressed plaints of her betrothed, upon her head. She smiled, with stiff lips and cheeks that felt as though they might crack.

"It is hard to believe! Almost like an elopement, in fact!"

"Did I not say it was the most romantic thing I have ever heard? Quite a fairy-tale, you might say!" Mrs. Hadfield, obviously, saw nothing improper in the proposal, and Mary thought that perhaps she was being old-fashioned, even a little priggish, in finding it shocking.

She turned back towards the tea-tray, automatically seeking a refuge in the safe normality of everyday forms.

"You dined on your way, I suppose? Will you have a cup of tea? There is plenty of hot water, and I can soon make some fresh for you."

"Something a little stronger, perhaps?" He glanced towards the tantalus. Mrs. Hadfield gave a little titter.

"My dear Mary, now that you are to be a married woman you must learn that a man who has just driven fifty miles should be offered something more stimulating than tea!"

"Of course. I beg your pardon." Mary rose in a flurry, but Jason forestalled her and took out the decanter.

"Brandy, I think. Your father kept an excellent cellar, my dear. Smuggled, I suppose?"

"Probably. He never said."

"I must find out his source, and see that we are kept as well supplied as he was. Will you join me in a glass, ladies?"

Mary, who disliked the taste of brandy, would have refused, but before she could do so Mrs. Hadfield clapped her hands with childlike delight.

"Oh, yes! A toast! We must drink a toast to the bride and groom!"

Smiling, he turned back to the table and poured more, making a little ceremony of it and taking several moments, so that when he brought her a brimming glass it seemed easier to Mary to accept gracefully. His eyes gleamed as he raised his glass to her, and once again the familiar magic stole about her, so that she lifted the glass to her lips as if in a trance, and sipped.

It tasted so unpleasant that it seemed better to be rid of the drink as quickly as possible, as if it had been medicine, so she schooled her expression to one of happiness and drank as fast as she could without choking on the fumes. To her dismay, when she set the glass down, Jason refilled it almost at once, without giving her a chance to refuse. She made an incoherent protest, but he smiled.

"It will do you good," he said. "We have a tiring day tomorrow, and you must be sure to get a good night's sleep." Gently and kindly he insisted that she must finish it, and by the time she had done so her head was buzzing, and when she rose to her feet they seemed unimaginably far away, so that she was not sure that she could control them.

"I must go upstairs," she enunciated carefully with a tongue that felt as though it were made of shoe leather. "I must tell Sarah to pack. Get things ready. For the morning."

"There is no need for you to worry about anything," he said soothingly, as to a fractious child. "I have already had instructions sent up to your woman to pack for you. We need not take a great deal, in any case, for as my mother has pointed out we may buy newer and better in Brussels. Just travelling clothes, for a few days, will suffice. I have told her that we are going to London—no need to say more. As you yourself so wisely said, there is no point in setting the neighbourhood by its ears, by announcing our intentions. And servants gossip, you know! If one should hear of it, I dare say it would be all round Sussex by tomorrow!"

"But...I must take Sarah with me! I cannot go without my maid!"

Mary could hear the note of rising panic in her voice, so it was certain that Jason did, too.

"My dearest girl, she shall come, if you like! I had thought to engage you a French maid, but after all a bride must be humoured! Only, I beg of you, say nothing to her of our plans, until we are on our way tomorrow!''

He led her to the foot of the stairs, and stood watching her as she made her slow way up. Reaching her room, she was not greatly surprised to find that Sarah was on her knees before a trunk, while gowns, pelisses, spencers and bonnets were laid round the room.

''Well, here's a start!'' she exclaimed. ''Off to London in the morning, without a moment's warning! What maggot has he taken into his head, may I ask?''

Mary removed a pile of neatly folded chemises, and three pairs of kid gloves, and sat carefully in the chair she had emptied. Her head felt heavy, and it seemed unfair that she should have to deal with Sarah's crossness on top of everything else.

''It is Mr. Hadfield's wish. Mr. Hadfield who is, I should remind you, the owner of this house, and my future husband.'' She leaned her head back and closed her eyes, but at once the room seemed to sway and whirl around her, so she opened them again. ''I should like to go to bed,'' she enunciated with careful dignity.

Sarah, frowning suspiciously, laid aside the gown she was folding and came to her charge.

''Have you been drinking, Miss Mary?'' she asked with incredulity. She could smell the brandy on her breath, but she still found it hard to believe.

Mary put up clammy hands and rubbed her forehead.

''I couldn't help it, Sarah,'' she said. ''Didn't want to but it was a toast, you see. You have to drink a toast, and then he gave me more, and I had to drink that. Celebrating. But I can't tell you the toast, not until tomorrow, and you're to come with me, come with us instead of a French maid.''

''So I should think! A French maid! The very idea!'' Sarah clucked soothingly as she bent to undo the ribbons of Mary's soft kid evening slippers, then helped her to undress and get into bed. There was a moment when she thought the girl might be sick, but it passed, and she stayed by the bedside until the alcohol-laden breath was steady and slow, and she was sure that Mary was asleep. Her eyes rested, thoughtfully, on the ruby that gleamed balefully on Mary's finger, which even in sleep was bent to restrain it. Then, frowning, she abandoned the packing and went to sit for a while in the chair that Mary had cleared. Whatever her thoughts, they did not please her, and presently she left the room and was gone for half an hour on an errand that she would have denied, had anyone seen her. They did not, however, any more than they heard the sound of galloping hoofs as one of the grooms rode away down the drive. Listening to the retreating sound, and somewhat reassured, she finished the packing, and went to her own bed.

In the cold dark of early morning Mary dragged herself, shivering and miserable, from her bed. Her stomach was queasy, she had a vile taste in her mouth, and her temples throbbed so fiercely that she thought that the sound of them must be audible to others, like jungle drums. Sarah was brusquely sympathetic and gave her a disgusting mixture that she had concocted expressly, which made Mary feel well enough to enter into an argument about what she should wear. Since she was not permitted to say that she was on her way to her wedding she could give no satisfactory reason why she should wish to wear her best silk dress to sit in a coach and travel, but she won by a mixture of tenacity and, had she known it, her pallid looks and slightly haunted expression.

The coach was crowded, since Mrs. Hadfield naturally wished to bring her own maid, and Jason wisely elected to ride alongside. Mary and her future mother-in-law sat side by side, rather silent, with the two equally silent servants facing them. There were hot bricks for their feet, and with warm wraps they were cosy enough, but the chill air, smelling of dust, of the worn leather of the seats, and of Mrs. Hadfield's cologne-scented handkerchief, was charged with unspoken questions and words. Mary watched the familiar landmarks, faintly illuminated by a pallid dawn, recede, then fell into an uneasy slumber, in which she was once more in the schoolroom, and facing a barrage of questions to which she did not know the answer.

They halted only once, at Croydon, where a cup of coffee revived her spirits and settled her insides, which were more upset than usual by the motion of the carriage. Mrs. Hadfield had been unwontedly silent since they had left the Priory, and for this Mary had been thankful. After Croydon Mary stayed awake, but her companion kept her eyes resolutely closed, only the occasional lifting of the scented handkerchief to her face betraying that she was not, in fact, asleep.

They went not to the London house where Mary had expected to make a halt, but to a hotel. It was a small, quiet, genteel place that Mary had never heard of, where they were greeted with the utmost deference, and shown up to a private sitting-room.

"Just a few minutes, my dear," said Jason, smiling at them meaningfully, "and then we must be off."

Mary tried to return the smile, but her legs were cramped and her headache had returned with new violence, and the prospect of another journey dismayed her. All she longed for was to climb into a warmed bed and hide her face in a pillow. Mrs. Hadfield, however, seemed to have a new energy, and bustled round, dismissing both the maids.

"There, you may go, we shall do very well without you! The girl will show you your rooms, and you may have a little rest. Have you my bandbox? Ah, good. We shall be going out in about an hour, with Mr. Hadfield."

"Shan't I stay with you, Miss Mary?" Sarah ignored the older woman, looking like a large sheep being harried by a small and yappy dog.

Mary found that she wanted to cling to Sarah, to beg her not to go away, not to leave her. She was tired, of course. She summoned what she hoped was a bright smile.

"No, Sarah. I shall be all right. I will call you if I need you."

Mrs. Hadfield removed Mary's bonnet with her own hands.

"Shall I send for some wine? You are rather pale, my dear. Of course, you must be feeling very excited."

"Yes," said Mary vaguely. "But a little tired, and the motion of the carriage... I should prefer some tea, if you please."

"I am sure Jason would wish you to take a glass of wine! It would make you feel much better, and you do not want to be fainting at the altar, do you?"

With some difficulty Mary managed to insist that she wanted only tea, and when it came she drank two cups, and felt a little better. The whole morning, however, had so unreal an air that she could scarcely tell how she felt. Not, certainly, like a bride on her wedding morning. Unless all brides felt like this? She called up an image of Jason's face, and like a lucky talisman it banished, for a while, the wreathing fogs of uncertainty and carried her back into the magic, fairy-tale world where he was her handsome prince.

Lost in this dream, she allowed Mrs. Hadfield to fuss over her, sitting unresisting as a lay figure while her hair was taken down, brushed, and rearranged. Obediently she washed her face and hands, submitted to having her gown tweaked and shaken into more becoming folds, her cheeks pinched to bring some colour into them.

"A bonnet veil, I think," said Mrs. Hadfield. "I have one in my bandbox, especially. You should go veiled to your bridal, my dear, and, besides, you would not want to have nasty, vulgar men staring at you, would you? The Church is near by, we are to walk there, and I should not care for you to experience any unpleasantness."

Mary could not imagine why any nasty, vulgar man should wish to stare at her, for even in her best gown and Russian pelisse she was aware that she cut an uninteresting figure. Nevertheless she submitted to having the black lace arranged over her bonnet, finding that the resultant restriction of her vision accorded well with her own feeling of unreality.

A knock at the door heralded Jason's arrival.

"Are you quite ready, my dear?" he asked. He, too, was in travelling clothes, and she felt a little pang of disappointment, quickly suppressed. "We must leave at once. The parson will be waiting for us. It is not far."

"Where is Sarah? I must ring for her."

"Sarah? Who is Sarah?"

"My maid, of course! You said I must not tell her of our plans, and I have not, but there can be no harm in her knowing now."

"Your maid! How very strange, my dear! You have me to attend you!"

"Yes, and of course I am very grateful, Mrs. Hadfield, but Sarah has been with me for so long, she is almost like a mother to me. I should so like her to be there."

"A servant, as a wedding guest! Still, you may please yourself, I suppose."

Mary rang, but no Sarah came. Jason was growing impatient, consulting his watch, his lips thinning. Mary rang again, anxiously, and this time Mrs. Hadfield's maid came running to the summons, with the news that Sarah was nowhere to be found.

"The young person went out, madam," she said, confining her lofty remarks to her mistress, "as soon as she had been dismissed. I thought it strange, but then she is no more than a farmer's daughter, after all! I supposed she had gone out to look at the sights."

"Sarah has been to London many times!" Mary snapped. "She has no need to look at sights she has seen time without number. Oh, where can she be?"

"Well, wherever she is, we cannot wait for her. As it is we are almost too late. After all, she does not know what she is missing! Ten to one she has run off to buy something, and doesn't realise how long she has been."

Mary realised that to insist on waiting for her maid would do no more than annoy her companions; nevertheless she could not help glancing behind her several times as they walked briskly down the narrow back streets. It was not an area of London that she knew; indeed it was not the kind of place she would have expected to be married in. The houses were poor, leaning against one another like drunks in need of support, and the narrow streets were dirty, so that they were forced to pick their way. Jason had her on his right arm, and his mother on his left, and his long legs made no concessions to their shorter strides, so that Mary was forced to increase her pace and his mother, at times, was almost running.

The Church, when they reached it, was dark, dank and cheerless. Though doubtless very old, its age was conveyed by worn dips in the dirty flagstones, by the greenish tinge of the glass in the windows, which made the light within dim, and by the smell of mice and dust, rather than by ancient monuments, carvings, or the delicate tracery of vaulting. Their footsteps sounded loud in the gloomy hush, as if they were the first people to venture inside for several centuries. A bent, black-clad figure materialised from the shadows, so silently that Mary jumped.

"Mr. Hadfield?" His voice was hoarse and shaking, nearly as unsteady as the bony hand that came out and received the shining coin that Jason slipped into it. "Thank you, sir. Thank you. Just wait here. Vicar'll be just a moment, just a moment."

He shuffled off in a miasma of dirty clothes and old, unwashed body. Mary felt her skin shiver, as if it had a life of its own.

"My dears, I am so happy, I am quite overcome!" Mrs. Hadfield was hanging on her arm, peering up into her face. Through the gloom and the dismal shadow of her black veil Mary looked down at her, seeing a white, disembodied face that seemed to float free of its surrounding black clothes. Unable to speak, she looked at her in silence, and the older woman hurried on, seeking to distract her. "Flowers! We should have had some flowers, Jason! At least a posy for the bride! I believe I saw a woman with a basket of violets, as we were on our way here. It was not far; I can run back for some! No, no, it is no trouble! Nothing is too much trouble, today!"

"It is too late for that now, Mother. The parson is coming, look. We must go up to the rail."

"Yes, yes, never mind about the flowers. Afterwards, my dear. Afterwards you shall have flowers, but now... let me straighten your veil—it is slipping a little. There...and your pelisse..." She tweaked at Mary again, but Jason brushed her aside as if she had been an importunate insect.

"Not now, Mother. Come, Mary, my dear." He took Mary's arm in a firm grip, which steadied her a little, and led her up the aisle. Something scuttled away from their approach, in the dirty darkness within the pews, but Mary scarcely noticed, though Mrs. Hadfield drew aside her skirts with a squeak of dismay. Then they were at the altar rail, and it was a little lighter. The priest stood waiting for them, and at first Mary thought her own eyes were at fault, until she saw that he was swaying gently. He breathed out a powerful waft of spirits, and eyed them blearily with little, bloodshot eyes. His linen was decidedly grubby, and there were unidentifiable stains down the front of his waistcoat and coat.

"Dearly b'loved brethren," he mumbled, "the Scripture moveth us in sundry places—"

"Not that, you fool," muttered Jason. "The marriage service, not Matins."

"Yes, yes, all right," he replied testily. "It was just habit, you know. Just habit. Now. Dearly b'loved we are gathered together here in the sight of God and in the face of this congregation..."

What am I doing? wondered Mary. What am I doing in this horrid old Church, with a drunken parson who cannot even remember what he is doing, and who gabbles out the words without any stop or sense? Seeking the comfort that she had always found before, in the sight of him, she lifted her eyes to Jason's face.

Aware of her movement, he looked down. His hand was still holding her arm, as if to support her, but now he released it and took her hand instead. His clasp was warm, but her fingers lay still and icy within his. He smiled at her, and

Mary stared up at him, her eyes fixed on his face. With a shock that went through her like a bolt of lightning she realised that she felt nothing, nothing at all. What, before, had been enough to cast a glamour over her mind and her spirit was now just a face. A handsome face, to be sure, even beautiful, but bereft of its magic it was no more than eyes, nose, mouth, put together by the exact rules of beauty but moving her to no more than a faint pleasure, as at a well-executed picture. It was as though she had slept and dreamed, and was only now wakened to everyday reality.

"No," she whispered. "No. I can't do it."

In front of them the parson, either unaware or simply not caring that they were paying him no attention at all, continued to drone out words that issued like a stream of dribble from his lips.

"Thirdly, it was ordained for the mutual society, help and comfort that the one ought to have—"

"You must. It is too late." Jason's voice was cold and hard. He made no attempt to lower it, nor did its sound interrupt the droning words of the service. Society, help and comfort? thought Mary. This man is a stranger to me!

She saw, now, that she had allowed herself to be blinded by a handsome face, and perhaps also by the knowledge of this man's position as her father's heir. Not that she had coveted his future possessions, even after her brother's death, but that she had always believed that her father's dislike of his cousins was unreasonable. There was an insidious pleasure in the idea of reconciling the feud, of being, perhaps, a Juliet to his Romeo. And it had brought her to this, that she was marrying a man she did not love, because she did not know him, and whose love for her she now found suspect.

"No! You cannot make me do it, Jason!" She struggled to free her hand from his, but he gripped it.

"Can I not? You would be ruined, my dear Mary. You have come to London with me, after all, of your own free will. If you will not marry me, you shall be my mistress. It is all one to me."

"You cannot do that! There are people! I can shout, or scream!"

"And have the truth about your brother known to all? Oh, yes, my dear cousin. Think what such a piece of gossip would do to your family name! The saintly rector, and dear Sir Anthony!"

"You could not! You would not!" Her voice was rising, but the priest paid no attention, merely raising his own monotone to be heard.

"...why they may not lawfully be joined together let him now speak or else hereafter forever—"

"Stop! I say there is an impediment!"

The voice, from the back of the Church, rang out as clear as a trumpet, so that the cobwebs in the rafters seemed to shiver. Startled, Jason's grip loosened, and Mary snatched her hand away from him, turning and already running to the large figure that stood waiting, outlined against the light streaming in through the opened west door. Mrs. Hadfield gave a little cry, but Jason stood frozen as Mary ran straight into the other arms that were already held out to receive her.

"...when the secrets of all hearts shall be disclosed that if either of you know any impediment—"

"Shut up, you drunken old fool," snarled Jason, knocking the book from the parson's hand with a blow. Like a musical box running down, the man continued for a few more words, until he finally ground to a halt.

"...ye do now confess it... Confess it... The lady's gone? Is there to be no marriage?"

"No marriage." Again the voice came. "Not to you, at any rate, Brother."

Mrs. Hadfield gave one small scream, and collapsed in the ungainly huddle of a genuine faint. Her son paid her no attention, but stepped over her and down the aisle.

"John? Damn it all, it can't be. You're dead!"

"Don't you wish I were?" said John Hadfield.

CHAPTER THIRTEEN

"It is a trick. I do not believe it." Jason Hadfield continued to walk towards them, lithe as a cat, his hands poised but empty. John Hadfield tightened his arms round Mary's trembling figure and turned her, slowly, so that his own body was between her and his brother. He did not take his eyes off the other, and spoke without withdrawing that steady, watchful gaze.

"Sarah," he said, pitching his voice to carry. Behind him another person, obedient to his call, slipped through the open door and waited. "Shut the door, I think. Is there a key?"

"Yes, sir. It's there, in the lock." At the sound of her maid's voice Mary lifted her head a little, and opened her eyes.

"Sarah? Is that you? Oh, thank goodness. Where did you go?"

"To fetch him, what else? Seeing as you hadn't the sense to send for him yourself." The rejoinder was tart: Sarah had been frightened, badly frightened, for her nurseling, and the relief of tension made her edgy. The key scraped in the lock as she turned it, and at the sound the ancient verger came hobbling from whatever dark retreat he had hidden in.

"'Ere! You can't do that!"

"Just see if I can't," said Sarah, pulling the key from its hole and placing it in John Hadfield's waiting hand. He slipped it into his pocket.

"But the marriage? What of the marriage?" The parson had retrieved the book, and was dithering by the altar rail. No one paid any heed to him, and his voice rose. "My money! I've not been paid my money! I demand that I be paid!''

Incongruously, he was climbing over the rail, bending to grip it with shaking hands so that he might lift one foot after the other without falling flat. He scuttled after Jason, tripping over the outstretched foot of Mrs. Hadfield without giving her a second glance, and clutching at Jason's arm. The other shook him off without looking at him, so that the parson fell heavily against a pew and struck it with his head. The verger came to his assistance, and together they hurried away. A little trickle of blood stained the wispy hair where the pew edge had caught. Somewhere in the gloom a door opened and was slammed shut.

Jason ignored them as he walked, stopping when he was a few feet short of his brother. His eyes were flat, unreadable. Slowly the other man released his hold on Mary, and unwound the arms that clung to him. Without moving his gaze he pushed her gently away from him.

"Sarah! Take your mistress. Go to Sarah, my love."

Mary was unwilling to leave the safety of that warm embrace, but she could see that he did not wish to be encumbered by her, so she moved obediently to one side, and felt the pull of familiar hands on her arm. She let Sarah pull her close, but her eyes were fixed on the two men, now within a few feet of each other. Seeing them together, now, Mary wondered why she had not realised that they were brothers. Though they could not have been more different in their colouring or in their dress, still there was something from their shared blood—the shape of the skull, of the ears, of their general physical appearance. She remembered, fleetingly, the day when she had seen Jason silhouetted against the window; she had seen it for a moment and discounted it.

Looking at the two men, she also wondered how she could have fancied herself in love with Jason. It was as if he had been some kind of sickness, some disease of the mind or the blood, of which she was now cured, so that she could look into her heart and perceive what had always been there, since their first meeting. Lazarus Smith or John Hadfield, it did not matter. He was her lover, and her friend.

"It is really you. I would never have believed it." Jason spoke conversationally, even affably. "When you no longer wrote, I felt sure you were dead."

"You knew that I had written, then? From my father?" A considering look crossed Jason's face. "No point in lying to me now. Whether he knew or not can make no difference now. And yet I find it hard to believe that he would not have replied, if only to tell me never to write again. You kept the letters from him?"

"Yes." The admission of truth seemed to surprise him for a moment, then he gave a shrug. "Yes, I thought it best. It would have made no difference, in any case. He would not have forgiven you lightly, you must know that. After all, he never cared for you, did he?"

"No. No more than I cared for him. But we owed a duty, each to the other. My father—our father—would not have shirked a duty."

"Then you should both be grateful to me. He, because I saved him from the unpleasantness of having to deal with you, and you because you did not suffer the pain of his rejection."

"I am . . . obliged."

"So, you see, you would do very much better to take yourself off again. There is nothing for you here. Not a penny from my father, of course, and as for Hadfield—a great millstone of a house, cumbered by debts? You cannot wish for that."

"And . . . Mary? You would give me her as well?"

"Willingly, so you take her abroad, and stay there. She has no money, of course, and her appearance is no more than passable, but then I suppose you have not been used to anything better, living as you must have been."

Once, Mary would have been cut to the quick at hearing herself described by Jason in such terms, but now they passed her by, though she felt Sarah's stir of anger. Her only thought was for John's reaction. It was true that his hands curled slowly into fists, but his expression did not change. His eyes were steady, fixed on his brother.

"So, we are to leave you in possession? And in exchange?"

"In exchange, my dear brother, your Mary and the rest of them may be assured that no word of scandal concerning her brother will ever sully the family name."

"Your name as well, surely?"

"Ah, but a different branch of the family, after all! No scandal attaches to me, do you see?"

John Hadfield did not turn his face to Mary as he spoke, and there was no emotion in his manner.

"Well, Mary, my dear, what do you say? Will you come with me? As my wife, of course. You said that you wanted a life of adventure."

"I will go with you wherever you choose." Her voice was low, but steady.

"And...Hadfield? You will never see it again, you know, if we accept my brother's offer."

"I do not care. But you—what of you? You are the eldest son. The entail falls on you. Why should you give up this great inheritance, to protect my sisters? They can mean nothing to you. I cannot expect you to make so great a sacrifice and nor, I believe, would they."

He was smiling, and for the first time Jason's assurance seemed to waver as he saw that smile.

"There need be no sacrifices, my darling. Neither yours, nor mine. Forgive me for testing you as I did, but I had to know what you really felt, what you really wanted. For myself, I have no need of great houses, of land and estates. But I will take my inheritance, not for my sake or yours, but because no man should gain by his own evil deeds. My brother shall never have Hadfield."

Jason took one more step forward and stopped again, folding his arms.

"You speak very confidently, Johnnie. Big brother Johnnie, poor Johnnie, he never joined our games. Didn't care for them, did you, Johnnie?"

"No. Not your childish games, with their small torments, small tricks, small evils. Nor your adult games, Jason. You were always good at them, weren't you? Always encouraging others to play, leading them, teaching them... And you had an apt pupil, in Giles. Eager. Already part way along the road, perhaps."

Mary bit her lip to keep back a wordless cry. Jason's face was ivory white, now, gleaming in the dusky Church. A sheen of sweat stood on his brow. He licked his lips.

"You speak in riddles, Brother John."

"You wish me to speak more plainly? Very well. I am talking about a man befriending a spoiled, impressionable boy. Encouraging him to gamble, more and more heavily, and lining his pockets with the boy's money and, later, his promises of money. Bad enough, you might think, even if the boy had not been his own cousin, and possessor of all that he coveted."

"You can prove nothing." Jason spoke through thinned lips, his voice sharp and high. "It is not a crime to gamble. It is certainly not a crime to win. And if he were my cousin, what of it? He did not care. He could have stopped betting any time he wanted."

"But he did not want, did he? He was already drugging himself, after all. I imagine he scarcely knew what he was doing, much of the time. But you did, Jason. You did."

"You can accuse me of nothing. None of this is of any consequence. He was my friend, we gambled together, and I won. Such things happen every day of the week, every week of the year."

"His friend?" John's voice was heavy and cold. It filled the musty dankness of the Church, coloured the dark shadows. Nearer the altar, there was stirring movement. Unnoticed by any of them, Mrs. Hadfield pushed her shoulders from the icy stones of the ground, holding herself painfully on forearms, then on braced hands as she raised herself up. She gave little, whimpering moans that were as little regarded as the rustling of the mice among the hassocks.

"His friend?" repeated John. "Say, rather, his seducer. His whore. His catamite. Brought by you to the gateway of hell, and then discarded. It was the betrayal of your love, your abandoning of him when he had no more to give, that led him to his death." The words fell from his lips like stones. Mary found that she had lost the power to feel surprise. Even disgust and anger were lost in a kind of aching numbness.

"And yet...you would have married me?" The words came without her conscious volition. Jason spared a quick glance in her direction, no more.

"Why not?" His tone told her that he was answering her to give himself time, no more. "I had to marry at some time, after all. And you would have brought me money, I then supposed. It was so easy, after all, to dazzle you—a little country mouse. Even easier than your brother. So romantic, was it not? Quite a modern Romeo and Juliet."

So, after all, she had seen it, then. And it had seemed good to her, to heal the breach in the two sides of the family. She remembered the coldness of his caresses, and shuddered.

"You came to me...straight from him? From Giles?"

"He was becoming such a bore. Always demanding, always complaining. It was quite a relief to be done with him."

"But then, when you learned I would have no money? Why not be done with me, also?"

"So I should have done. But then I had learned that someone was sniffing around, asking about the wretched Giles. If, by any mischance, there should be a scandal, then I would need you beside me. You, after all, were the only person who might have a claim against me. If there should be any trouble, where should my wife be, but at my side?"

"And afterwards? What was to become of me then? A wife, in name alone? While you pursued your other interests?"

"By no means. Although it is true that I prefer the company of my own sex, I am not averse, upon occasion, to the more usual pleasures. And I should need an heir, of course: several sons, to make my position secure. A child a year, and you would have been well occupied at the Priory, and only too happy to see me leave for more sociable climes. You would not have been unhappy."

"As a brood mare? I think I have deserved better than that. And Giles, too."

"Words! Words! It is all words, no more! There is no proof!"

"But it is true, none the less." John had stood silently by, while Mary questioned her erstwhile lover. Now his voice was tight with anger on her behalf.

"True. False. They are but words, also."

"I can bring proof. You were less clever than you thought, Jason. There were several who saw you together, who would not hesitate to condemn you. And Giles himself . . . he left a letter, did he not? A letter to you? And sent on to you by the landlord's wife." The hazel eyes flickered. "You destroyed it, of course. But you knew Giles, surely. The would-be poet, the writer. Even at such a time, particularly at such a time, he would be bound to weigh every word, to polish each sentence. There would be earlier drafts, half-written attempts, a rough copy made before the fair copy was penned. You had not thought of that?"

Jason's lip lifted a little, like a dog's, showing the tips of his white teeth.

"You lie. You whoreson bastard, you lie!"

John put his hand, slowly, inside his coat, drawing out a sheet of paper. Jason put out a hand and snatched at it, casting his eyes swiftly down the few lines of writing it contained.

"Maudlin rubbish. My name is not on it. It could be to anyone." He screwed the paper contemptuously into a ball, and flung it to one side. His arms returned to their folded position.

"Did you really think," John's voice was almost amused, "that it was the only piece? Or that I would carry them all with me, knowing you as I do now? There are plenty more and, yes, some of them have your name on them. Pieced together, they do not tell a story that you would like to be made known, I think. Nor, of course, would we. But which of us has more to lose?"

"So, why tell me all this? What do you want from me?"

"Surely that is obvious. Your absence. Now, at once, and never to return. You may go where you will, and I will even forgo any claim to the money you obtained from Giles. But, you may be very sure, I shall know where you are. I have many friends, in many countries, and your doings will be known."

"And this is your revenge, I suppose? Because you were sent away, you will do the same to me?"

"It *was* at your doing? I cannot say that I care, any longer. Nor that it is any surprise to me, for I have always suspected it. No, this is merely to protect Mary, and the rest of her family."

"And leave you to take the Priory?"

"I shall take it, though unwillingly, and do my utmost to break the entail, whatever it should cost. It has done damage enough."

"I will not do it! You shall not make me! I do no man's bidding, least of all yours, Brother!"

So quickly that Mary scarcely had time to see the movement, his arms left their twined position and he sprang forward, both hands upraised. Such light as there was gleamed dully on the blade that had appeared, as if by magic, in his right hand. Mary's hands came up to cover her lips, and at the same moment she felt Sarah's arms come up to support and restrain her. John, who had faced death in many forms and in many countries, had not missed the warning flicker in his brother's eyes, and had leaped back, his fist coming out to grasp the striking hand as it came.

There was a patter of feet, and a waft of air that lifted the dust in eddies from the floor and stirred the cobwebs, as Mrs. Hadfield ran forward. While the rest had talked, she had risen to her knees, and then to her feet. Unnoticed, she had listened to all that they had said, her mouth twisting in tearless anguish as her son condemned himself by his own words. Now, still without speaking, she darted to his side and hung with her full weight on his other arm. She was not heavy and he was a strong man, but she took him by surprise. In an instinctive reaction against her pull, he jerked his arm to free it. Her strength was so little that she could not hold him, and the force of his movement carried his uplifted arm across his body, and then down to the rigid arm which John held stretched high and straight.

For a moment they stood, the three of them, frozen as in a tableau. Then Jason's left arm moved as if of its own volition away from himself, with his mother still clutching it to her breast until he shook her off, as if she had been a puppy. The hand opened, its fingers splaying outward like the limbs of a starfish, and on the upturned palm a small penknife, scarcely longer or thicker than a bodkin, lay for a moment. The fingers curved away from it as if it were a red-hot ember, and then with a convulsive jerk the knife was sent clinking to the floor. Jason looked not at that hand, but at the other, which was still upheld by his brother, the cuff of shirt and sleeve falling away from the upraised wrist.

A thin cut, just beading with starting blood and no greater than a line ruled with a pen, bisected the fleshy pad at the base of the thumb, and ran down to where the tendons of the wrist stood out taut. Jason gave a high, shrill whine, and the larger knife slipped from suddenly limp fingers. Frowning, John released his grip, though careful as he did so to kick the weapon out of reach, but his brother showed no sign of wishing to retrieve it. He brought the injured hand up to his face, staring at it, the breath whistling through wide-stretched nostrils. He shook his head, whimpering, then put the cut to his mouth and sucked, hard. The cords of his neck stood out like ropes of steel, his cheeks hollowed until the lines of his teeth could clearly be seen. He stopped, spat, then looked again at the mark.

A few more drops of blood flowed sluggishly from the cut, which looked swollen and angry. He stood hunched over it, then raised his head and cast about like a dog, ignoring the people who watched him with surprise and disquiet.

"The knife! Where is the knife? Give me the knife, damn you!" His voice rose to a breathless scream, he wheezed slightly as he breathed, and his left hand came up to wrench the neckcloth off. Mrs. Hadfield, who had been staring up at him in incomprehension, crouched to the floor and scrabbled at it obediently, finding and retrieving the penknife. It had slipped into a crack between two of the stone slabs, and her hands in their fine kid gloves picked at it, until with a little exclamation of satisfaction the handle came up between her fingers.

"Here, dearest! Here you are!" She held it up to him, and he started back. His foot came up, hard, and kicked her hand so that she fell back with a cry, and the penknife flew through the air and landed, unseen, with a tiny, deadly clink. John's face showed the dawning of suspicion and horror.

"What have you done? For God's sake, Jason, what was it?" His brother ignored him. He was scrabbling at the cut, dragging at it and spitting out a froth of saliva and blood. His once handsome face was livid, the bones of his skull showing in highlights on the sweaty skin. His lips were slate grey, drawn back from his teeth in a rictus that was the parody of a smile.

"What is it? Oh, what is happening?" Mrs. Hadfield, nursing the hand he had kicked to her breast, crouched at her son's feet and stared up into his face. "What is the matter with you, Jason? Surely it was only a scratch!"

With an exclamation John turned away, and ran to where the larger knife still lay. It took him a few moments to find it, then he snatched it up and straightened to hurry back. Jason turned on his mother, his eyes so wide that the whites could be seen gleaming round the irises.

"Poisoned, you stupid bitch! You have poisoned me!" He thrust the hand towards her, and she recoiled from it and from the ghastly face that he turned to her. John reached his brother's side, the knife in his hand, and Jason cowered from him with a shriek that ended in a fit of gasping coughs.

"Don't be a fool, man," said John roughly, snatching Jason's right wrist in his hand and pulling his arm out straight. "I'll do what I can. What in heaven's name did you have on that blade?"

The other was shaking now, his teeth rattling together, his legs buckling. Tears ran down his face, ignored. On his knees now, he pawed at John with his free hand, clutching at his coat, dragging at his sleeve.

"Cut it, cut it," he snivelled. "It burns like fire. I can't breathe. Oh, God, I never meant . . . I'm sorry, I'm sorry, I didn't know...oh, cut it out, cut it deep, it's...help me..."

"Come and hold him still." John flung the order over his shoulder. Mary and Sarah started forward together. Jason's body was trembling so violently, now, that it took their combined strength to keep him still, while John drew the knife blade in a slashing cut along the line of the first. Mary watched in fascinated horror, unable to withdraw her eyes. Blood welled where the blade had gone, wobbled over, fell with a splash, but slowly, heavily.

"What are you doing? You are hurting him! Look how he bleeds! Jason! Jason! What are they doing to you?" Mrs. Hadfield cried.

He ignored her, and so did the rest. Jason was on his knees now, supported by Sarah behind him, while Mary held the top of his arm and John the forearm, just above the wrist. Mary could feel the weight of it dragging at her hands, and she heard Sarah gasp with the effort of holding him.

"Let his arm down, Mary," said John in a low voice. "It will bleed better if it is lower." She did so, not releasing her grip until the arm hung down by Jason's side. Another gout of blood splashed down, splattering the already dirty silk of her gown. The gown that would, she had thought, have been her wedding dress.

"Is it enough?" she whispered. "Will he . . . ?"

"I do not know," John answered wearily. He looked down, becoming aware that he still held the bloody knife in his hand, and he laid it carefully by. "I am afraid it was too late, if indeed it would ever had done any good. Whatever the poison, it is obviously quick, and deadly. I have seen such things before, in India, but I never thought to see them here, in London, in the hands of my own brother."

"He meant it for you," she said, answering his tone of voice rather than his words.

"Yes, and he would have done it, if his mother had not interfered. I should have realised something was wrong, when first he drew the knife. Let him down, Sarah. You cannot hold him like that." Between them they eased the dying man to the ground. John pulled off his caped great-coat, and spread it over the dank stones. Sarah, behind him, supported Jason's shoulders and head. Mrs. Hadfield looked from one face to the other, uncomprehending still, seeking reassurance that could not be given.

"You did not think he would attack you?" Mary had been puzzling over his last remark.

"Yes, I feared that he would. I knew what an unwelcome shock my return would be to him, particularly when he discovered that I was in possession of information that would be enough to send him to gaol, if not hang him. No, I meant that he was fighting with his right hand. I had been away too long, and forgotten that he was left-handed. That, you see, was where the real weapon was."

"It would have been you." Mary looked at him, seeing him lying on the ground as his brother now lay.

"But it is not. His mother saved me, all unknowing. And I fear that she has killed her son. Poor unhappy woman, what use will my gratitude be to her? She has never seen his faults; he has always been the epitome of perfection to her."

Mrs. Hadfield ignored them. She had taken a handkerchief from her reticule, and was attempting to bind up the wound that gaped on the hand that was now so swollen. Jason's other hand came across his body to clutch her.

"Make it better, Mother," he whined. "Make it better."

"Yes, yes, my dear. The naughty man has hurt you, and shall be punished. You will be better presently. It is a nasty cut, but Mama will tie it up for you, and soon the bleeding will stop."

He seemed satisfied, and lay still. The breath rasped in his throat, his chest heaved as he gulped for air. Mrs. Hadfield finished tying the handkerchief and sat back, keeping the injured hand in both her own. Already the white linen and lace were stained with blood.

"There!" she said brightly. His head was twisting from side to side, his mouth grinning wide. A terrible grunting sound issued from it and his lips moved, but he seemed incapable of speech. "Jason! Jason, what is it? Speak to me, Jason!" Her voice rose shrill as a knife on glass, and Mary gritted her teeth, then bent to put her arms round the other woman.

"Mrs. Hadfield! Madam, you should come away. Let me take you away; you should not be seeing this."

"Nor you, my dear," added John in a low voice. But Mrs. Hadfield would not leave go of her son's hand. She looked up at her stepson, and John wondered whether she would attack him again as the author of Jason's illness, but after a wordless moment she looked down again, her face suddenly sagging and falling into the lines of age.

"It was not true," she said, but her looks and voice belied her words. John, watching, prayed silently that the end would be soon. The eyes of the man on the ground were closed now, and he thought it likely that consciousness had already fled. He hoped that it was so.

As they watched, the body suddenly arched into convulsion so that Sarah was unable to hold it, and John moved swiftly round to add his own weight and strength to hers. The limbs threshed, jerking violently so that Mrs. Hadfield, clinging desperately to the hand she had been tending, was thrown from side to side, the feet drumming on the floor. Then, as suddenly as it had begun, the paroxysm ended and Jason lay still, limp and flacid, the only movement the slow, dragging rise of his ribs as he sucked air into his lungs with as much difficulty as if it had been treacle.

His eyes opened, and against all expectation there was consciousness there. They moved from face to face. There was neither hatred, nor fear, nor apology in his look, only surprise and annoyance. He frowned a little, then his chest lifted in one long, easy breath. For a moment Mary almost thought that the crisis had passed, and he would recover, so smoothly did the air slip down his throat. His mouth and nostrils returned to their usual shape, and there was even a little smile on the well-shaped lips. Then, as she looked at him, she realised that no second breath had followed, that the eyes were fixed and blank, the chest motionless. Sarah moved, so that he was lying on the ground, as still as the stones around him. A long moan came from Mrs. Hadfield. For her, looking with the anxious eyes of love, there was no moment of blindness. She fell forward across her son's body, sobbing and wailing. Mary would have lifted her up, but John stopped her, reaching across the body to take her arm in his hand.

"Leave her. It will do no harm now. Poor woman, she has lost the very centre of her existence."

"What will become of her? Where will she go?"

"Not to Hadfield, at any rate. Do not forget she has her own home yet, and another son still living. She is not your responsibility. But you are mine, and you cannot stay here."

"But . . . I cannot leave you here! What will happen? His death must be explained, somehow. You will not be blamed for it, will you?"

"I certainly hope not. You and Sarah may speak on my behalf, if necessary, but I hope it will not be. Never fear for me. I will send for Mr. Forester. I feel sure he will know what to do, and how this may best be resolved without scandal. It can be done, I think, but not while you are here! The presence of a young woman would be hard to keep quiet."

"I suppose so, though I do not know how we are to escape with no scandal at all. That, however, seems so unimportant to me now that I do not really care."

"But I do, for you, and for your family. Trust me, Mary, to know what is best."

"Yes, I do. But what shall I do?"

"You must go home. Sarah will go with you. Your own carriage and coachman are at the inn, it is still early enough in the day. If you leave at once, you should be home by nightfall, or soon after. Listen! I hear footsteps. The drunken parson, most likely. It is better that he should not see you again. He is drunk enough to remember nothing of what passed earlier, and we must hope that the verger has put himself into the same state. Come, now, be off with you!"

She rose and stepped back, pulling the skirts of her pelisse around the blood-stained hem of her gown. Sarah rose and came to her, taking the key of the door that John Hadfield held out. Putting her arm round her mistress, she urged her to the door, and Mary put out her hand. He looked at both his own, which were blood-stained, and shook his head.

"Go home, my dear. This is no place for you. I shall come to you, as soon as I may."

His eyes followed her as she went to the door, watching her as she stood for a moment, silhouetted against the daylight outside, looking back. He raised his hand in farewell, and she was gone.

CHAPTER FOURTEEN

OUTSIDE THE CHURCH, its door firmly closed behind her, Mary paused and looked about her. She was vaguely surprised to see that the world had not changed. The day was still grey and dank, the street dirty and crowded, the people were . . . people. Tall, short, thin, rich, poor, ragged, neat, old, young, healthy, or sick. People in all the thronging guises that a city street could offer, each with their hopes and fears, joys and worries, sins and virtues, each as liable as the other to sickness, to cold, to misfortune, or to death.

It came to her, as she stood unregarded by the passers-by, that this, in the end, was what had made Jason different from the rest. Not so much that he had been greedy, cruel, or depraved, for there were few people who had not at least the seeds of evil within them, but that to him other people had no reality. Titled or common, rich or poor made no difference to him. They were ciphers, puppets, tools to be used when necessary and then set aside.

She wondered, whether, unconsciously, she had always known this, and it had been part of his attraction. The spell he had cast over others, the enchantment he had laid on those who had thought to love him, had been in part the feeling of being able to get beyond that beautiful shell which isolated him from the rest of the world. To find the centre of the labyrinth, the heart of the maze, to be the only one to unlock the inner door of his being. And the centre of the enchantment was, of course, that it was empty. There was no inner door, no heart, no centre to find that was not purely and wholly concerned with himself.

It should have been a discovery to chill her soul, but instead she felt, deep within her, a glow of relief, of freedom. She looked into her heart, and found it not echoing and untended, until its roots had twined deeply through her, and it stood poised in its springtime, needing only the sun of one man's presence to burgeon into blossom, and ripen into fruitfulness.

It seemed to her that she had stood there for half a lifetime, but Sarah was still turning from closing the door behind them, and now her touch on Mary's arm brought her back with a start. Like one awaking from a dream, she looked round, her smile bemused but so full of joy that the servant, for all her worry, could do nothing but smile back. Suddenly the drops of damp that fringed every surface took fire, and shone like diamonds. A gleam of sun had come through the cloud, and even the beggar that crouched in the doorway across the street raised his face to its faint warmth, and stretched like a cat.

Without speaking, Sarah took her mistress's arm, and hurried her down the street and back to the hotel. A few swift words were all that was necessary, and in the time it took to order a post-chaise, and have the horses put to, they could be ready. Upstairs in the chamber Mary submitted, like a child, to having her blood-stained gown removed, and being washed and dressed in fresh clothes that Sarah hastily pulled from the still packed trunk.

The tea Sarah had ordered arrived while Mary was still in her clean petticoats and a wrap, and sitting by the fire as Sarah brushed out her hair. With no words spoken, it had seemed to both of them that Mary must be completely dressed afresh, as if she had just risen from her bed. Sarah swiftly pinned the hair into a simple chignon, then took a small bottle from her pocket and measured some drops into a glass.

"Here, now, Miss Mary. I think you should take this."

"Oh, Sarah, I need no physic. I am perfectly well."

Sarah, looking down at the pale face and the eyes with pupils still dilated, thought that her mistress was still under

the effect of the terrible events of the morning, and that
once the first numbing of shock had worn off she was liable to feel very ill indeed.

"I'm glad to hear that, my dear. But do take it, won't
you, just to please me?"

"If you ask like that, how can I refuse? I owe you everything, Sarah. If it had not been for you, I might have married him..." Her lips trembled, and her eyes swam with
sudden tears. The hand she put up for the glass shook so
that it rattled against her teeth until the maid put her own
warm hand over the cold one, and steadied it.

"There, there, my dear. You're safe now. Safe with your
Sarah. There, now, there. That's better, then." The old familiar words of comfort dropped murmuring from Sarah's
lips as they had done for as long as Mary could recall, as she
held the sobbing girl in her arms and let her weep out some
of the pent-up terror and relief. When the first paroxysm
had subsided into slow, shuddering sighs, she withdrew her
arms with a brisk, consoling pat, and proceeded to wipe
Mary's face with a cold sponge, and help her into her gown
and a warm travelling cloak, less fashionable than her pelisse but far more comfortable.

They were soon in the coach and rattling through the
streets. With good horses and a certain amount of luck,
Sarah thought they would be home before the end of the
lengthening day. Mary's eyes were heavy, her head nodded
with the motion of the coach. Two or three times she jerked
awake again, but soon Sarah was able to prop her comfortably into the corner with cushions, the cloak wrapped
warmly around her, and had the satisfaction of knowing
that her sleeping draught would keep her charge asleep for
most, if not all, of the journey.

They drove up to the Priory just as the last light of sun-
set shone, jade and primrose, in the western sky. The house
was dark and silent, with only a glimmer of light to show
that the servants had taken the opportunity of their master's absence to enjoy an evening in their hall. The sound of
their approach had been heard, however, and Sarah had not

long to wait before her knock at the door was answered by a startled Hampton.

"What is amiss? Have you returned alone, Sarah? Where is my mistress?"

"Miss Mary is in the chaise. Oh, Mr. Hampton, such goings on as I have to tell you! But first I must get my young lady upstairs and into her bed. She's asleep now, and I hope she'll stay that way, poor dear."

One of the footmen appeared, hurriedly pulling on his gloves and tugging at his waistcoat. Hampton told him to carry Miss Mary indoors—carefully, mind!—and sent a housemaid running to light the bedroom fire, and another to fetch a warming-pan with hot coals from the range. Mary never stirred as she was carried upstairs, nor while Sarah and Mrs. Turvey undressed her and put her into the warmed bed. Unwilling to leave her alone, Sarah withdrew into the little sitting-room, leaving the connecting doors ajar, and there regaled Mrs. Turvey and Hampton with a suitably expurgated version of events, leaving out the scandalous nature of the relationship between Giles and Jason Hadfield, but telling the rest and trusting to their own loyalty and judgement how much they would pass on to the rest of the servants.

"Well, whoever would have believed that handsome young man could be so wicked?" Hampton was truly shocked. He had enjoyed his minor role in what he saw as a romantic love-affair, and was bitterly disillusioned to learn that his young mistress had been so misled. "And this other gentleman, you say, is the rightful heir? The true Mr. Hadfield?"

"Yes, and a better gentleman never breathed. Saved her twice over, he did, our Miss Mary. Right from the start, I took to him, and now they'll be wed, sure as eggs is eggs, and in our own proper Church, too. None of this running off to London and special licences this time. Come Easter, or maybe Whitsuntide, our young lady'll be a bride for all the world to see!"

Mary slept the night through, and the following day did not wake until midday. Her body felt stiff and bruised as if she had been on the rack, or beaten all over, and every joint seemed to creak when she moved. It was an effort to leave her bed, and she was not sorry when Sarah forbade her to dress, and set her in a chair by the fire to eat the food that Cook sent up. She knew her household well enough, however, to gauge their feelings. When she saw the logs on her hearth were from the lime tree, scenting her room like incense; that her tray held every delicacy, in or out of season, that the kitchen could muster; and that the choicest blooms from the hothouse were bunched in profligate profusion on every available surface, her eyes filled again with the easy tears of an invalid.

A second night's sleep, however, restored her to her usual resilient state. This time she overruled her maid when Sarah tried to keep her from dressing, and insisted on going downstairs. In the empty house everything was so normal, the quiet ticking of the clock and the rustle of logs in grates almost the only sound, that she went from room to room, seeing the familiar furnishings with new eyes as a setting for her own future happiness. John Hadfield did not come to take possession of his house, however, and though she hovered all day within reach of the front windows, her ears straining for the sound of hoofs, no one came.

She went to bed early, as soon as she knew that she could no longer expect him that day, and as a result she woke before sunrise. For a few minutes she lay still, courting sleep with closed eyes, but they would not stay shut. Her whole body felt light and strong, and she could feel the blood coursing in her veins, and she could no longer stay in bed, or even indoors. Quietly she slipped from beneath the covers, and, stripping off her nightgown, washed with the cold water in her ewer, her bare flesh quivering at the icy touch of the cold sponge but rejoicing in the sensation. Tingling, she dressed in an old riding habit, and tied up her hair with a piece of ribbon. Boots in her hand, she crept down the back stairs and out to the door that would take her to the stable yard.

The empty stalls no longer saddened her; soon they would be full again. Jewel whickered a welcome as her mistress slipped into her stall, dropping her head into Mary's outstretched hands to lip up the apple pieces she had brought her. By the time the first light of dawn was dimming the stars and greening the sky, Mary had saddled her up and led her out to the mounting block in the yard.

She rode down the drive, where the tree shadows were bottomless pools of inky black, and out of the gates, turning towards the paths that would take her to the heights of the forest. It was still dark beneath the trees, and she kept her horse to a walk, finding her way by instinct rather than by sight. Higher up the trees were fewer, and the ride went between patches of gorse and birch that were still grey in the dawn light. Now she could urge Jewel to a canter, her hoofs thudding softly on the short, rabbit-nibbled turf. If Mary heard the echo of hoofbeats behind her she did not turn, but rode on to where a group of Scotch pines stood crowning the mound of a small hill, dark against the sky.

As she reached them the sun came over the horizon, and in the instant their trunks came to life in a glow of gold and red, the bark gleaming like amber. She slowed the mare to a walk, and they climbed the sloping hillside until they stood among the trunks that surrounded them like the pillars of some ancient Byzantine church. A clamour of birdsong rose from the surrounding woodland, and the air was sweet with the smell of new grass crushed beneath the horse's feet.

Mary lifted up her head to watch the sky, as the last star paled and faded in the light of the new day. The man behind her did not speak, but she was so aware of his presence that he might as well have announced himself with a fanfare of trumpets. Jewel, feeling her inattention, dropped her head to snuff at the grass. The silence between them stretched to an eternity.

"Mary," he said at last, very low. "Mary." She thought she had never liked her name so well. He had dismounted

and looped his horse's reins over a branch; now he stood at
her side, looking up at her. The warm light cast a glow over
his face, making him look suddenly young and almost vulnerable. He held up his arms, and without a moment's hesitation she let herself slide down into them, making no
attempt to dismount but trusting him to catch her safely.

He held her to him, and without any false modesty she
raised her face for his kisses, returning them with an ardour that shook him to the core. He felt healed of an old
hurt that he had not even noticed until now, her love filling
an echoing gap within him that must always have been there,
so familiar as to be unperceived. When his hands caressed
her, feeling the soft contours of her body through the covering of her clothes, she did not shrink from his touch with
maiden coyness, but smiled with lips reddened by his kisses
and heavy-lidded eyes with pupils black and dilated with
pleasure. He buried his face in the warm hollow of neck and
shoulder, breathing in the faint flower scent that hung about
her, stilling his wandering hands and willing the clamour in
his blood to subside.

"Mary," he whispered again, his voice hoarse. "Oh,
Mary."

"You say my name," she murmured back to him, kissing the scar that crossed his cheek, "yet I hardly know what
to call you. I cannot, yet, think of you as John."

"You may call me what you will, so long as you kiss me
between words."

"Lazarus, then. Oh, Lazarus, what if we had never met?
What would have become of us then?"

He felt her shiver, and held her close. He had put on a
heavy riding cloak, and now he wrapped its voluminous
folds round them both and led her to where the trunk of a
fallen tree made a convenient seat. The sun was higher now,
its strengthening beams appreciably warm on their backs as
they sat pressed together.

"No need to think of that. We did meet, and as soon as I
set eyes on you I knew..."

"You knew! And I did not. Yet you did not speak. What a deal of time we have wasted."

"How could I, when you as good as told me you were in love with someone else? And that someone else my brother!"

"But you knew him! You knew what he was like, and said nothing."

"I knew what he had been like, as a child. But children grow, and change. When we were younger I was jealous of him, because he had all my father's love. As a man, absent for so many years, how could I be sure that the faults I remembered were not coloured by that jealousy? I did not really even know why I had returned to England, after so long a time. Certainly I had no intention of presenting myself to my family. I thought I would get news of them, and see that all was well, but I did not want to make myself known to them. All the more so when I heard that your brother was dead, and my father must inherit. To turn up then, like the proverbial bad penny, just in time to make my claim on the inheritance—unthinkable! Particularly if, in so doing, I must deprive you of your home. I knew you too well, even at the very first, to think that you would abandon your love, and ally yourself to me, merely to gain the Priory."

"But you did not go away."

"I knew that I should do so, but it was already too late. I could not rid myself of the hope that you might come to need me, perhaps even learn to love me!"

"I did, oh I did! Only I did not realise it!"

"If I had found that my brother had grown up a good and an honest man, one who would love you as you deserve to be loved, then I would have gone at once, and never have crossed your path again. But from what I learned it seemed very clear that my letters had never reached my father, and that it had been Jason who intercepted them. I spoke to an old servant, who had known me as a child, and she confirmed what I had already suspected. Knowing that, I could not leave you to marry him. But I never expected to discover what I did!"

"About poor Giles? I never thought that I would come to pity him, but now I do. My father was much at fault, in giving way to his every whim. But I felt the fascination that Jason could exert. What I felt was not love—I see that now. But for my brother..."

"We shall never know, perhaps. So powerful an influence could have worked for good, if it had chosen, instead of for evil. For Giles's sake, and for what he tried to do to you, I regret nothing. My brother carried the seed of his own destruction within him, and he has rightly perished by his own hand. I could not have killed him, even then, but perhaps death was the kindest end for him."

"Was it all planned, do you think? Giles, I mean, and me?"

"Possibly. Probably. Certainly he meant to have as much money as he could get from Giles, even if he did not intend his death. Though I think he would have hoped for that, as well, and that is why he encouraged him to take the opium. Then, of course, you were a tempting prize. Not only for your riches, though he would have wanted that, but because with you as his wife his position would be unassailable. That is why, when he learned you would have no fortune, he still wished to rush you into marriage. He feared what you might learn of his influence over Giles, and what better way to protect himself than to bind you to him as his wife?"

"What will happen now? You will not be accused of his death, will you?"

He soothed her with a caress.

"No, no, I shall be quite safe. My friend Forester has seen to everything. He will be found to have died in a street brawl, and nobody will be greatly surprised."

"And his mother? Will she agree to that?"

"Poor woman, she is quite broken by his death. In spite of everything he was, of all that she heard him admit with his own tongue, she is heartbroken. To protect his memory she will say nothing, and we must hope that the company of her younger son will comfort her, at last. I remember him as a quiet child, not overly intelligent, but with no malice in him. He will farm the acres my father left, and do it well, I believe."

There was a little silence. Mary sat held close and warm in his arms, at peace as she had never been since Martha's death. At that moment she would have gone with him, without a second thought or a glance behind her, have joined her life to his and travelled to any quarter of the globe that he might choose, so long as he would love her. She could almost have wished that the earth might swallow up the Priory for ever, so that they might be free of it.

"I am afraid your legacy is not much to your taste," she said. "It brings you nothing but debts."

"They do not matter. I told you before, I am a wealthy man, though I do not choose to display it. As for my inheritance, I cannot turn it down, but I meant what I said about the entail. The Priory shall be yours, your very own, as is only right, since you have cared for it all these years, and your own money has gone into helping it."

"I do not want it. I would rather be free from all such responsibilities."

"You say that now, but I do not think you will always feel this way. Where else, after all, should we raise our children? It shall be a home, now, for us and our family. The shadows of the past will be cast out. One need not travel the world, my dearest, to find adventure."

She sighed.

"I suppose you are right. But we shall travel a little, shall we not?"

"Certainly, if you wish it! But the Priory will always be there for us. It is waiting for us now. Do you think they will send out search parties for you?"

"I hope not! How scandalised Sarah would be if she could see me now! And yet she always liked you. She was wiser than I, I think, and saw that you were the right one for me long before I knew it."

"Intelligent woman. And to think that you offered her to me as my bride!"

"That offer is rescinded. You will have to make do with me."

"Well, I hope I shall be able to make the best of it." He kissed her again, a lingering kiss that left her breathless. There was a snuffling sound, and something cool, hairy and damp tickled their two faces. The mare Jewel, who neither of them had remembered to tether, had abandoned her grass and come to find them. Unheard on the soft, short grass, she had ambled up and was standing right behind them, her head lowered to breathe lovingly down their necks. Mary laughed, and put up a hand to caress the velvet-soft nose and lip.

"That wretched creature!" exclaimed John Hadfield. "I should never have sent her to you if I had known she would be so good a chaperon. Worse than any dowager, I declare!"

"You sent her to me! But I thought...oh, of course! And her name was Juno, was it not?"

"Yes, it was. I was afraid I had betrayed myself, when I said that, but of course you merely thought I had misheard her name."

"I should have realised," she said with remorse. "And he let me thank him for her, and never said a word! He must have wondered where she had really come from! How did you know I was in want of a horse?"

"I saw the stables, the first time I came to visit you, and could see there was nothing there that was fit for you to ride. I was worried about you—you looked so pale—and thought it would do you good to ride."

"How very good you were! And without a word of thanks!"

"Well, you may thank me now, if you wish."

She did so, but with the mare still breathing over her and tickling her neck it was impossible not to laugh. "She is quite right, you know! We must go back. Will you come with me? It is time you saw your house, I think."

"I will come, but only for a few hours. I cannot stay there alone with you."

"Then I shall do as I had wanted, and go to London with my sister Georgina. You, I think, should get to know the Priory. I think you will find a welcome there, particularly if you mean to put right some of my poor father's desperate little economies."

"I shall do my best. I know little about the management of such a place."

"Then do not be afraid to say so. No one will think any the worse of you, if you are honest, and they will be pleased to teach you."

They stood up, still clasped together beneath the cloak, knowing that they should return, but lingering, reluctant to leave this island of joy and go back to the everyday cares of the world. At last, however, he lifted her up into the saddle and then mounted his own horse. They rode side by side, but how different was this ride from the last they had taken together! Now their talk was in low, confidential murmurs, much interrupted by halts when they paused to kiss. When they reached the gates of the drive he did not, as before, turn back. Together they rode up to the front door, and as the watchful Hampton opened it for them John Hadfield lifted Mary once more down into his arms, and under the butler's astonished gaze proceeded to kiss her once again.

Flushed and laughing, Mary led him to the door.

"Here is your master, Hampton," she said. "He is come home at last."

Together they walked in, and the house folded its walls around them, as a mother held her child in her arms.

Harlequin invites you to the most
romantic wedding of the season.

Rope the cowboy of your dreams in
Marry Me, Cowboy!

A collection of 4 brand-new stories,
celebrating weddings, written by:

New York Times bestselling author

JANET DAILEY

and favorite authors

Margaret Way
Anne McAllister
Susan Fox

Be sure not to miss Marry Me, Cowboy!
coming this April

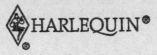 HARLEQUIN®

MILLION DOLLAR SWEEPSTAKES (III)

No purchase necessary. To enter, follow the directions published. Method of entry may vary. For eligibility, entries must be received no later than March 31, 1996. No liability is assumed for printing errors, lost, late or misdirected entries. Odds of winning are determined by the number of eligible entries distributed and received. Prizewinners will be determined no later than June 30, 1996.

Sweepstakes open to residents of the U.S. (except Puerto Rico), Canada, Europe and Taiwan who are 18 years of age or older. All applicable laws and regulations apply. Sweepstakes offer void wherever prohibited by law. Values of all prizes are in U.S. currency. This sweepstakes is presented by Torstar Corp., its subsidiaries and affiliates, in conjunction with book, merchandise and/or product offerings. For a copy of the Official Rules send a self-addressed, stamped envelope (WA residents need not affix return postage) to: MILLION DOLLAR SWEEPSTAKES (III) Rules, P.O. Box 4573, Blair, NE 68009, USA.

EXTRA BONUS PRIZE DRAWING

No purchase necessary. The Extra Bonus Prize will be awarded in a random drawing to be conducted no later than 5/30/96 from among all entries received. To qualify, entries must be received by 3/31/96 and comply with published directions. Drawing open to residents of the U.S. (except Puerto Rico), Canada, Europe and Taiwan who are 18 years of age or older. All applicable laws and regulations apply; offer void wherever prohibited by law. Odds of winning are dependent upon number of eligibile entries received. Prize is valued in U.S. currency. The offer is presented by Torstar Corp., its subsidiaries and affiliates in conjunction with book, merchandise and/or product offering. For a copy of the Official Rules governing this sweepstakes, send a self-addressed, stamped envelope (WA residents need not affix return postage) to: Extra Bonus Prize Drawing Rules, P.O. Box 4590, Blair, NE 68009, USA.

SWP-H395

Fifty red-blooded, white-hot, true-blue hunks
from every State in the Union!

Look for MEN MADE IN AMERICA! Written by some
of our most popular authors, these stories feature some
of the strongest, sexiest men, each from a different state
in the union!

Two titles available every month at your favorite
retail outlet.

In March, look for:

UNEASY ALLIANCE by Jayne Ann Krentz (Oregon)
TOO NEAR THE FIRE by Lindsay McKenna (Ohio)

In April, look for:

FOR THE LOVE OF MIKE by Candace Schuler (Texas)
THE DEVLIN DARE by Cathy Thacker (Virginia)

You won't be able to resist MEN MADE IN AMERICA!

This April, Harlequin and Silhouette
are proud to bring you

Just Add Children

How do you guarantee a lively romance? Take a
handsome, single man and a successful, single woman—
then...*Just Add Children*.

Three complete novels by your favorite authors—
in one special collection!

BABY, IT'S YOU by Elise Title
NATURAL TOUCH by Cathy Gillen Thacker
TO LOVE THEM ALL by Eva Rutland

Available wherever
Harlequin and Silhouette books are sold.

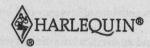

Bestselling Author

Janice Kaiser

Look in on the secret lives and loves of a powerful family in

Private SINS

Brett— the brilliant young attorney who dares to fall in love with her husband's son.

Amory—a supreme court judge who will have to put his heart and life on the line.

Elliot—a man trapped by his contempt for his wife and his forbidden love for his father's bride.

Monica—the bitter wife who will make her husband pay for daring to love another.

Harrison—a senator whose scandalous affairs may cost him more than his career.

Megan—the senator's aide and mistress, whose dreams may be on the cutting block.

Get to know them intimately this March,
at your favorite retail outlet.

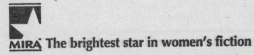

MJKPS